50p

THE OC

If he didn't [...] him, he cared for them. He [...] mit. Deliberately he used the code which meant the message went to OSS rather than British headquarters. He remembered that snide, cold-blooded English Colonel; the request he was going to make wouldn't have an icicle's chance on a hot shovel if it went to him. He used General Heidsecker's code name. 'Geronimo. Geronimo from Apache. Mission completed, total success. Imperative assistance sent prevent reprisal against area. All children in village due extermination. Request drop of small arms, ammunition at Lavallière field by dawn, repeat dawn tomorrow. Reply confirming soon as possible. Apache.'

THE OCCUPYING POWER

Evelyn Anthony

THE SHERIDAN
BOOK COMPANY

This edition published in 1993 by
The Sheridan Book Company

First published in Great Britain by Hutchinson 1973

Arrow edition 1983
Random House UK Ltd, 20 Vauxhall Bridge Road, London SW1V 2SA

Reprinted 1983, 1985, 1987 and 1990

Printed and bound in Great Britain by
Cox & Wyman Ltd, Reading, Berkshire

ISBN 1–85501–460–2

To
NICHOLAS AND DENISE
with my love

1

It was a wide, quiet street, lined with chestnut trees; the houses were protected by walls and wrought-iron gates, and there were few of them. It was a place where the rich lived, but not those who had recently acquired money and wished to make a display. It was a little faded, reserved, very conscious of its status as an address in one of the most status-conscious cities in the world. The taxi cruising slowly down its length came to a halt outside a pair of tall iron gates. There was a gilded crest at the top of them, a circle of oak leaves and a boar rampant, with a coronet above. The driver leaned out and opened the passenger door.

'This is it,' he said. 'Rue de Varenne.' A woman climbed out; she moved clumsily, a heavy-set body on thick legs. She was dressed in a dull coat and skirt and flat shoes, her greying hair showing at the edges of an unflattering felt hat. She opened her handbag and gave the driver the exact fare; after a moment's hesitation she added a very small tip. He took the money, slammed the gears and drove off without thanking her. She stood on the pavement looking up at the gates. A house was visible beyond them, a three-storied grey-stone building with a graceful classical façade, the work of an eighteenth-century architect. There was a small paved courtyard, and two huge stone urns stood at the foot of a flight of steps, filled with flowers. The woman didn't move; she stood as if she were uncertain what to do, looking through the gates. She had arrived in Paris the night before, booked into a modest tourist pension on the Left Bank, and spent a miserable evening sitting in her room. She had never travelled abroad before; her youth had been spent in pre-war Germany where foreign travel was actively discouraged, and then the war had come, binding her to home and a part-time job in a hospital.

While her husband had gone to France, she had kept his letters, all the weekly news sent from his posting outside Paris, full of enquiries about her and the children, prosy, serious letters which she read over and over again to ease her loneliness while he was away. She still had them, yellow and ragged at the edges, tied up in a cardboard box. They had been married thirty-two years and she still loved him. That love and the extreme of desperation had brought her from her homeland to Paris and to the house of a woman she had never seen. A woman who might try not to see her if she knew who she was. Under the ugly hat her blue eyes narrowed. The face was lined and its contours blurred by middle age, but it showed traces of a vanished prettiness; the colour of her eyes and the shape of her mouth were pleasing. When she married she had been a gay and attractive girl of twenty, with a nice rounded figure and a tiny waist. Now she was coarse and shapeless, the result of all the post-war years of hardship, worry and hard work. While the other woman, the one who lived in the elegant house behind her crested gates—how had she survived the onslaught of the years? Was she as beautiful still as she had been when her own husband had first met her—Louise, Comtesse de Bernard.

She said the name under her breath. An aristocrat, smart and spoiled, a prominent figure in Parisian society. On an impulse she opened the gate and went into the courtyard. Her expression was hard, hostile, masking the inward fear of facing the unknown with such a brutal sense of disadvantage. Only for Heinz, her husband . . . for him she would have faced anyone in the world. Even the woman with whom he had fallen in love, all those years ago. She crossed the courtyard and rang the bell.

Louise de Bernard was on the telephone. She used her small boudoir as an office; there was a plain desk and a small filing cabinet, and a telephone with an internal system. A large desk diary was open beside her. Long fingers with beautifully polished nails held a pen and wrote in a name and a time on a day two weeks ahead.

As she talked she smiled. 'Of course Raoul; I'll be delighted. And thank you again for the flowers. Yes. Goodbye.'

The door of the study opened and a girl who somehow looked like Louise de Bernard and was yet completely different in type, put her head round and shook it at her mother.

'Is that the faithful Raoul again?'

'Yes, you know it is; don't be nasty, darling. He's very sweet.'

'He's a stuffy old bore.' She came in and sat on the edge of the desk. She was painfully slim in the modern fashion, casually dressed in trousers and a shirt, her feet in canvas shoes and her ankles bare. Long straight hair hung down past her shoulders and there was no make-up on her face. She put an arm round her mother and kissed her.

'Don't marry him for God's sake! He's a dreadful old reactionary.'

Louise de Bernard glanced up at her daughter. 'He's the same age as me. And I'm not going to marry anyone, as you know perfectly well. Don't sit on those papers, darling, I haven't read them yet.'

Sophie de Bernard slipped off the desk, fumbled in her breast pocket and produced a flattened packet of cigarettes. She flicked at the desk lighter and blew a cloud of Gauloise over her mother's head.

She was thirty but she looked younger, almost coltish. The expression on Louise's face was tender as she looked up at her. Sophie was the younger of her two children, the most physically like her father, and the most temperamentally akin to her. She was unmarried, living with a left-wing writer whom Louise considered an offensive boor, with whom she quarrelled and became reconciled at regular intervals. She was a Maoist who sincerely believed that her mother's generation and all it stood for should be swept away by force. At the same time there was a deep and devoted relationship between them which nothing, neither Louise's disapproval of her mode of life or Sophie's revolutionary convictions, could ever undermine. They loved and understood each other and were far closer than Louise could ever be with her son. Paul was steady, conventional and immersed in his own family life. As Sophie said, and Louise didn't disagree with her, his marriage to Françoise de Boulay had stifled an individuality he might have had. He was a good son, an excellent father and husband and, in his sister's merciless description, a catastrophic bore. Married to a woman whose personality wore a strait-jacket. They were pleasant, dutiful to Louise, who never interfered, and frankly horrified by the antics of Sophie, whose lovers and political activities caused them agonising embarrassment.

'Mother, I didn't mean to disturb you. How's the appeal going?'

'Very well,' Louise said. 'I'm holding a meeting here tonight. I think we may raise more than our target.'

'At least you work hard,' Sophie said. 'But you know what I think of organised charity, don't you?'

'Oh yes,' her mother said. 'I know all about that. Give me a cigarette?'

'Here.' She lit it for her. 'What did Raoul want? Dinner again?'

'The opera; there's a gala performance of *Norma*. I said I'd go.'

'I think it's extraordinary. Half the men in Paris are sniffing round you, and you choose to go out with that pompous idiot. Why don't you take a lover—somebody glamorous and exciting. It would be good for you, darling. Much better than all this committee work.'

'I don't want a lover,' Louise said firmly. 'And I like Raoul; he's an old friend. I also like committee work. Now go away and don't lecture me.'

'You only stick to him because he's safe,' her daughter remarked. 'Papa wouldn't want you to waste your life. You can't go on forever living in the past.'

'Please,' Louise said. 'Don't start all that this morning. I'm happy, Sophie. I have a busy life and I've no intention of having a lover or marrying Raoul. Now let me get on with some work! We can lunch together if you're free.'

'I am,' Sophie admitted. 'I'm furious with Gerard, he can get his own lunch today. And his own dinner!'

Louise, who had heard this threat before, only smiled slightly and said nothing. The bombastic Gerard had a feeble streak, which had so far claimed Sophie's ready sympathy. The day she discovered that it concealed a contemptible character, there would be no more meals and no more relationship. Louise, who had seen the pattern repeat itself, without her daughter suffering any apparent harm, was content to wait upon events.

'I'll go and leave you in peace,' Sophie announced. 'But actually I came up to tell you something—there's a woman downstairs, asking to see you. I told Gaston I'd give you the message.'

'What woman—I'm not expecting anyone this morning. Who is it?'

'I don't know,' Sophie said. She had gone to the door and opened it. 'I've never seen her before. She's a German; she said her name was Minden.'

Louise de Bernard still held the pen balanced between her fingers; the cigarette burned in an ashtray in front of her. Now the pen dropped, spattering ink across the blotting pad. 'Minden?'

'Yes.' Her daughter changed her mind about going out. She pushed the door shut. 'My God, Mother, what's the matter?'

'Minden,' Louise repeated. She got up slowly and turned round. 'Are you sure that was the name?'

'Perfectly sure. Mother, what is it—what *is* the matter?'

'Oh, Sophie—it's not possible, it can't be!' The girl came towards her quickly.

'For God's sake, who is this Minden woman—why are you looking like that?'

Louise didn't answer for a moment. Minden. It wasn't possible after all these years. After so much pain and suffering . . .

'What did she say?' she asked. 'What does she want?'

'To see you, apparently. That's what Gaston said. I saw her waiting in the hall. She looked very ordinary, a dumpy kind of frump . . . Mother, will you please sit down and tell me what this is about? You look as if you'd seen a ghost. Who is Minden, what does it mean?'

'Minden,' Louise said slowly, 'is the name of the German officer who was billeted upon us during the war. Heinz Minden. Now do you understand?'

Sophie de Bernard went up to her mother and put her arm around her. 'I'll send her away,' she said. 'I'll say you're not here. Don't worry; you just stay up here. I'll get rid of her.'

'No, Sophie.' Louise shook her head. 'If it's a woman it must be his wife. I'll have to see her. I'll have to find out what she wants.'

'No you won't,' her daughter said fiercely. 'You're not having the past brought up again—you've gone through enough because of that bloody war. You and Papa! I don't care what she wants—you're not seeing her. I'll go and get rid of her now!'

'No,' Louise repeated. 'No, I'll go. I'll see her. Tell Gaston to show her into the salon and say I'll be down in a few moments. Don't argue, Sophie, do as I say. I don't know what she wants or why she's come here, but I've got to see her!'

'Why?' her daughter demanded. 'You don't owe her anything! How dare any of them come here!'

'I'll come down in a moment. Ask if she wants anything—some coffee—please, go and do as I ask.'

'All right,' Sophie de Bernard said. 'But you're not seeing her alone. I'll be there with you!'

The door closed and Louise could hear her hurrying step go down the passage and run down the staircase to the hall. Minden. She hadn't thought of him for years. There was no association with him in the Paris house. That had been bought after the war ended, when she wanted to escape from St. Blaize and never see it again. He came into the eye of memory and it was as he had been, as a young man in his thirties, neat and efficient in his uniform, with that expression she knew so well in his eyes as he watched her, following every movement she made. And there were other memories, pictures she refused to see, fighting to shut them out. Hands reaching out, words whispered to her in the darkness. Shame and fear and love. Above all, love. But not for him. And not for the father of Sophie and Paul.

That memory, more than any of the others, she had struggled to suppress over the years. Her daughter, sweet, undisciplined, immature at thirty, talked of lovers, without the least understanding of what love itself could mean. But Louise knew. The moment of panic passed; when she was arguing with Sophie her hands were trembling, now they were still. If Heinz Minden's wife had come to see her, then she wasn't going to run away. She paused for a moment, smoothing her hair, steadying herself. If the past had come back then it had to be faced. She opened the door and went downstairs.

Ilse Minden had refused to sit down. She followed the tall French girl into a large room, splendidly decorated in shades of pale green with touches of blue, and some gilt furniture which she recognised instinctively was very valuable. She shook her head when it was suggested that she might like to have coffee, or wait in comfort. She stood in the middle of the carpet looking round her, holding a large plastic handbag in both hands like a shield. Sophie offered her a cigarette. Minden's wife could sense her hostility in spite of an attempt to be polite.

She refused, her tone abrupt because of nervousness.

'Thank you. I don't smoke.'

She couldn't have afforded to smoke, even if Heinz had approved of the habit. She didn't smoke and they lived so sparingly that she had forgotten the smallest luxuries of self-indulgence. It was so long ago since she had been to a hairdresser, or bought new clothes. Everything they had went to their children, who seemed to take it for granted and were busy running as far away from them as possible, now that trouble had overtaken them. Bitterness bolstered her courage. Underneath her timidity there was a worm of hatred, slowly uncoiling as she waited, taking stock of the wealth and good taste in the room, of the casual self-confidence of the young woman, in spite of her mannish clothes and bizarre appearance. Ilse Minden moved towards a table, covered by a blue velvet cloth. There was a small Louis XVI ormolu and porcelain clock on it, and two photographs. One was a studio portrait of a young man, dark and good-looking, smiling towards the camera. The other showed a woman standing with a little boy and girl on either side of her, a fountain in the background. The woman wore the long skirt and clothes of twenty-five years ago. She turned towards Sophie.

'Is that your mother?'

'Yes. With my brother and me. Taken at our home in the country during the war.'

'I see. Does she still look like that?'

'I think so. But you'll be able to judge for yourself. I hear her coming now.' There was something in the German woman's face that made Sophie uncomfortable, a look of sullen menace mingled with uncertainty. And the menace was predominating, as she gained confidence. Ilse Minden turned towards the door. The picture showed a young woman, very beautiful . . . When the door opened she stiffened. A tall woman walked towards her; a beautiful woman in an elegant brown dress, with a silk scarf round her throat and pearls knotted through it. Dark hair and eyes, expensive scent. Hate suffocated Ilse Minden at that moment; jealousy constricted her so that when the woman held out her hand she couldn't move to take it.

'Madame Minden? I am Louise de Bernard. What can I do for you?'

'I have to talk to you.' The woman facing her spoke with a thick accent. She glanced towards Sophie.

'This is my daughter,' Louise said.

'I am Heinz Minden's wife; I've come from Bonn to see you.'

'Please,' Louise said, 'won't you sit down. Did Sophie offer you some coffee, Madame?'

'She didn't want anything,' Sophie said. She walked up close to Ilse Minden. 'Why do you want to see my mother?'

The German didn't answer her. She walked across and settled herself in a chair, clasping the ugly handbag on her knees. She spoke to Louise.

'I don't speak very good French,' she said. 'I would like to speak to you alone.'

'My daughter knows about your husband,' Louise said slowly. 'You can speak in front of her. Why have you come here?'

'She knows about my husband?' The blue eyes turned to Sophie; there was a sarcasm in them now, stronger than the hostility which had been there before. 'All about him?'

'Yes,' Louise answered her. 'There are no secrets in our family, Madame.'

'How lucky,' Ilse Minden said, 'that you have nothing to hide. Please let me talk to you alone. I've come a long way.'

'Sophie,' Louise said quietly. 'Leave us alone, darling.

Please.' There were times when it was unwise to argue with her mother. For a moment Sophie hesitated. Her lover said that being a rich American gave Louise de Bernard her authority. But to Sophie that was a superficial lie. Her mother commanded others because she was fully in command of herself. Which was something that Gerard, riotously self-indulgent, would never understand. She got up and went out.

'Thank you,' Ilse Minden said. There was a pause; they looked at each other. Jealousy was rending the older woman's purpose. She was beautiful, she looked young, she would turn any man's head as much now as she had done then . . . Suddenly tears came into her eyes and overflowed. She dug into the handbag and brought out a paper handkerchief. She pressed it tight against her face.

'Don't, please.' The American woman's voice was gentle. She felt a hand on her shoulder and took the handkerchief away. She had a speech prepared, rehearsed over and over during the long journey overland from Bonn, repeated in front of the mirror in her dingy pension bedroom that morning. Now she remembered none of it. Old sorrows and present fear came out in a rush of words.

'You've got to help him! You've got to pay back what you owe him—he sacrificed everything for you! Oh God, God help us . . .'

'Don't cry,' Louise said. 'Try and calm yourself.' She pulled a chair next to Ilse Minden and sat down. 'I don't understand,' she said. 'How can I help your husband now? I haven't seen or heard of him since the war.'

'No,' the other woman said, using the handkerchief. 'No, you wouldn't. You didn't need him any more, did you? You were safe then because we'd lost—while he . . . Do you know what he's suffered for all these years, do you know how we lived after the war was over? How could you . . .' She spoke with angry vehemence. 'You had everything you wanted. You were the victors!'

'Madame Minden,' Louise said. 'I knew your husband many years ago when he was living in my house. You talk about a debt; all right, I owe him a great deal. You say you've come to ask for help. Would you please explain what kind of help you want? And try not to be so hostile towards me; I never did you or your husband any harm.'

She moved away and got a cigarette. She felt disturbed and distressed. There was something ugly about the other woman's tears, something more than emotional turbulence which is always disconcerting to a stranger. There was hatred, and there was a subtle suggestion of threat. For all her tears, there was a determination and a toughness about Heinz Minden's wife which made Louise uncomfortable. She had come to demand something, rather than to plead.

'You say you never did him any harm?'

'Never. If he told you anything different, then I'm afraid he's lying.'

'Oh, he wouldn't describe it that way!' She gave a short, unpleasant laugh. 'Everything you ever did was perfect, Madame de Bernard. You couldn't do wrong in Heinz's eyes —surely you know that?'

'You're talking about years ago,' Louise pointed out. 'About the distant past. None of that matters anymore.'

'Not to you, of course. But it matters to us. It's mattered to me, Madame, knowing my husband didn't love me any more because of you! It may be years ago for you, but it's day to day for me! How do you think I felt, living in dirty back rooms, taking what jobs I could to support us, starving myself and him to give our children a chance, and knowing that nothing I did, *nothing*, stopped him thinking about you!'

'I'm terribly sorry.' Louise looked away from her, from the anguish and bitterness assaulting her from so close. 'Please believe me, I did nothing to encourage this . . .' And then she stopped, remembering. 'I'm sorry,' she said again. She put out a hand to Ilse Minden, who jerked back from being touched.

'Helping you caused all the trouble,' she said. 'When the war was over the organisation which took care of people like Heinz found out about it, and they threw him out. They stopped helping him. We were on our own then, hiding, running from place to place frightened to settle anywhere. We could have been in South America by now if he hadn't compromised himself for you!'

She could have argued with Ilse Minden; she could have pointed out that what her husband had done only reflected credit on him, that it was not because he was in love with her. Any man, anyone with decency or sensibilities would have done the same. But she didn't say anything. To the woman facing her, it was an incomprehensible folly, committed by an infatuated man for a woman he loved. And the knowledge of this made Madame Minden, dull and plain and tearful, a very frightening person.

'Surely by now that kind of thing is over,' Louise said. 'There are thousands of people living in Germany without having to fear for what they did. Or what they were.'

'My husband was a brilliant man,' Ilse Minden interrupted. 'You call working in a pharmacy, selling tubes of toothpaste and bars of soap, living without fear? And that's only in the last five years. Before that he was doing odd jobs, sweeping, digging, anything he could find where nobody would notice him. And now, Madame de Bernard, even that miserable life is over. He's in prison!'

Suddenly the German woman's tears were dried up; she looked calm and grim waiting for Louise to react. In all the years of running a large household, managing her family and the complicated affairs of a large fortune, Louise had never felt as lost and disconcerted as she did now.

'Why is he in prison? What's the charge?'

'War crimes,' his wife said. 'For all these years they've been hunting him; that filthy Jew in Vienna had his name on a list. And two months ago they found him. He was arrested and he's in jail waiting to be tried.'

'It shouldn't be,' Louise said slowly. 'Your husband wasn't like the others—he didn't . . .'

'He did his duty,' Ilse Minden broke in harshly. 'He fought for his country and his Führer as we all did. Then it was patriotism, now it's a crime. The only time he failed was when he put you first.'

'It wasn't me he put first,' Louise said. 'Surely you can see that?'

'Can't see anything but my husband facing a sentence of fifteen or twenty years,' came the reply. 'That's why I'm here. I've used my savings to get here and see you.'

'What do you want me to do?' Louise asked. 'If you need money for his defence . . .'

'No thank you,' Ilse Minden said. 'Money would be easy for you, wouldn't it? I don't need money. There are lawyers in Germany who will undertake a defence for someone like my husband. Someone who's being persecuted by the politicians and the Jews. No, Madame de Bernard, I need a different kind of help. I want you to stand up in court and tell them what my husband did for you. I want you to testify that he saved lives, and risked his own. His counsel knows what happened. He says that if you appear for the defence it will make all the difference. He could get a suspended sentence.'

'I can't give you an answer.' Louise stood up suddenly. 'I've had no time to think about it, no warning. I can't just promise to go to Germany and stand up in a court—I'll have to talk to my family.'

'I see.' She opened her handbag, took out another paper handkerchief and wiped her mouth with it.

'You had a sister-in-law, didn't you?'

Louise stood very still. 'Yes.'

'Her name was Régine, wasn't it?'

'Yes it was.'

'You look upset, Madame,' Ilse Minden said in a quiet voice. 'Why don't you sit down again? I'm not leaving here yet. Shall I tell you about your sister-in-law? Shall I tell you what my Heinz told me about her?'

'Are you threatening me?'

'Of course not; I need your help. Heinz needs it. One thing the defence counsel said to me—there'll be a lot of dirt and scandal when this case comes to trial. People who've been living a lie and pretending to be what they weren't are going to look very sick by the time it's all over. Don't you think that's true?'

'You are threatening me,' Louise said slowly. 'You're trying to blackmail me. Well, you've made a mistake. I won't be blackmailed. I'll show you out.' She stood up and went to the door. The German woman got up.

'Your husband,' she said. 'The Resistance hero. I believe your son is running for deputy for your home region, isn't that so? Before you throw me out of your house, Madame, think carefully. All we need is a few words from you, to save an old man from spending the rest of his life in jail.'

'If you'd put it to me like that first, I might have testified,' Louise said quietly. 'Now will you please leave my house.'

'You're very grand, aren't you, Madame de Bernard? You can turn a poor woman away, and leave the debt you owe my Heinz unpaid? Very well. But here is my address. I'll be there for the next two days. Let me know when you change your mind.' She walked past Louise to the door and let herself out, leaving it open. Her thick shoes made an ugly noise as she crossed the marble hall. There was a snap as the front door shut.

For some moments Louise didn't move; it was as if the presence of the other woman hadn't left the room. Hate hung in the atmosphere like cigarette smoke. She went to the door and closed it. She pulled the chair away from the sofa where Ilse Minden had sat down; she lit a cigarette and deliberately calmed herself. She straightened a cushion and made a note to replace one of the hothouse plants.

'Mother? I heard that woman go out. Darling, what's the matter?' Sophie de Bernard came towards her. 'What in God's name did she say to you?'

'Not a lot,' Louise said slowly. 'But enough. Her husband's in prison in Germany; he's going to be tried for war crimes. She wants me to go and give evidence for him. She wants me to tell the story in court.'

'That's ridiculous! You're not doing anything of the sort! You can give written evidence, an affidavit and send them that. You're not going near any war crimes trial!'

'Darling, you don't understand. She threatened me. She threatened to make a scandal.'

'And can she make one?' Sophie asked the question boldly. Her attitude was defensive, determined not to care. 'Not that I give a damn,' she said. 'You know that.'

'Yes, I do. But you're not the only one. What about Paul?'

'Don't tell him,' Sophie said. 'Look, Mother, be sensible. She's just trying to frighten you. There's nothing she can rake up now that would matter to anyone. It's over and done with —nobody cares any more. Let her go to hell. And so what if he did do one decent thing? What about the rest of it? Come on, forget about it. I'll take you out to lunch today.'

'She left me her address,' Louise said. 'She said she'd be there for two days and to let her know when I changed my mind. When. Not "if".'

'That's just bluff,' Sophie said angrily. 'You'll never hear another word about it.'

Louise looked at her daughter. She was brave and loyal and loving, ready to battle the world for her mother. Would she be so ready, so trusting if she knew exactly what the woman Ilse knew? Probably; there was a generous spirit there and a capacity for understanding which was rare in the modern *avant garde*.

She held out her hand to Sophie and forced herself to smile.

'You're right, I expect. I won't hear any more from her. Give me half an hour to telephone and finish that wretched report upstairs and then we'll go and lunch together.' Reassured, Sophie preceded her mother out of the salon. She had a capacity for believing the best would happen rather than the worst. Upstairs in the study, with the mechanics of her normal life to be attended to, Louise stared at the telephone and the papers, unable to apply herself to either. Sophie had tried to comfort her, and had succeeded in lulling herself. Louise thanked God for what she felt was only a respite. When you change your mind. Heinz Minden's wife had chosen her words with care. The piece of paper with the address of the pension was on her desk. She had brought it upstairs with her. Subconsciously. She put it away carefully in a drawer, and knew as she did so, that the first part of the battle had been won by Ilse Minden.

• • • • •

There was a three-hour delay on calls to Bonn. She sat in the dreary little sitting room of the pension, waiting for the call, looking through old copies of *Plaisir de la Maison* and a tattered edition of *Elle*, which was six months out of date and featured an article by film stars who had undergone abortions and were championing the cause. She hated the French. Their lack of morality disgusted her. She disliked their food and their fashions, their architecture annoyed her because it was so grandiose and nothing could take away from the people of the country the splendour of its history and the strength of its traditions. She could never forget that they had been beaten; that she had worn stockings and scent and a smart fur coat which Heinz had brought her after his posting to France. For a brief period they had had their hands in the till, fingering the luxuries. Twenty years of deprivation had followed that fleeting indulgence. Defeat and humiliation, shame and fear. She hated her country's enemies, and above all she hated the woman who had received her that morning. It had been a catharsis to go and see her, to spill out some of the venom which had corroded her spirit for so many years. Now she could hate the real woman, not the figment which was all Heinz's unhappy confessions had created for her. Now she knew the colour of Louise de Bernard's eyes, the shape of her face, the gestures she used. The enemy had taken on flesh. When the call came through she hurried to the outer office and dropped into the chair behind the reception desk. She gave a glare at the proprietress who seemed inclined to linger and try to listen.

'Herr Kopner? Frau Minden. Yes, yes I've seen her.'

There was a pencil on the desk and a note pad. She began to draw little lines, crossing and recrossing as she talked. 'Yes, I had a long talk. No. She refused. Well, we expected that. Of course. No, no, I didn't say anything too obvious. Now I will make the next move. I'm sure of it. Certain. How is my husband? He mustn't suspect anything—he wouldn't agree—yes, yes, I've told you, I shall do it immediately. I gave her two days. I will telephone to you as soon as I have any news. Good. *Auf Wiedersehen.*' She hung up. The proprietress came back, her expression curious. 'You wish this call to be put on your bill, or would you like to pay for it now?'

'On the bill,' Ilse Minden said. 'Can you help me please—I need a directory for the Houdan region. Do you have one here?'

'The directories are under the shelf there. Can I get the name for you?'

'Thank you, no. I can look it up myself.' She ruffled the pages, uncertain at first where to look, refusing to satisfy the old woman's curiosity by letting her find the number. She ran one finger down the page; her nail was filed short and the cuticle was rough. She found the name and the number, and wrote it down.

'I want to make another call,' she said. 'Also on the bill. Do I dial direct?'

'For Houdan and that part, certainly, yes. Shall I get it for you?'

'No. Thank you.' Ilse Minden dialled slowly, checking the figures against the number scribbled down on the pad. There was a pause.

'Hello?' She raised her voice unnecessarily, as foreigners do when speaking on the telephone in a different language. 'I wish to speak to the Comte de Bernard. Thank you. Yes, I'll wait.' She glanced at the proprietress, who looked preoccupied and went out of the hallway. 'Good morning,' she said. 'Monsieur de Bernard? You don't know me. My name is Ilse Minden.'

. . . . .

In his office on the Hofgarten Strasse in the centre of Bonn, the defence counsel, who was preparing his brief for Heinz Minden, put back the telephone and lit a cigarette. He smoked the cheapest brand; it was a curious idiosyncrasy and quite out of character; he lived extremely well and bought the best for himself. His practice was flourishing, he owned a smart house in the best residential area, out on the Bahnhof estate; ran two cars and had a well-connected second wife, who was fervently advancing his political ambition. He was a good-looking man of forty-two, just the right age to seek office. Too young for the war and yet old enough to appeal to those who had fought in it, and for whom the old wounds still smarted. His name was Siegfried Kopner. He had visited Heinz Minden the previous afternoon. He found him a pathetic specimen, and Herr Kopner did not equate pathos with pity. Minden was broken, his resignation infuriated Kopner, who had staked his reputation in public upon saving him. And more than him, much more than the liberty of one listless old man who actually looked back on his past with regret.

Kopner had been looking for a platform from which to deliver his political viewpoint. The trial of someone like Heinz Minden was exactly what he needed. In the court he could say all those things and ally himself with attitudes which would have been unthinkable as part of an election formula. And yet they supplied a need and expressed the feelings of thousands, perhaps millions of his countrymen. Fortunately, if the husband's spine was snapped, there was plenty of determination in the woman. Kopner thought his client's wife was an unpleasant type, embittered and sexless, fastened like a leech upon the uncaring corpse of the man she was married to; but she presented him with the weapon he needed. During the long, tearful consultations about Minden's defence, she had told him, little by little and with increasing self-pity, the story of her husband's infatuation for the Comtesse de Bernard, and of the effort he had made on her behalf. Nothing would convince the woman, so blinded by jealousy, that Minden had acted out of anything but a desire to ingratiate himself with the Comtesse. To Kopner it was a gift; the kind of story which properly presented, could diminish his client's responsibility for the crimes charged against him, and show him in the kind of heroic light which the liberals found so satisfactory. And at the same time there in the courtroom would be a representative of the enemy; the old enemy, but still very much a symbol, not only of their own heroism but of the iniquity of their opponents. Louise de Bernard. He had checked on the family after listening to Ilse Minden and in the dungheap of marital discord and old infringements of international law, he had found a shining political pearl. He had smoked the meagre cigarette down to its buff coloured tip. He rubbed it out in an onyx ashtray. He had sent Minden's wife to Paris. It was too compromising to go himself. Her initial failure had disappointed him but he appeared undaunted by it. She possessed the confidence of the obsessed. She wanted her husband's freedom; that was the reason she gave to herself. But equally, and probably more, if motives were honestly analysed, she wanted her rival humiliated and destroyed in public.

Which was exactly what Siegfried Kopner wanted too. He

lit another cigarette and spoke to his secretary on the intercom.

'Telephone to my wife,' he said.

There was a dinner party arranged in his honour that evening; he decided it would be simpler if his wife brought a change of clothes to his office and he dressed there. He had a great deal of work to do and he didn't want to leave early.

His wife was the daughter of a former Admiral; her family were of a higher social class than his own, but the war had deprived them of their Eastern estates and she was eager to marry him. She was a hard, determined woman whose ambitions were centred upon him. She had devoted herself to his comfort and his career from the start of the marriage, and he was very happy with her. He slept at regular intervals with a delightful, amusing little dress designer he had met at a party, and considered himself to have the best arrangement any man could want.

His wife came through on the line. He told her to bring his evening suit; she agreed immediately. 'Any news from Frau Minden?' She knew everything about the case. He always discussed his work with her; she often had valuable comments to make. 'She phoned not long ago,' Kopner said. 'The Comtesse wouldn't agree. I don't think she handled her very well. But she's going to carry out the second plan, and she thinks this will work. I think so too.'

'Excellent,' his wife said. Her voice came through high pitched through the receiver. He held it a little away from his ear. 'They'll give in,' she said. 'I'm very confident. I'll be at the office at six-thirty; that will give you an hour to change. We mustn't be late. I've sent flowers to Hilda.'

'Excellent,' he said, imitating her. 'Until six-thirty.'

A senior member of the Bundeswehr would be present at the dinner. It was hoped to enlist him as a sponsor for Kopner's candidature. The evening would be very important in his career. At about the same time as his wife arrived with the suitcase, carrying his beautifully pressed dinner jacket, Ilse Minden got off the train at Houdan railway station and took a taxi to the Château St. Blaize.

2

SOPHIE DE BERNARD was a fast driver; she took the autoroute out of Paris, following the signs to Versailles and swung round past the town onto the Chartres road. For the first twenty minutes Louise sat beside her without speaking. The traffic was always heavy, and although they were ahead of the evening rush, the pace was sluggish; there were few opportunities for Sophie to unleash the Mercedes and drive at her usual speed. Finally they cleared the slow-moving line of cars and lorries, and the car shot forward. Louise looked at her.

'Don't go too quickly, darling. We'll be there soon enough.'

'He makes me sick,' her daughter said furiously. 'You shouldn't have come down; they're only going to make things difficult for you.'

'They won't mean to,' Louise said. 'Besides, I've made it difficult for them. Paul sounded terribly shaken on the telephone.'

'Only because that damned Françoise had been at him. "Think of your career, think what will happen if there is a scandal"—I can just hear her saying it!'

'You've got to promise me not to quarrel with them,' Louise said. 'I've got to talk to Paul and find out what he wants me to do.'

'He'll want you to protect him,' Sophie said angrily. 'That's obvious. He should have thrown that woman out of the house instead of listening to her! I shouldn't have called you to the telephone! Anyway, whatever you say, Mother, I'm not going to stand by and let them bully you.'

Louise didn't answer. Her son's anxious voice on the telephone the night before had been completely unexpected. She had never thought for a moment that Ilse Minden would go direct to him. But she had, and the worried man, trying to seem calm, had begged her to come down to St. Blaize and discuss the problem with him. And with his wife, whose voice she could hear murmuring in the background. They would both be there, frightened and surprised, not knowing how to cope. The unexpected seldom disturbed their lives. She allowed herself to wonder how her son and his wife Françoise would have behaved had they faced the same situations as she had done. And her husband, whose portrait had been commissioned by Paul and now hung in the main hall of the Château. He was very proud of his father, who had been a hero of the Resistance. If she wore her own Legion d'Honneur ribbon, he was visibly gratified. She thought of the coming interview and shuddered. Not for herself. Since the telephone call last night her feelings for herself were numb. All she could feel now was sorrow for the others, the innocent whose safe illusions had been shattered. How much had that woman told Paul—how much would she have to tell Sophie, who might not be as immune as she pretended . . .

They had left the autoroute behind and were travelling fast along the country roads, passing through St. Leger en Yvelines, where her husband Jean used to hunt before the war, on to Houdan, and then across to St. Blaize, down the narrow road she remembered so well. It was a long time since she had been there, almost three years. Visits for the christening of her first grandson, then a grand-daughter, one painful Christmas spent with the family, who hadn't known how to entertain her, because her distress at being in the Château was so obvious. They had meant to be kind, Paul and Françoise, and Sophie, at that time in the first stage of a violent love affair with a popular guitarist, had been in America with him on a tour. She couldn't spend Christmas in Paris alone; it would be too painful. Against her will, and only to please them, Louise had allowed them to persuade her and she had come back to the house which had been her home, and which she never wanted to see again. Now, passing through the wrought-iron gates and turning up the drive, she saw the familiar turret, clothed in ivy and the handsome façade, surrounded by sweeping green lawns, the old trees giving their magnificent shade, unchanged by centuries. Dogs rushed out to meet her, the lean grey Weimaren hounds that her daughter-in-law kept, and which had replaced the spaniels which she and Jean had loved. And then her son, tall and anxious-looking, with his wife's slight figure, suitably dressed in tweed and English cashmere emerging from behind him. They kissed her; he was affectionate and warm, and pretended not to notice his sister's aggressive attitude as she walked into the house. Inside, Louise paused for a moment.

There was the hall, a large room with a Norman ceiling, the sixteenth-century tapestries which had been there since they were woven, and the portrait of Jean de Bernard, with a light over it, dominating the room. Françoise advanced towards her; she had a special tone for her mother-in-law, of whom she was very much in awe. It suggested that whatever happened she had to be humoured, and it never failed to make Louise feel like an intruder.

'Would you like to go upstairs to your room, first, Louise? Then we can talk in the library?'

'Yes, that would be nice. Where am I sleeping? The little blue room?'

'Well, no,' Françoise explained. Her smile was strained and she looked as if she hadn't slept. 'We've had that done for Christiane. You're in the second guest room. It's all been decorated; it's very pretty now.'

Louise smiled back at her and followed her up the staircase. A manservant was carrying her small case. They had insisted that she and Sophie stayed the night. It couldn't be discussed in a hurry. She walked slowly up the winding stone stairs and outside the bedroom door she hesitated. Her bag was inside, the servant stood waiting for her to go in. It was a room she hadn't seen for over twenty years. A room which held memories of such anguish and such longing that she felt her colour fading as she stepped inside it.

Nothing remained the same. The walls were a different colour, the old-fashioned four-poster bed had gone, the armchair, the Empire furniture, the ugly pre-war chintzes. 'Thank you,' she said, not turning round, and the door closed. She was alone in the room which had been Roger Savage's bedroom. She went to the window and looked out. He had done the same, that morning in June, in 1944, drawing back the curtains and looking down. She hadn't thought about him, she hadn't let his memory return to spoil the last few years. Now there was no defence. Suddenly she dropped upon the bed, and found that she was crying. No defence at all. Her daughter-in-law had made the changes, turning the room into a pretty, chic guest bedroom, but she couldn't paint out the past, and it rushed at Louise, sharp and so real that the present seemed to have no substance. Roger Savage. And down the corridor Heinz Minden's room, and the room where Régine slept. They were all there, the ghosts and the living, crowding in upon her, demanding to be recognised. And Savage was the most real of all. She could see him standing by the window, tall and broad, the sun shooting rays of light around him as he blocked it out, looking down at the forty-foot drop below. She put both hands to her face and wiped away the tears. He had hated to see her cry. Even at the end when she was weeping in agony for him, he had been hurt by her tears . . .

There was a knock at the door. It opened without waiting for her to answer, and it was not Sophie, as she expected, but her son Paul.

'Mother,' he said gently. 'I had a feeling you'd be upset. Come downstairs; we're all waiting for you. We'll talk about it and find a solution together.' He put his arm around her, and they left the room.

There had been a row between Sophie and Françoise; she could feel it as soon as she went into the yellow salon. They were apart, the Comtesse de Bernard sitting very upright, her face pink and her eyes bright with anger; Sophie lounging like an urchin, a cigarette dangling from her mouth. Louise looked at them both and gently disengaged herself from Paul's arm. He couldn't support her. He belonged to his wife; he had a family of his own, a life apart from hers. His was the future. Ilse Minden had come into their lives, and the past was threatening them all. She was the direct link with it; the responsibility must be hers alone. But first, before any decision could be taken, there was something she knew she had to do. She had known in that upstairs room, as clearly as if Savage had come back and told her.

'Let's all sit down,' she said. 'Paul, my dear, get me a drink, would you? A whisky and Perrier.'

'Of course.' He looked relieved at having been asked to do something.

'Françoise? Sophie?' Both women shook their heads. Louise took the glass from him and lit a cigarette. For once her daughter-in-law didn't rush forward with an ashtray.

'I don't know what that woman told you,' Louise said quietly. 'But I can imagine you've found a lot of it distressing.'

'We didn't believe it,' her son said. 'We would never believe anything . . .' He stopped, embarrassed. 'We just wanted to discuss what should be done.'

'You're not going to bully Mother into giving evidence to keep that bloody woman's mouth shut.' Sophie turned on him fiercely. 'And that's what I gather you're proposing to do!' She gave her sister-in-law a look of fury.

'No we're not,' Paul de Bernard said. He avoided his wife's anxious glance. 'We're going to behave in a sensible fashion and talk this out. Nobody's going to do anything to upset Mother. So you needn't talk like that.'

'None of you need get angry with each other on my account,' Louise said. 'There's no need. I'm sure Ilse Minden told you she'd been to see me. She tried to blackmail me. As she obviously did to you, Paul. One thing is certain; she doesn't intend to give up. What we have to decide is whether to give in to that blackmail, or whether to resist it.'

'There is another point.' Françoise de Bernard spoke for the first time. There was an expression on her face as she looked at Louise which had never been there before. 'And that's whether, in conscience, Mother shouldn't do as she asks.'

'That's true,' Louise answered. 'And there's only one way to decide. And that is for me to tell you exactly what happened. The truth.'

'Mother . . .' Sophie began, 'we know . . .'

'No, darling,' Louise interrupted. 'I'm afraid you don't. But I am going to tell you. Then we will make up our minds what I must do.'

• • • • •

The Château de St. Blaize lay some fifty kilometres from Paris, and forty kilometres from the great medieval city of Chartres. The village of St. Blaize en Yvelines was dominated by the Château which watched over it from a slight rise in the ground. It was a small, turreted château of grey stone with a slate roof, a tower at its north side, approached from the road by a long gravel drive. For nearly six hundred years it had been the centre of life for the village, and the same family had lived there without interruption except for a period of exile during the Revolution. The bigger houses in the area were under German occupation, their owners quartered in a small portion of their homes, but St. Blaize belonged entirely to the de Bernards. The village, observing everything that happened at the Château, congratulated the Comte on having kept his home intact and admired his facility for coping with the occupying forces. He showed remarkable tact and foresight for a comparatively young man, and his lack of false heroics relieved the citizens of St. Blaize of any feeling of guilt for their own complaisance towards the enemy.

One experience of German anger had been enough for the most reckless of the men who sat round boasting and grumbling in the wine shop. They followed the example of the Comte and showed their wish to co-operate with the German authorities. As a result, their lives were undisturbed, and only one German officer, more of a guest than an intruder, lived at the Château with the Comte and his family. It was known that the Comtesse held different views from her husband and had never hesitated to express them, but since she was an American, her example was ignored. Nobody in St. Blaize wanted trouble, or to be forced to fight the Germans. They wanted to survive, like the Comte de Bernard.

One evening at the end of May in 1944 Louise took their coffee into the salon; for the last three months Jean de Bernard had insisted upon the German dining with them instead of in his room, and staying for an hour or two afterwards. Eating with him had been bad enough for Louise; his presence in her drawing room only increased her disgust with her husband. There was nothing obviously offensive about Major Minden. He was a quiet man in his thirties, unobtrusive and embarrassed by his being billeted upon them. He had gone out of his way to be self-effacing and when the Comte de Bernard offered him hospitality, he responded by generous gifts of things which were unobtainable for the French. He was always polite, tactful, appreciative of everything. He apologised for the situation in which they found themselves without ever putting his guilt into words, and he followed Louise with his eyes, mentally fornicating, until she could have screamed.

The meal this evening had been simple; food was short and luxuries like butter and sugar tightly rationed. Not even Minden's ingenuity could get them the rich veal and cream, the pork and game and poultry which had made the food at St. Blaize famous before the war. The cook had died in 1941, and now the cooking was done by Louise or Marie-Anne, who showed remarkable skill with vegetables, eggs and an occasional chicken. There was a splendid cellar at the Château, and they bottled a light white wine from their own vineyards in the Loire. After dinner, Minden produced a bottle of fine cognac and offered his host a cigar. Louise looked at him as he pierced and lit it. It was May, but the weather had been wet and cold; a log fire was alight in the wide stone grate, and the light flickered over the face she had loved, and caressed with her hands. He had changed very little in the eight years they had been married. His manner was the same; gentle, courteous, a little aloof but his laugh hadn't lost its warmth or his eyes their charm. She could see Minden responding to it, smiling and talking, leaning a little forward, the cigar jutting through his fingers. For a moment he was concentrating on the Comte and not slyly glancing at her, his tongue slipping over his lips. She hated the way he treated her, the spring to his feet when she came into a room, holding out her chair when they sat at the dining table, always polite, with his head a little on one side as if he were concentrating on every word. And she said as little as possible. She showed him that she resented him and disliked him, but his skin was elephantine. Nothing she said or did to convey her feelings made the slightest difference. He responded by bringing her a large bottle of the most expensive scent at Christmas which was exclusively exported to Germany. She would have respected him more if he'd tried to put his hand down her dress.

He and her husband were talking about the war; the room was full of the smell of cigar smoke; Louise poked at the logs and listened.

'I didn't believe they'd ever invade,' Jean de Bernard said. 'I still can't take it seriously.'

'It's very serious indeed,' Minden said. 'It's said there must be quarter of a million men waiting to leave England and land over here. Of course, it's the Russians pressing for a Second Front that's forced them into it.' He tapped his ash into a silver bowl.

'You don't seem concerned, Major,' Jean de Bernard remarked.

'I can't see them winning,' Minden said mildly. 'I foresee terrific casualties and complete defeat.'

'Aren't you being a little complacent?' They both looked at Louise.

'I don't think so,' the Major answered. His tone implied that it wasn't a topic on which she would have anything sensible to say.

'After all, the British Empire and the United States are a pretty formidable combination,' Louise went on, knowing how Jean hated her to goad the German. 'You won't just flick off a quarter of a million men like a speck of dust.'

Minden nearly smiled. He had to be careful not to show the extent of his confidence but it was so much a part of him now that he couldn't pretend to be afraid. Invasion didn't trouble him. Victory was certain. He stared for a moment at the Comtesse's beautiful legs. American women had the best legs in the world. And the best teeth; hers were perfect. In spite of her colouring, brown hair and hazel eyes, she couldn't have been a Frenchwoman. She was too tall, too slim.

'You must forgive me, Madame,' he said. 'I believe our soldiers are the best in the world. I think we will beat the invasion forces when they come.'

'And will you be going to fight them?'

His half-smile was still there, the light of admiration in his eyes as he answered her. Jean de Bernard re-lit his cigar, without looking at his wife. 'Unfortunately, I shall still be attached to General Brühl. Believe me, I would like to be a combatant, but someone has to do the staff work.

'It may be dull but it's better than being sent to Russia.' Louise lit a cigarette. Jean de Bernard got up bringing his cup.

'Could I have some more coffee?'

She ignored the warning in his eyes. He was a coward. He was her husband and now she despised him as much as she had looked up to him and loved him. Let him crawl to the conquerors; she didn't glance at him. She poured the coffee which was real instead of the filthy mixture of acorns and chicory which was all the non-collaborationists had to drink, and gave it gack to him.

'I think I'll go to bed,' she said. 'I'm rather tired tonight.'

Immediately the Major was on his feet, his heels snapped together. She went out of the room, savouring the small exchange which was already beginning to look petty and pointless as she thought about it. Scoring off someone too insensitive to feel it was small compensation for the misery and shame which tormented her every time she saw him. He wasn't a brute, there was nothing of the strutting Nazi about him; he was an ordinary man, not remarkable in any way, but he was a German, the symbol of the disgrace of France and the capitulation of the man she loved. Jean had collaborated and the village had done the same. French girls walked the lanes with German soldiers and their families accepted cigarettes and food. France had lain down for her conquerors, it was not so much a rape as a seduction. Louise, who had loved all things French and embraced the culture and even, within two years of marriage, the faith of her adopted country, watched in horror as people she respected set about ingratiating themselves with the invaders, as the homes of their friends were filled with German officers on social calls, and there were dinner parties and murmurs of love affairs with women whose husbands had not yet been repatriated. The first shock had come that summer's day in 1940, four years ago, when she and Jean had stood together in the Château with his sister Régine, then a girl of fifteen, and seen the German scout car come skidding up the gravel drive, scattering the stones, and slam to a stop before the entrance. There were black and white crosses painted on its sides and as they watched through the window, three men got out in field grey uniform. He had held her in his arms, and she had gripped him tight, ready to die with him if he asked her. 'Oh my God,' she had whispered to him. 'What are we going to do . . .'

'Learn to live with them,' Jean had answered. 'Live with them and survive. And keep our home.' She hadn't believed him, she hadn't really understood. When the salon door opened and the first German officer stepped inside, she waited for Jean to move, to show resistance. Instead he had disengaged himself from her and walked towards them, one hand extended.

'Gentlemen,' he had said. 'Welcome to St. Blaize.' There were two of them, young men with anonymous faces under their peaked combat caps. Tears had come rushing into her eyes; she had caught Regine by the hand and dragged her past them and upstairs. As she ran into the hall she heard her husband say, 'You must excuse my wife. She is upset. Please sit down.' From that moment the disintegration had begun.

When Louise had gone out, Minden stretched and sat down again. Jean poured some brandy into his glass and offered the bottle, but the Major shook his head. 'I've got some work to do,' he said. 'Brandy makes me go to sleep. I'm glad your wife went up early, I wanted to talk to you in private. You know there was an alert tonight?'

'No,' Jean de Bernard said. 'They must have been on their way somewhere else, nothing was dropped near here.' The Major had come back late; to Louise's irritation Jean had insisted upon waiting dinner for him.

'It was a single plane,' the Major said. 'We've had them come over before. Personally I believe it was a reconnaissance flight. On the other hand it may have been a drop.'

'A drop—what do you mean?'

'Enemy agents. It's not likely but we have to take precautions. There'll be road blocks tomorrow and a search. I wanted to warn you. I didn't want to worry Madame de Bernard.'

'They won't drop anyone here,' Jean said. 'It's two years since they tried that. Nobody at St. Blaize wants any trouble.'

'We know that,' Minden said seriously. 'There's no resistance in this area. Now that the resistance at Chartres has been broken . . .' He paused, regretting having mentioned the incident. 'But I just wanted to ask you to use your influence with the village. If anyone should have landed here—I hope you'll impress on them how foolish it would be to shelter them. As I said, I'm sure it's a reconnaissance plane that probably went astray. It may have crashed somewhere nearer the coast; that's the official view, but we have to be careful.'

'Don't worry,' Jean de Bernard said. 'We're at peace, we get along with you extremely well. The last thing anyone wants to do is to spoil our relationship with the military. You have my personal assurance that I'll go down and speak to the mayor tomorrow. If the Allies have been stupid enough to try and involve us by dropping any agent here, they'll be given up to you immediately.'

'Thank you,' the Major said. He got up. 'I should make sure all doors are locked. I hope your wife won't be frightened; really there's no need to mention it. There'll be a routine search tomorrow, but I'll make sure you're not disturbed.'

'That's very considerate of you,' Jean de Bernard said. 'Louise wouldn't be alarmed but it might upset my father. He's getting so confused so quickly.'

'I'm sorry to hear that. I must go and have a talk to him one evening. He isn't getting any worse?'

'Not physically; age is a sad thing, Major. He's becoming more and more of a child.'

'I'll say goodnight,' the Major said. 'If you should hear any rumours tomorrow you will let me know?'

'You can rely on me,' the Comte de Bernard said. 'Goodnight.' He didn't leave the room after Minden; he stayed on beside the sinking fire, finishing the brandy. Enemy agents. A quarter of a million men waiting on the other side of the English Channel to launch themselves against the coast of France. A rain of shells and bombs falling on French homes and killing the innocent inside them. The giants squaring up for a fight to the death, with his people and his country as their battleground. Above all he didn't believe the Germans would be beaten. Their vengeance upon any who had turned against them would be too terrible to contemplate. Thanks to his efforts St. Blaize en Yvelines had suffered only two casualties since the occupation, and they were the direct results of night warnings like this one, of a parachute drop by the British . . . No more French lives were going to be sacrificed to the ruthless strategists in London. He finished his brandy, and lit a cigarette. He had better follow Minden's suggestion and make sure that every door and window was locked. And then he had to go and see his wife. In his youth there had been fifteen servants at the Château; now there were two, Marie-Anne and Jean-Pierre, husband and wife who had started working in his parents' time as kitchen maid and undergardener. They were in their sixties and Jean-Pierre had a stiff knee. Soon after Minden arrived he pressed his batman, a surly Rhinelander with a milky eye, into helping them and doing odd jobs in the garden. It was part of his plan to ingratiate himself. Jean de Bernard had accepted it as he did everything the Major offered. Cigarettes, the few petrol coupons that were more valuable than banknotes, brandy, cigars; the clumsy ogling of Louise . . . And so St. Blaize survived, his father lived in gentle senility upstairs, his son and daughter played on the green lawns and chased each other through the shrub gardens just as he had done. The village and its people lived in peace. Shortages would not last for ever nor would their occupation by a conqueror. France would outlast the Nazis; the Château with the scars of old sieges on its outer walls would stand intact when the occupation was just a section in the history books. What he was doing had to be done. It had cost him his pride, his self-respect, and the love of his wife.

He smoked his cigarette down and thought about her, his brow furrowed with unhappiness. They were completely different in temperament. She was passionate, impulsive, with the pride he recognised as truly American. Compromise disgusted her; unlike so many of her sex she never lied, or demeaned herself by petty actions. She was a woman of daring and character, bold and fiercely loyal to those she loved. Soon after they met in New York he had teased her that a hundred years earlier she would have taken a waggon out West and fought the Indians. Although it was a joke, he had come to recognise how accurately he had described her. She was truly the child of her New World, and he the product of the Old one. Now she despised and hated him for a cowardice she couldn't understand. She had expected him to fight; expected the people of St. Blaize to rush against the Germans with flails and scythes, like the mobs in a Hollywood movie about the Revolution. After eight years of living among them, Louise hadn't understood the villagers any more than she did him. He threw his cigarette away, placed a wire guard in front of the smouldering fire and fastened the window shutters before turning out the lights. It took a long time to bolt the windows on the ground floor, to lock the back doors and the massive entrance door with its iron hinges He checked that the little door leading from the cellar was also locked. Jean Pierre always fastened it from habit. Then he began to climb the steep stone stairs that led to the tower, built by an ancestor in the sixteenth century as a fortification for the house and the only means of reaching the upper floors. A nineteenth-century Comte de Bernard had built a back stairs to accommodate his staff, but the massive stone steps, hollowed in the middle by hundreds of years of use, had never been replaced. On the first floor Louise de Bernard slept in what had been their bedroom. At the top of the stairs he paused. In the first few months when Louise kept the door locked, he had taken a mistress. Outraged and bitterly hurt, Jean had turned to the wife of a neighbour who had been considered for him when they were both children, but it had been a tepid affair which died away in mutual disappointment. He wanted Louise; her substitute proved to be a vain and vapid shadow of whom he quickly rid himself.

Since then he had accepted the situation and only once tried to force a reconciliation when he got drunk sitting alone in the library one winter. His need and his loneliness had driven him upstairs to batter on the door. Her rejection of him had been angry and contemptuous. He hadn't tried again. Now she no longer used the key. It was finished for ever between them. He came to her room and knocked.

. . . . .

In London, blacked out against German air attacks, two men were sitting in the coffee room of the Garrick Club, smoking cigars and drinking liqueurs. To one of them the surroundings were familiar; it was a club patronised by the Stage and the law, famous for its unique collection of theatrical portraits and mementos, for the excellence of its food and service and the quality of its membership. The English Colonel had joined many years ago after establishing himself at the Bar; he hoped that his American guest was impressed by the grandeur and originality of the coffee room, and by the atmosphere of calm gentility which was not altered even by war.

There were a dozen people seated at the side tables, all of them male. The rule excluding women except as guests on Thursdays had not been relaxed, nor the tradition reserving the long central table in the dining room exclusively for men. They had eaten as well as rationing had permitted and drunk an excellent wine, which the Colonel appreciated and the American General tended to ignore. Colonel Fairbairn asked his guest for the third time whether he liked the brandy and the General said he did. He made no attempt to hide his preoccupation with something other than cognac and the history of the eighteenth-century portraits which the Englishman had been describing to him. General Frank Heidsecker was a big man, inclined to fat in spite of rigorous exercise and attention to diet, with a round, bland face, hair so crew cut that he seemed almost bald under the light, and mild blue eyes. He was a third generation American, his ancestors having come over in an emigrant ship to work the Pennsylvania mines. His grandparents had spoken German all their lives, his own mother's people came from Düsseldorf and he had married a girl called Susan Schwartz. In type and attitude, Heidsecker personified the humane, unpretentious American commander whose epitome was Dwight Eisenhower. Heidsecker disliked military pomp, ignored protocol whenever possible, and cared passionately about the men for whom he was responsible.

He was happily married with three sons, and a daughter who was still in high school in St. Paul, and he believed with the simplistic passion of an early Christian in the rightness of his country's cause, and the sanctity of its way of life. He was as completely different from the English Colonel as it was possible for one human being to be from another. The Colonel was tall and thin; his knees stuck up through his well-creased trouser legs, his hands were long and bony at the wrists, with nervous fingers always fiddling with buttons or the buckle of his Sam Browne belt. His face was gaunt and patterned with freckles; he had sandy hair which was receding, and short-sighted eyes covered by horn-rimmed spectacles; he plucked them off and waved them about when he wished to emphasise a point. They were whisked off his nose and began making circles in the air, as the Colonel leaned towards the General. 'You mustn't think about it, you know,' he said. 'Once they've gone, there's nothing one can do.'

'This man is different,' Heidsecker said. 'You know his reasons for volunteering? I damned nearly didn't accept him.'

'With respect, sir,' the Colonel said, 'they made him the best possible choice. We can't afford to fail in this mission. Too much depends upon it.'

'Everything depends upon it,' the American corrected gloomily. 'If our guy doesn't get through . . .'

'Then we'll send one of our chaps,' Fairbairn said. 'I'll have plenty of candidates for you.'

'You don't mind sending your people in, do you?' Heidsecker asked him.

'No,' Fairbairn said mildly. 'I suppose I don't let myself think of them as people. I look at the mission, I weigh up its importance, and then its chances of success. I don't allow myself to get involved. This sort of work would be impossible. Think of when it is a charming young lady . . .' He laughed, which made the General positively dislike him.

'In fact, I think your man was one of the toughest characters I've ever come across. We should be drinking to his success, you know.' He raised his glass, and reluctantly the General did the same. 'He must be nearly there by now—probably landed. I know that part of France, it's very pretty.'

'I doubt he'll appreciate it,' Heidsecker remarked. The Colonel's attitude of callous irony was irritating him into remembering the difference in their rank. There was a short silence, while Fairbairn accepted the rebuke. Heidsecker sucked at his cigar; the Colonel made peace by striking a match for him.

'There are so many damned "ifs" to this whole mission,'

the General said suddenly. 'For something as vital as this, the whole plan seems plain crazy. Supposing the Comtesse de Bernard has changed her attitude—all we have is the word of some village priest . . .'

'As a Presbyterian,' the Colonel said, 'I don't exactly rely on Roman Catholic priests as a source of credibility, but in this case, this priest has done some very useful work for us. I'm sure the lady hasn't changed her mind and gone over to the Germans. She'll help our man. That cigar isn't drawing very well—let me get you another . . .'

'No thanks,' Heidsecker said. 'You know what he said when I wished him luck—Come back safe and sound, that's what I told him. He looked me right in the eyes. "I don't give a damn about coming back, just so long as I get in and do the job." And he meant it too. He doesn't expect to get out.'

'Oh Lord.' Fairbairn looked pained. 'Not false heroics, I hope? That's awfully dangerous—he didn't seem that type to me.'

'He isn't,' the General said. 'But if you had his motive, would you give a damn about what happened to you?'

'No,' the Colonel said. 'I don't suppose I would. But I find it difficult to visualise; I'm not a man of action.'

The General's next remark astonished him. 'I'm not a blood and guts commander,' he said quietly. 'I mind like hell what happens to my men. I have to admit that this guy is a certain loser. But it's not just him. There's a much greater responsibility involved. What about the French?'

'The French?' Fairbairn's voice squeaked. 'What about them?'

'If we succeed,' Heidsecker said, 'what the hell do you think the Germans will do to those civilians? Or hasn't that occurred to you?'

'It hasn't,' Fairbairn admitted, 'and now that you mention it, sir, I can't say it worries me. There'll be the usual reprisals.'

'Not for this,' the General said. 'Not if our man gets through and does his job. God knows what they'll do to them. I tell you, Colonel Fairbairn, we're going to have a terrible responsibility for the consequences.'

'Sir,' Fairbairn said with what he hoped was patience, 'at any moment the weather may change and our invasion fleets will set out. Hundreds of thousands of Allied and American lives depend upon that man we sent out today and whether he can get through. Whatever happens to the French civilians, whatever the cost to them or anyone else, the invasion depends upon it!'

'Women and children,' the General said. 'It'll be on our heads.'

'No,' the Colonel said. 'It won't. If we fail, we could lose the war. We must think of nothing but the success of this mission, General. The consequences are no concern of ours.' He raised one finger to the club waiter and ordered the General a large Scotch and water. With ice. The subject was not resumed between them.

. . . . . .

'What do you want?' Louise de Bernard was brushing her hair; she turned as the door opened and she saw her husband standing there. He never came to her room except in an emergency. The last time his father had been taken ill during the night.

'What is it?' she repeated. He came inside and closed the door. He didn't move towards her. 'I want to talk to you.'

'All right.' She put the brush down and got up from the dressing table. 'Come in.'

In the last four years his hair had become quite grey. She remembered how thick and black it used to be. He looked tired and unhappy. She stifled an impulse to be gentle, to ask him to sit down. Their ways had parted. There was no going back.

'Minden told me something tonight,' he said. 'There's been an alert; it was a single plane. It may have dropped enemy agents here.' Louise looked at him. He saw the bitterness in her eyes.

'God help them then,' she said. 'After what happened to the last one. Why have you come to tell me?'

'Because I know you,' he said slowly. 'I know how you feel about what happened before. I have to be sure you won't do anything foolish.'

'Like helping them? With you in the house how could I—I'd be sentencing them to death!'

'Recriminations are no good,' her husband said. 'I know you'll never forgive me, but that doesn't matter now. What does matter is to prevent another tragedy. I don't want people shot as hostages for some reckless British plan to sabotage or kill Germans round here. I won't stand by and see it happen. I just want your promise that you won't get involved in anything. I'm trying to protect you too.'

'I don't want your protection.' Louise stood up. 'We had this two years ago, when that poor devil came here and the Palliers sheltered him. Was it you who gave them away, Jean? I've asked myself that question and I've never been able to believe you!'

'You know I didn't. You don't choose to believe me.'

'The night the Palliers were executed you had the German commandant to dinner here,' she said. 'That was the night our marriage finished. Two of your own villagers were dragged away and put against the wall and shot in front of everyone. And you did nothing to save them. You say I've never forgiven you. In God's name how could you forgive yourself?'

'He would have shot more,' the Comte said. 'He was talking of fifty hostages. You judged me, Louise, because I disappointed you. You turned me out of your bed and you've kept me out for two years because I didn't behave as you expected! You wanted heroics, didn't you? A grand gesture, flouting the German commander, and fifty people lying dead in the square instead of two!'

'How do you think that Englishman died?' she asked him. 'What do you think they did to him? That Nazi, sitting here with his feet under the table, you eating and drinking with him. Oh no, Jean, whatever your reasons, there was no excuse. As for asking me not to involve myself, you're wasting your time. My country's at war with these brutes. And I'm an American. You've collaborated. You've given the example to St. Blaize and they've followed it. To think I used to be shy about coming from the States! I was so proud of France and her great traditions! God, what a fool I was. If you've finished, then please go away and let me get to bed.'

'Paul and Sophie,' Jean said angrily. 'And Papa. Would you sacrifice them? Would you see your own children and my father dragged off to some concentration camp to be murdered? Is that what you wanted me to do? Was that the price of being loved by you?'

'You've gone all the way with them,' she said contemptuously. 'You declared yourself the first time they came to this house. And then you stood by when that old man and his son were butchered. I've never asked you—what did you and that German talk about over dinner that night? It must have been a charming conversation!'

'We talked about the future of this village,' her husband answered. His anger had gone; a dull despair was in its place. 'We talked about whether the wholesale murder he proposed was really necessary to teach the people to collaborate. I convinced him that it wasn't. I lost two lives and saved many more. And we are all alive and safe, with our homes still standing. That counts with me, Louise. Whenever I walk through St. Blaize and see the people living and working in peace, the children playing, everything normal, I thank God. And I collaborate. You can despise me if you like.'

'Believe me.' She turned to him. 'Believe me, I do. From the bottom of my heart. Now you've delivered your message from your friend Minden, will you please go away? I want to go to bed.'

He didn't answer; he went out, closing the door behind him.

Louise stripped off her dressing-gown, turned off the light and pulled back the curtains. It was a brilliant moonlit night outside. She opened the window and the cold air made her shiver. If anyone had been dropped they wouldn't have a chance unless they reached the woods at Chemire. If they ventured into the village asking for help, the people would give them up. Someone had denounced the unknown Englishman who came one similar night two years ago, and with him had died the two Palliers, father and son. Was it her husband Jean? The informer had never been found but the German commander who ordered their execution had been her husband's guest that night. She shut the window and pulled the curtains.

What had happened to the man she married—why had she never seen the flaw? It was a question to which there was no answer. All she could remember were her mother's arguments against the marriage. 'He's different, he's a European. He doesn't think or feel like us.' And it was true. When total crisis came their priorities had been light years apart. When he left to fight in 1939 she had hoped she might be pregnant, to carry part of him with her in case the unthinkable happened and he didn't come back. But there was no child and she had thanked God for it. Everything in her, her traditions of pride and independence, the fierce American preoccupation with justice and liberty rose up against the rational acceptance of a loathsome enemy and an ignominious defeat. He might learn to live with the Nazis, but she never would.

And yet she ate the food that Minden gave them, used his petrol coupons to drive their car, tolerated him, albeit with hostility. Collaboration was insidious; fighting alone was not as easy as she had imagined. Little by little the corruption of the spirit spread, gaining in little ways over her resolution. She felt weak and filled with self-disgust. The Allied invasion was coming and yet everyone she knew regarded it as doomed. If they were right and the armies of the free world perished, then the future held nothing but darkness and oppression and men like Jean would be responsible. For a moment she had pitied him, seeing the signs of strain, noticing the grey hairs. But she could never afford to forgive him or to try to understand his attitude. If she weakened, she would become a traitor to herself, to her own sense of what was valuable in human life.

She thought of the aircraft which had passed over them that night, its engines throbbing with the distinctive note so different from the German planes. No bombs had fallen; the noise had died away. Enemy agents. Somewhere out there in the cold, clear night, a man or several men might be stranded in a hostile countryside, hoping for shelter. And there was nothing she could do to help them. She turned over, fighting back tears. It was useless to cry; in spite of her conversion to Catholicism she hadn't prayed for years. God was deaf, or dead. Tomorrow would be like all the other days. Routine, helping Marie-Anne with the cooking, looking after her father-in-law and the children, Paul and Sophie. Régine was coming for the weekend; she had forgotten about her. Jean's sister was nineteen, a student at the Sorbonne who lived with an aunt in Paris and occasionally got home to see her family. Louise had never liked her, even when she was a child. She was cold and secretive, resentful of the newcomer whose attempts to win her confidence had failed. Like her brother she was very dark and slight, with a face that was too pale and set to be attractive. The disease of collaboration had been mortal to her. She was passionately pro-German.

If she was fond of her brother she concealed it, only with the children and her father did she show any feeling. She loved the children, and for this Louise tried to tolerate her and avoid a confrontation. And her devotion to her father was a contrast to her indifference to everyone else. She adored the old Comte, and spent most of her visits sitting with him in his room. He was prematurely senile, and Régine was the child of his own age.

He lived on the floor above in a room whose windows had been lengthened to give him a view over the countryside, with a gramophone and a collection of books. He was a beautiful old man, gentle and confused, who played the same record over and over again, beating time to the music, his head a little to one side. His wife had died just before Louise came to St. Blaize and something had gone with her, some spark of life without which he began to wither mentally. His dependence upon his son was like that of a child, loving but intrinsically selfish. He clung to Louise because she was there, but there was no gauge of his real feelings. Food and comfort and security were all he needed. She gave them to him and he seemed grateful. Whenever she came into his room he looked up and gave his charming smile, holding his hand out to her. It was doubtful if he understood what had happened, whether he appreciated the significance of Heinz Minden coming to sit with him, being respectful and polite in order to win friendship in the house. He was a ghost who hadn't died. The night the Palliers were executed and their murderer sat in the dining room below with Jean, Louise had taken refuge in the old man's room, listening to a record of Caruso singing Pagliacci, which the old man played again and again, while she wound up the gramophone. She had cried that night but he hadn't noticed or if he did he made no comment. Like all old people he ignored the grief of others for fear it would disturb his own placidity. There had been a Requiem Mass offered for the Palliers in the village church, a brave gesture by the priest, Father Duval, which Louise had never forgotten, even though she seldom went to Mass.

Jean and his sister Régine had not attended. Louise had knelt alone in the de Bernard stall, with pathetically few people in the body of the little church, and the widow weeping only a few feet away from her. There had been no sermon: not even Father Duval dared preach against the murder of his parishioners. The Requiem Mass itself was a risk, but the influence of Jean and the effect of his conciliatory invitation appeased the military commander and there were no consequences for the priest or the few worshippers. As the wife of a prominent collaborationist, Louise was permitted to strike her attitude and escape investigation. As a woman she wasn't regarded as important in a world so essentially dominated by men. After the executions the village had quickly returned to normal. The troops drove away, business was resumed, the children went back to school and the rumours died.

But Louise and everyone else had heard them. It was said that the body of the elder Pallier was so badly beaten as to be unrecognisable when it was collected for burial. The fate of the British agent could only be imagined. He had been last seen driving away in a car with four Gestapo agents, his wrists handcuffed behind him and a look of despair on his face.

It could happen again. Louise pulled the covers close and tried to sleep. She found herself praying that it was only a reconnaissance plane, and that no second victim had come floating down to torture and death at St. Blaize en Yvelines.

. . . . .

In the village itself all the lights were out. It was a country community and they kept early hours. Only the cats and a single scavenging dog roamed the streets. In the back room of Madame Pallier's bakery, a man sat eating a meal by candlelight. The curtains were drawn and a rug had been pinned over the window to keep any fraction of light from showing through. The heavy-set figure of a woman, dressed in black, was seated in a wooden chair close to the door.

'You have no right to come here,' she whispered. There was a gun on the table, near the man's right hand. He looked at her.

'They killed your husband and your son. You ought to want to help.'

'I never wanted them to get involved,' she hissed at him; her face was grey and her eyes sharp with fear and anger. 'I told them it was madness. I told them you dirty British were just making use of them and nobody would care what happened to them if anything went wrong! But they wouldn't listen—no, they were full of politics and all that wind—and look what happened. Dead, both of them, and me left alone with nobody to help me, running this shop, working just to keep alive in my old age. You get out of here! Go somewhere else!'

'And have you call the Germans?' the man said. 'Like hell! You make a move or a sound and I'll shoot you, understand that? I'm no English gentleman, Madame. I wouldn't hesitate.'

'They'll get you,' she sneered. 'They'll cut your balls off when they find you. That's what they did to the other one, the man who came here. They tore him to pieces making him tell . . . I'm not afraid of you! And I won't help you!'

'You are helping me,' he said. 'And you'll go on doing it, just for tonight. I'll be gone by tomorrow. You be a nice old lady now, and nothing will happen to you.'

'And when you're caught,' she demanded, 'and they make you tell where you were hiding? What becomes of me then, eh?'

'You get shot,' the man said. 'But if you try anything while I'm here, I'll do it first. So you've got trouble either way. You make good bread. I'm hungry.'

'You're eating my rations,' Madame Pallier accused. 'You come in here and steal my food . . .' She called him an obscene name. He went on eating, watching her. He was in the early thirties, a fair-haired man, with irregular features and blue eyes. He had a small suitcase and a smart leather attaché case with initials in gold. R.B.S. He wore a French roll-necked oatmeal sweater and casual trousers. His shoes were two-tone calf and suède, made pre-war. He looked a well-off member of the professional class who was in the country for the weekend.

At that moment his mind was occupied by the problem of Madame Pallier. London had supplied his chiefs with her name and address in St. Blaize. There was no Resistance in the district, no Communist activity because it was miles from major industrial development.

There was a chance of assistance from the widow of a Frenchman shot for hiding a British agent two years earlier. He could either try her or hole up in the woods at Chemire till the hunt had died down. He had elected to trust the widow. The London-based branch of the American Office of Strategic Services had provided him with the vital contact, upon whom the whole plan would depend.

Fortunately it wasn't Madame Pallier. He poured out some wine; he had to decide what to do with her. The solution was obvious, but being a reasonable man, he tried not to jump to it too quickly. He didn't want to kill her till he was certain that he had to. She had a hard, shrewd face; everything about the way she sat, the tightness of her clenched hands, suggested a desire to rush into the street and scream for help. The moment he left the house in the morning, she would find a telephone and get through to the local army headquarters. He couldn't trust her even if she promised. Her own skin was at risk. Her husband and son she regarded as fools who had thrown their lives away and her remembrance of them was a grudge. He couldn't take the chance.

There was a mental adjustment to be made before you killed a woman. He had been taught this. They had to be depersonalised; you had to get them out of focus, so that it was just a shape, an object. It made it much easier. 'I'm sorry about the rations,' he said.

She didn't answer; she hugged herself and glared at him.

'You'd like me to go now, wouldn't you?'

'Yes!' She spat it at him, coming forward in the chair.

'If I did, how do I know you won't raise an alarm? Would you give me your promise?'

She didn't hesitate. 'Yes, yes, of course I would. I wouldn't tell anyone, I don't want trouble, that's all. You go. I won't say anything.'

There wasn't a hope in hell of trusting her. He had an assignment on which a quarter of a million lives depended. One old woman—he stood up from the table and picked up his gun. 'Okay then,' he said. She was becoming a dark shape in front of him, the embittered face was a blur. 'You open the door first and make sure it's clear.' She turned her back on him and he fired.

• • • • •

Heinz Minden had not gone to bed. He liked to work late; he found it difficult to lay everything aside and leave something until the morning. Unanswered questions spoiled his sleep. He was methodical by nature and this trait had been developed by his training into an obsession. He had been on General Brühl's staff at the Château Diane for six months, and it was certainly the most satisfying part of his career. He leaned back in his chair and stretched; his shoulders were stiff from stooping; he shuffled his papers together into a neat pile, fastened them with a clip, stacked them in his briefcase and closed it. It was self-locking. He wore the key round his neck with his identity disc. He had enjoyed the evening. For eighteen months he had been stationed near enough to Breslau to spend weekends at home. The move to France had distressed him; he hated leaving his family. He disliked a mess atmosphere; like his chief, General Brühl, he was not a professional soldier, and his attitude to the rigidity of military life was tolerant but not enthusiastic. He liked privacy and the company of women in the evenings. He missed his own two children badly. He wrote to them both twice a week. Photographs of them all stood in a frame beside his bed. He judged that within another six months, he would be back with them again. 1943 had been a bad year; he remembered the sense of despair that grew in him as the Russian campaign disintegrated and the rumours of collapse crept through the corridors of the informed. Food was short, casualties mountainous, air raids transformed the nights into a hell of modern making. Germans like himself began to tremble. But now he was confident. Now he knew that victory was certain for his people. He carried this knowledge with him and it made him invulnerable. Land, sea, air, blockade, invasion. It would still end with Germany as master of the world. He didn't see this in terms of a Wagnerian triumph, a funeral pyre of subject races presided over by the men gods of the Reich.

To him it was a state of order, a peace and continuity which would envelop Europe and in which the German virtues would be generally adopted. It was a return to his home, a rebuilding of the cities, a life in which the children grew up without fear. And it would come. He knew this now. He thought of Frederick Brühl. He was the son of a Hamburg butcher; Minden's own father had been a solicitor's clerk. They had many traits in common. They were in their thirties; Brühl looked older. He too was quiet, and although a bachelor, untouched by the fashionable smear of homosexuality. He painted for relaxation, and in Minden's opinion showed some talent. He didn't swagger and he didn't shout. He surrounded himself with his own people and, blessed by the personal protection of Heinrich Himmler with whom he was on friendly terms, he carried out his work. He had a weakness, which the upper-class officers derided, but which Minden thought amusing and quite harmless. He was a romantic snob. Grandeur appealed to him, and he surrounded himself with the trappings of greatness which belonged to a vanished age. For this reason he had made his headquarters in the Château Diane, the magnificent house built for the most famous royal courtesan of the sixteenth century, Diane de Poitiers, mistress of Henri II. In many ways it was extremely suitable; it was built in semi-fortress style, with a superb gateway, surmounted by Diane herself in stone, flanked by stags. The General occupied the royal apartments; he took his meals with his officers in the state dining room, at a refectory table twenty feet long, with Renaissance candelabra and superb tapestries; he had insisted on having the original four-poster bed fitted with a proper mattress so that he might sleep in it. There was a large contemporary portrait of Diane de Poitiers which had been moved from the marble hall into the General's sitting room.

It showed her in the guise of Diana the huntress, naked and voluptuous, the crescent moon, symbol of the goddess, gleaming in her hair. The General liked to sit and stare at it, entranced. It was not a picture that aroused any sensual response in Heinz Minden. Nude voluptuaries were not his type.

Whereas the slim and elegant Comtesse de Bernard would have driven him to any folly. When he first came to the Château St. Blaize, she had avoided him, making no secret of her hostility. Being a man of sensitivity he appreciated her resentment and made himself as unobtrusive as possible. He thought the Comtesse the most sexually attractive woman he had met in his life. When she walked into a room or stood near him, he broke out into a fine sweat; his hands, normally so sure and steady, trembled. He lay awake at night, forgetting his pretty wife with whom he had been so happy and dreamed hot, lustful dreams of possessing the Comtesse in unlikely erotic situations. He was a patient man and doggedly determined. He wanted her and as the weeks went by and she was forced by circumstances into accepting him, he felt that one day his desire would be realised.

He set out to be a benefactor; he made friends with the two children, whom he genuinely liked, and was flattered by their response. He even went up and talked to the old Comte; he brought presents for Jean de Bernard, choosing those luxuries which he knew were unobtainable on the open market. Cognac, champagne, cigars. He ordered his batman to help the two servants, he made himself part of the family in spite of themselves and little by little he was taken for granted. When he first arrived, Louise de Bernard used to leave the salon rather than sit in his presence. Now she talked to him over the dinner table, and it wasn't long before he sensed the deep hostility which she felt towards her husband. Minden was not a particularly immoral or ruthless man. He had his own code, which was ethical and middle class. He wouldn't have deliberately put himself between husband and wife. But this wife, whom he wanted to the point of agony, didn't even share a room with her husband. The batman had soon discovered that. The knowledge diminished the stature of the Comte de Bernard in his eyes. No self-respecting man would have allowed his wife to lock him out. Minden, normally mild and considerate, with an exaggerated view of women's frailty, would have soon put an end to the attempt. The situation increased his hope of ultimate success. She must be lonely; she was young and beautiful and living like a nun. He brought her a present of scent at Christmas, and began very carefully to disclose his interest in her. He had to be careful, because she was spirited, and a premature move would spoil his chances.

He treated her with friendliness and courtesy, but he let her know, by a touch against her, a smile when she came into the room, by the scent which was the most expensive and exotic he could buy, that he found her irresistibly attractive, and that the moment she held out her hand, he would be there.

He went to the window, after switching off the lights and opened it wide. He knew the value of fresh air for healthy sleep; for a moment he looked out over the countryside, illumined by the same bright moon Louise had seen two hours before.

There was a red glow to the left, a finger of fiery orange in the middle of it. He leaned out, and on the wind he smelt smoke. There was a fire in St. Blaize. He watched for a few moments and then withdrew. He had no curiosity about the village or its people. They were co-operative and peaceful. If they needed help beyond the capacity of the primitive local fire engine, they would call upon the German military. St. Blaize was a good place for a German. No assassins lurked in the streets or sprang upon them in the lanes. There was no trouble. Which was exactly why Brühl had picked the district to set up his headquarters. Minutes after he was in bed, Minden was deeply asleep.

. . . . .

'Mama! Mama, wake up!' Louise felt her son's arms round her neck, and his mouth pressing excitedly against her cheek.

She hadn't heard the maid come in and draw the curtains back; the room was filled with a pale sunlight. 'Darling, what is it—why haven't you gone to school?' She sat up, and the little boy climbed onto the bed.

'I'm going,' he said. 'Fritz is downstairs.' There was another of the Major's gestures. His batman drove the children to the village school each morning before taking him to the Château Diane.

'There's been a fire,' her son announced. 'A big fire in the village!'

'In the village? Where—Marie-Anne, is this right?'

'Yes, Madame.' The maid came towards her. 'Poor old Madame Pallier's house. They couldn't put it out; everyone was asleep when it happened. She was burned to death, poor old soul.'

'How terrible.' Louise shuddered. She looked at her son's excited face. 'Go down now, darling, or you'll be late. Where's Sophie?'

'Getting her books—you know, Mama, she's always late.'

'Go on.' She kissed him. 'Don't keep Fritz waiting.'

'How awful,' she said to the maid. 'That poor woman. After losing her husband and son like that too.'

'They're an unlucky family, Madame.' Marie-Anne paused at the door. She was fond of the Comtesse, and she enjoyed calamity. Without words the two women understood each other. Marie-Anne hated the German Fritz, and she knew that Madame hated the Major. Yet they could not get rid of either of them. She and her husband had served the Comte's father and mother since they were brought up from the village in their teens. They were glad to survive, but they were not proud of the price the Comte had paid for it.

'Very unlucky,' she repeated. 'Two sons lost in the First War, poor Gaston was the only one left, and then he gets himself murdered by the Germans and *his* only son goes too. Now the place burns down. I heard she was found by the door; she must have been trying to get out. Old people like that shouldn't live alone. There's always trouble.' She shook her head, filled with enjoyment.

'Where's Monsieur?'

'Gone down to the village,' Marie-Anne said. 'He left as soon as we woke him with the news. He's gone to see the Mayor.'

Louise got up and dressed. They had only one car and a tiny amount of petrol. The coupons were another of the

Major's gifts. There was no way of getting to St. Blaize. Jean should have woken her and taken her with him. She'd had the courage to go to the Palliers' Requiem while he stayed at home. She wanted to go down, to show herself. She ran down the stairs to the hall, hearing a car come to the front. At the foot of the stairs she almost bumped into the Major. He was dressed in his field grey uniform, his cap under one arm, drawing on his gloves. He was a tall, well set up man, his dark hair cut close to a fine-shaped head.

'Good morning, Madame.' He smiled at her.

'Good morning.' Louise disliked meeting him alone, even in the hall. 'I'm looking for my husband, I thought I heard his car.'

'That was Fritz, I'm afraid,' the Major said. 'Coming back from the school. Is there anything I can do?'

'No,' Louise said. 'Thank you. There's been a fire in St. Blaize and an old widow died. I wanted to go down myself.'

The Major looked at his watch and then at her.

'I'm in good time this morning,' he said. 'I'd be delighted to drive you.'

'Thank you,' Louise said again. 'But it wouldn't be possible.'

'Why not?' He had placed himself in front of her. 'You're looking very charming this morning. Why can't I drive you to the village?'

He was making the first move in the silent game, the first acknowledgement that there was a game in progress. She decided to play it in the open too.

'I can't go with you, because the woman who died lost both husband and her son two years ago. They were shot by your military. I'm sure you realise how inappropriate it would be for me to go to the village with you.'

'If you think so. But please remember they must have done something criminal. We don't shoot people for nothing.'

'A British agent was dropped here. The Palliers sheltered him and got caught. That was their crime. And from what Jean tells me it could happen again.'

'It wasn't necessary for him to tell you,' the Major said. 'I just asked for his co-operation, that was all.'

'And I am sure you got it,' Louise said. 'But don't expect it from me.'

'I'm sure you're very brave,' the Major said gently. 'But please, dear Madame de Bernard, don't be foolish. Leave this unpleasant kind of thing to men. Personally I don't think anyone was dropped round here. It was just a reconnaissance, that's all. If I can't be of service, then I shall go. Until this evening.'

He bowed and gave her a smile for which she could have slapped his face. Then he went out into the morning sunshine.

. . . . .

There was a German patrol on the road junction between St. Blaize and Houdan. He watched it through his field-glasses, lying on his stomach in some bushes on a rise in the fields about three hundred yards away. The bicycle lay in an irrigation ditch, covered with leaves. He had spent the night hidden there, wrapped in a thin waterproof sheet, eating some of his K rations, watching the fire he had lit in the Palliers' kitchen grow from a flicker in the darkness to a full-scale beacon. A funeral pyre, he thought, for a heroic mother of heroic France. He bit into the bar of chocolate. Christ, he hadn't any right to judge. Nobody had occupied *his* home town. It wasn't till you heard the tanks rumble past the door that you could say how you'd behave in the circumstances. It was a pity about the old lady, but he refused to think about it. The fire must be attracting a lot of attention. It was only when he scouted the roads in the morning and saw the improvised check point that he knew they had heard the plane hovering overhead and guessed its mission.

He swore. His papers described him as Roger Bertrand Savage, Swiss national, domiciled in Berne, born in Ohio, USA, by profession a company lawyer in the firm of Felon, Brassier et Roule, an internationally famous company with offices in Geneva, Berne, and a subsidiary in Philadelphia.

It was an excellent cover, worked out from the New York end and confirmed by their contacts in Switzerland. Felon and Brassier had substantial US interests and were secret supporters of the Allies. Anyone checking with them would get the same information. Roger Savage was a senior member of their staff, an American who had graduated at the University of Lausanne and taken Swiss nationality before the war. He was at present visiting a client in France. It would hold up against all but the most detailed investigation, and he felt confident in the role. He spoke excellent French and German; he had a marvellous ear, not only for languages but for nuances of accent.

He watched the soldiers moving lazily round their road block. He had a survey map of the district and he got it out and studied it carefully. He knew all the main routes into the village. The one he could see through his glasses led in from the north. If that one was blocked then for a certainty so were all the others. The bastards had put a net round the area. They had cut off the roads as an escape route, and that meant they were getting ready for a patrol sweep through the fields and around the smaller wooded hills. It was eight o'clock in the morning. At any moment the first group would be setting out. He turned back to the map. The railway line was a very small branch line of the Paris to Chartres route which was heavily marked. St. Blaize was a community big enough to merit a small sub-station. Few trains would be running. The line was marked to the west, about three-quarters of a mile away. It was hidden by a belt of silver birch trees. He crawled backwards to the irrigation ditch, dragged the bicycle upright and keeping in the shelter of the ditch, began wheeling it away towards the birches. He came out of the shelter of the dip, focused on the patrol once more, and saw no sign of anyone sweeping the area with glasses. He jumped on the cycle and pedalled quickly over the edge of the field towards the trees. When he reached them, he dismounted, walked out to the other side and reconnoitred again. There was no sign of German military presence. There was no road, only the undulating fields and the thin ribbon of railway track. He pushed on, using the cycle when the terrain was possible, but moving as fast as he could. He slid down the slight embankment to the track, dragging the bicycle with him. He mounted, carrying the suitcase tied on his back; inside were a change of clothes, the ground sheet folded very small, the handsome leather briefcase embossed with his initials and a radio transmitter set. He carried his gun stuck in the waistband of his trousers. The L pill, that release from torture above bearing, was concealed in his left cuff link. He was a brave man, but he wouldn't hesitate to take it.

He cycled along the edge of the track for a mile and three-quarters. It wound and twisted in the way of branch lines. Sometimes he glanced back, listening for the rumble of a train, looking for a pencil of smoke. Nothing came. The morning grew warm, and he hummed to himself, his nerves calm. Sufficient unto the day is the evil thereof. The old tag came into his thoughts and he changed it. Sufficient unto the hour; the minute. The sun shone and the way was downhill. And his mission had begun. By nine-thirty he had reached the outskirts of the station at St. Blaize. He pulled the cycle up the incline and wheeled it slowly towards the first group of sheds and outbuildings. Further on the slope became a platform, with the ticket office and waiting room. He tried the first shed, but the door was locked. He could see nobody about. The second building was a store room of some kind. The door was open and it was empty inside. He slipped in with the bicycle and a moment later came out without it, closing the door. It could be weeks before anyone looked in there.

He walked slowly up the platform and stopped at the time-table board. A printed sheet with pencilled alterations showed that there was a train due in thirty minutes. He recognised his own good luck. It was the only train that day. He went into the waiting room, and then stopped. Two young women were sitting inside, one of them was knitting. They both stared at him. He smiled.

'Pardon,' he said. 'I'm looking for the toilets.'

'Through there,' one of the girls said. Her companion smiled back; she showed an interest he didn't find flattering. He went through to one of two doors, marked with a vague male silhouette. Inside the smell was urinous and stale. He unpacked his bag, and quickly stripped out of his clothes. In underpants and singlet his body was muscled and vigorous, the body of a soldier at the peak of training. He changed into a plain white shirt, Swiss made, like the dark suit and the tie, the calf shoes, combed his hair down and put on a soft black Homburg hat. He looked at himself in the spotted mirror. Herr Savage from Berne. He repacked his sports clothes in the suitcase, slipped the loaded gun into his trouser band, and looked at his watch. The train wasn't due for ten minutes. There was nothing to do but go out and face the two women. He came into the waiting room; they were still there and they both looked up at him, registering surprise. He lifted his hat to them and sat down, folding his hands on his lap and closed his eyes. He could feel them looking at him and he heard them whisper. He shifted a little till his right hand was over the hard outline of the gun. He lifted one eyelid a fraction to see if either of them had moved; they were still sitting, murmuring together. He heard them giggle and immediately he relaxed. Everything was going his way. The open shed, the train timetable, the solution of fire for disposing of the old woman. He suddenly saw her face, the hatred and cunning in her eyes, the downward pull of her mouth as she denounced her husband and son . . . He had felt no pity at the time and he felt no remorse now. He had a job to do. He had a primary objective to reach and it was coming closer. There was a clanging of a signal bell and then the rattling roar of the train. The women jumped up, hurrying as women do when they are travelling. He yawned, straightened his hat and got up slowly. They were on the platform when he reached the door. A moment later they had disappeared inside the train. Four passengers alighted. Savage walked through the waiting room door and joined them at the barrier.

He paid for his ticket, explaining that he had come through from Paris without time to buy one. Nobody even glanced up at him. Outside the station he looked round. A decrepit Peugeot with a gazogene waited by the side of the road. He saw two of the passengers hesitating. He took a chance and rushed past them to the motorcar. The driver was inside reading a copy of *La Dépêche des Yvelines*.

'You are a taxi?' Now Savage was speaking like a Swiss. The old man nodded.

'I am the taxi, Monsieur. The only one. I have a limit of four kilometres.' Savage opened the door and got inside, throwing his suitcase ahead of him.

'The Château de St. Blaize,' he said.

'That's outside the four kilometres,' the driver said. 'Sorry, I can't take you.' The other passengers were approaching the cab. Ten francs came at him from behind, held between the finger and thumb of the man in the rear.

'Take me there. Five more when we arrive.'

'What about these people here? How do they manage?'

'I don't know,' Savage said. 'Take the money and let's go. I have an appointment.'

The engine started and the old car bumped forward; Savage lit a cigarette, the first he had allowed himself since leaving the Palliers' house smouldering from coals raked out of the stove onto the carpet. He checked his passport and papers and sat back, tipping the Homburg a little back on his head. He hated hats.

They passed the first German patrol on the way out of the village. He showed his documents, the taxi driver vouched for his arrival on the train from Paris, and from then on the way to the Château was clear.

3

HE rang the old-fashioned iron bell-pull outside the door and waited for what seemed a long time before it was opened to him. Jean Pierre, garbed in a green baize apron, with his sleeves rolled above knotty elbows, showed him into the salon on the ground floor. Savage presented a business card and asked the old butler to give it to the Comtesse. Left alone, he paced quickly round the room, taking stock of the fine eighteenth-century furniture, and the pictures. Ancestral faces, some simpering, some arrogant, looked down at him, and Savage remained unimpressed. He was more interested in a photograph which showed a very pretty dark haired woman posing beside a fountain with two children. He picked it up. She certainly photographed well. He was still holding it when the door opened behind him and he heard a light step cross the floor.

'Monsieur Savage?'

Louise held out her hand and he kissed it, making a little bow. The room faced south and the sunlight fell directly on her; he had placed himself to be in shadow. It was the right woman, no doubt at all about the large brown eyes and the cast of face which was so palpably American. Even after so many years, she spoke French with a Boston accent. He smiled at her.

'You must forgive me for descending on you,' he said, 'without any warning: I would have telephoned, but unfortunately I arrived very late in Paris, and there was some difficulty getting through here this morning.'

'The lines are terrible,' Louise said. 'Please sit down; let me offer you something. Would you like to sit in here or in the garden? It's quite warm outside.'

'The garden would be very nice,' Savage agreed. Less chance of anyone listening in the open air. She seemed relaxed and friendly. He felt she was excited to see a stranger. Life must be dull, he decided. He followed her out into the sunshine.

The butler brought wine; it was pale and dry, with a slight *pétillance*. 'It's our own,' she explained. 'It makes a nice apéritif. You will stay to lunch, of course.'

'You're very kind,' Savage said. 'You will have had Monsieur Felon's letter, so you know why I'm here.'

'No,' Louise said. 'I've heard nothing. Of course, I know your firm, Monsieur Savage, because of my family trust, but I never received any letter.'

'Oh.' He made a gesture of annoyance. 'How ridiculous—it must be the censorship. It will probably arrive after I've left. I shall have to explain it myself.'

'It's about the trust?'

'Not exactly.' Savage offered her a cigarette. The sun was warm and he watched her close her eyes for a moment, lifting her face to it. She had a fine profile. She opened her eyes and turned to him.

'What do you mean, not exactly?' Her father had died before the war; with America's entry into the conflict, her affairs had been placed in the hands of the Swiss lawyers whom Savage represented. She knew M. Felon personally.

'I haven't come about money.'

'No? Then what is it—is something wrong?'

'No.' He shook his head. 'Can I ask you a question, Madame de Bernard? A very personal question.'

'I suppose so. I won't guarantee to answer it.' Her mother was inclined to interfere. For a moment Louise wondered whether some rumour of her estrangement from Jean had reached Boston, and the repercussions had found themselves at St. Blaize via Switzerland. She gave Savage a hostile look. 'What is your question?'

'What are your feelings towards the Allies?'

Louise didn't answer him. She got up. 'I'm afraid I never discuss the war.'

He didn't move; he blew a smoke ring at her.

'You haven't answered the question,' he said. There was nobody near them; trees, lawns, the fountain in the photograph, but no lurking gardener, no passing maid. He spoke in English. 'Sit down and take it easy. I've got news from home.'

She stared at him. She did as he suggested.

'You're American!' she whispered. 'What is this? Who are you...?'

'I saw your mother before Christmas,' he said. 'She's fine; remarkable woman. You look like her. There wasn't any letter from Felon. There isn't any trust-busting to be done. I'm here on my own. Now—how do you feel about the Allies?'

London said she was reliable. Their information was gathered through an unlikely source. Father Duval, parish priest of St. Blaize en Yvelines, was a gossip, and priests visiting the area paid a call upon him, which he encouraged because it gave him the opportunity to talk. He was a stubborn man in his mid-fifties, devoted to his parishioners and disdainful of the Germans whom he had fought in the First War. He had given a young curé from Paris a complete picture of the conditions in the area and the attitude of the people of the village. He had mentioned the Comtesse's presence at the Palliers' Requiem, and lamented the collaborationist stand taken by the Comte. Within two hours, the curé had picked up enough information to relay it back to London through a radio operator hiding in Chartres, one of a thin chain of Allied secret communication that stretched across France and was being constantly broken up by German intervention. The operator only worked another two weeks before the detector van caught up with him, and he was killed in a gun battle.

Savage hoped that London and his OSS chiefs had been correct in their assessment. It was one thing to make a gesture from the safety of marriage with a known collaborator. It might be quite different for the Comtesse de Bernard to actively help an Allied agent. Women were fond of adopting heroic poses or just being bloody-minded. Watching her now, he felt more confident. There was nothing exhibitionist about her; she even looked frightened, which was reassuring.

'I hate the Germans,' she said quietly. 'I hate them for what they're doing to the world, for what they're doing to the Jews. I hate their arrogance and I hate their beliefs. If they win this war it'll be the end of civilisation. Does that answer your question?'

'I guess so,' Savage said. 'I need to stay here for a few days. I need to operate from here. I've got a perfect cover story and everything will check. You've nothing to fear from that angle.'

'Then you're not with Felon and Brassier . . .' Louise said.

'I was,' Savage answered. 'For about three years before the war. Now I'm working for a bigger firm. Will you help me?'

He saw emotions changing on her face; she was a woman who showed her feelings. Surprise, fear, hesitancy. And then resolution. It was in her eyes as she looked at him. London had been right about her. For some reason, apart from his own skin, Savage was glad.

'I'll help you. I'll do anything I can.'

'Thanks.' He leaned over and refilled their glasses; when he gave one to her he felt how cold her fingers were. But the resolution was still there.

He raised his glass to her. 'Thanks,' he said again. 'I can't say you won't regret it, because if anything goes wrong you may. How long can you keep me here?'

'As long as you like,' Louise said. She was already seeing Jean in her mind's eye, hearing his questions . . . Why should a Swiss lawyer stay with them—couldn't he finish his business in a day—food was short . . .

As if Savage knew her thoughts he said, 'I'm your cousin. I have all the family data. Your mother was a great help. I'm the son of your father's first cousin, Roger Savage. He married a Swiss girl, Marie Thérèse Fielharben, daughter of a rich glass manufacturer. The family weren't exactly pleased, and after I was born the couple divorced. I was brought up in Berne and I became naturalised before the war.'

'That's right,' Louise said. 'There was a Roger Savage . . . Did my mother know what this was for?'

'She didn't know you were going to be involved,' he said. 'She was asked for details for a cover story and she gave it. She'd no idea we'd ever meet up.'

'What have you come for?' Louise asked him. 'What are you going to do?'

'Sorry.' Savage shook his head. 'No questions; no answers.

I'm your cousin from Switzerland and you've asked me to stay a while. Just act naturally.'

He smiled constantly, but it was without warmth; there was an alertness about him even in repose. She started to exclaim out loud and then stopped, suddenly. The plane circling overhead, the German alert. That must have been him . . .

'Oh my God!' she said. 'I forgot—you can't stay here! We've a German officer billeted on us.'

'I know,' Savage said. 'Major Minden. That's okay.'

'How do you know?' Louise said. 'How could you know about him . . . ?'

'No questions,' Savage reminded her. 'How about your husband?'

'He's for Vichy,' she said bitterly. 'He went over to the Germans in 1940. He couldn't be trusted with anything.'

'He'll accept the story; so long as you act naturally,' he repeated. 'Does he come home for lunch?'

'He may not today,' she said. 'He's in the village with the Mayor. There was a fire last night and a poor woman was burned to death. Jean takes that sort of thing very seriously. He does what he can for the people.'

'I'm glad to hear it.' Savage sounded unimpressed. 'Tell me about the Major.'

'There's nothing to tell.' Louise dismissed him; the subject embarrassed her. 'He's at the staff HQ at Château Diane. He doesn't obtrude and that's all I can say for him.'

Not quite all; Savage noticed how that pretty mouth had tightened, the look of wariness in her eyes. Major Heinz Minden. She needn't have warned him; he knew more about the Major than she did. The old manservant appeared beside them, wearing a faded alpaca jacket, and formally announced lunch.

They talked about the weather, about Switzerland and the Marshall Trust Fund, Savage giving a good performance for the benefit of Jean-Pierre who shuffled in and out of the dining room. He noticed that Louise de Bernard was uncomfortable; she said as little as possible, leaving the major role in the deception to him. He didn't falter in it. Years ago he had been an enthusiastic amateur actor at college; his histrionic talent had taken him to the bar where a peculiarly incisive mind promised a brilliant future in the law if he ever got the chance to go back to his practice. It wasn't a chance he would have bet good money on. He didn't expect to get out alive and he didn't care. He had told as much to his own General who had looked worried and responsible, as if the life of one man were important in their kind of war. Savage enjoyed his wine. He believed in taking what was on offer, like the warm sunshine during his trek across the fields that morning. What had happened hadn't soured him for the good things, for food and drink and women and the pleasure he derived from an ironic joke. Just because you expected to die you didn't have to reject life prematurely.

And for him it would be easy; he carried death in his cuff link like a talisman. But only when he had finished what he had come to do. He hadn't pretended it was patriotism. He had told his worried General exactly why he had volunteered and what made him such a suitable choice to go to St. Blaize. The General had been distressed. Not so much by the reason, Savage suspected; stories like this were not uncommon. But by the hate he had showed the General when he talked about his mission. Personal, burning, obsessional hatred. The same feeling had brought him into the special OSS unit, and made him the most promising trainee of his group. He was rougher, quicker, more ruthless than any of them. He learned to kill with his hands, to silence with a single blow. To use many types of weapons, to handle explosives. His French and German were fluent; like many with a natural acting talent he was also a good linguist, with an ear for dialect. He could pass for a Swiss in Switzerland, after his three years spent working there. They took their coffee in the salon, because it had turned colder outside and clouded over. He glanced at the grey skies through the window. The weather must break soon. Clouds and rain, holding back that fleet of barges, keeping the armies on the leash . . . He looked across at Louise de Bernard and smiled. She had been watching him silently for some minutes.

'You're doing it again,' he said.

'Doing what?'

'Asking questions. I can see it on your face. "Was he dropped last night when the plane came over—what's he going to do here . . ." Stop it. Stop thinking about me as anything but your cousin from Switzerland. Otherwise you'll never make it stick.'

'I'm sorry,' Louise said, 'but it's not easy.'

'Nothing like this is. Tell me about Major Minden.'

She shrugged. 'There's not much to tell. He's been billeted here for six months. He gets on well with Jean, my husband. I see as little of him as I can.'

'I take it he's not the strutting Nazi type?' He had cold eyes; however much he smiled, it stopped at his mouth. There was something about him which made Louise uncomfortable.

'No, he's certainly not that. He's rather quiet. He's a staff officer.'

'I know,' Savage said. 'Reliable, a bit stuffy, tries to show it's not his fault the others are such bastards. I can imagine.'

'He wants to be friends,' Louise said. 'He brings us things—luxuries—my husband takes them. I hate him.'

'That must be distressing,' Savage said. 'Since I guess you're the one he wants to be friends with . . .'

'That isn't true!' She felt herself changing colour.

'It ought to be,' Savage said. 'Unless he's a fag. Married, isn't he?'

'Yes. How did you know?'

'Never mind. Go on talking about him. What happens here in the evenings?'

'He has dinner with us; Jean insisted on it. I couldn't stop him. Then he comes and sits in here; I often go to bed early, I hate sitting with him. Sometimes he goes straight up to his room and works.'

'How much work does he bring back?'

'I don't know. He has a briefcase with him; I never go near his room, I don't know what he does.'

'And he gets on well with your husband. What do they talk about—the war?'

'Sometimes. Books and music. He likes music very much. He gave my father-in-law some records.'

'He sounds ideal,' Savage mocked. 'When does your husband get home?'

'Soon now. It must be nearly three. What am I going to tell him—if he thought for one moment you were . . .'

'Don't even say it.' Savage stood up. 'Don't say it and don't think about it. You don't need to explain about him; I know all about him, so don't worry. You just stick to the story. I'll be up in my room when he gets back. It'll be easier for you if I'm not there. He won't be surprised; the Swiss are hogs for sleep. Just remember I'm your cousin Roger.'

'The real Roger Savage never visited the States,' Louise said. 'How did you know about him?'

'Through contacts,' he said. 'He died in Lausanne two years ago. Motor smash. Actually he was a drunk. We did our homework properly. Nobody can pick any holes. Play it straight and your husband will believe you.'

'I won't have to go into much detail,' she said. 'We haven't much to say to each other any more. He goes one way and I go another.'

'Good,' Savage said. 'That makes it easier. Let's find my room.'

She took him up the broad stone stair, past her room and to the floor above. His suitcase, securely locked, was on a chaise longue by the end of the bed. It was a large room, furnished in old-fashioned floral chintz; it had a Victorian atmosphere, emphasised by a mahogany four-poster bed. There was a faint smell of must and stale air. Louise apologised and opened the window.

Savage went and looked out.

'I'd hate to leave here in a hurry,' he said. 'That's a forty-foot drop. Who sleeps near?'

'I do,' she said. 'On the floor below. My husband's two rooms away from mine; Minden is down the passage, my sister-in-law is next to you.'

'You haven't mentioned her,' Savage said. He sat on the edge of the bed and bounced gently up and down. 'Comfortable mattress. Where is she?'

'In Paris,' Louise answered. 'She's a student at the Sorbonne. She lives with Jean's aunt and she comes home for odd weekends. She'll be here for dinner this evening.'

'Is that nice, or nasty?'

She shrugged, as she had done when he asked about the Major. 'She doesn't bother me. We've nothing in common and we know it.'

'How would you describe her as far as I'm concerned? Friend or foe?'

'Foe,' Louise said slowly. 'I'd say definitely—foe. For God's sake, watch yourself!'

'I will, don't worry,' Savage said. He got off the bed and came towards her. 'I'll unpack now. You go back downstairs and look like somebody with a long-lost cousin.' He closed the door and locked it. He hung his coat over a chair back, and went to the suitcase. The clothes were innocent, the ammunition for his gun was concealed as a box of cigars. Each cigar held four bullets; built into the false bottom of the suitcase was a small two-way radio transmitter set. Savage went to the window again and looked out. The view was so beautiful he paused. Chequerboard fields of green wheat and bright yellow mustard, belts of trees outlined against the sky, bending in symmetry before the wind. Below him the gardens of the Château, hedges and yew walks, flower beds—from above it wasn't possible to see the weeds and the signs of neglect. In the courtyard the stone fountain threw up a meagre spray.

There were no ledges, no windows near him; if anything went wrong he was as effectively trapped in the room as a prisoner in a cell. Transmission from there was impossible. He would have to get on the roof; and for that he would need Louise de Bernard's help. It had been easy to say he wouldn't tell her anything, to pretend she could be kept on the perimeter. It was a glib lie in one sense but a necessity in the other. The less she knew the less she could tell the Gestapo if she were arrested. But without her help he couldn't hope to complete his mission. Frederick Brühl. Savage knew the face as if it were his own. There were few pictures of him, many were pre-war civilian snapshots. The latest showed him among a crowd, wearing his peaked cap, a blurred and grainy image which had lost outline when it was blown up. Spectacles, a stubby nose, small mouth with rather full lips. A most unremarkable man. Savage stood by the window with the panorama of a peaceful countryside below him, and saw nothing but that face. And then another face, laughing and with hair dishevelled by wind, streaked across the forehead. Eyes that were wide and bright, half closed against the sun, a brown hand raised to shield them. And then the image changed. Savage slammed imagination's door. Brühl . . . He could think about Brühl, and his hands curled into fists, he could let the hate rise in him. It was safe to think about Brühl, it was like giving the batteries of his purpose a recharge. If he had been afraid for himself or concerned for other people, like the American Comtesse de Bernard, the old woman in the village he had shot in the back the night before, he had only to think about the reason why he was in St. Blaize. Nothing and nobody mattered but to succeed. He pulled the window shut. His chiefs in OSS had chosen well. They had chosen a man with a personal reason, knowing that the force of motive would send him on when other men might have turned back.

And they had made a wise choice when they picked on Louise de Bernard as his liaison. She was brave and she was honest; would hold up well enough to reasonable pressure. She was reliable. She was also going to help him more than either of them knew. He had been sent to St. Blaize because a member of Brühl's staff was living in the house of a collaborator with an American wife of Allied sympathies. Major Heinz Minden. What he made of his situation was up to him. Time, as the sarcastic English Colonel had impressed on him, was not on Savage's side. He had a few days, a week at the most, to make the invasion safe. A tremendous burden. He could hear the pedantic voice, unmasculine in pitch, repeating the remark. The responsibility was almost too much to place upon one man. If he had any doubts—Savage hadn't believed in the offer; they had told him too much to let him off the hook. It was part of the game, part of the tests applied to agents like him. He had given the Englishman a look of contempt and not bothered to answer. Major Heinz Minden. Not the strutting Nazi type; unobtrusive, Louise had called him, anxious to be friends. He remembered the colour coming into her face when he suggested that Minden might be interested in her. Which of course he must be. She was a beautiful woman. Her hostility probably intrigued him. Some men were like that. He would need her help in setting up the transmitter. It was to be used once only. To report on the success of his mission. If he failed there wouldn't be a message. He took his shoes off and lay on the bed. Somehow he had to use Minden in his plan. Possibilities flitted through his mind, but didn't stay. Until he met him and could make a judgement, it was premature. He had a strong intuition that the part Louise de Bernard was going to play would be a vital one. He couldn't afford to be sorry about it, but he was. He liked her. But that wouldn't stop him. He didn't hear the Comte de Bernard's car come up the gravel drive. He was making up for the sleep he had lost in the fields the night before.

• • • • •

Jean de Bernard had spent the morning in the Mairie; he and Albert Camier were shut up in the little office on the first floor, and the air was blue with cigarette smoke. Camier had sent for wine.

'We don't want trouble.' The Mayor repeated it again. 'We have to think of the village. Trade has improved since they came to the Château Diane; my own business is doing very nicely. We don't want any Allied agents here!'

'Even if there is an invasion,' Jean de Bernard said, 'it could fail—nobody beats them on equal terms. Russia was different. That was the winter. They'll throw the Allies back into the sea, and who will suffer then? We will. If we've turned against them, they'll crush us to pieces.'

'They haven't taken our men,' Camier said, sipping at his wine. 'We've no Jews here, thank God, so that's no problem. They buy from us and so long as we obey the law, we're left alone. There are no more Palliers in St. Blaize, Monsieur, depend on it. If someone's come to this district to make trouble, they've picked the wrong place!'

'They've given me this proclamation to put up.' He pulled a roneoed sheet out of a drawer and handed it to Jean. 'I thought I'd write something myself and sign it.'

The sheet of paper informed the inhabitants that anyone found sheltering enemy agents would be shot; it was signed by the district commander. A different man to the indignant German who had dined with him the night the Palliers were executed. He had been very indignant; Jean remembered how hard it had been to calm him. He looked up at Camier.

'You put a notice up,' he said. 'Warn the people.'

'Why should we die for the British?' the old man said. 'What have they ever done for us—I remember my father saying, they'll fight to the last Frenchman! If we do have to live under the Germans it's not that bad.'

'The Comtesse would not agree with you,' Jean said. He refused more wine.

'With respect for Madame,' Camier said, 'women aren't the ones to judge. We men have the responsibility. Thank God you've given such a good example; it's made a great difference.'

'We're a tired people,' Jean said slowly. 'Bled white by wars. We need peace, and time to recover ourselves. They won't be here for ever. France will survive them. That is what matters. I must go now. Since Madame Pallier had no relatives, there's nothing we can do.'

'It's a pity about the shop.' The mayor shook his head. 'It was a nice little place, good position. She did quite well. Mind you, it could be rebuilt . . .'

He spoke more to himself; he owned the grocery and wine store, and he supplied the officer's mess at Château Diane. If he were to buy the site of the Palliers' bakery and build—it wouldn't be easy. He'd have to get permits for labour and building materials, but then he was on good terms with the district headquarters; someone there might recommend him. He was known for his co-operation with the Government and the occupation forces. He might open a second grocery store, or else employ a baker. He got up quickly as Jean prepared to leave. He shook the Comte's hand, making a little bow. He was not in such awe of the family as he might have been if the war hadn't changed everything. They held comparatively little power. That was in German hands.

Jean started his car and drove slowly back to the Château. Camier's wine was sour on his stomach; the stench of smoke from the smouldering ruin of the bakery clung to his clothes. He had talked to people, taken council with Camier, who was typical of his class and age. Cunning, commercial-minded, concerned with the realities of survival. Men like him abounded, and they made the task of governing France so easy for the conquerors. He remembered his short war service, the overwhelming numbers and efficiency of the enemy, the sense of being swept away like sand before a tidal wave. Men he had known since childhood had thrown their weapons away and turned for home. His people's spirit waned and died; for some it was not so much a rape as a seduction. They welcomed the German strength as an anti-dote to their own national weakness. France could be great again, and powerful again; what had revived a crippled, beaten Germany within twenty years might well be the saving medicine for ailing France. He knew many who believed this. He had friends who were more Nazi than the S.S. whose attitudes they imitated.

The Jews had always been unpopular; now they were hated. When the Germans asked for Jews, their French neighbours helped to round them up. He frowned, deepening the line between his brow, ashamed of his own knowledge. The Comte in his Château, the Mayor in his grocery store, the people going about their work and living their lives in St. Blaize. For what should they fight, at this late stage? For Allies who were their hereditary enemies, and who blamed them for their surrender? For a place in a world which would be dominated by outsiders, by Americans who had stayed neutral until Japan attacked them—by England, the foe of centuries . . . He turned into the driveway and slowed down, protecting the loose-laid gravel. Louise thought he was a coward. But then they judged by different standards. The difference in priorities was as fundamental as her desire to fight a war which was already lost and thereby lose the chance of gaining from the peace. She despised him; he didn't blame her. He loved her, as he had always done. He accepted her rejection because he knew she couldn't change. He accepted his own suffering for the same reason.

If it was borne with patience, some good would come out of it. He went into the dark entrance hall, and shivered. It was high vaulted, stone walled, with two large Flemish tapestries hung down one side; the temperature was chill.

'Jean?'

He turned and saw his wife facing him, standing in the doorway of the salon.

'I wanted to come with you this morning. You should have waited.'

'I'm sorry; you were still asleep. There was nothing you could have done. The poor woman was dead long before they got to her.'

'It's horrible,' Louise said. He had followed her into the room and they were both standing. She had a cigarette in her hand, and she found an ashtray at the other side of the room, where she could turn her back on him for a moment. He had a way of looking directly at her, watching her face. She had found it attractive once; he had fine dark eyes, full of expression. Now it made her falter. He was an enemy, not to be trusted.

'I had a surprise,' she said suddenly. 'Do you remember I had a cousin Roger, father's first cousin—Roger Savage?'

'I heard him mentioned, but I can't remember meeting him. Why?'

She turned and faced him. 'His son arrived here this morning. From Berne. He works for the family trust lawyers. He's upstairs. I said he could stay with us for a few days.'

Jean de Bernard took a cigarette from his case and slowly lit it.

'Of course,' he said. 'How nice.' He didn't have to look at her. He didn't ask for explanations. He knew with infallible instinct that she was lying.

'Excuse me,' he said. 'I'm going upstairs to see Papa.'

• • • • •

At six-thirty a car drew up at the gates of the Château. The lodge was empty, its windows shuttered. There was no gatekeeper and the gates stood open. The car was sleek and highly polished; the driver sprang out and stood at attention by the back door. Inside two people turned towards each other. The man was in his forties, clean-shaven, with close-cropped brown hair and high cheekbones, deep-set eyes.

He slid his arm round the shoulders of a girl, much younger, with dark hair down to her shoulders and a rapt expression on her face. He bent and kissed her, opening her lips; one hand closed over her breast. Outside the car, his driver stood at attention, staring straight ahead.

'I shall miss you,' the man said. 'I shall think of you with your family while I'm alone.'

Her face was pale, like a mask, the eyes closed. 'I have to come,' she whispered. 'You don't know how I hate it. You don't know how I hate every minute I'm away from you!'

'One day I shall come up to the house,' he said. He searched her mouth again. 'Let me drive you now. Why should you walk, carrying that bag . . .'

'No,' she murmured, holding on to him. 'No, Adolph, not yet. Give me time to talk to them. Let me talk to my brother first . . .'

'All right.' He drew away and opened the door. 'I won't force you, my darling. I won't embarrass you. Till Monday.'

Régine de Bernard got out. The driver handed her her week-end case and saluted. The rear window of the car was down. She blew a kiss through it. The man replaced his black cap, the skull insignia of the Death's Head division of the S.S. gleamed above the peak.

'Till Monday,' Bernard's sister whispered. The Mercedes waited till she had gone through the gates. Then it did a U-turn in the narrow drive and headed back towards Paris.

Régine went upstairs to her own room. Whenever she returned to St. Blaize she cried herself to sleep because she could have been with Adolph. She banged her door shut, sighing deeply, and touched her breast where he had caressed her. They must never know, of course. Her brother and her sister-in-law, whom she hated. They wouldn't understand the fire in the loins that drove her mad, when she was separated from him. She was a de Bernard, a well brought up Catholic of impeccable family, and it wouldn't be conceivable that she copulated with a German old enough to be her father. The only person with whom she felt comfortable was in fact her father. He was frail and wandering, a dying child, who asked no questions and was content to sit and hold her hand. Her brother had become a stranger. The world was full of strangers now, of people who wouldn't understand how she could be the mistress of a Colonel in the S.S. Privately Regine jeered. She knew friends of her aunt who were having affairs with the upper-class officers of the Wehrmacht.

It was only the black uniform that frightened them. It didn't frighten her. She loved it; she loved the inference of force and cruelty, the way he hurt her when they were making love. She wanted to crawl and kiss his feet. She threw the little case on the bed and began to pull out her clothes. There was a noise from the room next door. She stopped, listening. Nobody slept there; it was always empty. Her fool of a brother, whom his wife had turned out of her bed, occupied the room below. Somebody was staying in the old guest room. She stood still; the walls were very thick, they muffled and distorted noise. There was a faint bang, which she thought must be the window; her own made a similar noise because the frame was heavy and it swung on its weight. Régine went outside and paused by the door. She was tense, curious as a cat. She knocked and then opened it.

A man was inside, knotting his tie in front of the dressing table. He turned round and looked at her. She saw a smile which didn't come from his eyes.

'Hello,' he said. 'You must be Régine. Come in.' She found herself shaking hands. He had taken the initiative away from her.

'I'm Roger Savage, Louise's cousin. I'm staying for a few days.'

'I didn't know anyone was here,' she said. She could feel the colour in her face. 'I heard the window bang. Please excuse me for bursting in . . .'

'That's quite all right.' He smiled down at her. There were deep rings under her eyes and she looked plain and tense. 'What time is dinner? I'm afraid I've been sleeping.'

'Seven-thirty. I've only just arrived.'

'From Paris,' Savage said. 'Louise told me about you. How is it there?'

'How should it be?' Hostility flashed at him.

Foe, he reminded himself. Definitely foe. 'I'm asking you,' he said. 'I haven't been there since the occupation. I hope it hasn't changed.'

'I don't think so; perhaps you ought to go and see for yourself.'

'Perhaps I will,' he said. 'We Swiss are such dull fellows; it would be good for me. I might even take you out to lunch.'

'I'm at the Sorbonne,' Régine said. 'I wouldn't have time.' She made a little movement, awkward and unwilling. 'Thank you.'

'I'll see you downstairs,' Savage said. He opened the door for her.

Louise hadn't misjudged her attitude, but he felt her dismissal of the sister-in-law was a mistake. She reminded him of an animal living on its nerves. It was ridiculous, but he had a prescience of danger. He inspected himself in the glass. Hair brushed down, clothes conservative and neat, expression relaxed. The Swiss were dull fellows; he must remember that. He heard voices in the salon and opened the door to find Louise in front of it.

'Oh,' she said. 'I was coming to call you.'

Savage took her hand and kissed it; he felt her fingers tremble.

'I hope I'm not late.'

'Of course not, come in. We're having a drink.'

She wore a yellow printed dress with a long skirt; the cut was pre-war.

'My husband Jean. This is Roger.'

He shook hands with the Comte; he formed a quick impression of a good-looking dark eyed man with prematurely greying hair and a firm grip, and then his stomach knotted quickly. A man in grey uniform moved forward.

'Major Minden, my cousin Monsieur Savage.'

Minden. Heinz Paul Minden, Major in the 23rd Infantry Corps, aged thirty-seven, married with two children, home in Breslau. Savage bowed. Nothing remarkable, pleasant-looking in a clean-cut way, tall, well built. They shook hands. Louise handed him a glass of the dry wine he had drunk before lunch. The Major offered him a cigarette; he could see Jean de Bernard watching him. He felt Régine come in, and forestalled an introduction by announcing that they had already met.

She accepted a drink and retreated into a corner seat.

'This is my first visit to St. Blaize.' Savage spoke to the major. 'It's beautiful; it must be pleasant to stay here. Do you work in Paris?'

'No, my office is at the local headquarters,' Minden said. He didn't like the Swiss. He was surprised and irritated to find another man in the house. His eyes strayed from Savage, who was describing the train ride from Paris in tedious detail, and followed Louise as she moved round the room. She seemed restless; her cousin's visit appeared to have unsettled her. He thought she looked very beautiful in the yellow dress. Regine was as quiet and withdrawn as usual. Minden paid her no attention. He was wholly absorbed by the older woman.

The voice of Savage recalled him. 'I was stopped on the way here,' he said. 'It looked like a road block. I must say your troops were very polite.'

'I'm glad to hear it,' the Major said. 'There's an alert on for enemy agents in the area. But it's only a formality. I don't think it's a serious possibility.'

'Roger.' Louise had appeared beside them suddenly; she linked her arm through his and pressed fiercely with her fingers. Savage looked down at her. He gave her arm a friendly squeeze.

'You don't know how interesting I find all this,' he said. 'Imagine how quiet it is, living in a neutral country. Enemy agents! That sounds very exciting.'

'I disagree.' Jean de Bernard spoke directly to him. 'The last time these people were dropped round here, they involved a local family and two of them were shot. It was a useless, irresponsible act, and it cost French lives. We don't want any more of it. If I found anyone hiding here and trying to cause trouble for the occupation forces, I shouldn't hesitate to give them up!'

There was silence then; Savage felt Louise stiffen beside him. The Major looked embarrassed. 'And quite right too,' Savage said. 'You French are sensible, like the Swiss. You prefer peace. Just think, if I hadn't become a citizen when I was younger, I could have been fighting in the American Army!' They were all looking at him. He patted Louise's hand; he could feel the German wince. He'd noticed the wandering look that followed her, the contracting of jaw muscles when she held his arm. The Major didn't like the cousin from Switzerland handling what he wanted to touch so badly himself.

'Of course,' Minden said, his voice unfriendly. 'I didn't realise you were American.'

'Only my father,' Savage explained. 'My mother was from

Lausanne. I've spent all my life in Switzerland. Do you know it?'

'No,' the Major said. 'I've never been there.'

'We used to ski at Verbier before the war,' Jean de Bernard said. 'My father skied extremely well.'

'How is he today?' The Major channelled the talk away from Savage and Louise led him to a sofa which was set back by the wall. She sat beside him. He lit her cigarette and saw that her hand trembled.

'You must be mad,' she said quickly. 'Talking about enemy agents . . .'

'Mad to ignore it,' he said. 'Why shouldn't I mention it? I've nothing to hide; stop looking frightened or they'll notice something. Smile. And put that cigarette out, your hand's shaking like a leaf.'

'It's terrifying,' Louise whispered. 'There's something odd about Jean. I don't think he believes me. How did you meet Régine?'

'She came into my room; said she heard a noise. I'd watch your step with her. She's sharp as a tack.'

'She's completely wrapped up in her own life,' Louise said. For a moment she glanced across to where her sister-in-law sat, holding a glass of wine in both hands, not drinking it and watching her brother talking to the Mayor. 'She's just young, self-centred. I don't take any notice of her.'

'Well, I shall,' Savage said, 'and you should. My hunch says she's dangerous.' He leaned against the sofa, one arm stretched out along the back. Louise looked at him and suddenly he smiled. It made him look different.

'I like your dress,' he said. 'Try to relax with me, don't look so strained.'

'I'm sorry,' she said. 'I'll try my best. I won't let you down. Aren't you scared yourself? Sitting here with that man across the room . . .'

'No.' Savage shook his head. 'He interests me. Put me sitting next to him at dinner. I want to make a good impression.'

'You ought to avoid him,' Louise protested, 'keep out of his way. I think you're taking unnecessary risks. I've calmed down now, give me another cigarette. It was just when you mentioned the alert . . .'

'Here.' He lit it for her and for a moment their hands touched. His were warm and steady. There was nothing about him to make her feel protective, and yet she said it. 'Be careful. Please.'

'Don't worry.' Savage got up, and slid his hand under her elbow. 'Your manservant has just come in. And don't forget, put me next to Minden.'

Louise sat at the end of the table, with Jean at the head, candles burning between them, lighting the faces of Savage and Minden and Regine.

Savage was talking; he talked to Jean, to Régine, who hardly answered, and most of all to the Major, who was dour and unresponsive. Watching, Louise felt herself relaxing. He was so confident, so bold in his assumption of the role. And so Swiss that she could hardly believe it was acting. She ate little and only sipped the wine, aware that Jean was glancing at her from the other end, with an expression which she couldn't analyse. Did he suspect anything? It was impossible to tell. She had no practice in lying to him, or to anyone; she had been brought up to tell the truth and to despise evasions. Now she had agreed to live a terrifying lie and to deceive people so close to her that every mood and look was known. And if she failed, if Jean suspected that Roger Savage was not her cousin, that he was in any way connected with the air-raid warning of the previous night, then the man she had promised to help was already dead. 'I'd denounce them immediately', that was what Jean had said, and she knew that the words were directed at her. And he'd do it; she had to remember what happened to the Palliers, to reject the hope that he had been incapable of the final infamy.

And if that happened beyond doubt, then even the chill compromise of living under the same roof would be impossible for her.

Savage's voice interrupted her thoughts. 'What excellent brandy,' he said, talking to his left to the Comte. 'I didn't know you could still get it in France.'

'Major Minden was kind enough to give it to me for Christmas,' Jean de Bernard said.

'And the cigars too? How very generous.' Savage made the German a little bow. 'And are you stationed near St. Blaize?'

'I am at the headquarters, at the Château Diane,' Minden said. 'About half an hour's drive from here.' He looked up at Louise and his expression softened. 'Even if it were Paris, I should prefer to live here.'

'The Château Diane? Haven't I heard of it?'

'It belonged to Diane de Poitiers.' Jean de Bernard answered Savage's question. 'It was built for her by Henri II. It's only a part of the original building; much of it was destroyed after the Revolution. But it's very beautiful.'

'Most of the original furniture is still there,' Minden said. 'Wonderful tapestries—my General uses the State rooms.'

'How interesting—does he like history?'

'I don't think so,' Minden laughed. He had drunk a lot of wine and he felt suddenly bold. The presence of Louise sitting so close, and the faint drift of cologne she wore acted as a delicious goad upon his imagination. He wished she would open his scent and use it . . . 'He doesn't care for history much but he's madly in love with Diane de Poitiers!'

'Really?' Jean de Bernard said. 'You never mentioned this before.'

'It's quite amusing,' Minden said. He felt a moment of disloyalty but suppressed it. He wanted to interest Louise. 'There's a portrait of her as Diana the Huntress—you know the kind of picture, a naked allegory, very voluptuous. He had it moved into his sitting room. He sits in front of it, staring. He's read everything written about her; he even sleeps in her bedroom, in her bed!'

'He sounds as if he's a romantic,' Savage said. 'What's his name?'

'General Brühl,' Minden answered. Nobody had laughed or even smiled at his account of Brühl's obsession. Perhaps he had merely sounded coarse. He looked anxiously at Louise and found her watching her cousin. He felt irritated. He felt obliged to defend his General to these people, for whose benefit he had just held him up to ridicule.

'He's a very talented man,' he said. 'He paints in his leisure time—very well. And apart from this little foible about Diane de Poitiers, he's very interested in antiquities.'

'Then we have that in common,' Savage said. 'I should love to see the Château. I suppose, Major, it wouldn't be possible?'

'Not inside, I'm afraid,' Minden said. 'I'd invite you as my guest, but unfortunately non-German personnel are not permitted. I'm so sorry. However, there's some very fine carving on the outside, you could see that. The gateway is remarkable;, it's Diane de Poiters again, as Diana. Three times life-size, supported by a stag.'

'I must certainly go,' Savage said. 'Louise, could you find time to take me tomorrow?'

'Yes of course. We could go in the morning. But we'd have to bicycle. We have a little petrol but it has to be saved for emergencies. Would you mind that?'

'I haven't cycled since I was a boy.' Savage smiled round at them. 'I'm sure the exercise would do me good.'

'Not at all,' Minden spoke to Louise. She tried not to look away, but the moist brown eyes with their message of desire disgusted her. 'Madame, you can use my car. I'll send it back for you and you can drive over and spend as much time as you like. It will be my pleasure.'

'Thank you,' she said. 'You're very kind.'

'Wasn't there a story,' Savage said, 'that Diane de Poitiers had a skin like a young girl when she was sixty?'

'I read that somewhere.' Régine spoke suddenly, and because she hadn't joined the conversation everybody looked at her. There was a polite little smile on Savage's mouth. 'I read all about her; eternal youth and the rest of the nonsense. Personally I don't believe a word of it. Women like that are just myths. As for being in love—those sort of women aren't capable of it!'

'What sort of women?' Louise asked her. 'Kings' mistresses?'

'Professionals,' Régine said. 'The sort of French woman who only exists in the minds of foreigners. A kind of national whore.'

'Régine!' Jean de Bernard spoke sharply. 'That's not a word for you to use. Please . . .'

'There isn't another,' she said coldly. 'I'm not a child, Jean. Please don't rebuke me as if I were.'

Louise pushed back her chair. 'I think we'll go into the salon.' Before she could leave the table, Minden was beside her, pulling the chair away.

'A wonderful dinner,' he murmured.

Louise brushed past him. 'Thank you. I'm glad you enjoyed it.' Régine followed her; she looked pale and there were dark pits under her eyes. For a moment Louise was tempted to ask her if she were feeling ill. But the eyes looked at her and through her, opaque and hostile, the sullen mouth set in a stubborn line.

'I'm very tired,' Régine said. 'Would you mind if I went to bed now?'

'No, of course not. You look tired.'

'Say good night to Jean and the Major and your cousin for me. How long is he going to stay?'

'I don't know,' Louise said. 'A few days. He's come on business over my family trust.'

Régine looked at her for a moment and then away. It was a way she had of being rude. 'He doesn't look at all like you,' she said. 'If he's a cousin he can't be very close.' She walked out of the room before Louise could answer.

They settled in a little group close to the fire; Louise had a frame of embroidery which she worked on in the evenings; both Minden and Savage looked at her. The fire was alight; the light flickered over her as she sewed, casting soft shadows over her face. Both men examined her, but in different ways. The German's eyes ranged over the line of her neck, down to the outline of her breasts and the curve of one leg crossed at the knee. Before his imagination the yellow dress disappeared and the hair caught up behind her head was loose and flowing over bare shoulders. He shifted in his chair and forced his thoughts away from her. To Savage she was more complicated. Sexually attractive, remote and independent, vulnerable and yet brave. There was no need for mental stripping, for the laboured erotic imaginings of the other man. He looked at her and he was stirred.

She had done well that evening. She had kept the balance between them, hiding the fear which he alone had seen. Her hands were steady as she used the needle; the fingers were long and graceful, the nails unpolished. She looked serene in the firelight, removed from them all, as her husband and the Major talked together, excluding him. Once she looked up and caught him watching her. He left his chair and came over to her.

'What are you making, Louise? Show me . . .'

'It's a stool cover—for Papa's room.' He bent over her. 'That's very nice. It must take a long time.'

'About three months, if I do some every night.'

'I want to talk to you,' he said quietly. 'I'll come to your room later.' He went back to his chair, stretched out his feet and gave a little grunt.

'This is so pleasant,' he said. 'I never imagined life was so peaceful in France.'

'It is peaceful,' the Comte de Bernard said. 'And that is how we want to keep it.'

Louise went upstairs first; she paid a visit to her father-in-law and found him sleeping deeply, his bedside light still on. She arranged the bedclothes round him and switched it off, leaving the door a little open. Jean-Pierre and Marie-Anne slept on the same floor within his call. Then she went downstairs to her room to wait for Savage. She heard Jean and the Major come up; she heard Savage saying good night. The minutes went by until an hour had passed, and then a knock sounded on her door. She opened it and he came in.

'I thought you weren't coming.'

'I gave them time to get to sleep; do you have a cigarette?'

'Over there on my dressing table, help yourself.'

Savage sat on the bed. He lit two cigarettes and passed one to her. Again their fingers touched. She wore a dressing-gown, and he noticed how much younger she looked with her hair down.

'I learned a lot tonight,' he said. 'You were terrific. Come and sit down here.'

'You took so many risks,' Louise said. 'I haven't stopped shaking yet. All that business about enemy agents—I nearly died!'

'It was quite natural to talk about it,' he said. 'A real Swiss would have been indignant as hell, being stopped and questioned. I wanted to be convincing.'

'You were certainly that,' she said.

'That Kraut can't take his eyes off you,' Savage said suddenly. 'Why didn't you tell me it was like that?'

'Why should I?' She was surprised and then angry. 'It's bad enough for me having him here, seeing him looking at me like that. I hate him; I hate myself for even speaking to him!'

'And your husband—how about him? How does he like having that goon licking his lips over you?'

'He ignores it,' Louise said. 'Minden will never try anything and Jean knows it. It's part of the price he's willing to pay. For St. Blaize, for being safe.'

'He'd better make the most of it,' Savage said. 'It may not last long. I'm going to need a lot of help from you. How frightened are you? Maybe I should put it differently. How brave?'

'Not brave at all.' Louise shook her head. 'Thinking about this kind of thing is not the same as doing it. I'm scared to death. But I'll still help all I can. You may think this is funny, but I'm grateful to you for the opportunity.'

'To risk your life? It's a hell of a thing to be grateful for.'

'I've been living this life since 1940; living with capitulation, with people thinking of nothing but their own skins. I came here full of pride in being married to a Frenchman—a fine old family, you know the kind of thing. I thought St. Blaize and the Château were marvellous and I was just so lucky to be part of it. Well, I don't feel that any more. I despise them. I despise my own husband. And I was getting like them, taking that man's food and drink, letting him lend his car tomorrow. At last I've got a chance to do something to help. And whatever happens I can keep my self-respect. I mean it. I'm very glad you came.'

'If things go wrong,' he said, 'you will be sorry. I hope you realise that.'

'I do. That's why I'm scared.'

'It's a good way to be,' Savage said. 'It makes you careful. Do you have any books on local houses here? I want something on the Château Diane.'

'I'm sure we have—there's a huge library. But why there? Surely you're not thinking of getting in there! It's Brühl's headquarters—it's guarded like Fort Knox!'

'That figures,' Savage said. 'What do you know about Brühl?'

'Nothing. He doesn't mix socially; nobody's ever met him.'

'No,' Savage said. 'I don't suppose they have. Can you look out some books for me tomorrow?'

'I wish you'd tell me what you're going to do. I could do so much more if I knew. Why can't you trust me?'

'If you're arrested,' Savage said calmly, 'you can't tell them what you don't know. I do trust you. I believe you'd be brave and hold out as long as you could. I trust any woman to keep her mouth shut except when someone is using an electric probe inside her.'

'And what about you? Are you so sure you'll hold out?'

'Damned sure,' Savage said. 'Because they'll never take me. Within two seconds I'll be dead. That means if I fail to do the job, somebody else can try.'

'Is it so important? Is it really vital, this thing you've come to do?' She shivered; it was past one o'clock and the room was cold.

'Here,' Savage said. 'You're freezing.' He dragged the quilt off the bed and wrapped it round her. 'Keep this on. Okay, I'll answer that question. It is important. It's more important than you or me or anything that may happen to us. It's the difference between winning and losing the war.'

'I won't ask you any more,' she said quietly. 'You know I'll do anything I can.'

'I know,' he said. 'I only hope you don't regret it. But at least I've warned you. You'd better get to bed now.'

He got up and stretched himself. 'Put your light out before I open the door.'

Louise sat in the darkness for some moments after he had gone. He hadn't touched her or said anything, but she knew that there was a moment when he wanted to stay. She got into bed, pulling the quilt into position. There had been something in his face when he wrapped it round her. Some current of communication, sharp and shocking in its implication. Moments before he had talked about her being tortured as coolly as if he were discussing someone far away. Then there was that sudden blaze inside him, which was as quickly dampened down. Something had answered him; sparks had struck between them without words, without touch. If he had stayed she would have let him. The moment of self-knowledge showed her that she had reached a time of total crisis in her life.

4

'You look tired, Régine. Didn't you sleep well?' Jean de Bernard got up and kissed his sister; he was sitting on the terrace in the brief morning sunshine. She took the chair beside him.

'I'm all right. It's this weather, it's so unpredictable . . .' She shaded her eyes.

'Are you working too hard?' he asked her. 'You haven't looked yourself for some weeks. There's nothing wrong, is there?'

She didn't answer immediately. She was tempted to tell him. She had reached the stage with Vierken when she wanted to stabilise the relationship. She wanted to bring him down to St. Blaize and present him to her family. Her motives were not clear; she had plunged into what seemed to be an exciting affair, and found it becoming more and more important to her. Vierken had shown her to herself; she knew now what she wanted and that nothing else would ever satisfy her. It was a discovery which had changed her life.

'No, there's nothing wrong. I've met somebody I like. I just thought I'd tell you.'

Jean de Bernard came forward in his chair. 'Oh? Aunt Pauline hasn't mentioned anyone—who is it?'

'She hasn't met him,' Régine said. Instinct told her to go slowly. 'He's a German.'

'I see,' her brother said. 'Where did you meet him?'

'At a concert.' They had been sitting next to each other at the Conservatoire, and he had picked her up. She wondered what her proper-minded brother would say if he knew that. 'It's nothing serious, Jean. But he's nice and I thought I'd like to bring him home one weekend.'

'Why haven't you introduced him to Aunt Pauline?'

'You know how she feels about Germans. She'd make him uncomfortable. It's different with you.'

'Not when it comes to my sister,' he said. 'I tolerate them because I don't want trouble. But I don't like you associating with them. Who is this man, what service is he in?'

'The army,' Régine said. 'I told you, it's not serious, you don't have to get so worked up about it. I won't bring him here either if he's not welcome.'

'If it's not serious, then there's no point in bringing him down to meet your family. It would certainly upset Louise.'

'And you'd mind about that, wouldn't you? Even after the way she's treated you?'

'I'm not going to discuss that. She's entitled to her feelings.'

'But you're not entitled to yours, or me to mine,' his sister pointed out. 'She won't have you in her bed, because you haven't been out blowing up railway bridges and getting a lot of people killed! Oh, don't look at me like that, we all know how it is here. Everyone knows. You've no courage, Jean. You shouldn't let her get away with it!'

'You don't understand, Régine,' he said. 'How could you? You haven't lived yet; you haven't been in love.' She thought of the afternoons spent in Vierken's suite in the Crillon, of the breathless, frantic violence of their lovemaking; of the sick pain of mental and physical longing to be with him. Oh no, of course she wouldn't understand . . . She looked at him.

'You're saying you still love her, aren't you?'

'I'm not saying anything. I won't talk about it.'

'She's gone off sightseeing with her cousin, I suppose.'

'Yes. Minden lent them his car.'

'How long is the cousin staying?'

'A few days. Not long.'

'Why should he suddenly come here? There's something funny about it.'

'There's nothing funny.' He sounded irritated. 'Her trust is administered in Switzerland and he works for the lawyers.'

'Oh well.' She shrugged and got up. 'If you're satisfied. But I couldn't sleep last night, and I heard him go out of his room and down the stairs. I wonder what he was doing? I'm going to play with Paul and Sophie.' She walked away to find the children; he could hear her voice calling to them in the garden. She loved them as much as she hated Louise. He lit a cigarette and settled back to wait for his wife and her cousin to return.

The Château Diane was half an hour's drive from St. Blaize. Savage and Louise sat in the back; he praised the beauty of the countryside, and spoke Schweizerdeutsch to Fritz the driver, who was not amused and said in French that he couldn't understand a word. Savage was in a good mood. He had slept well the night before, and he was feeling confident. Whenever the sun shone, his optimism grew.

The car drove through the little town of Anet; it was worth seeing in its own right, for the cobbled streets and sixteenth-century houses, many with their original outside gabling. They turned down a hill, and swung left. There in front of them towered an enormous grey stone gateway and a high wall; the turrets of the Château pointed above it like fingers.

The car stopped. Fritz opened the door for Louise. They got out and Savage stood looking at the gateway. Above the door there was the magnificent naked sculpture of Diane de Poitiers, as Major Minden had described. Huge carved wooden gates enclosed the entrance porch; two red and white sentry boxes were on either side of them, and barriers strung with barbed wire surrounded the outer perimeter of the wall. A vast dry moat surrounded the whole building. Louise touched his arm.

'You see what I mean,' she said. 'This is just the outside. Think what the Château must be like. It wouldn't be possible.'

Savage took her arm. 'Let's walk round a bit, make it look authentic. They would grab this, wouldn't they? It's so beautiful. If you do have any books on it, could we find them after lunch?'

'I was thinking about it,' she said. They walked slowly, his arm pressing against hers. 'We can ask Jean. He'd know where to find something. You haven't seen the library; there are over a thousand books.'

'Are you still scared?' Savage asked.

'Yes. Aren't you?'

'Not particularly. By the way, you've got to show me how to get out on the roof.'

'The roof? Why . . .' She paused and he walked faster, pulling her on with him.

'I want to look at the view,' he said. 'When does your sister-in-law go back to Paris?'

'Sunday night,' she said.

'Hell.' Savage frowned. 'I don't like her being around. She worries me more than your husband.'

'She wouldn't like you, because she doesn't like me,' Louise said. 'And she's very pro-German, I know that. But there's nothing to worry about from her. She doesn't care what happens here.'

'She cares more than you think,' he said. 'Let's turn back now; and don't look like that. I'm not planning to vault over the Château wall and take it single handed.'

'But you're going to try and get inside, aren't you?' Louise said.

'Yes,' he admitted. 'No harm in telling you that much. I've got to get into Brühl's little fortress. Nice and snug, isn't it, tucked away here . . .'

'You'll never get out,' Louise said slowly. 'You'll be killed.'

'Maybe. So long as I've done what I came to do it won't matter a damn.'

'Isn't there anyone back home who'll miss you?' They had stopped by the Château wall; the gateway towered above them, casting its shadow over them. Two sentries marched between their boxes; a military car came to the entrance and they snapped to attention. Two more guards approached the car and examined the papers of the driver.

'There's no one,' Savage said. 'This isn't a game for married men.' There was a tensing of the arm linked through hers that made her look at him.

'Have you been married?'

'Yes. But I'm not now. Come on, there's the car over there.'

'I'm not trying to pry,' Louise said. 'I shouldn't have asked.'

'No,' he said. 'You shouldn't.'

They drove back to St. Blaize in silence; his mood of cheerfulness had disappeared. He sat turned away from her, looking grimly and blindly out of the window. His hands were clenched tight on his knee. She leaned back and closed her eyes; tears stung behind the lids and she didn't know why.

Suddenly a hand covered hers. It was warm and it pressed her fingers. 'Stop thinking,' he said. 'And worrying. I can feel you doing it.'

'I'll try,' she whispered. 'I'm sorry; I know I upset you.'

'Not you,' he said. 'Nothing to do with you. You're a good girl.'

He went on holding her hand for the rest of the journey. As soon as they sat down to lunch he was back in his role; he asked so many questions and showed so much enthusiasm for the Château Diane and its architecture, that Jean de Bernard could do nothing less than take him to the library and help him find the books he wanted. The afternoon passed quietly for Louise. She had a headache but was too restless to lie down. The children went upstairs to play with their grandfather after his midday rest; they climbed the stairs with their mother, each holding her hand; Sophie, who had her father's dark hair and large brown eyes, broke away to run to the old man's bedroom first.

She was a true de Bernard, shy, intelligent, affectionate only to those she knew. Her love for the senile old man always touched Louise. They sat together holding hands while the Comte talked to her in his thin voice. By contrast the visits to the upstairs floor bored Paul, who was boisterous, and hated sitting still.

That afternoon Alfred de Bernard was in his big leather armchair, with a rug over his knees, his gramophone on a table within reach, and a book open beside it. He was a beautiful old man, with transparent white skin stretched over his fine bones, black eyes that looked into a past of his own, hair as fine as down, and the smile of the old who are content. He glanced up as Louise came in. She bent and kissed him. He had been a kind and gentle father-in-law, stricken by the loss of a much younger wife; his affection for her had been real, but already he was withdrawing from the world. Within three years of her marriage, Louise was taking care of him. He loved his grandchildren; but had they not come to see him every day, he would have soon forgotten them. He depended upon his son, whom he bullied in a timid way, but he loved his daughter above everyone else.

'Dear Régie,' he said to Louise. 'She spent such a long time with me this morning. She doesn't look well. I wish she'd come home. Pauline doesn't look after her properly.'

'I'm sure she does,' Louise said. The Comte drew the little girl into his arm.

'Sophie and she are so alike,' he murmured. 'Régine was such a beautiful child. She's gone back, hasn't she?'

'No, Papa,' Louise answered. 'Not yet. She goes to Paris tomorrow. She'll come up and see you before she goes.'

'I wish she'd stay.' He shook his head. 'Take care of her, won't you . . .'

'Of course I will.' She patted his hand. 'I'm going to leave the children with you for a few minutes. Paul, you can read something for Grandpapa. I won't be long.' Outside the room she hurried down the stairs to the floor below and along the passage to the guest room. She knocked on the door and went in.

Savage was lying on the bed, the leather-bound books spread round him. 'I found just what I wanted,' he said. 'Come in.'

'You wanted to get on the roof,' Louise said. 'I've left the children with my father-in-law. Hurry and I'll show you. I'll have to go back to him in a few minutes or Paul will run downstairs. He gets restless after a while.'

She took him up the stairs, past the door of the old Comte's room; pausing for a moment they could hear the sound of the little boy's voice reading aloud. Then on down a corridor that twisted; Savage pointed to the closed doors on one side of it. 'Who lives up here?'

'The two servants, Jean-Pierre and Marie-Anne; that first door on the left. They're all staff rooms and there's nobody in them. Here.' She stopped in front of a small wooden door and opened it. Another flight of stone spiral steps was immediately inside. 'Go up there and you'll find the entrance to the roof. It's bolted from the inside. And for God's sake be careful; I've only been up there once, to show someone the view. It's very steep and the valleys are slippery. What are you going to do up here?'

'Set up a two-way transmitter,' Savage said. 'And I can only use it once. We don't want one of their detector vans picking up a signal from here. You go back to the children. I'll go up and look around.'

The view was magnificent; he stood for a moment in a wide leaded valley, looking out over twenty miles or more of countryside. The village of St. Blaize crouched like a stone animal to the left, its church spire fingering the sky. And to the north the roofs and squares of Houdan seemed no bigger than his hand. Further still was Anet with the distinctive pink and grey of the Château Diane on its perimeter. There had been no ground plan available in London. It was not one of the great monuments of France; only a small jewel set in a country full of minor treasures, the tribute of an enamoured king to his courtesan. And now General Friedrich Brühl used it as his headquarters. It had taken British Intelligence a year to discover where he was; a year of careful research into the smallest fragments of information, a word here, a rumour, the tracking down of officers with certain specialist qualifications.

It had sounded such an anticlimax when Louise said it the night before.

'That's Brühl's headquarters,' and the casual reference the Major made to the man who was top on the list of all Allied Intelligence services.

'My General's in love with her. He even sleeps in her bed.' Savage stood looking out towards the Château; at that height the wind went through him. He looked round for the best position, given the slant of the rooftops. The big trees which had worried him because of interference were some distance away. He chose a place near the edge. Heights had no terrors for him; he stepped to the rim and looked down. This was the best place from which to transmit. He went back, down the spiral stairs and to his own floor. There was nobody moving, no sound coming from below. It was the hour between dusk and evening when the upper floors were deserted. He got his suitcase out, and dragged the waterproof covering from the top of the clothes cupboard. Less than five minutes later he was back on the roof, the transmitter in position, covered by the waterproof.

He bolted the roof door shut and slipped down the spiral stairs. On his way to his own landing the old Comte's door opened and Louise came out. Two children followed her; a boy of seven and a smaller, very pretty girl, who reminded him immediately of Jean de Bernard. He shook hands with Paul, and asked Sophie if she would kiss him. Shaking her head, the child hid behind her mother. Savage looked at Louise and smiled.

'She's got the right idea. Never kiss a stranger.' They walked the rest of the way together.

. . . . .

On Sunday the de Bernard family went to Mass. To their surprise Louise accompanied them. Savage found himself alone with the Major. He discovered him reading in the salon, looking quite different in civilian clothes. He glanced up as Savage came in and frowned.

'Good morning.' Savage wore his broadest smile. 'The sun is shining and I'm going for a walk. I hope you will keep me company.'

Minden lowered his book. 'I'm reading,' he said.

'You can read this afternoon,' Savage said. 'It's cold in here. Come and get some exercise.' With a sigh the Major put his book aside. He followed him out into the garden. It was indeed a lovely morning, the sun was exceptionally hot and the first cabbage white butterfly of the season fluttered past.

'Let's go this way.' Savage pointed round the side of the Château. 'There's a pleasant walk through here; I found it yesterday. I find this more beneficial than going to church. You're not a Catholic?'

'I was brought up a Lutheran,' Minden answered. They were walking side by side down a shaded path towards an avenuc of lime trees. 'Personally I'm an agnostic.'

'The religion of the scientist,' Savage remarked. 'And the law. I prefer the rational law to metaphysics. One could say our society is substituting pharmaceuticals for prayers.'

'I hope that's not a sneer,' Minden said. His tone was sharp. He didn't like Savage; he hadn't wanted to be dragged away from his book to take this walk. Now he detected a sarcasm at the expense of what he most believed in and he reacted angrily.

'A sneer?' Savage repeated it with surprise. 'My dear Major, why should I sneer at the greatest science of them all? Man is controlled by chemistry. That is a fact, not an accusation.'

'It's not a theory people like,' Minden said. The apology had mollified him. Both men began to quicken their pace towards the avenue of trees. 'Nor to be fair, is it completely proven. Certainly most human reactions can be altered by chemical means, but it's not yet certain how decisive a part chemical balances play in the basic behaviour patterns of man. This will be the study of the future.'

'If there is a future,' Savage said. 'The world has been ravaged by war, and there is still the major battle to be fought.'

'It will be won,' the Major said. 'I have no doubts about the outcome. And then there will be peace for the next five hundred years. Time for rebuilding, for re-shaping Europe.'

'You're very confident that the Allies' invasion will fail,' Savage said. Over their heads the sun broke through the trees, dappling them with light. Minden's face was blotched and leprous, as if he had a skin disease. Then the trees closed over them and the illusion passed. 'How can you be so certain of a German victory? I must tell you frankly, Swiss opinion has begun to veer towards the Allies.'

'Then it is mistaken,' Minden said. He spoke without emphasis, coolly, from a position of knowledge denied to a neutral. He had a profound contempt for Swiss money-making and dealing with both sides. Minden didn't need to be on the defensive; Savage recognised the absolute certainty in his answer and the skin on his body pricked.

'You're facing an invasion; a huge Anglo-American army will be thrown against you. And you must admit, your best troops were lost in Russia. It's not the old Wehrmacht defending Europe today. There are unfortunate parallels to be drawn with Napoleon.'

'That's understandable,' Minden agreed, 'but it happens to be the wrong conclusion. Certainly our manpower is not what it was. But this won't be the deciding factor. The invasion will fail. England and America will have to capitulate. If Switzerland backs the Allies she will regret it. Shall we turn back now?'

'Are you suggesting that Hitler really has a secret weapon? I can't see what else would make America and England ask for peace.'

'VIs and rockets are already falling upon England,' Minden pointed out. 'The Führer keeps his word. He's promised victory and we shall have it.'

'Then there must be something else, some other weapon,' Savage said.

'If there is,' the Major answered, 'I wouldn't know about it. I'm only a simple staff officer.'

'You're not offended by this conversation?' Savage sounded concerned. 'I felt we could discuss it openly.'

'And why not? I'm not a political fanatic. I enjoyed our talk. Beautiful grounds, aren't they? It's a pity the gardens have become run down. My batman helps with the vegetables but he hasn't time to do more.'

'They must be glad to have you here,' Savage said. 'You've been very helpful to them.'

'I've done what I could,' Minden said. 'They're a nice family. The Comte is a sensible man; we get on very well.'

'My cousin has become very French,' Savage remarked. They were within sight of the Château. 'I'm surprised; Americans don't usually lose their identity so completely. I have the feeling she resents you. You don't mind my saying that?'

The Major did mind, and his frown showed it. However, he shrugged. 'I suppose so. No woman likes a stranger in her home. I think she's grown used to me. One day we will be friends.'

'I'm sure you will. I met my little cousins yesterday. They're delightful children. I've always heard that American children were monsters; I'm afraid my views on upbringing are very strict.'

'With an American father?' the Major couldn't resist it.

'My parents were divorced. My mother raised me. And she had the old-fashioned ideas. I hear the car; they must be back from church.'

'Ah,' Minden said. 'Yes, they're back. I promised to play with the children before lunch.' He began to walk very quickly towards the Château.

They turned the corner and there was the car, with Jean and Régine, the children and Louise. As soon as they saw Minden the children ran towards him. He went down on one knee and gathered them into his arms. Savage could see him laughing. He looked up and saw Louise watching him; Jean and Régine had gone inside. He went acros to her; she looked girlish and pretty in a hat. He put a hand on her shoulder. 'Good morning. Did you say one for me?'

'I couldn't,' she said in a low voice. 'I felt if I mentioned it at all, something awful will happen. Besides, I haven't been to Mass for months. I told you, I was a coward.'

'I know,' Savage said. 'I believe you.'

'Look at the children,' she said. 'He always makes such a fuss of them.'

'So I see.' Minden was standing upright, the children, one on each side of him, swinging from his hands. They were looking up at him and laughing.

'Mama,' Paul called out, 'Mama, Major Minden wants to play ball with us!'

'That's very kind of him,' Louise answered. 'Lunch is in half an hour.' The three of them began to run across the lawn.

'So he's a child lover, is he?' Savage said softly.

'There's nothing I can do about it,' Louise answered. 'They'll grow up thinking the Germans are nice. Why are you looking like that?'

'They're not nice,' Savage said. 'They're a race of bloody schizophrenics, and that bastard is a good example. When can we talk?'

'Not now,' she said. 'Jean will be getting us something to drink. After lunch, go to your room and wait for me. I'll say I've got a headache.'

• • • • •

'I can't find either of them.' Régine faced her brother. 'He's not in the house and Louise isn't in her room. I looked.'

'And what is that supposed to mean?' He looked up at her, his face wary, an expression of anger in her eyes. 'Régine, I warn you, before you say anything, be very careful.'

'All right, I know you want to close your eyes to it,' she said angrily. 'That's the trouble with you. But I'm different. I know there's something wrong with this so-called cousin, coming out of the blue! I watched them together this morning when we came back from Mass. I looked out of the window and saw them; he had his hand on her shoulder and they were looking at each other. And it wasn't like cousins! She says she's got a headache and she's going to lie down, he pretends to go for a walk. He went walking this morning, the Major told me. They've gone off somewhere together!'

'So you went to spy on Louise,' Jean de Bernard said slowly. 'You couldn't find her in her room, so you come running down to me to make trouble.'

'He's not a cousin,' Régine said defiantly. 'He's a lover. I know it. I know by the way he looks at her!'

'You know nothing about it.' Jean got up and suddenly he seized his sister by the arm. 'I told you this morning and I'll tell you now. Mind your own business! Louise is my wife and I won't have you snooping and telling lies. Roger Savage *is* her cousin; I know who his parents are, I know everything about him.'

'He's sleeping with her,' Régine sneered. 'At this moment I expect she's flat on her back under some trees!'

With his right hand he slapped her hard across the face. 'Shut your mouth,' he shouted at her. 'Get out of this room!'

She backed away from him, one hand against her cheek. She had begun to cry. 'I'm going,' she said. 'I'm going back to Paris now!'

The door slammed after her; Jean de Bernard stood for a moment, not moving. Régine was right about Roger Savage. Her reaction to him had been instinctive, her deduction wholly feminine. There was nothing Jean could define about Savage that accounted for his suspicion. His performance, if that was what it was, had been faultless; it was Louise who had failed to convince. He knew his wife and their estrangement hadn't changed her personality. She had the natural frankness of her race. The role of deceiver didn't fit her. He walked across to the window and lit a cigarette, staring out. If they had gone for a walk they would return that way.

Minden was wrong. There *had* been a drop of enemy agents, and the man who passed himself off as Roger Savage was the parachutist. Whatever Savage was planning to do, it could only mean death and destruction, with its attendant reprisals against the French. Everything he had worked for and sacrificed so much of his happiness to preserve was now in mortal danger. He had lost his wife and his self-respect, but he had kept St. Blaize and the village intact. He loved the Château above mere stones and trees and an old heritage. It was the house where he was born, where he had played on the lawns and ridden his first pony down the bridle paths. It had survived the Revolution, watching over the village for six centuries. Everywhere he looked there were reminders of the past and of his responsibility for the future. The portraits of his ancestors, the photographs of his grandparents and parents as children, the large studio study of Louise, by the fountain with his son and baby daughter. Standing by the window, waiting for them to come into view, Jean remembered that day four years ago when he had seen the first German scout car drive to the door, and the first Germans to set foot in St. Blaize en Yvelines walked across the gravel. He had been so disillusioned and heartsick, returned from total military collapse to protect what was left of his family's future. At that moment there had been no middle way, no compromise between the decision to step forward and hold out his hand to the ravishers of France, or take out his army revolver and shoot them dead. He had made his choice and paid the price. Now it was threatened with destruction. His old father slipping peacefully out of life upstairs, loved and protected, his sister whom he had slapped across the face like a slut, because she had panicked him, his children, Louise herself. They would all be taken and questioned, before they were dragged before a firing squad.

Jean knew what happened to the dissenters, to the resisters. He didn't feel anger any more; now fear possessed him, fear for the people he loved. Fear for the wife who had betrayed them all by her blind obstinacy, and whose danger he couldn't bear to contemplate. There was only one thing to be done. He had made one choice four years ago. He made a second then. He went to the bureau and from the back of the drawer he took his army revolver and a clip of bullets which had been hidden there since the capitulation of France. Then he went to find Savage.

. . . . .

Savage had his mouth pressed hard against hers; she had stopped resisting him, her lips were open and her eyes closed.

He could feel her heart beating fast under his moving hand. It had happened between them without warning. He had gone upstairs and waited for her; he was sure that his mind was occupied by nothing but the Major. When she came into the room his body moved; it came close to her, one hand pushed the door shut and the other caught her by the shoulder. Without speaking, he leant his weight against her, pinning her against the wall.

He hadn't meant to make love to her; equally he was sure she hadn't expected it. The fact was that it had happened. He raised his head and looked down at her.

'This is breaking all the rules,' he said. 'They didn't teach me about this in training school . . . I want you very much. I feel you want me.'

The muscles pinning her against him were steel knots. And yet there was a warmth in the eyes and for all his strength he hadn't hurt her. 'Oh God,' Louise whispered, 'you know I do. Let me go.'

'No,' Savage said. 'We're going to make love. We nearly did last night. It's going to happen anyway. You know it is.'

'Take your hands off my wife!' Jean de Bernard stood in the open doorway, his revolver pointing at Savage. He spoke in English. Savage moved a step back; his eyes flickered to the door, judging the chance of crashing it shut on the Comte and jamming him against the lintel. The gun was too close. He stood clear of Louise.

'I ought to kill you,' Jean de Bernard said. 'I would have done if I hadn't been afraid of hitting Louise. Get away from him.'

'No,' she said quietly. She moved to Savage and took hold of his arm. 'Put down that gun,' she said. 'Nothing happened between us.'

He didn't look at her; he said slowly to Savage, 'I heard everything. You're no more Swiss than I am. You've come to this house and brought us all into danger. My foolish, romantic-minded wife let you stay. You know what the Gestapo would do to her, don't you? But you don't care! You'll use her and try to sleep with her, and never think of what could happen to her—to all of us!'

'All right,' Savage said coldly. 'So I'm not Swiss. You've found out. But I'm here and I've been made pretty bloody welcome. So what do you tell your German friends?'

'I tell them,' Jean said grimly, 'that I became suspicious. That I confronted you, you admitted you were using false papers; you tried to escape and I shot you.'

'Very tidy,' Savage said. 'But where does that leave your wife? You think she won't be questioned? You'd better shoot us both. Unless you're ready to give her up too.'

'No!' Louise cried out. 'Jean—for God's sake . . .'

'He won't shoot,' Savage said. 'Right now he'd like to, but he knows he can't. He knows you won't alibi him if he does, and he doesn't fancy the boys getting their itchy hands on you. Why don't you put the gun away? There's nothing you can do about me that doesn't give Louise to the Gestapo!' He turned away from them both and dropped into a chair.

'You bastard,' Jean de Bernard said. 'You blackmailing bastard . . .' He turned to Louise. 'You see now what you've done! You see what these people really are!'

'He's a soldier,' she said slowly. 'He's here to do something important. He can't let anything stand in the way. I don't blame him.'

'No good trying to enlist her,' Savage said. 'She's on my side. I tell you something, Comte de Bernard. She's got more guts in her finger than you and forty million bloody Frenchmen like you.'

'You're getting out of here,' Jean said. 'I don't care where you go, but you're leaving here!'

Savage waited; his instinct counselled him to wait, to leave the initiative to the woman. She had been taken by surprise, but he noted with admiration how bravely she had reacted. He looked at her and smiled slightly. Her scent was still on his hands, a faint suggestion of flowery powder and cologne. He would have liked to take that gun away and bring it butt downwards onto the Comte's skull.

'Jean,' Louise said slowly, 'he can't leave here. He's got to stay in this district. If you turn him out, I'll go with him. Then you'll be sure of one thing. We'll be arrested together.'

'I see,' de Bernard said. 'I see how it is. He's seduced you completely. You're putting the children at risk, you realise that? And my father? You're quite prepared to do this, just for him.'

'Not for him, no,' Louise said quietly. 'What you saw shouldn't have happened. I'm sorry it did. It was just as much my fault as his. I'm going to help him because I want to see the Allies win. I want to see your country free of Germans. It's too late for me to turn back. And now it's too late for you too. You'll have to help whether you like it or not.'

'That's sense,' Savage remarked. 'You believe in neutrality, that's okay by us. Just forget you came up here.'

'My wife's in danger,' Jean blazed at him. 'My whole family's in danger because of you!'

'It so happens,' Savage said quietly, 'that they're in greater danger than you think. Why the hell don't you put that pop-gun away and listen?'

Slowly the gun lowered. 'What do you mean?' Jean said. 'What danger?' Savage took a packet of cigarettes out of his pocket and lit two. He held one out to Louise. Her hands were quite steady.

'I came here to do a job,' he said. 'I was picked for it and trained for it. And I tell you this. Nothing on God's earth is going to stop me. Get that clear first. I could make a deal with you now but I've no guarantee you'd stick to it. All right, you'll protect your wife even if it means helping me. But for how long? You'd think of some way to cross me up and get yourselves in the clear. I can't take that chance. I can't take any chance that could stop this going through. So I've got to trust you. You think you can live with the Nazis and survive, don't you? You think if you keep your nose clean and don't get into trouble they'll let you alone and you can go on living here, bringing up your family?'

'I know I can,' Jean de Bernard interrupted furiously. 'It's people like you—you talk about being trained—trained to kill! To destroy, to come into my country and throw away French lives because of some scheme thought up in London! You may be expendable, maybe you don't mind being killed, but my wife and family aren't going to suffer because of your mission or whatever it is. You say they're in danger—I don't believe you. You're the danger.'

The gun was raised again, pointing to Savage.

'You can shoot me,' he said coldly. 'Go ahead. But first I'm going to tell you why I'm here. Then you can make your choice.'

. . . . .

Adolph Vierken had taken a suite at the Crillon. When he came to Paris six months earlier he had been very tired, unable to sleep, suffering from the combat fatigue which was common among men who had served on the Eastern front. His service in Russia had been almost eighteen months. He had come back two stone lighter, suffering from dysentery and exhaustion. He and his men had fought a savage rear-guard action against the advancing Russian armies, and performed their function of punitive expeditions against the civilian population with a brutality which had earned Vierken the Iron Cross with oak leaves. He could account for thirty thousand executions and the destruction of a hundred villages with every human inhabitant slaughtered, by mass machine gunning, gassing in mobile vans and public hangings. He was weary and melancholic when he arrived in France after a home leave which hadn't helped his nerves at all. His family were strangers, his wife and children irritated him, the least noise caused an explosion of tension; he had even threatened them with violence. He had applied for and received a non-combatant posting; the plum assignment in France was his reward for duty unremittingly performed. Music was his favourite relaxation. In the first few weeks he went alone to the Paris Opera House or to the Conservatoire and listened to concerts; slowly he relaxed. He began to sleep again, his appetite returned. He brought a ruthless efficiency to his police work which reorganised the S.D. section and he began to enjoy life. Since his return from the East he hadn't touched a woman. He felt drained, impotent; his manhood was suspended, and the knowledge made him savage. His interrogations were ferocious even by Gestapo standards. He fled the cellars of the avenue Foch and soothed himself with Mozart, Brahms, and Beethoven, with a luxurious suite in the splendid French hotel, with superb food and wines. But it was when he met Régine de Bernard that his cure was complete. She was sitting next to him at a concert and for the first half hour he hadn't noticed her. A concert of Schumann's romantic *lieder* held him rapt, unaware of anything or anyone, until the interval. When he noticed her first the impression was unfavourable. He had always liked tall women with big breasts and Aryan colouring. Stupid, subservient women, like the wife whose docility had almost driven him mad when he came home. This was a girl, slight and dark and not even pretty. He didn't know what made him speak to her. Perhaps it was the nostalgic effect of Schumann's beautiful love songs. He had felt a surge of loneliness. He opened the programme and asked her which of the cycle she liked best.

When the concert ended he took her to supper. They talked, politely and casually about unimportant things. He found her intelligent, intense in a disturbing way. He noticed her small hands and the neatness of her body. Interest began to stir in him. He saw her home, very correct, holding his excitement in check. The next day he sent his car to the Sorbonne and took her out to lunch. By the end of that week she came back to the Crillon with him and they went to bed. She was a virgin; uncertain, eager, clumsy. Desire for her and satisfaction, followed a wild unleashing of the pent-up force of imprisoned sexuality. He found his manhood with Regine; she found with him a self she never knew existed.

Cruelty, force, possession; she wanted love in the terms which most appealed to him. Her intellectual cleverness made her submission all the more exciting. She kissed his hands and worshipped him for being what he was; there was no shame, no inhibition. They were twins in their desires, and out of their sexual sympathy a curious love grew up between them. He had never been loved like that by a woman before. He discovered tenderness, outside of making love; it pleased him to be nice to her, to play records together in his sitting room, to buy her beautiful clothes which she could only wear for him. They liked poetry; she taught him to appreciate the plays of Racine and Molière, she went to museums and art galleries with him. Sometimes they wandered along the banks of the Seine, he in civilian clothes, holding hands and looking at the timeless beauty of the city at night. But most of all they made love. The night she left St. Blaize they were together in his bedroom, exhausted and complete. She had gone to his hotel as soon as she reached Paris. She had taken a bicycle to the station and sat miserably waiting for a train, rubbing her cheek where Jean had slapped her, crying with anger and jealousy. She had disliked her sister-in-law from the moment she came to the house. Her own mother she hardly knew; the memory of a delicate woman, dying upstairs in a room full of flowers, was already dim. Her father's grief and withdrawal had been more of an agony to her than the loss of her mother. The arrival of Jean's wife caused a furious upheaval of adolescent jealousy and the fear of being superseded. Dislike had become hatred, but it was silent, secretive, feeding on imagined wrongs. Nothing Louise had done could expunge the crime of coming into the family and taking the place which Régine believed would have been hers.

She leaned on an elbow and stroked Vierken's chest, playing with the coarse dark hair. And she told him what had happened.

'He hit me,' she said. 'He slapped my face. The first time in my life he's ever touched me. Even when I was a child he never did that. Just because I told him the truth about her.'

'You're jealous, sweetheart,' Vierken told her. 'You shouldn't feel like that about a brother. You have me now. I want all your jealousy.'

'How can he defend her?' Régine said. 'I thought he had more pride. She hasn't slept with him for years! I know that man isn't her cousin, I know it!'

'How?' he asked her. 'How can you know?'

'Because of the way he looks at her,' she said. 'It's like the way you look at me. I know what that means . . . Jean had never met him before, he just arrived, no warning, nothing. There's something wrong about him; I felt it as soon as I saw him!'

'And if he is her lover,' Vierken said, 'what does it matter to you? If your brother were a man he'd know how to deal with them. Why make yourself unhappy? Look at you, your eyes are full of tears . . .'

'Swiss,' she went on obsessively. 'A Swiss lawyer—he didn't look like a lawyer to me!'

Vierken rolled over on his back, his arm around her. He

pulled the pillow straight under his head. 'What did he look like then?'

'I don't know,' she said. 'But they were lying, both of them. I'll never forgive Jean for taking her part against me. Never!'

'Hush,' Vierken said. 'Forget about it. I love your little breasts. Come here . . .' Early in the morning he sent her to the Sorbonne in his car. He bathed and shaved, whistling to himself. He had an appointment with the Military Governor at ten o'clock. His dislike for General Stulpnagel made these meetings difficult. He resented the arrogance of the military, their ill-concealed snobbery towards his troops and his officers. A middle-class German from a small town near Cologne, he hated the Prussians and the class they represented. He and his élite had taken the place of the Junkers in the German hierarchy. They meant to keep it. He went to the writing table in the sitting room and made a few notes. Then he put a call through to his office and was connected to his aide.

'This is a Obergruppenführer Vierken. I want a security check run on a Swiss national. Yes. Number one priority. The name is Roger Savage, living in Berne, works for a firm of Swiss lawyers, Felon et Brassier. Find out if he's visiting France. If he isn't, send a message to the S.D. at Chartres to arrest a man staying at the Château St. Blaize under that name. Good. I'll be in at midday.'

He rang off, crumpled the piece of paper on which he had written the details Régine had told him, and threw it away. Her family quarrels didn't interest him; an affair between her sister-in-law and a cousin was no business of his. But a stranger with a suspicious background story suddenly arriving near to General Brühl's headquarters was very much the concern of the S.S.

• • • • •

'I don't believe it,' Jean de Bernard said. 'It's impossible.'

'You don't want to believe it,' Savage said. 'Because if you do you'll have to get off the fence.' Louise said nothing; she looked at them both, Jean stunned and disbelieving, the American contemptuous and bitter. It was incredible. Now that Savage had told them she wanted to reject it. It was too horrible to be true. Not even the Nazis . . .

'You could be lying,' Jean de Bernard said slowly. 'You could be inventing the whole story, just to keep me quiet, to make me help you . . .'

'I could but I'm not. Use your head; nobody makes up something like this. We've known they were working on it. They made the break-through last year; Brühl found a formula. Using concentration camp prisoners for experiments.'

'Oh my God,' Louise broke in. There was something terrible in Savage's face now. Even Jean saw it and was silent.

'Auschwitz,' Savage said. 'He was in charge of the I. G. Farben complex there. He started this project and tested it on men, women and children. My wife was one of them. And my child. She was four years old.'

Jean de Bernard opened the revolver; slowly he took out the bullets one by one. He dropped the gun and the ammunition into his pocket.

'I volunteered,' Savage said. 'I'm going to get that bastard. I'm going to kill him.' He opened and closed his hands. 'But that's nothing to do with you. It's not your problem what happened to my family.'

'It is!' Louise broke in passionately. 'It's the most horrible thing I've ever heard—of course we'll help you!'

'The point is, that what they did to my wife and child they'll do to the population of every French town and village on the coast. As a nerve gas this one's a beauty. It causes panic, hallucinations, convulsions and death. Its effect on children is the worst. They go mad with fear, they tear themselves to pieces . . . This is their secret weapon, not the VIs or the rockets. It's Brühl's formula XV. With this they can wipe out the invasion force in a few days. Killing hundreds of thousands of French civilians is just incidental.

'And we know through intelligence that they're on the point of perfecting the gas. It's not the conventional kind that blows away on the wind. It's a chemical spray that releases its poisonous substance into the atmosphere on making contact with the ground. We don't know how long it lasts, but we do know it's easy to manufacture and can be stockpiled very quickly.'

'How did you discover this?' Jean de Bernard said. 'How did you find out?'

'Coincidence. My General called it the hand of God; he's the sort of man who'd see it that way. A number of Spanish Jews were arrested when France surrendered. They went to Auschwitz. The Spaniards are a touchy people; they didn't like their Jews being pushed around. So some of them who hadn't died in the camp were repatriated. One went to the American embassy in Madrid with a story. There were rumours of an experimental centre deep in the complex; there was a man called Brühl in charge of it. And prisoners were being taken there and never coming back. The word got out that it was gas. And then this woman saw a burial detail. From the description of the corpses, skin discoloration. self-inflicted injuries, and other symptoms, our people realised the guess was right. It was gas, but not the normal kind. Since then we've been tracking Brühl down from the time he disappeared from Auschwitz. We knew the bastard had gone into hiding somewhere to complete the formula. He didn't need any more guinea-pigs. And then we found him.'

'How?' Louise said. Savage lit a cigarette; he let the match burn for a moment.

'Your friend Major Minden,' he said. He spoke to Jean. 'He's no staff officer. That's part of the masquerade. He's one of Germany's leading biochemists. He was with Brühl at Dresden before the war. When we heard he was here we knew the General Brühl at Château Diane and the scientist were the same man, putting the final touches to his project. There are four airfields within a hundred kilometres of here,' Savage said. 'They'll be able to get the stuff to the bomber squadrons in a matter of hours.'

There was silence then; Savage went on smoking. Jean stared at the ground. 'What do you plan to do?'

'Get into the Château. Find Brühl. Without him they'll never finish it in time. And they can't use it in Germany without slaughtering their own people. So time is vital. Once we push through occupied Europe the gas will be no use to them. I've figured out a way to get inside the Château. But I'll need your help.'

'Jean.' Louise stood up. If he hesitated now . . . She was surprised at the way her heart raced.

Jean de Bernard raised his head and looked at the American. 'Tell me what you want us to do.'

Us. It was a committment she had never thought he would make. Even faced with the nightmare Savage had disclosed to them, Louise had feared he might try to find some compromise.

'I've got to get past the sentries, and whatever security they have inside the Château,' Savage said. 'If I start shooting I'll never get near Brühl. It's got to be done on the level. And that's where Minden comes into it. He has a special pass; I saw them examining a car when Louise and I went over there yesterday. Nobody gets through the outer sentry post without one. I've got to get Minden's pass. All I need is a few hours, time to get there, go inside and do the job. Then get out and get back here.'

'We'll help you,' Jean said. 'Tell us how.'

'Keep Minden occupied this evening,' Savage said. 'Get him to stay downstairs and give me time to search his room. That's all you have to do.'

'I can do that,' Louise said. 'We all have cold supper on a Sunday night; he often takes his up on a tray and works. I'll ask him to join us. He'll come.'

'Make it a family party,' Savage suggested. 'Bring your father down; we'll all be there. Then I can slip out. If I can get that pass I can put it back during the night and he'll never know it was gone.'

'And if you don't get back?' Jean asked him.

Savage shrugged. 'They'll be here in the morning. If that happens I hope to God you'll shoot Louise and then yourself.'

'Very well.' Jean moved to the door. 'We'll get Minden downstairs and keep him there. We'll give you any help we can. But there's one thing.'

For the first time he looked at Louise; then back to Savage. 'If you touch my wife again I'll kill you. I just want you to know that.' He held the door open for Louise. 'Go and find Minden,' he said. 'He'll come if you ask him.'

He went out of the room and without waiting for Savage to say anything, Louise followed him.

• • • • •

'This is very nice,' Heinz Minden said. He looked round him and smiled; at the Comte de Bernard and his father, sitting with a rug over his knees and a glass of champagne in one frail hand, at Louise whom he thought looked especially beautiful in a simple blue dress and a long row of pearls. Even at Savage who raised his glass to him. The party, so Jean de Bernard said, was really in Savage's honour. It was a pity Régine had been called back to Paris and couldn't be with them. Minden had been surprised and delighted when Louise came to his room. He could hardly believe it when there was a knock on the door and he found her standing there. For a moment he had lost his composure and stammered, wondering why she had come. The explanation was simple and he found her manner charming. The family were gathering and they wanted him to join them. She hadn't given him a chance to excuse himself. She had held the door open and stepped aside to let him follow her. On the way down the stairs he brushed against her and his manhood surged at the contact. In the elegant salon, drinking champagne with the family around him, the Major felt more at home than he had ever done before. He missed being part of a domestic unit. He had a sentimental character which liked to be in harmony with other people. He forgot his contempt for Jean de Bernard and his dislike of the Swiss cousin. He didn't regret the work which was neglected for that evening; he kept his eyes fixed on Louise and enjoyed himself. He moved towards her.

'Madame de Bernard,' he said. 'It is so kind of you to include me in your family gathering. I drink to you.' He raised his champagne glass and Louise did the same. The smile on her face felt as if it were stitched on; she did something she hadn't thought possible. She stroked the seat beside her and said, 'Sit down here, Major, next to me.' She felt Savage's eyes on her but they moved quickly away. He was talking to her father-in-law, who seemed animated and cheerful. He was so cool, so in control of himself. She thought of his wife and the child, of the hate and agony in his face as he spoke about them.

And yet in spite of it he had held her in his arms, hungry and demanding . . .

'My mother,' Minden was saying, 'is a remarkable woman. Do you know I'm one of eight children?'

'Really? No, I didn't know that.' She wrenched her thoughts away from Savage, pinning the false smile onto her lips and turned to give the Major her attention.

'She was so good to us all,' he was saying. 'My father died when we were all young. She went to work, Madame de Bernard. It may seem peculiar to you, but she paid for my education and my three brothers'. She was a hospital matron in Breslau where we lived. We didn't see much of her, of course; my grandmother lived with us, you see, and she took care of us. But I owe everything to my mother.' He finished his champagne.

'I'm sure you must be grateful,' Louise said. She took the glass out of his hand. 'Let me give you some more.' She poured from a bottle on the side table. Roger Savage came beside her.

'Your father-in-law would like some,' he said. His voice dropped to a whisper. 'Keep him busy. I'm going upstairs now.' With their backs to the room he gripped her wrist, just for a moment. Then she was on her way back to sit beside the Major.

'Tell me,' she said, turning fully round to him and blocking Savage out of sight, 'tell me about your father, Major Minden. Do you remember him at all?'

Savage went up the stone staircase at a run. Outside the Major's bedroom door he stopped and glanced round quickly. There was nobody in the corridor; the old servants were huddled in their bedroom on the floor above. He opened the door and went in. It was a similar room to his own, with a solid four-poster bed and ugly chintzes, large and comfortable, with a washstand and porcelain basin in one corner. Minden had scattered his possessions round; family photographs, a shelf of books, a travelling clock. There was a mahogany writing table by the window. Before going downstairs he had stacked his papers into a neat pile; the briefcase was lying beside them. Savage grabbed it, snapping at the lock. Nothing happened. He tried again, pushing furiously at the catch. It held fast. It was locked. He searched on the desk's surface for the keys, but found nothing. A glance at the papers proved them incomprehensible, covered in meaningless symbols. He pulled out the table drawers but there was nothing in them but yellowing headed writing paper and a box of paper clips. No keys. He opened every drawer, felt in the pockets of the Major's uniform jacket and trousers which were hanging, with a twin pair, in the wardrobe. He found a handkerchief and wisps of fluff, a cigarette packet and a box of matches. No key. At last he stopped looking and recognised that any further search was useless. There was no reason for Minden to hide the key. He felt he was among friends. He had left his papers on the table. The briefcase was probably self-locking. Obviously he must have the key on him. Savage looked round quickly, making sure he hadn't left anything disturbed. The room seemed exactly as it had when he came in. He closed the door and hurried back to the salon.

Minden was deep in conversation with Louise; Savage dropped into the seat beside the Comte. When Jean de Bernard looked across at him he shook his head.

A little before ten o'clock the old Comte signalled that he was tired. Immediately Jean de Bernard helped him up, Minden came over to say goodnight and Louise kissed him. 'I'll come up with you,' she said to Jean. Each took him by the arm and guided him out of the room.

'I have enjoyed myself,' the Major said. 'What a delightful family they are—ah, it makes me miss my own!'

'Perhaps you'll be with them soon,' Savage suggested.

'Perhaps,' he agreed. His right hand came up and fumbled with the scarf he wore tucked into his shirt neck. Between his fingers there gleamed a metal chain. As Savage watched he drew it out, playing with it. 'My wife gave me this,' he said. He showed Savage a locket held between finger and thumb. 'I keep her picture in it.' Beside the locket he dangled, hung a key. Savage lifted his eyes slowly from it to the Major's face.

'How nice,' he said, 'to have a memento like that.' Just then Louise and Jean came back into the room. He could see by the Comte's face that his message of failure had been passed on to Louise.

The Major sat on with them for another hour. To Louise the

time seemed to crawl; her head ached with tension, the effort to keep up a conversation drained her now that the reason for it was gone. She watched her husband with amazement.

He laughed, he encouraged Minden to talk more and more about himself, he exerted his charm until she felt the German would stay up all night. Yet he was being very clever. It had been a party and parties did not suddenly tail off into embarrassed gloom. Savage avoided her anxious signals; he too was playing his part, only she was failing, overcome by worry and the knowledge of his failure.

'You look a little tired,' her husband said kindly. She had no idea how white and strained she appeared. 'Go up to bed; we men may sit and talk for a while.' Gratefully she followed his suggestion. As she said good night to Savage, his lips formed a single word. Wait. She lay on her bed fully dressed until she heard him come to the door.

'You couldn't find it?'

'No. But I know where it is.' She watched him come towards her. He dropped on the end of the bed, close enough to reach out and touch her, but he didn't move. 'It's round his bloody neck,' he said. 'I saw it tonight. I've got to get it off him.'

'You can't,' Louise said. 'If he's wearing it round his neck it's impossible. Why can't you break the lock?'

'And have him find it had been forced? He may fancy you, but not enough to let something like that pass. You'd have the S.S. coming here.'

'What are you going to do?' she asked him.

'Try to get it when he's asleep. He may take it off at night.'

'It's too dangerous,' Louise said slowly. 'If he wakes up and catches you . . .'

'I'll kill him,' Savage said. He searched his pocket for a cigarette and swore because his case was empty.

'And that will certainly bring the S.S. to St. Blaize,' she said. 'You can't do that. There is another way.' She got up and brought the cigarettes from the silver box on her dressing table. Over the flame Savage looked up at her.

'How? How else?'

'I'll get it for you,' she said quietly. 'Go upstairs and wait for me.'

'There's only one way you could get it,' Savage said. 'I don't want you to do it.'

'I'm thinking of the children. Children like Paul and Sophie, dying in agony. Tearing themselves, going insane. I'll get that key for you. Just go and wait.' She got up and began to unfasten her dress. Savage reached out and held her arm. She pulled away from him. 'No,' she said. 'Don't touch me. Do as I've asked you. Go away. I'll bring it to you as soon as I can.'

. . . . .

'You're so beautiful,' Heinz Minden mumbled, 'so wonderful . . . Why did you cry out? I didn't mean to hurt you . . .'

'That thing round your neck,' Louise whispered. 'It cut into me. Please take it off.' In the darkness he fumbled with the chain and it slid away; she took it out of his hand, feeling the little key between her fingers. She let it drop on the floor beside the bed. Then she closed her eyes as his arms clamped round her. An hour later she stood in the doorway of Savage's room. She held the chain with the locket and the key.

'He's asleep,' she said. 'Take what you want. He's in my room.'

'Don't cry,' Savage said. He took the key from her. 'How long can you give me? How long can you keep him there?'

'As long as I like,' she said. She put a hand to her face for a moment and then brushed back her hair. Savage saw her hand trembling. 'He said he loved me,' she said suddenly. 'I feel as if I'll never be clean again. For God's sake go—I'll have to get back in case he wakes.'

'Wait here,' Savage said. 'I'll bring the key back when I've opened the case. Then go back to him.'

Five minutes later he had come back. She took the key from him.

'It's one-thirty now,' Savage said. 'Give me till four.'

'Good luck,' Louise said. 'I'll pray for you.' She turned to go back to her own room.

Minden stirred in the bed, reaching towards her.

'Where were you—darling . . .'

'I'm here,' she whispered. 'I'm with you. You were sleeping. It's early still; we have all night to be together.'

• • • •

General Friedrich Brühl had finished dinner. He was not a glutton, but he appreciated the quality of food. He had developed a taste for wine and rare liqueurs, which was far removed from the days when he had lived on sauerkraut and beer as a young man. It amused him to imagine the pride of his parents, good solid artisans from Munich, if they could see their son's elevation in the world. He sat at the head of the long sixteenth-century refectory table, and glanced at his officers; there were six of them, intimates chosen as his personal staff. The light from candles in solid gold Renaissance candelabra flattered their faces and reflected on the General's thick-lensed glasses. Three of them were scientists, like himself, the others were his aide, a liaison officer with the military commander of Paris, and his nephew, whom he had saved from service on the Russian front. He raised his glass and tasted a mellow Château Yquem. The cellars had been stocked with magnificent wines; Brühl had ordered their careful removal to the stable block, where it was cool and the precious vintages wouldn't be disturbed again. He caught his nephew's eye and smiled. His sister and he were very close; she wrote regularly and he replied with affectionate enquiries about the family, details of the weather and the continued progress of her son, who was proving just the sort of young man Brühl approved of most. Reliable, obedient, sober-minded. In his uncle's service he would have a fine career. Brühl had begun his working life at fourteen as assistant in a chemist's shop, sweeping out, running errands, cleaning the counters and bottles for a few marks a week. In the evenings he studied; he had never been aggressive or athletic, his eyesight was poor and his inclination was solitary. He was a bookish boy, a disappointment to his father, who was a boisterous, lusty man, and one of the earliest recruits to the National Socialist Party. He grew up in the violence and mob politics of Munich in the 20's, saw his father come home with the brown uniform of the Nazi Sturmabteilung stained with the blood of Communists and Jews who had been beaten up.

He listened to the exposition of the new philospohy and recognised the superiority of the tough fanatical men who were its prototypes of the new Germans. He couldn't be one of them; nature and undernourishment had prevented that, but he hero-worshipped and admired. It was a party member, a wealthy furniture manufacturer, who heard of his interest in chemistry and science, and paid for his education. Brühl found his *métier* in the University. He excelled at his studies, and he gave his services to the Party who had befriended him, by pointing out Communist elements among the students. He was made treasurer of the Nazi student organisation and he was admired for his administrative gifts. His nickname was the Owl; he emerged with an honours degree in physics and chemistry and went on to achieve a doctorate. When Hitler became Reichschancellor, he was given the post of professor, after its former occupant, an elderly Jew, was bullied into resignation. Friedrich Brühl, the butcher's son, became one of the new élite; a fanatical party organiser, an intellectual whose achievements embellished the Nazi image among a people who worshipped academic titles. He also met, and formed a friendship with another mild myopic, Heinrich Himmler. The result of that friendship was to bring him into brief contact with the Führer himself, an occasion which to Brühl could only be compared with the Beatific Vision to a Christian Saint. He was overwhelmed, enslaved; rational political belief became obsessional faith. There was nothing Brühl couldn't equate with service to his leader and his country. At the outbreak of war he was immediately placed in charge of all chemical research and given full facilities at the I. G. Farben chemical plant at Dresden.

One of his minor contributions was the development of ZkI, which came into use in the gas chambers of Auschwitz; it was quicker and left the corpses less noisome to handle than Monoxide. Exposure to Brühl's gas killed within four minutes.

But the perfection of the ultimate in chemical warfare lay before him; after two years of intensive study and research and highly secret experiments, also undertaken within the concentration camps, Brühl was able to offer to his old friend Himmler a means of repulsing the Allied invasion, of rolling back the advancing Russians, of reducing any country to submission. Victory, Brühl announced to Hitler's personal representative, could be within German grasp inside a year. Hysteria, convulsions, panic and death. Armies, entire populations would be destroyed. Everything he needed was put at his disposal. Brühl himself rejected the facilities at I. G. Farben; he didn't need large laboratories for his work, but he did need absolute secrecy and immunity from Allied bombing. It was decided to establish his research centre in France, in a quiet rural district near enough to Paris to be easily accessible to the defensive bomber squadrons, and in an area where there was no resistance and negligible risk of local curiosity. Brühl had chosen the Château Diane as his headquarters, picked a small, highly qualified staff, and assumed the rank of General in the Wehrmacht. His staff were also given military rank, and the Château was officially designated an Army Headquarters for the areas around Dreux, Houdan and St. Blaize en Yvelines. The security was so efficient that the district headquarters at Chartres had no idea of Brühl's real function or of the existence of his research laboratory in the Château cellars. He had enjoyed every moment of the time spent at the Château Diane; he indulged in romantic daydreams of a vanished age, and lusted over the memorials of a woman who had died four hundred years before. He felt like a king, sleeping in the bed where a Valois had coupled with his mistress, sitting at the same table, taking a mid-morning walk through the gardens where they had wandered together. In the laboratory the perfection of his work was near. He gave the signal and the company of men rose to leave the dining room.

On this night he did not invite them to take coffee with him. He didn't believe in spoiling his subordinates. In the splendid marble hall he said good night, and went to the red salon to have his special brandy and coffee alone. The mess waiters were S.S. men, in army uniform. Even the chef, specially imported from Germany, was a member of the fanatical Nazi Police. Logs were alight in the fireplace; his coffee and a superb Champagne Cognac waited for him. Brühl relaxed into an armchair, sipped his cognac, and gazed at the portrait of Diane de Poitiers.

Red hair in delicate ringlets, a pale Aryan face and a body like white silk, erotically exposed against a dark background. Brühl closed his eyes for a moment and thought about her. He had never wanted a living woman and his sexual impulses were feeble even in youth. Now he copulated in imagination.

By the time he had finished his brandy, he was thinking about his research. Only one factor remained unresolved. The gas was affected by rainfall. On contact with soil, or any greenery, it became noxious and pervasive. Water, or waterlogged conditions, prevented it from rising. As it had a limited effectiveness on exposure to the atmosphere, this was a serious problem. Bad weather could nullify a gas offensive for some hours; after which the poisonous content would be dissipated. Brühl was a perfectionist. He had to present a weapon without weakness. Its strategic importance depended upon its swift annihilation of the enemy. It could not be subject to the vagaries of weather. The strategy had already been worked out; it was the Führers intention to offer token resistance to the Allied invasion force, allowing a major advance along the entire front. It was calculated that a quarter of a million men would be in France within a week. When the target was large enough, Luftwaffe squadrons would saturate the area with gas bombs, working from the immediate coastal front inland to a depth of two hundred miles. The result should end the invasion attempt and a massive gas raid on selected cities should cause England to surrender. But the vital elements were surprise and timing. If the enemy were not completely destroyed at a safe distance from the German border, the gas could not be used. Brühl frowned; he had a particularly able assistant in Heinz Minden, who had put forward several solutions to the problem of the gas reacting to water, but unfortunately none of them were viable. Without boasting, Brühl recognised that no member of his team possessed the scientific genius which distinguished his own work. He alone would be able to find the answer. He yawned a little, and squinted up at the massive ormolu and ebony clock which stood on a bracket beside the fireplace. It showed eleven-thirty. He rang a bell and the waiter appeared. The tray was removed and the General went up the marble staircase to the state bedroom on the first floor.

There his batman undressed him, placed a glass of hot milk and an apple beside the bed, saluted and went out. By ten minutes past midnight Brühl was asleep.

• • • • •

Savage shut himself up in Minden's room. The briefcase was open and he had taken out the papers, carefully keeping them in sequence and was examining them. All Minden's identification papers were there; the special pass into the Château Diane was a small yellow card, with his photograph on the inside. It was quite different to any form of identification used in any of the German armed forces. His controller at OSS had suspected that a special pass would be issued to the members of Brühl's staff, but there was no way of obtaining a specimen. Savage had to get the genuine article and substitute his own photograph. He carried that photograph, full face and showing the upper portion of a Wehrmacht major's uniform, concealed in the lining of his inner breast pocket. It lay on the table beside him. The size was correct, it would fit over the Major's picture. It was firmly pasted in and there wasn't time to remove it without the risk of damage. But it was the papers themselves that occupied Savage. He had glanced at them quickly; most consisted of scientific data which he didn't understand, but there was a copy of a recent memo, obviously circulated among the staff and signed by Brühl. 'Gentlemen, I have received instructions from the highest authority to produce a specimen of the formula XV for testing before the end of May. I cannot comply with this command until we have overcome the problem of the formula's reaction to rainfall. I urge everyone to apply themselves with increased diligence to this most urgent matter. I have assured the highest authority that we will succeed in our efforts. There will be a meeting in the conference room at four o'clock this afternoon. "Brühl".' Savage looked at the date. It was two days old. The formula's reaction to rainfall. It could mean anything in scientific terms. Practically, it meant that whatever the reaction was, it prevented the gas being tested for final approval. So unless they had found their answer in the last two days, he was in time. There was a green leather notebook; inside it was a meaningless jumble of chemical symbols, with Minden's observations jotted down. But the last two pages were straight notes. Again, much of the language was too technical for Savage to understand in detail, but the sense was clear enough.

Water had a nullifying effect on the nerve gas. The final comment, scribbled and underlined, said simply, *'We must find a solution'*. He shut the book and began replacing everything in its original place in the briefcase. With a pinpoint of adhesive at each corner, he affixed his photograph on top of Minden's. Then he went to the wardrobe and began to dress in the Major's uniform. It was tight and the sleeves were an inch too short, but the greatcoat covered this, and the peaked cap fitted. He paused for a moment, catching sight of his reflection in the mirror. Then he went out and down the stairs. The major's car was in the garage, adjacent to the stables at the one side, and out of earshot of the Château. The batman Fritz slept in the chauffeur's flat above.

Savage slipped behind the wheel and started the engine. He just hoped the servant didn't wake and look out of the window. Minutes later he was through the rear gate of the Château and on the road to Anet and the Château Diane.

5

THE two sentries at the main gate of the Château had come on duty at midnight. There was a four-hour rota system throughout the day and night. It was two-thirty and both men were sleepy and unalert. Two cars had turned into the Château since they took up their posts; both contained officers returning from trips to Dreux, where there was a discreet little brothel run by a respectable widow. The lights from another car dazzled them for a moment as it swung into the gateway and stopped. The left-hand sentry approached and as he did so, the window on the driver's side slid down and a hand came out, holding the distinctive yellow card which the sentry recognised immediately. As a matter of form he shone his torch, saw the photograph, glanced in the interior of the car and saw a German officer in the semi-darkness.

Savage's hands were stuck to the wheel with sweat. 'Hurry! Open the gates!' The angry command brought the sentry to instant attention; he saluted, gave back the pass, and ran to do as he was told. Savage let in the clutch; he forced himself to drive slowly. The main courtyard was deserted, but the left-hand side was in deep shadow, overhung by the building. The moon, which had been full the night he arrived at St. Blaize, was now on the wane but the light was bright enough to show him everything. He swung the car round and left it in the patch of darkness, its bonnet pointed to the gate. As he switched off the ignition, he wondered briefly whether he would ever get the chance to drive it out, and then dismissed the thought. There was no time for speculation or for premonitions. He had got in, and that was the first obstacle overcome. The second, and equally dangerous, was the entrance to the Château itself.

Walking across the courtyard, he felt naked and conspicuous in the moonlight. The entrance was level with the courtyard. As a senior staff officer perhaps he should have a key. Cautiously he tried the ring handle. It didn't move. There was nothing he could do but press the modern bell-push on the wooden lintel. It seemed a long time waiting there in full view. When the door swung open it made no noise and Savage jumped as the yellow shaft of light fell full upon him. Two soldiers stood in the entrance, both wore revolvers and one had unbuttoned his holster, his right hand poised over the gun butt. There was no question of palming the yellow pass in front of them. And if that pass was examined the name and the face wouldn't match. Instinct fired in him like a rocket. He stepped across into the hallway and shouted, 'You idiots! Where the devil have you been—why weren't you by the door?' The guards stiffened immediately. The man who had been about to draw his revolver snapped to attention. Savage swung round on them, scowling. 'Names! You'll be on report for this!'

'Vogel, S.S. korporal, Herr Major!'

'Schumann, S.S. Mann, Herr Major!' Neither was looking at him, their heads were rigid, their eyes fixed in front. Savage paused for effect. His heart was pounding.

'You'll hear about this in the morning!' He snarled the threat at them. Both flung up a stiff arm in salute, petrified by discipline. The reaction to an officer had saved him; fear and habit threw them into confusion when he reprimanded them. They were used to being shouted at, abused, even struck, by their officers. Numbed by his accusation of negligence, they never thought of checking on him. The German military system might have its faults but disrespect for superiors wasn't among them. He'd have been a dead man by now if it had been. He was in a huge entrance hall, a lofty ceiling with marble walls. Tapestries and paintings glimmered in the lowered electric light; a massive console table of carved and gilded wood was directly in front of him, with a red tortoise-shell clock that showed the time as 2.40 a.m. The massive marble staircase rose on his left, there was a pair of double doors to the right. For a moment he stood, hesitating; the ground plan he had studied in Jean de Bernard's reference book refused to focus in his mind. He heard the sound of one of the guards on duty moving behind him. He took off his cap, pinned it beneath his arm and turned to the door on the right, opened it and went inside. The room was in darkness; he felt for a light-switch, found it, and an overhead chandelier bathed everything in light. It was a spacious room, obviously in use as a mess; besides some fine period furniture, there were leather chairs and sofas, newspapers and magazines arranged on tables, and flowers by the windows. Savage stayed still, looking round. He pulled at Minden's collar; the jacket was too small for him and it was tight.

'Who the devil are you!' He spun round. A figure had risen from behind one of the sofas; the jacket hung open, the face was red and the eyes peered suspiciously. The man wore Colonel's badges. He must have been in one of the chairs. Savage came to attention and saluted.

'I'm sorry, sir! Excuse me for disturbing you.' You fool. You bloody fool. You won't bluff your way past this one . . . He turned back to the door. The German was a big man, thick necked and bald; Savage noticed that he swayed a little. Drunk and sleeping it off.

'Stay where you are!' Savage waited, watching the officer come nearer. He had picked up his holster belt and was taking out the revolver. There was nothing Savage could do; if he tried to leave the room the Colonel would raise the alarm, or even fire. He was not quite sober, and suspicious as an angry bull. He came close to Savage, glaring, the revolver held loosely in his right hand.

'What are you doing here? I've never seen you before! Who the hell are you?'

'Major Friedman, sir.' Savage gave the first name he could think of; his football coach at college had been a man called Friedman. Freddy for short. 'Friedman,' he repeated. 'I've just arrived from Paris.'

'At this hour? What the hell do you mean by coming here in the middle of the night? Friedman—I want to see your papers.' The muzzle of the gun came up and pointed at Savage. Colonel Von Gehlen was sober enough now.

'Certainly, sir.' There was no way out. He had Minden's pass in his pocket and the moment the Colonel saw the name he was discovered. Savage took the pass out, stepped up to the Colonel and gave it to him. There wasn't a hope of grabbing the gun, because it would go off in the struggle. He couldn't afford shouts or noise. The Colonel snatched the pass and looked down at it; not long enough for Savage to move. He breathed in sharply.

'Put your hands up,' he said, 'and turn round. You're under arrest.' Savage raised his hands and turned his back. Once they reached the door he was finished.

'Slowly,' the Colonel warned. 'Go to the door. One move from you and you'll get it in the back!'

'All right,' Savage said. 'I surrender. I won't try anything.' They reached the door. Now. He had one chance, and only one. When that door opened they were in sight of the guards on duty at the entrance. If the Colonel knew what he was doing he would stay just behind out of reach. But his brain wasn't quite clear; he took two steps forward because they had come to a stop by the door. Savage heard him breathing heavily and made a guess. He aimed a violent kick behind him, and caught the Colonel on the shin with his heel. Savage had registered that he wasn't wearing boots. He gave a cry of pain and at the same moment Savage swung round, his right arm curved back from the elbow, his hand stretched out, the fingers rigid. The blow was so fast the German didn't even see it. It caught him across the cheekbone. The revolver fell out of his hand, and Savage kicked it across the carpet. He struck again, and this time the blow was lethal. It hit the Colonel across the side of the neck. He gave a choking grunt and his knees sagged; Savage caught him before he fell. There was an open wound across his face and blood was running down it. His eyes were open but the eyeballs showed white. Savage dragged him across the room, looking for a chair in a corner. He propped him in it; he stood over him for a moment, making sure there was no heart-beat, no breath. But the Colonel was dead. Savage turned his head to one side, hiding the ugly slash across his face. He picked up Minden's pass and found the revolver. He threw it into the chair with the Colonel. Then he remembered that cry when he cracked the German's shin. They had been close enough to the door for some sound to penetrate through to the guards outside. But if they'd heard anything they would have come by now. He rubbed the heel of his right hand. In training they had hardened it by constant hammering against wood. He glanced once more at the dead man. At a casual look he seemed to be asleep. Savage crossed the room, opened the door and switched out the lights. The two soldiers were seated by the door; they saw him and immediately jumped up, standing to attention.

He ignored them and turned to the right. The stairway was a magnificent sweep of marble, with a wide balustrade, curving up from the main hall to the upper floors. Savage had plotted the route so carefully before, that the lapse of memory when he first came into the hall seemed extraordinary. But the initial nervous tension had disappeared. Killing the Colonel had triggered off the reflexes of his training. He was cool and confident, and inside him burned the beacon of hate. He mounted the steps and began to climb. It seemed a long way up. Electric sconces on the walls gave a subdued light. He had reached the first floor; a long corridor stretched in front of him, with more sconces lighting the way on low-watt electric bulbs. Three more doors; there was a thread of light visible under one of them. He crept past it. Diane de Poiters' bedroom. It was at the very end, exactly as it had been marked on the plan, identifiable by its massive oak doors, gilded and carved, with the initial D and the crescent moon in a cartouche above it. So far, he said inside himself, so far and you have got away with it. He's on the other side of those doors. The face in the blown-up photograph, the murderer of your wife and your child. The handle turned without a sound. He stepped inside, keeping the door ajar, trying to see into the room by the light in the corridor outside. It took some seconds before his eyes became accustomed and could distinguish shapes. The bed towered like a tent directly in line with the doorway. He carried a pencil torch in the greatcoat pocket; the tiny beam picked out a gilt chair, a narrow table with ornaments and flowers on it. And then it crept towards the bed, moving over the draperies; he closed the door behind him and began to follow the small bright light. By the side of the bed he stopped and very slowly moved the torch upward. Brühl's head lay on the pillow, turned a little to one side. No spectacles, more hair than in the photograph where he had worn a cap; a younger man than Savage had imagined him. He slept with the innocence of a boy. The torch moved again, finding a table by the bed. It lit up a glass with an inch of milk at the bottom and a plate with an apple core. And a bedside light. Savage switched it on and sprang. He caught the hair in his left hand, jerking up the head, exposing the throat. As Brühl woke, he died. Savage's right hand smashed down and shattered his windpipe. There was a horrible gurgling sound, and his body threshed about under the bedclothes. Then it collapsed, quivered for a moment and didn't move again. Savage looked down at him. It was so quick, so painless. Patricia had died in agony, torn by convulsions, wrenched out of life in the midst of unthinkable terrors as the gas attacked her nervous system. He couldn't imagine his child . . . He stood without moving for some moments. He had lived for this act of retribution, dreamed of it, longed for it, lain without sleep fighting the pain of his grief with the antidote of hatred and revenge. Now it was done. His personal debt was paid. Hundreds of helpless victims had been sacrificed, the wives and children of other men, husbands, fathers, old and young, the human guinea-pigs selected to perfect the final infamy against the human race. He looked once more at the lolling head on the pillow; blood was trickling steadily out of the corner of the mouth, staining the white pillow. He had paid his personal debt. Now he was going to settle the others. Quietly he began to search the room.

There was a desk, a modern roll-top in a corner by one of the big windows. It was unlocked; inside were files and papers neatly clipped together, several small leather note-books, and a letter written to Brühl's sister which had been put aside for posting. In the inside drawer he found what he was looking for. The General's personal oddments, a gold lighter, a matching cigar case and a pencil and a bunch of keys. He took the keys. It was a chance. It wasn't part of his mission but he was going to do what even his superiors had thought impossible.

He was going to find the laboratory. Outside in the corridor he stopped, freezing against the wall. He could hear voices coming up the stairs, they were low, and someone laughed. Some of the staff coming up to their rooms . . . He stepped back into Brühl's room and waited by the door, listening. Footsteps didn't reach him, they ceased further up, doors opened and closed, somebody called out goodnight.

When he came out again the corridor was empty. He put his cap on, pulling it low over his face, brought Minden's revolver out of its holster and slipped it in his pocket. The cellars. The laboratory must be below ground, hidden and well protected. On the ground plan they were reached from the main hall, through the kitchens. It was all too easy to walk down the stairs and out past the guards who had let him in. But to walk through the main hall, and go towards the top security area in the building in the middle of the night—he wouldn't get through without being stopped and he knew it. They had refused to give him explosives; the risk of setting off the gas and killing the French inhabitants for miles around wouldn't be countenanced by his superiors, although the English Colonel had tried to argue in favour of a single sabotage operation in which the Château was destroyed. For this reason they hadn't used bombers. The gas couldn't be unleashed. Killing Brühl, the genius of chemical destruction, was the most that they had hoped for. Savage had nothing but a revolver and his manual skill at silent killing. It couldn't be so simple; down through the main hall, on to the kitchens and down again to the cellars. The Germans would never have left such a primitive arrangement to house their hopes of victory over the world. There must be another, more sophisticated way for Brühl to reach his work. And then he saw the other door. Beside Brühl's bedroom. It was a narrow door, much narrower than the others, newly constructed to the same basic design so that it blended in.

He went and tried the handle. It was locked. The third of Brühl's keys opened it. Savage found himself standing in a three-man lift. There were two buttons, one marked 'ground floor', the second, 'XV centre'. That meant there were two entrances to the cellar by the lift shaft, one on the main floor for the staff and the one above, which allowed Brühl direct access from his room. Savage closed the door, shut the steel grid which came up to waist level, and pressed the button marked 'XV centre'. The decent was soundless; for a moment he had feared the hydraulic whine which must surely have attracted attention at that hour. But there was nothing. German efficiency had anticipated that.

Softly the lift came to a stop. There was a red light on the wall by the buttons and it glowed. Savage was on the level with the laboratories. He pushed back the grill, opened the door and stepped out. He found himself in a short corridor, constructed of concrete blocks, with soundproofed ceiling and fluorescent lighting. There was no other exit that he could see. The entrance to the laboratory was at the end of the passage. Savage left the lift door ajar; so long as the little red eye was alight, the lift couldn't be called upstairs, leaving him trapped.

The door to the cellar was steel. He examined the lock and couldn't see any signs of an alarm system being attached to it. If anything existed like an electric beam, he had already broken it. He began to try the keys on Brühl's chain, and with the second try he was successful. The massive door was on a weight mechanism; it swung open and then closed behind him. He felt for a light switch, found something and clicked it down. Instantly there was a flood of brilliant light. Six enormous strip lights bared what had been the château cellars and was now a single room some sixty feet in length. Savage stood for a moment, looking round him. A part of his brain registered that no alarm had sounded. There were long tables with scientific instruments, drawing-boards, some of the paraphernalia of all laboratories. Along the left-hand wall hung a row of twenty gas-masks, suspended like gargoyles from hooks, under each of them a white overall. He stepped into the room. There were two big steel cabinets down the centre, with rows of drawers. He went to one and pulled; it opened, disclosing a thick hessian file. The other drawers were the same. He wandered round the tables and the drawing-boards. He understood nothing which was written on them. Formula XV was in that room; the gas-masks proved it. But where? In what guise? He walked from one end to the other and could see nothing. Back to the filing cabinets again. Records; millions of words, the history of their researches, carefully documented. There must be a safe, a vault below the present level where what they were working on was kept . . . It was in the middle of the wall of steel cabinets. A large square box standing at chest height. There was nothing marked on it to indicate what it contained, only a single word in German, printed on a pasteboard slip inside a slot on the front. *Caution.* The lock was inset into the top, covered by a metal flap. Savage went to where the gas-masks hung, stuffed Minden's hat into his pocket and put one on. For a moment he couldn't see clearly; he wiped the goggles with a handkerchief. There was an odd-looking key on Brühl's chain, a thick key with a stubby snout and two irregular-shaped teeth. It fitted the lock.

And there, sitting squat on a shelf inside the steel box, were two glass containers. The contents looked like water. Completely colourless; he tipped one slightly and the formula moved sluggishly, like oil. A pure concentrate, enough to stock hundreds of bombs, to throw hundreds of thousands of people into the violent paroxysms that preceded death. If he spilt the stuff on the floor it would kill the German garrison at the Château. And it would seep out and destroy the people in the area, spreading God knew how far, carried like the plague. He couldn't do it. Savage put the container down. He didn't think of his own life; frustration brought a sweat of agony out on his body; it ran down his face inside the mask, making his eyes sting. He had the formula there, a hand's reach away. All he had to do was destroy it. But how? How? He almost shouted the word, and it came muffled through the filtered mouthpiece. There was an answer and he couldn't find it—there was something, something he knew . . . And then he saw them, up above his head. A dozen eyes in the ceiling, round and black, at five-foot intervals in two rows. Water. Water neutralised the gas. That was what Brühl's memo said, what Minden's notes had repeated. The formula was still imperfect because rainfall would render the gas harmless. 'We must find a solution.' Minden had underlined those words. And there, right above him, was a sprinkler system, installed in case of fire. He pulled off the mask, slipped the rubber headstrap over his wrist, and began to run to the near end of the room. There was the little glass box, with the lever behind it and the instruction in Schrift printed above in red. *In case of fire break glass and depress lever!* He paused for a few seconds, deciding how best it could be done. Water would destroy the formula. And the records. Two years of work and research on how to murder millions of people in the extremity of agony. All neatly documented in those filing cabinets. He went to the first of them and opened every drawer to its length. He did the same with the second. Then he took out both containers of the formula and stood them on top of the steel safe. He pulled on the gas-mask and went to the emergency lever; lifting the glass flap, and taking the handle, he pulled. Immediately there was a drenching downpour from the system overhead. Water cascaded from the sprinklers. Savage drew Minden's revolver, cocked it and took aim. He fired twice; the glass jars shattered, their deadly contents spurted outwards, lost in the flood pouring from the ceiling. Savage turned and ran to the exit. He locked the steel door and pounded down the passage to the lift. Inside, he slammed the gate shut and punched the button marked 'ground floor'. He tore off the gas-mask, smoothed Minden's cap and pulled it on; he suddenly noticed that his hand was shaking. The lift stopped in its noiseless way. Carefully he opened the outer door; the dimly lit main hall was silent. Nobody had heard the two shots, buried down beneath the floor. If the corridor had been soundproofed, so was the laboratory itself.

He stepped out of the lift and pushed the door closed behind him. If nobody heard anything or went near Brühl till the morning, that laboratory would be under ten feet of water. Everything in it, every record, every drawing, would be destroyed. And the murderous fluid floating in globules on the surface of the water could harm no one. Not even its creators, when they discovered what had happened. The two guards were at the entrance; they were sitting down, one had his head sunk forward, lightly dozing. Savage didn't hesitate. He walked towards them. 'You!' He barked the word. 'Sleeping? Stand to attention!'

They leaped to their feet, rigid; the man who had drifted off for a few minutes gasped out loud with fear. 'Open the door,' Savage snapped. 'Immediately!'

He stepped out into the night and into the courtyard. For a moment he couldn't see the car; it was hidden in a patch of shadow. He slipped his hand into the greatcoat pocket and came out with Brühl's keys. One quick movement flung them into the darkness. He got into the car; there was a horrific moment when the ignition wouldn't fire. He pressed the starter and there was nothing but a sleepy rattle. Then suddenly it burst into a steady throb as the engine turned; the chassis trembled, and he let in the clutch. He stopped at the gate; two guards came up to him, their torches shining. He fumbled for Minden's card, swearing furiously, thrust it through the window and, on an impulse, punched the horn. The gates were opened quickly, the guards were at the salute as he swept past them. Not until he had turned away from the Château and was on the road to St. Blaize, did he realise he had forgotten to switch on his lights. He also realised something else: the shoulders of Minden's greatcoat were soaking wet. He swore, more from a sense of petty anticlimax than from anxiety. A wet coat was no problem. Nothing was any problem now. He had done the impossible and come out of it alive. So far. He found a cigarette and lit it. Perhaps now he could think about Patricia. Never about his child. That was impossible, the mind couldn't endure it. But his wife, whom he had failed in all that really mattered. Perhaps now he could think about her, because Brühl was dead, and what had killed her was destroyed. He looked at his watch; it was three-thirty. He had told Louise de Bernard to keep Minden occupied until four o'clock. His inclination was to drive fast, but he restrained it. Steady now. No accidents, no stopping, no puncture. The idea almost made him laugh. It was three-forty-five when he glided into the garage under Minden's batman's sleeping quarters, his engine cut off, the car coasting home on its own impetus. The Château was completely dark; he moved very quietly, using the little torch to find his way upstairs. Outside Louise's door he paused; there was a line of light showing under it and he could hear soft voices. He went on upstairs to Minden's room, stripped off the uniform, pushing the wet greatcoat to the back of the cupboard, changing Minden's second coat to its place on the rack. The briefcase was there; he removed his photograph from the yellow pass, put it back in the briefcase and closed it, snapping the lock shut. A look round the room showed everything in place;

there was no sign that anyone had been there or that anything had been moved. Savage went out, closing the door without making a sound and slipped into his own room. Four-ten. He lay on the bed, waiting; his body felt stiff, his neck ached with the onset of tension. He tried for a moment to think about his wife, but a strange inhibition closed her image out of his mind. Out of the weariness, the mingled sense of exultation and the inevitable let-down after so much pressure on the nervous system, Savage found that he was thinking of Louise de Bernard as if she were the only woman he had ever known in his life.

. . . . .

'I'm very happy,' Minden said. 'I hope you are happy too.' He stood by the bed looking down at her.

'Yes,' Louise said, 'of course. But I really must sleep now.'

'I've tired you.' Minden bent over her, one hand stroked her shoulder. 'I'm sorry. You're the most beautiful woman in the world. I adore you.'

Louise raised her arm; her watch showed four-fifteen. 'Here, your chain. You'd better put it on.'

'It wouldn't do to lose it,' he smiled, fastening the chain with the locket and the key round his neck. 'Let me kiss you once more. Then I'll go.'

'No,' Louise said. 'Please—I'm so exhausted.'

'Good night then,' he whispered, taking her hand in both of his and pressing it to his mouth. He murmured something in German which she didn't understand. When the door closed, Louise lay back and for a moment her eyes closed, and real exhaustion overcame her. The first time he had made love like a pig; the second time, after he woke from sleep, he had decided to arouse her; she didn't know which had been the worst. He had become very emotional; the mixture of sexuality and sentimentality nauseated her. She ran her hands over her body and shuddered. The back of her hand was still moist from his kiss. When she went to his room she had expected some query. He had been in bed reading, when she opened his door and stood just inside it. 'I'm lonely,' she had said. 'I thought you might be too.' He had thrown the bed-clothes off and come to her; immediately excited, he had wanted to take her there, and it was with some difficulty that she persuaded him to follow her to her room. He hadn't asked a question. Four-fifteen. Four-twenty. She got up and put her nightdress on and dressing-gown. She had begun to tremble; the sense of degradation passed into panic as she thought of Savage. Had he come back—if she went to his room and it was empty, would that mean he had been caught, and had he swallowed the lethal pill in time . . . ? Or was he at that moment in the hands of the guards, carrying Minden's pass and wearing Minden's uniform? She hadn't faced the reality before; her decision to seduce the Major was an emotional one, like giving Savage shelter, taken without a proper calculation of the risks involved. If Savage failed, then they were all doomed, she and Jean and the helpless old Comte, even the children . . . Her husband was right. To risk her own life was one thing, but to put Paul and Sophie at risk . . .

When the door opened and she saw Savage she gave a cry.

He didn't say anything; he came and put his arms round her. He could feel her trembling. 'It's all right,' he whispered. 'Everything worked. All thanks to you.'

'I was so terrified,' she said at last. 'I stood here and suddenly realised what would have happened to us all if you'd been caught. To the children too. I must have been mad.' She shook her head. 'Quite mad to do it.'

'Maybe.' Savage lit a cigarette and gave it to her. 'But you've just helped to win the war. Calm down now and listen to me. My job was to kill Brühl, to stop him getting the gas to the production stage. Without him, it would take months. And they haven't got months. The invasion is only weeks away. I did my job and I did more. I wrecked the laboratory and destroyed the stocks. Okay, you've slept with a German and you risked the lives of your whole family. But it was the right decision. Even if it went wrong, it would still have been right. Look at me.' He bent down and kissed her mouth; her lips were cold and they didn't open.

'Quit worrying,' he said.

'You killed him,' she said. 'It doesn't worry you . . .'

'No,' Savage said, 'it doesn't. You forget. He murdered my wife and child.'

'I'm sorry,' Louise said. 'I didn't mean to say that. I'm just not used to people being killed.'

'Let's hope you never have to be,' he said.

'Would you tell me about her?' He didn't answer at once. He drew hard on the cigarette and blew the smoke out with violence.

'I've been trying to think about her tonight,' he said. 'And I can't. I've had a picture of her in my mind, ever since I knew what had happened. We had a boat, a nice thirty-footer, I used to take her sailing round Cape Cod. She loved the sea; it was the only thing I did she really enjoyed. I remember her sitting up in the bows, with her hair blowing all over the place, looking out to sea. She used to tan very dark. She was Belgian. Her name was Patricia.'

Louise took the cigarette stub out of his fingers. 'What happened? Why wasn't she in the States?'

'Because she left me,' he said. 'We'd been married four years, she was never happy in California; I tried moving to New York to practise, but that was worse. I met her in Switzerland. I married her when she was just a kid, straight out of convent school. She didn't know what had hit her. But she tried; goddam it, we both tried. She was sweet and gentle, and full of guts. Your kind of guts, all heart and no head.

'But I wasn't what she wanted and she went home, taking the baby with her. She was two years old then. I don't want to talk about her.'

'No,' Louise said. 'You couldn't. Why did they arrest your wife?'

He turned and looked at her. 'Because she did what you're doing. She got herself mixed up hiding Allied airmen. Someone betrayed the network and she was caught and sent to Auschwitz. With my daughter. That's all I knew for two years. I tried everything; the International Red Cross, the American embassy in Geneva, contacts in Spain—everything. Nobody could get her out. I was in the army in the Judge Advocate department. I kicked like hell, I wanted to fight. But they needed lawyers and I stayed at my desk. Then I was sent for; there was my senior officer, who looked like somebody had knocked all his teeth out, and another man, a

Lieutenant Colonel in the Intelligence Corps. They told me to sit down, gave me a cigarette and offered me a Scotch.

'Then they told me about Patricia and my child. The Spanish Jewess who got out of the camp had got to know her there; they became friendly. Then Patricia was moved to the special compound. The other woman didn't see her again for some weeks, till one day she happened to be on her way to the medical centre and she saw a burial detail going across the special compound, outside the wall and near the wire fence. She saw the bodies, and she saw Patricia. She was still holding the little girl in her arms.'

'Oh God,' Louise said. She put her arm round him. 'Oh God, how terrible—I'm so sorry . . .'

'I left the JA,' Savage said. 'I joined a special unit attached to OSS and I told them why. So when they wanted someone to take this on, they chose me. Just before I killed him tonight, that bastard opened his eyes. I think I went on living just for that moment.'

'You mustn't blame yourself,' Louise said. 'It wasn't your fault.'

'I didn't make her happy,' Savage said. 'When she wanted to go back to her family I said Okay. Six months after she left the war broke out. I should have gone over and brought them both back.'

'You didn't love her, did you?' Louise said. He turned and looked at her.

'No,' he said. 'That's why I let her go. And that's what's been driving me crazy ever since. I just didn't love her, and that's why she died like that. Why they both died.' He put his head down in his hands suddenly. 'I'd like a drink.'

Louise got up. 'I'll get you one.'

She found the bottle of Minden's cognac and brought it upstairs. She poured some into her own water glass and gave it to him.

'You mustn't cry about it,' Savage said. 'I don't like to see you cry. Come here and sit beside me.' He put his arm round her; it was a hard grip.

'What did that Kraut do to you?'

'Nothing that matters,' she said slowly. 'I was sitting here, waiting for you, feeling frightened and sorry for myself. As if I were so special. You were right. I just slept with a German, that's all. Don't let's talk about it. It's what you've done that matters.'

'Yes,' Savage said. He drank the brandy down. 'Yes, I killed Brühl and I wrecked the laboratory. By the time anyone goes down there in the morning they'll need a boat.'

'What are you going to do? You must get away at once.'

'I'll go tomorrow,' Savage said. 'I'll leave quite normally. There'll be a massive security check in the area but my Swiss passport should get me through. I'll go to Paris and on to Berne. I don't want to hang around here. With Jean's record and Minden to back it up, you won't be suspected.'

'You must get out,' Louise repeated. 'Whatever happens you mustn't be anywhere near here. I wish you could go now, tonight!'

'No transport,' Savage said. 'And respectable Swiss cousins don't disappear at five in the morning. Our friend Minden might start asking questions. I'll see him tomorrow and say goodbye. I don't want any loose ends here for you.'

He turned her face towards him and kissed her. Louise shivered and he let her go. 'I'm cold,' she said. 'I'm sorry.'

'You've had enough for tonight,' Savage said. 'Get into bed.'

She lay while he pulled the bedclothes over her and tucked them in, watching him. Her body was cold and her courage suddenly low. She put out a hand and held on to him.

'I'm frightened,' she said. 'I don't know why but I have the most awful feeling—why don't you take Jean's car and go? Now! Please, Roger. Don't wait till tomorrow.'

'You go to sleep,' he said. 'Don't worry.' He switched out the light and left her. Louise lay in the darkness. Everything had gone well; Savage had succeeded and returned safely; there were only a few hours to go through before he left the Château. By that time tomorrow he would be miles away. There was no logical reason for the insistent, strident panic in her which cried out that this was not how it would end.

6

FRANZ ZERBINSKI had been Colonel Von Gehlen's batman for two years. He had served with him in Belgium when the Colonel was with the occupation forces, and spent a year in Brussels. When they moved to Paris, Franz was delighted. He sent his wife French scent and silk stockings, and set himself up with a girl he had picked up one Sunday morning at a café on the Champs-Elysées. She was seventeen, a plump little tart who cuddled up to him and made him feel at home. His Colonel's posting to the Château Diane had disturbed this happy relationship; he didn't see her so often, and he had an unhappy feeling that she had found another friend.

He had been asleep for an hour, or so he thought, until he woke up feeling cramp in his left leg, and discovered it was after four o'clock. He had been dozing on a chair in the Colonel's bedroom, waiting for him to come upstairs and be undressed. It was a nightly ritual, getting his officer out of his clothes and into bed. He was always drunk and irritable, and sometimes he punched out at Franz, who had learned how to dodge him. As an officer he wasn't too bad; he was generous to his batman. His one disadvantage was his habit of getting drunk every night and Franz having to sit up till he came upstairs. Four-twenty in the morning. He had never been so late. Franz got up and stretched himself; he felt worried. If the Colonel were asleep in the mess, he must have taken on a bigger load than usual. It wouldn't do for him to be found there in the morning when the orderlies came. He hesitated, not knowing what to do. If he went down and woke the Colonel he'd probably get a bollocking. If he left him there, he was sure to be blamed.

There was a little loyalty in him. He didn't want his officer to be disgraced. He decided to go downstairs to the mess and bring him up to bed. Because of this decision, Brühl was discovered several hours earlier than Savage had anticipated. In the confusion that followed, nobody went to investigate the laboratories until much later in the early morning. By which time the water had risen so high it flooded the corridor. But long before this, the S.S. had arrived at the Château.

By six o'clock that morning, Obergruppenführer Knocken, head of the S.S. in Paris, was holding an investigation at the Château Diane. He had brought seven staff officers with him, and Adolph Vierken as his second in command. He chose the dining room, where Brühl had loved to preside over his intimates, and sat at the head of the refectory table. He was an ugly man, his hair so close cut that he was almost bald, with short-sighted eyes further distorted by strong pebble glasses. He held a gold pencil in one hand and at intervals he tapped his teeth with the end of it. Before him stood the two soldiers who had been on duty inside the main entrance during the night. Both stood at attention and their faces were grey with fear. Knocken had taken statements from the guards at the gate; their entry book was on the table in front of him. Vierken sat on his right-hand side, smoking, listening to the interrogation. He had been awoken an hour earlier by the emergency call from the Château. Brühl had been discovered almost immediately after the Colonel's body had been found. Instantly the Château was placed on a full alert, and Knocken was notified. He and Vierken and their officers had arrived within the hour.

As senior officers in the German security forces, Knocken and Vierken knew the significance of Brühl's death and what it meant to the Nazi war effort.

'Now,' Knocken said. 'I want you to think before you answer. I have here the report from the guards on duty at the main gate. Seven officers left the Château between nine p.m. and midnight. All had returned by two in the morning. Then an eighth officer was admitted. He passed through the main gate. You say you let him into the Château at about that time. Is that correct?'

Both men nodded. 'Yes, Herr Obergruppenführer.'

'How long have you been posted here? You . . .' He spoke to the private soldier.

'Five months, sir.'

'And you?'

'Four months, sir.'

'I see.' Knocken tapped his teeth with the pencil. He spoke in a quiet voice.

'This officer that you admitted,' Knocken said quietly. 'You say he arrived back at two-twenty-five. Did you recognise him?'

'No, Herr Obergruppenführer.' The most senior of the soldiers answered; he was a regular S.S. man with ten years' service behind him and he had been decorated for gallantry in the Polish campaign.

'Why not?'

'He was wearing his cap pulled down, sir.'

'And what was his name?' Knocken had a list in front of him. On it were thirteen names. Seven of these were members of the staff who had gone out after eight o'clock and returned during the night. All had been checked out and in. The six remaining names, including Minden's, were all officers billeted outside, none of whom had yet reported for duty. 'Well,' Knocken repeated, 'what was his name?'

'I don't know, Herr Obergruppenführer.'

'You didn't check his pass?'

'No sir.' Knocken drew a circle on the sheet of paper and placed a dot in the middle of it. 'Why not?'

'We were slow to open the door, sir. He took our names and said we'd be reported.'

'I see.' Knocken made another dot in the circle. 'So he took your names and you forgot to ask for his pass or for any identification?'

'Yes, sir.' The man's voice croaked with fear.

'What did he do—where did he go?'

'He went to the mess, sir.'

Knocken turned to Adolph Vierken. 'Where he murdered Von Gehlen.' He drew a line through the circle. The stony eyes glinted at the soldier.

'You saw him come out?' The corporal nodded. 'And where did he go then?'

'Upstairs, Herr Obergruppenführer.'

'Exactly,' Knocken remarked. 'He went upstairs. And he killed General Brühl, without anyone hearing.'

'It's incredible,' Vierken said. 'He passes the guards on the gates, he bluffs his way in here, murders two men and gets to the cellars, without anyone stopping him!' The gas-mask had been found in the lift, Brühl's keys were recovered from outside.

'He had a pass,' Knocken said. 'The guards at the gates checked him in, but unfortunately they didn't notice the name. A number of officers go out for the evening and they get careless. Very careless. In fact,' he spoke to the others grouped round the table, 'the security arrangements seem to have been extremely lax.' He looked at the senior S.S. officer present, whose task had been the safety of Brühl and his project. The man didn't dare to look at him. 'I shall hold you responsible, Gruppenführer Brandt. Entirely responsible.' The officer blanched to a sickly colour.

'Yes,' he said. 'I am responsible. But you must realise we had no reason to think any attempt...'

'There was an alert here on Friday night!' Vierken suddenly shouted at him. 'You ordered a search of the area with the regular military at Chartres! You found nobody and you assumed, *assumed* it was a reconnaissance flight! That assumption was wrong, Gruppenführer Brandt! It was careless and slack. Somebody was dropped. And that man came in here last night and killed General Brühl.'

'And lost us the war,' Knocken murmured, too low for them to hear. He addressed himself to the quivering Brandt. He tapped the list with his gold pencil. 'There are thirteen names here. Seven regular officers who have all been accounted for, six who live outside and have not reported for duty. But an eighth man came in and went out again. A man whose name is not on any list. That is our murderer. You let him out again?' He spoke to the corporal.

'Yes.'

'Describe him. Remember everything you can.'

The corporal made a visible effort. 'He was tall, sir, about my height. He wore his cap pulled down; I didn't see his eyes or what colour hair he had. He was a German. I'd swear to that. He had a major's rank on his collar. That's all, Herr Obergruppenführer.'

'He would speak perfect German. That means nothing. So we have a tall man in a major's uniform. Not very helpful.' Knocken looked at the corporal and at the private soldier, who had not spoken a word.

'You're under arrest,' he said quietly. 'Report yourselves.'

They sprang to attention and saluted. 'Heil Hitler!'

'And you, Gruppenführer Brandt, will do the same.'

The officer got up, stretched out his arm and said loudly, 'Heil Hitler!' He was dead and he knew it. He left the room with some dignity.

Knocken turned to Adolph Vierken. 'I am putting you in charge of this operation,' he said. 'I want this man found! You can have what troops and facilities you need, on my authority.'

'Thank you, Obergruppenführer,' Vierken said. 'But first I must point out that the murderer left here at least four hours ago. In my opinion he will have left the area. I can't promise to find him.' Knocken allowed himself a tiny smile. Vierken was no fool; he wasn't going to commit himself to something he might not be able to do. And four hours was a long start. Nobody but a madman would stay within a hundred kilometres of the Château Diane.

'I agree,' he said. 'I agree it's unlikely we'll get him. But I'm convinced of one thing. He was landed here on Friday night. Somebody sheltered him for Saturday and Sunday. Somebody, somewhere in this district, has been hiding him. And that car came from the direction of St. Blaize en Yvelines. Somebody hid him there.'

'I'll find them,' Vierken assured him. 'I propose to close off the entire area. Nobody enters or leaves the district within a radius of fifty kilometres. All telephone systems and transport comes under S.S. control; the regular military authority is suspended. There will be a complete communications blackout. And I want the seventh battalion to supply me with three hundred troops, and the necessary armoured vehicles. I shall set up my headquarters here and conduct the investigations myself.'

'Very good,' Knocken said. He took up his pencil and

tapped it against his lower teeth; he looked round the table at his staff officers. Their faces were stiff and grave. 'Gentlemen,' he said. 'I have to tell you something. What happened here this morning has cost us the war.' There was a murmur from them, a wordless protest. He held up his hand. 'I'm not exaggerating. Frederich Brühl and his work are irreplaceable. Both are destroyed. All that is left to us is vengeance. These people'—he turned to Vierken, grim and scowling beside him —'these people helped our enemies. We've treated them with softness. Our occupation has been gentle. And this is the result! Weakness, gentlemen, has brought this terrible disaster upon our Fatherland. But they are going to pay for it.' His clenched fist slammed the table. 'You,' he said to Vierken, 'are going to make an example of them that will go down in history! I want them punished . . . I want it to be a punishment to fit what they have done!'

Vierken stood up. 'I promise you that,' he said. 'I promise you the French will pay a price for this that will never be forgotten!'

'Good,' Knocken said. 'Good. I am relying on you.'

'I shan't fail you,' Vierken said. 'I'll think of something really special for them.' The meeting broke up; Knocken gave two orders which were to be carried out immediately. An S.S. firing squad executed the four soldiers who had been on duty on the gates and inside the Château, and Gruppenführer Brandt was handed a revolver with which he shot himself. A message detailing the disaster was sent direct to the Reichs-Chancellery in Berlin. Knocken and Vierken returned to Paris, where Vierken went to his headquarters for an hour to clear his desk. Among the messages and memos waiting for him was a brief note from the German Embassy in Berne. 'Felon & Brassier confirm that Roger Savage has left for France. He can be located at the Château de St. Blaize en Yvelines where he is dealing with the financial affairs of the Comtesse de Bernard. His date of arrival was May 30th; he is expected to return to Berne early this week. He is a Swiss national, resident in the city for the past five years. Message ends.'

Vierken had forgotten about Régine's cousin-in-law. He was still stunned by what had happened at the Château

Diane, still struggling to reconcile himself to the disaster of Brühl's murder and the destruction of the laboratory. His rage was mounting, with a sense of frustration which could only find an outlet in savage cruelty. He read the report on Roger Savage twice. For a moment suspicion had reared in him, only to subside regretfully in the face of that confirming evidence. There was nothing wrong with the Swiss staying at St. Blaize. Their source in Berne was beyond question. Felon & Brassier were international lawyers of repute. The address given as Savage's home had confirmed his absence. There was nothing there.

He made arrangements for his Parisian commitments to be looked after and went to the Crillon to collect his belongings. A week at St. Blaize from where the killer's car had come—ten days. Time enough to question and search and then, with an ingenuity which was just beginning to suggest itself, devise a punishment meet for the crime . . . He had an appointment with Régine that evening. He had arranged to collect her from the Sorbonne, and bring her back to the hotel. He thought of her disappointment and was sorry. He telephoned and left a message for her. He had a little time left; just enough to explain, to hold her in his arms. Just as he had decided to leave the hotel, Régine arrived. She was breathless and untidy. He opened the door of the suite and she ran into his arms.

'My darling—I came as soon as I could get away. My tutor was furious . . .'

'Kiss me,' Vierken demanded, pressing her small body hard against him. 'Kiss me!'

Moments later she looked up at him, her face streaked with tears. 'How long will you be gone? I miss you so much—I can't bear it!'

'Not long,' he comforted. 'A week, a few days more perhaps. It won't be too long.'

'It'll be eternity to me,' Régine declared. Sometimes the extent of her passion surprised him. She was so small, so slight and pale. He stroked her hair with tenderness. His wife, that placid, obedient cow, had less fire in her whole body than the frail girl possessed in one of the fingers he was kissing.

'It won't be long,' he repeated. 'Don't cry, sweetheart; I

shall miss you too. When I come back we can be together again.'

'Where are you going? Why can't I come with you—I could make an excuse to my aunt . . .'

'No,' Vierken said. 'This is official business. I can't tell you where I'm going. It's police work.'

'You won't be in danger, will you?' The thin arms circled his neck, clutching with desperate strength.

'No,' he assured her. 'I've told you, it's a police operation. Resistance.'

'Give them hell,' she said fiercely. 'But come back safely, that's all I care about. You will be careful, won't you? You know if anything happened to you I should die?'

'Would you?' Vierken asked her. 'Do you love me so much?'

'You know I do.' She leaned her head against him and he kissed her hair.

He thought suddenly that he would never, ever go back to his wife. If the war was lost, as Knocken said it was, then his escape was planned. Spain and then Central America. He had money hidden away against the treachery of fate. He would forget about his wife. He would take Régine with him.

'You mean a lot to me,' he said suddenly. 'I want you to know that.'

'I worship you,' she said simply. 'I couldn't live without you now.'

'You have such passion,' he muttered, holding her against him; the muscles of his thighs were taut. 'Such fire, for such a little girl. I could break you . . .'

'Do it,' she whispered, her eyes closed. 'Do it now—we've got time . . . Love me, Adolph. Love me . . .' He swung her up into his arms and took her to the bedroom. Afterwards at the door of the suite they said goodbye. He held her very close. And he broke the discipline of twenty years. 'Promise me you'll stay in Paris. I don't want you to go home to St. Blaize. Stay here.'

'Why not?' Régine asked. 'Why mustn't I go?'

'Because I order you not to,' he said, using the sexual language which had such power over them both. 'I command you understand me? I love you, Régine. Promise me you'll stay here, with your aunt, till I get back?'

'If that's what you want,' she said. 'I'll do it. I'll do what you say.'

'Good,' Vierken said gently. He kissed her eyes and lips. 'Good. Remember, wait for me. We'll be together soon.' He left immediately after she did; his chief interrogator, a young S.S. Captain in his twenties, sat beside him in the car.

By the time Heinz Minden arrived at the Château Diane troops of the Waffen S.S. were in command, and since Vierken's first orders had been issued just after nine o'clock, the area had been completely sealed off from contact with the outside world.

. . . . .

'I can't understand it,' Jean de Bernard said. 'Half an hour ago I telephoned through to Louis Malle and now the line is dead.' He banged the receiver rest up and down. 'This is a real nuisance; Malle promised to get me some supplies of roofing felt; I told him I'd pay the black market price but we've got to get the tower roof insulated; there's so much damp coming in we'll have serious damage.'

He glanced at Louise without really seeing her. He had spent a night sleeping uneasily, disturbed in the small hours by a nightmare in which he saw his father and his children choking to death. His temper was frayed and his nerves on edge. He struck the telephone and swore. He hadn't noticed how pale his wife looked, or the nervous glance she gave Savage when he appeared for breakfast; they hadn't had a chance to speak alone. Last night had been a failure. That was all Jean knew. But something about her silence irritated him. He looked round at her.

'They must have cut the telephones off,' she said. They were alone in his study.

He frowned at her. 'What do you mean—who's cut the telephones?'

'The Germans,' Louise said slowly.

'What makes you say that?' He walked towards her. 'What do you mean?'

'Savage got the key,' she said. 'He got into the Château. He did what he came over to do. They must have found out by now.'

'My God,' Jean de Bernard said. 'My God—I thought you said he'd failed . . .'

'He didn't,' she said. 'He killed Brühl and he destroyed the gas.' For a moment there was silence; he didn't move or speak Suddenly he made a gesture.

'Thank God,' he said in a low tone. 'Thank God. He must get away from here.'

'He's going,' Louise answered him. His reaction had surprised her. She had expected fear, reproach, even though he had tried to help Savage. 'When did he tell you this?' Jean asked.

She answered without thinking. 'When he got back; about four o'clock.'

'He came to your room?'

'Oh for God's sake, Jean! How else could he let us know!'

'He could have come to me,' her husband said. 'Did he touch you again?'

She turned on him bitterly. 'And what the hell does it matter? What do you care about a thing like that when we're all in danger of our lives! No, he didn't make love to me, if that's what's worrying you. He went straight to his own room.'

'I must talk to him,' the Comte said. 'I've got to know what he plans to do. He ought to leave immediately.'

'He's going,' Louise said. 'He's upstairs packing now—someone's coming up the drive.' Louise was on her feet, looking out of the window. 'On a bicycle. It's Camier!'

Jean stood beside her, watching the Mayor of St. Blaize pedal to the front door, dismount and wipe his sleeve across his sweating face. The sound of the bell pealed through the outer hall. 'Why has he come?' Louise turned to her husband.

'We'll soon see. He may have tried the telephone. Ah! Albert—come in.'

'Monsieur le Comte—Madame la Comtesse.' Camier bowed to them both. He was out of breath, and he carried a cap in his left hand. When he shook hands with Louise she felt him trembling.

'You look very hot,' Jean said. 'Sit down; we can offer you some wine.'

'Monsieur, the town is full of S.S. troops—they've taken over the telephone exchange at Houdan, the railway station is closed, there are road blocks everywhere! Do you know what has happened? Why are they doing this?' He was so frightened that a dribble of saliva appeared on his lips and ran down his chin.

'I have no more idea than you,' Jean de Bernard said. 'We have heard nothing. This is terrible, Albert. Are people staying calm?'

'The Mairie was besieged,' Camier said. 'I was at my shop as usual when I was sent for and this German officer was sitting at my desk in the Mairie, banging a riding whip and shouting. I just stood there, Monsieur. I didn't understand it. There's been no trouble—we've done nothing! People were trying to get in to see me, and the troops were pushing them back and hitting them.' He wiped his face again, all pretence of manners forgotten. He looked incongruous in a blue suit and a tie. The peasant of a thousand years, cunning, stupid and fearful of forces from outside, mumbled and sweated, hoping blindly that help would come from the seigneur.

'Will you come down and see them, Monsieur! That pig in my office wouldn't tell me anything—he treated me like a dog!'

'I'll come,' Jean de Bernard said. 'But I doubt if they'll pay much attention to me.' He turned to Louise. 'Don't worry,' he said. 'Don't worry, my dearest. We've nothing to fear; our consciences are clear. I'll come down with you, Albert.'

'It's a calamity,' the Mayor lamented. 'When I saw those black uniforms I nearly pissed myself . . . Oh, Madame, I beg your pardon—I am so worried I didn't realise what I was saying . . .'

'It's all right,' Louise said quickly. 'I understand. Please don't apologise.'

Even as she spoke the door opened and Savage stood there. He looked at them in turn. 'I've interrupted something,' he said. 'Excuse me.' He gave a very Swiss bow.

'No,' Jean de Bernard said. 'No, come in, Roger. This concerns you too. This is the Mayor of St. Blaize, M. Camier.

There's some emergency; the town has been occupied by the S.S., the telephones are cut off, and no one is allowed to leave the district.'

'And there's a curfew!' Camier burst out. 'They posted the notice up outside my office . . .'

'How very awkward,' Savage said. He raised his brows at the mayor. 'Does this apply to neutrals? I am a Swiss national.'

'I don't know, Monsieur,' Camier quavered. 'I don't think they'd care what you were—my God, it was like a nightmare! Will you come down, Monsieur le Comte—see what you can do.'

'I think that's a mistake.' Savage spoke curtly, addressing himself to Jean. 'I wouldn't seek them out. They'll come and find you soon enough. After all,' he shrugged at the unhappy Mayor, 'they may arrest you both. You have to go of course, Monsieur, but I think the Comte should stay here with his family.'

'I have a responsibility to the village,' Jean de Bernard said. 'I must see if there's anything I can do. No harm will come to Louise and the children.' He kissed Louise on the cheek; she started to say something in support of Savage, but he left the room too quickly.

'He's a fool,' Savage said. 'He shouldn't draw attention to himself. They haven't wasted any time!' It was the usual German practice to take hostages and shoot them in reprisal for acts of sabotage. The going rate in human life was one hundred French for a single German soldier. He didn't say anything about it to Louise.

'You can't get out!' she said. 'Don't you realise, they've closed the roads—you're trapped here!'

'If the Mayor's right,' Savage said calmly, 'and I expect he is . . .'

'I hate that man,' she burst out. 'Crawling round the Germans from the day they arrived—now he sees what they're really like! And he comes running here, whining for help . . . You don't think they'll arrest Jean?' She turned to Savage and the anguish on her face surprised him.

'I don't know,' he said. 'I don't know what they'll do. My guess is that they'll pay us a visit here pretty soon. You'll need to keep your nerve, Louise. If they see any sign of cracking, they'll have you down to their headquarters. You know your story and all you have to do is stick to it. Don't worry about what I say or Jean says—just keep to your own line.'

'But you can't stay here,' she protested. 'You've got to get away before they come round asking questions! Can't you make contact with London—what can you do?'

'I can radio them,' Savage said. 'If the routes are all closed I can ask for a pick-up plane. That was part of the deal. It's bloody risky but it may be the only way.'

'You should have gone last night,' Louise said. 'Now you're trapped here . . . Oh my God!'

'I couldn't do that,' Savage said. He came and caught her by the shoulders. 'For Christ's sake, I wanted to go normally, catching the early train. If I just disappeared after what had happened, don't you think Minden would have seen the connection? He may be in love with you, but don't think he'd hesitate to turn you in! It's my bad luck they acted so quickly. They must have discovered it very early this morning.'

'If they arrest you . . .' Louise whispered.

'They won't,' Savage said quickly. 'I'll put a call through to London for a pick-up.'

'They can't land here, it's madness,' she protested. 'The plane will be shot down!'

'You'd be surprised,' he told her, 'how many times we've landed people on a field not far from here. It can be done. Don't be afraid.'

'I'm so frightened I feel quite numb,' she said. 'Numb and sick. Aren't you afraid?'

'Not for myself,' Savage answered. 'I've done my job. I'm satisfied. If they catch me I'll swallow my L pill and that's the end of it. But you're different. Your husband's a man, he can take care of himself. But I don't want anything to happen to you. I was thinking about it last night. Get on the plane with me. Come to England.'

'I couldn't,' Louise said. 'You know that—the children . . .'

'They'll be all right,' he insisted. 'It's only a matter of a week or so before the invasion. You can come back to them afterwards. We'll smash the bastards back to the Rhine. They'll be all right till then.'

'No.' She shook her head. 'No, I could never do that. I couldn't leave them behind.'

'I'm not sure you'll hold together,' Savage said. He held her against him. 'If you show any sign . . .'

'I won't,' she said. 'I'll hold together. I promise you that. I won't break down.'

'I love you,' Savage said. 'I'm trying to tell you so. This marriage is over; we could be together. If you won't come back with me, then I'm coming back for you. I want you to know that. We'll take the kids to the States. Kiss me.' His mouth was warm; she felt the strength of his arms around her and for the brief moments while they stood together, fear receded. Escape offered itself, not the flight back to England, leaving her family behind, but the escape of losing herself with him, of letting his desire control them both. I love him . . . The knowledge overcame her, impossible to deny. I love him and, oh God, how I want to be loved by him while we have the chance . . . She never knew what made her think of Jean de Bernard at that moment. He came unwanted into her mind; the grey in his hair and the lines of worry round his eyes, going down to face the Gestapo in the village. Abruptly she pulled herself away from Savage.

'When do you think Jean will come back? How long has he been gone?'

'About an hour,' Savage said. 'If he doesn't come back soon it won't look very good. You care about him, don't you?'

'He's my husband,' she said. 'It's not just the children; I couldn't walk out on him now either.'

'I see,' Savage nodded. 'How about afterwards—when the war's over?'

'That would be different,' Louise said. 'If we get through this, I would feel free to go with you. If you still wanted me.'

'I'll want you,' Savage said. 'Make no mistake.'

. . . . .

It was late afternoon when Jean de Bernard came back to the Château. Louise and the children were at the front door to meet him; Paul, whose ears were tuned for engines, heard the car first. Jean kissed them both. Louise tried to question him with her eyes, unable to speak before the children, but he only shook his head. Louise watched him playing with them for half an hour, listening to their tales of what they had done at school, one balanced on each knee. He looked from one to the other, smiling and calm, the Papa that they expected to find when they came home. 'We saw a lot of soldiers,' Paul informed him. 'They were in black, with skull and crossbones on their caps. We waved to them but they didn't wave back. Why are there so many of them?'

'I don't know,' Jean said. 'Perhaps they're going on manœuvres.'

'I wish I could watch them,' Paul said. 'I'm going to be a soldier and have a skeleton on my cap.'

When they had gone upstairs to see their grandfather, Jean de Bernard sank back in the chair; he looked old and exhausted.

'The Death's Head Battalion, that's what they've brought in here,' he said. 'The execution squads. Louise, would you get me a drink, please? I waited three hours in the Mairie to see the officer in charge. I'm very tired.'

She got up immediately and brought him some of Minden's cognac. 'Drink it down,' she said. 'Oh my God, Jean, what's going to happen, what did you find out?'

'Nothing. When he did see me, he just took down my name and told me the whole area was under curfew and S.S. authority. I asked him what had happened—what was the reason for it. He just looked at me. Then he shouted, "Sabotage and murder. Assisting enemy agents. You'll learn what it means to touch German lives and property. You'll pay for it round here, I can promise you that!" '

'He didn't question you?'

'No. He was in charge of the military operation. The questioning will be done by others; professionals. That cognac was good. Thank you. You know it was curious today. I watched those swine taking over the village, I saw the people's faces, white with fear; Camier gibbering like an old woman, and I thought this is what I tried to stop. This is what I've been afraid would happen for four years, and now it has.

And I helped to bring it about. I brought the Gestapo here in the end. Ironic, isn't it?'

'*I* brought them,' Louise said slowly. 'It's not your fault. What do you think they'll do?'

'Try to find the saboteur. They were already searching the houses when I left. Then they'll make arrests. Hundreds of men, I imagine. And then they'll shoot them unless the agent is denounced to them. That's what they usually do.'

There was silence between them; he held his hand over his eyes, shielding them and Louise didn't move. When she did speak her voice trembled. 'These hostages—they won't take you, will they?'

'They may.' He spoke calmly. 'Poor Camier is certain to be chosen; they always take the mayor, the doctor, the priest. After that it's indiscriminate. Don't worry about that. Where is Savage?'

'I don't know,' she spoke impatiently. 'I'll go to Major Minden; I'll ask him to protect you . . .'

'I'm sure he would,' Jean de Bernard said gently. 'He's not a bad man. But he has as much influence with the S.S. as I have. He couldn't do anything.'

'Jean.' She came and knelt beside his chair. She laid her hand on his arm. 'You won't give Savage up to them?'

'If I could save the lives of Frenchmen, yes I would,' he said. 'I'd give myself up with him. But not you. You are the reason I will stand by and see innocent people murdered and do nothing. You and father and the children. We are caught; there's nothing now to do but wait and see what they will do.'

'You hate me for it, don't you,' Louise said. 'You blame me for what's going to happen. I can see it on your face.'

'The gas had to be destroyed. The monster who made it had to be killed.' He put one hand over hers but there was no warmth in it. 'A million French could have died when the Allies invaded. Nothing can alter that; we did the right thing. But seeing what I saw today, I can't feel anything but horror. Horror for the few hundreds in this area who are going to die because of what we had to do. It may sound stupid and sentimental, but I can't help it. I feel like a murderer.'

There was nothing she could say to him; silence continued.

At last she spoke. 'When will we know what's going to happen?'

'By tomorrow—perhaps even tonight. They move very quickly. I wish I could get you and the children away.'

'Don't, Jean,' she whispered. 'Nothing can happen to us. You're the one who could be in danger. Roger was right; you shouldn't have gone down and made yourself conspicuous!'

'That won't make any difference,' he said. 'There have been de Bernards at St. Blaize for five hundred years. They would know where to find me. You mustn't worry; we have to be brave and calm. It's our only chance now.'

He got up, and stretched; as he crossed the room his step was slow. 'I'm going upstairs to see Papa.'

Louise lit a cigarette; she was in control of herself again. The effect of fear was to numb, after a time. She felt cold and tired, with a sense of anger spreading under the dread of what was coming. And yet it seemed unreal. Jean talked of people she knew being taken and shot in cold blood: Camier, Father Duval, Doctor Joubert . . . Intellectually she accepted it, emotionally she resisted. It couldn't happen. Something, somehow, would prevent it. She went and stood by the window, the cigarette in her right hand, watching for the unknown. 'There have been de Bernards at St. Blaize for five hundred years . . . they would know where to find me . . .'

They wouldn't take Jean as a victim. He was a well-known supporter of the Vichy Government and an open advocate of collaboration with the German occupation forces. They wouldn't take him. She rationalised it calmly, unaware that the hand holding the cigarette was shaking and spilling ash on the floor. They wouldn't drag Jean away watched by Paul and Sophie, screaming and struggling to go to their father . . .

She was still standing there when Savage found her.

'They're going to take hostages; Jean thinks it will be hundreds of people. People from the village here, from all over the district.'

'That figures,' Savage said. 'I warned you in the beginning it was going to be nasty. Don't worry about Jean; I think he's safe enough. His record will protect him.'

'I wish you could get away tonight,' she said. She turned round suddenly and clung to him. 'Jean thinks they may come here at any moment. Couldn't you just go into hiding . . . ?'

'No,' Savage said. 'Everyone knows I'm here. If I disappear that puts the finger on me, and I'd be flushed out like a rabbit. And where do you think you'd stand—all of you? Forget it; if they come here and ask questions that's okay. I've got answers ready. I've got to clear my escape with Minden tonight. I'm going to make a hell of a fuss about being kept here.'

'That's him now, I think,' she said. 'I hear a car.' Savage went on holding her; her back was to the window.

'No,' he said and his voice was gentle. 'No, darling, it's not Minden.'

There were two cars, black and long bonneted, with the swastika pennant flying from the radiators. He watched the men in S.S. uniform spring out, and the rear door of the first car open. A tall man with the insignia of a Standartenführer got out and stood looking up at the Château for a moment. The bell began to peal, and someone was hitting the front door with a pistol butt.

'They've come, haven't they?' She didn't turn to look.

'Yes,' Savage said. 'Yes they have. You've got to be a very brave girl.'

• • • • •

Minden was given his clearance to leave the Château Diane at five that evening. He had no work to do, he and his colleagues were helpless, confined to the Château while the laboratory was pumped clear of water.

Late that day a group of Brühl's staff had stood in inches of water, looking at the destruction of their work. The laboratory was a shambles of broken glass, sodden materials, filing cabinets with their drawers open and the contents reduced to pulp. Electrical failure had followed submersion and they were on emergency lighting from a small generator. There was an overpowering smell of chemicals and damp. Gasmasks were worn as a precaution, both by the pumping crew and the staff; they were discarded when the atmosphere was proved unpolluted. This was done by bringing a junior officer's pet dog into the area. The effect of the gas upon animals was as ferocious as upon human beings. The spaniel stood in the water up to its flanks and sniffed unhappily, its brown eyes rolling with fear, but it showed no reaction. Nothing proved the efficiency of water in neutralising Formula XV more than the immunity of the dog. Minden could have wept; one of Brühl's favourite assistants, a man who had worked with him from the start of the project in Auschwitz, stood with his face hidden in a handkerchief, and sobbed. Nobody was allowed to see Brühl; an autopsy was performed inside the Château by the doctor on the staff. The cause of his death hadn't been announced. Secrecy covered everything, and the rumours multiplied. He had been stabbed, shot, poisoned—a dozen different men were said to be arrested—the saboteur had been caught; it was a team of parachutists who were being hunted throughout the countryside; it was the *maquis* group who had been hiding in the Château—Minden heard it all and didn't care. His work was ruined. But more, much more than a sense of personal loss, was the agony of knowing that the war could not be won. In the flood water lapping through the laboratory, he saw the fall of Germany. There was a terrible incongruity about it which numbed him.

At three he was questioned by a team of two S.S. officers, a Major and a Lieutenant. It was a preliminary investigation; anyone who didn't satisfy these two was passed on to the man in command, a high-ranking S.S. officer called Vierken. Minden had vaguely heard of him; he was attached to General Knocken in Paris. He had a reputation for severity. The S.S. Major was a genial man with red hair, and a face so thickly freckled that it looked brown. He told Minden to sit down. The lieutenant was pale with a narrow face and a long nose. He gave Minden a glance of chill suspicion.

'Your movements yesterday, Major Minden, until you reported this morning. You may smoke if you like.'

Minden thanked him. 'I went back to the Château St. Blaize on Saturday, where I'm billeted on the family. Sunday was quiet and I spent the evening there.'

'And how was it spent? What exactly did you do?'

'I did some paper work for an hour; then I joined the family for drinks . . .'

'The name of the family,' the S.S. Major asked.

'De Bernard. Comte de Bernard.'

'Continue please. You joined them for drinks.'

'We had dinner together; I dine with them every evening. We talked and about eleven o'clock we went to bed. I left at my usual time this morning.'

'I see.' The Lieutenant was writing on a pad.

'You never left the house?'

'No.'

The Major cocked his red head on one side.

'Can you prove this?'

Minden hesitated for a moment. 'Yes, I can. But I'd prefer not to go into details.'

'I'm afraid you will have to,' the Major said. 'What were you doing that proves you didn't leave the Château between midnight and, say, four, four-thirty in the morning?'

'I was with a lady,' Minden said stiffly.

The Major gave a cheerful laugh. 'So were a lot of the officers who were out last night! They can produce their witnesses—can you?'

'I'd rather not, for obvious reasons.' Minden looked disturbed. 'The husband—it would be very difficult and unpleasant for her, but of course if it had to be corroborated, then she would have to tell you we were together. Until well past four o'clock.'

'How nice,' the Major smiled. 'The name of this lady?'

'The Comtesse de Bernard.'

'Thank you, Major. Only a formality these enquiries, we know all General Brühl's officers are loyal Nazis, but we have our duty to do. We have to find this murderer.' He turned to the Lieutenant. There seemed to be an unusual rapport between them; Minden smelt homosexuality in the big red-headed man. 'And the people who sheltered him. Don't we, Oberleutnant?'

'Yes, Herr Major. And when we do, God help them.'

'God help a lot of people,' the Major said. He stood up and saluted Minden.

'You can go now. This report will be submitted to the Standartenführer and if he is satisfied, you'll get permission to leave the Château. Heil Hitler!'

Minden snapped his heels together and flung up his arm. 'Heil Hitler!' He went back to his office to wait.

Vierken read through every report; four of them were unsatisfactory in that the officers billeted outside had been absent and maintained that they were in bed but had no witnesses to prove it. He decided not to see them; his expert, Captain Kramm, would quickly uncover any evasion. So far his operation had run with absolute smoothness. The whole area was cordoned off, its communications silenced, its municipal offices occupied, and house to house searches well advanced. His men were experts, as efficient in their duties as the excellent Captain Kramm, who could question a man for hours with patient mildness, and then subject him to tortures which never failed to extract the truth.

They had carried out police operations in Poland, in Holland, in Russia; they could uncover a mouse if it were concealed in a building. Vierken felt by instinct that this part of his plan would produce nothing. The man who got into the Château Diane was a trained expert; personally he believed that the agent had already left the district. His ultimate destination would be the South, to an area strong in Resistance supporters like Marseilles, where he could attempt an escape by sea in a boat, or the even more daring pick-up by an Allied submarine. Vierken didn't think he would find Brühl's murderer in the district or that his apprehension was as important now as the total intimidation of the local population. When the Allies invaded, they must be cowed completely. This act of defiance, the succouring of an enemy who had incidentally done unparalleled damage to the German war effort, must be punished with awful ingenuity.

When he came to Minden's report, he paused. Comte de Bernard, Château St. Blaize. Régine's brother. Régine's sister-in-law. He looked down again at Minden's report. His alibi was a woman. Vierken played with his pencil, sucking at it in unconscious imitation of his chief. Minden had spent the night with a lady. It was common enough; a lot of women had affairs with Germans. But it didn't tally well with Régine's description of the household. He had pictured a conservative aristocratic family, dominated by its traditions, to whom Régine dared not introduce him. He had a clear image of the brother and sister-in-law of his mistress, and the lady mentioned in Minden's account didn't suggest the Comtesse de Bernard at all.

Régine had said that Louise was sleeping with the cousin. Perhaps she was. Perhaps she was also sleeping with Minden. And this was interesting, because Régine had conveyed to him that her sister-in-law was very anti-German. He folded the report and made another telephone call. Teams were out investigating in all the villages. He decided to go to the Château St. Blaize and confirm both the Swiss cousin and the Major's alibi for himself.

· · · · ·

'Louise!' Minden found her in the drawing room. The curtains were drawn and the room looked intimate and warm in the light of the fire.

She sat in an armchair, her profile illumined, both hands clasped, and Minden felt his pulse leap. He had seen the S.S. cars in the driveway, and impelled by an instinctive fear, came rushing into the house to find her. Lust stirred in him at the curve of her neck and the line of her legs under the skirt, but something stronger brought him to her side, dropped to one knee, his hands reaching out for hers. He didn't think to analyse the feeling, or to associate her with the enemy.

'My darling—what are you doing here alone?'

'You saw the cars outside,' she said. 'They've been here since five; Jean has been questioned and they've kept him in the dining room with a guard. Roger is in there now.' She moved her head towards the study. 'They're keeping us separated till the questioning is over.' She pulled her hands away from him. 'I'm next,' she said. She reached into the box for a cigarette and immediately he held his lighter to it.

'Don't be angry with me,' he said. 'Please—it's not my fault. There's been a serious act of sabotage and my General has been murdered. Everyone has to be questioned. Try to understand; and don't blame me. They won't hurt anyone who isn't guilty.'

'Not even hostages?' The look on her face shocked him. 'If they don't find this man they're looking for, Jean says they'll shoot hundreds of innocent people.'

She could smell the cologne he used, and she felt nauseated; his hands, with the dark hairs growing from the wrist, were touching hers again. She resisted an impulse to rip at them with her nails.

'Please,' he said again. 'Don't blame me for it.' Before she could stop him he had brought her hands to his mouth and was kissing them. 'It was so wonderful,' he mumbled, holding them tight against her struggles, 'so beautiful—I've been thinking of you and hoping tonight . . . Don't turn against me, don't pull away . . .'

'Let me go!' She wrenched herself free and got up. 'Don't ever dare touch me again!'

'I understand,' he nodded, controlling himself. 'I understand, I don't blame you. This must have been a great shock. But you mustn't be frightened. When they send for you, just tell them the truth. Don't be difficult with them . . .' He swallowed, anxiety tightening his throat. 'Don't show hostility. Just tell them the truth. They questioned me today, and I'm afraid I have something to confess to you.'

'I don't want to hear it.' Louise turned away from him.

'You'll be angry,' he said unhappily. 'But I hadn't any choice. I told them I had spent the night with you. I had to account for myself between midnight and four in the morning, and I had to tell them I was with you. I'm very sorry.'

'Oh I don't mind,' she said. 'I don't mind being classed with all the other whores who sleep with Germans. Would you please go away and leave me alone now?'

'Don't talk like that,' Minden said quietly. 'Don't use that word. I love you. I've been in love with you since I came to this house. I told you so last night and it's the truth.'

'Love?' Louise turned round to him. 'You talk about love? Coming from a German it's an obscenity! You'd like to go to bed with me, wouldn't you—you'd honestly expect me to make love while your bloody butchers are shooting innocent people in hundreds? You wouldn't even see anything incongruous in it, would you? I think you're mad. All of you. You're mad and evil, and the thought of what I did with you makes me want to vomit. You can go in and tell those swine in there exactly what I've said. I don't give a damn.'

'You're upset,' he said. 'You don't know what you're saying. I understand, I really do. I shan't take any notice. As for reporting you . . .' He shook his head, his expression pained. 'How could you think I'd do anything to hurt you?'

'Oh, for God's sake,' Louise said, 'go away. Leave me alone.' He stood for a moment, looking at her. She had turned her back on him and was standing by the fireplace, nervously smoking. She heard him cross the floor and then the door closed.

When they arrived, the S.S. officer had introduced himself as Standartenführer Vierken. Saluted them and bowed to her. He was polite, his attitude exaggeratedly correct. His men had made a brief search of the house, and in response to Jean's protest, the old Comte had not been brought downstairs. Vierken had taken the little study as his interrogation room; he phrased it tactfully, suggesting that it would be suitable for discussions with each member of the family. There was a younger man, with a cherubic face and little eyes, mild as milk, who followed Vierken everywhere.

Jean had gone in first: they were not allowed to speak when he came out and passed through the drawing room to get to the hall. Louise had jumped to her feet, but an S.S. man accompanying her husband had gestured her to stay back. Now Savage was in the interrogating room. She hadn't spoken to him since the S.S. had come into the house. 'Stick to the story. And don't let the bastards see you're frightened.' They were his last words to her, whispered as the door burst open and Jean appeared, grey and shaken, to announce the Germans' arrival.

Before he had time to announce them, the figures seen through the window were in the room. Black suited them; the skull and crossbones embroidered on their caps glittered with silver thread, their boots shone like glass. The tallest and most senior was dark, with brown eyes; it seemed to Louise that he was looking at her with special interest.

What in God's name was happening in the study . . . ? She dropped back into the chair and threw the butt of the cigarette into the fireplace. Minden had worried her; she hadn't known how to reject him without arousing his suspicion. The invasion of the S.S. gave her the excuse to expunge some of her own self-disgust by abusing him. She shivered, thinking of the brown eyes moist with sentiment, the hard hands grasping at hers and the greedy kisses sucking at them. Love. He talked of loving her, and the horror was that she believed him. In his own way and within his own definition, he loved her. He had been working on a gas that would have killed her and her children, but he would still have loved her. He was the second man to tell her so that day. I love you. Savage had said it too. There was no sentimentality there; no compromise. Strength and toughness, the kind of sexuality which would completely dominate her if she ever gave it the opportunity. A man with whom she would live a very different life from the ordered, tranquil years of her marriage to Jean de Bernard.

Was he convincing them? How secure was his cover story, how astute was that sinister man with the perfect manners who had stared at her with eyes like stones...?

Behind the study door, Roger Savage sat in front of the desk which had been used by three generations of de Bernards, one leg crossed over the other, facing Adolph Vierken. Physically they were rather similar. Both were big men, powerfully built, in the best of condition; Savage with his cropped Swiss hair-cut could have passed for German. He showed no sign of nerves because he felt none. Nothing could alter the astounding success of his mission; the destruction of the laboratory and the corpse of Germany's premier scientist lying with his larynx smashed. His safety was not important beside that. He hoped to escape if he could, but he had long faced the possibility that his was a one-way mission. He had come to look on those lethal cufflinks as friends. Carelessly he stroked one with his finger, looking coolly into the Standartenführer's eyes, and knew he didn't give a damn about the outcome for himself. And so long as he was in that room, he couldn't think about anyone else, not even Louise. His best weapon was his confidence; he was sending it out to do battle with the German's suspicions and he sensed that he was winning. Pity or fear for anyone or anything else, could stem that flow between them.

'And how long have you been dealing with the Comtesse's financial affairs, Herr Savage?'

'I haven't been dealing with them,' Savage said. 'It's a very large Trust, there is a considerable sum of money to be administered for her. Normally Herr Brassier looks after her interests, but he didn't feel able to make this trip so he asked me to come instead. I studied the details for a few days and I believe I am sufficiently knowledgeable to be able to deputise for M. Brassier on this occasion.'

'And you came through from Berne direct?'

'I took the train from Berne and crossed the frontier into France on the 30th at about 9 a.m. After that I proceeded to Paris; it's a very tiring journey and the train was stopped at the station for two hours—then I came direct to St. Blaize.'

'Your documents, please.'

Savage raised his brows. 'I've already shown them to you but if you insist on seeing them again . . .'

'Have you any objection?' Vierken's tone was sharp.

'Only to what seems a waste of time,' Savage said. 'You'll see everything is in order.'

Vierken glanced through the passport, studying the entry made at the frontier; the stamp was dated the 30th and initialled by the frontier official. His entry permit from the German Embassy in Berne was stamped and dated in the same way. He looked at the photograph on the passport, checking the details for the second time with the list in front of him. It contained the information on Roger Savage which the S.S. had received from Switzerland. They checked. Slowly he closed the passport and replaced the permit in its envelope. He didn't hand them back. Instead he lit a cigarette and let the silence become an awkward pause. Savage shifted his position and gave a little cough to attract his attention. Vierken looked at him.

'You realise, Herr Savage, that you arrived in this district on the day after an alert for enemy agents?'

'No,' Savage said. 'How should I know a thing like that? I came here on business, and now that all this unpleasantness has happened, I am extremely anxious to go home. I must emphasise that I'm a neutral and none of the restrictions apply to me.'

'They apply,' Vierken said coldly, 'to whoever is in the area. Which you happen to be. Doesn't it occur to you, Herr Savage, that your arrival was an unhappy coincidence?'

'Not at all,' Savage said stiffly. 'I arranged the date well in advance—how could I know that there'd be an alert? If there's any doubt about my credentials, why don't you check with my firm in Berne?'

Vierken looked at him. 'I already have,' he said. 'That's why I'm asking you these questions here instead of at my headquarters.'

For a blind second Savage faltered. He couldn't have checked him—there hadn't been time since his arrival at the Château that afternoon . . . He decided to attack instead of retreating.

'How could you check my credentials when you didn't know I was here? I don't understand this.'

'But we did know,' Vierken said. 'I personally knew all about you, Herr Savage. From the day you arrived. Would you like a cigarette?'

That was an old dodge to show up a shaking hand. 'Thank you.' He took time to take it out and light it, holding the match flame for longer than he needed. His hands were rock steady. He glanced straight at the German. 'How did you know about me? Was it reported?'

'Not officially,' he said. 'Mademoiselle de Bernard is a friend of mine. She mentioned your arrival to me.'

Savage didn't hide his surprise. 'You know Régine?'

'Very well. She is a charming girl.'

'Very charming. She spent the weekend here.'

'I know,' Vierken said. 'She was very suspicious of you, Herr Savage.' Savage drew on the cigarette and placed one hand across the wrist of the other; his fingers pressed lightly against the flat surface of the cuff link. Pressure would release the metal square which concealed the L pill. So Régine de Bernard was a friend of the Standartenführer. Such a close friend that she reported on what happened among her own family. Charming. Very charming indeed.

'Indeed?' He showed resentment, even a little colour appeared under his skin. He glared at the Standartenführer. 'Suspicious of what, may I ask?'

'Not of your credentials,' Vierken said. 'It was your relationship with her sister-in-law that worried her. She seemed to think that for a cousin from Switzerland looking after money matters, you were much too intimate. Are you?'

'If you're suggesting that there's anything improper in my relationship with the Comtesse . . .'

'I am suggesting it,' Vierken said. 'She seems to be a promiscuous woman who doesn't discriminate. Is she your mistress, Herr Savage? I know that she is sleeping with Major Minden, who lives here. Does she divide herself between you? Alternate nights?'

Savage's hands were separated; for a second his fist began to double. He had a violent impulse to leap from his chair and smash his knuckles in that sneering face. Minden. They knew what had happened with him. Now he was sweating and it was cold, chilling his skin under the clothes. Louise. They were going after Louise. That bastard would hunt her through a labyrinth of questions, probing, insulting, threatening . . .

'I'll answer your question,' he said. 'Though it seems to me to be irrelevant. I am not Madame de Bernard's lover, and I know nothing about Major Minden. I have the highest regard for her character and as her cousin, I thoroughly resent your imputations!'

'Naturally.' Vierken smiled his sour smile. 'When do you want to leave, Herr Savage?'

'As soon as possible. Tomorrow would suit me.'

'I'm afraid that won't be possible,' Vierken said. 'You will need authority from me, or you won't be allowed to leave the area. And I do hope you won't be foolish and try to leave without my written permission. You'll only be arrested, if nothing worse happens to you. My men are in a resentful mood. They would just as soon shoot anyone who breaks the restriction. Here are your papers.'

'I certainly shan't take any risks,' Savage said quickly. 'This is nothing to do with me. I'm Swiss and strictly neutral. I want to get out of here as soon as possible. Could you please let me have the permit soon?'

'I'll think about it. Thank you, Herr Savage. You can go now.' There was a flash of malice in his look as Savage got up. 'I'll see the Comtesse now.'

Vierken didn't send for her at once. He shuffled his papers and drew patterns on a note pad. Captain Kramm was sitting in the corner; he had taken a record of everything Savage had said. After a moment Vierken spoke to him.

'What's your opinion, Kramm?'

'He seems to be genuine. He's very Swiss.' There was a note of contempt in that last comment. 'He showed no sign of nerves, he didn't hesitate or contradict himself.'

'His story checks exactly,' Vierken said. 'If it weren't for that Swiss report I'd take him back to the Château Diane and let you talk to him. But he's a neutral and we can't afford to get rough with him. His firm vouched for him and gave this address. It can't be faulted.'

'He didn't like the questions about the woman,' Kramm said. 'You got a reaction there.'

'No,' Vierken said, 'he didn't like that at all. But that's not the issue. I thought he was lying when he said they weren't lovers.'

'I'm not so sure of that,' Kramm said. 'If you can't put pressure on him, perhaps you could use the woman against him. If you have any doubts.'

'I wish I had,' Vierken said. 'I wish I could find one hole in his story and I'd have them both face to face in the Château and see which one of them broke first. But there's nothing, Kramm. He came here as her lawyer and he's still here. He wouldn't be, if he was in any way connected with what happened to Brühl. Write out an exit permit and I'll sign it. The sooner he leaves here the better—I don't want any damned neutrals hanging round here, making complaints through the Red Cross.'

He looked down at his papers again. There was Minden's report. Minden's alibi. Vierken would have accepted it without more than a superficial check with the Comtesse, if she had not been Régine de Bernard's sister-in-law. Everything Régine had said about her was becoming emphasised in his mind. It was as if his presence in the Château had given the prejudice of his mistress a new substance.

His mental picture of Louise de Bernard hadn't prepared him for the attractiveness which was so evident. She wasn't the type that appealed to him. She would never submit, like Régine, or fawn in an ecstasy of excitement, when he asserted his supremacy over her. Régine had described a cold, arrogant woman, deluding an indulgent husband, a bitter anti-Nazi who had refused to cohabit with him because of his collaboration. Looking at her, and noting the mingled fear and loathing in her expression, Vierken believed every word of what Régine had told him. And this was the same woman with whom Minden said he had spent the night.

It didn't fit. It didn't fit with Louise de Bernard. Which meant that either Minden was lying or she was acting so completely out of character that it needed an explanation. He looked up; his lips were drawn tight, the pencil in his right hand tapped the desk.

'Right,' he said to Kramm. 'Let's have her in.'

. . . . .

'Why did you go to Major Minden's room?'

'I've told you. I wanted to make love.' He had asked her the question so many times in different forms, that she had no idea if she were repeating herself. Behind the desk he played with his pencil and narrowed his eyes at her. The light shone on the surface of his dark hair.

'I don't believe you. I don't believe he was with you last night. Why are you lying?'

'I'm not lying.' She thought her voice sounded calm, but she couldn't be sure. She had begun to shake after the first few minutes, and now it was part of her, sitting on the little French chair with its aubusson seat and back, wishing to God it had been made with arms. She shook and she answered; she could hear the other man moving behind her, taking notes.

'You hate us, Madame de Bernard, don't you? Why would you sleep with a German officer when you hate all Germans?'

'I don't hate anyone.' That sounded feeble, a hollow protest, made through fear.

'I know that's a lie too. I know you're anti-Nazi; I know you've turned against your own husband because you don't agree with his attitude. I know all about you.'

'That has nothing to do with it.' She glanced over her

shoulder; the mild young officer with glasses was watching her, his pencil suspended. He looked like a student at a lecture.

'You were overcome with love for the Major?'

'If you like to call it that.' The sweat was running down between her breasts; the front of her blouse felt damp.

'Why didn't you choose your husband? Or your cousin; he's a well set up man. Why not?'

'I'm not on good terms with my husband.'

'That's right,' Vierken said. 'You hate Germans so much you won't go to bed with your husband because he's a collaborator. I find this very interesting, Madame. Don't you, Kramm?'

Louise glanced back at the young man. He was smiling at his superior. He didn't say anything.

'Are you sleeping with M. Savage?'

'No.' She raised one hand to her face, her fingers were trembling. 'No, I'm not.'

'Only with Major Minden?'

'Yes.' She saw Vierken get up from the desk and panic leaped inside her. Calm. Stay calm. Don't let him see your hands are shaking. Sit still. Think of the children, think of Papa lying helpless upstairs, of Jean and Savage—all their lives depend on you . . . He's coming round the desk to face me. They haven't hurt me yet but I know they're going to; it's coming very near. There's pain and violence in the room. I sense it in that man with the notepad, right behind me. If he moves . . .

'I don't believe you,' Vierken said. He put out a hand and caught Louise by the hair. She winced. He jerked her head back, pulling until the tears ran down her face. Behind them Kramm had laid down his notebook. 'I don't believe you went to bed with Major Minden,' Vierken said. 'Why are you lying?' He gave a vicious jerk that forced a cry of pain from her. It felt as if the hair were being torn out of her scalp.

'I'm not,' she said, almost sobbing. 'I'm telling the truth . . . Oh God, you're hurting me!'

'Kramm—she says I'm hurting her. She hasn't felt your soothing touch yet.' Just as suddenly he released her. Louise fell forward. She kept her balance and clung to the chair.

Vierken stepped away; he half turned his back and lit a cigarette. 'Kramm,' he said. 'Take her blouse off.'

'No!' Louise sprang up. 'No! Don't touch me.'

At a signal from Vierken the young officer paused.

'Tell me the truth,' Vierken said quietly. 'Otherwise he'll strip you naked and I shall personally put a match to your pubic hair. You didn't sleep with Major Minden, did you? You're giving him some kind of alibi, aren't you?'

'No.' Louise collapsed back into the chair. She raised a face streaming with tears. 'I did sleep with him. I'll tell you the truth—I'll tell you why I did it! I haven't had a man for two years—I was all right till he came here. Then he started looking at me—wanting me. He'd brush against me, try to touch me. It was driving me mad! In the end I couldn't help myself. I went to his room last night. I went in and begged him to take me! And I hate him! I hate all of you!'

She hid her face in her hands. If they don't believe me this time—if I haven't been convincing . . . Oh God, don't let that creature touch me . . .

'Like a bitch on heat,' Vierken said. 'But then all American women are whores. Do you feel like it now—I'm sure Kramm will oblige, won't you, Kramm? Come and put your hand up Madame's skirt, she'd like that.'

'Please.' Louise shrank back in terror. 'Please . . . I told you.'

'I know,' Vierken said. 'And now I believe you.' His look was full of contempt. Women of her type had always irritated him with their unconscious air of equality, even superiority. She hadn't been too difficult to break; the sight of her miserable weeping gave him satisfaction. He enjoyed seeing her humbled, degraded. And he believed her. So much for Régine's independent sister-in-law, the rich American who had bought herself a crumbling château and a useless title. She sat crying and trembling, revealed as a slut who couldn't control her own appetites. Vierken was content. Suddenly he had lost interest in her. Tormenting her now would be a waste of time. And he hadn't time to waste in letting Kramm play games. 'Go into the cloakroom through there,' he said. 'And wash your face. Don't try and pretend we've hurt you. Hurry up!' Inside the little room Louise held on to the basin for support, seeing her own reflection in the mirror. It was white and her mouth trembled. She cupped some water in her hands and splashed her face. The top of her head felt raw and burning. She shivered. It had been so close, so terribly close. And Savage was right. She wouldn't have held out. If that man had touched her, taken off her clothes . . . For a second the little room reeled. Then she steadied herself. It was over. She hadn't failed them. There was a little ivory brush and comb; she brushed her hair back and composed herself. She came back into the room and waited. Vierken was sitting on the edge of the desk. He waved his cigarette at her. 'You can go, Madame de Bernard. Kramm, go and talk to the servants. Look in on the old man.'

'Oh please,' Louise begged, 'please don't, he'll be so worried—he's senile and he doesn't understand . . .'

'Shut your mouth,' Kramm said. He had an unexpectedly loud, harsh voice. It was the first time he had spoken. He jerked his head towards the door. 'You heard the Standartenführer. Get out!'

Louise stumbled past them through the door, and into the salon. There was an S.S. man on duty there now. He pointed to the dining room.

'In there. And no talking!'

As she came in, both Jean and Savage sprang up. Another S.S. man swung his carbine round and pointed it. 'Don't move! Stay where you are!' Louise looked instinctively at Savage. He didn't draw back at the threat; instead his whole body tensed, balancing for the assault. Involuntarily, Louise cried out.

'No—don't do anything—for God's sake! I'm all right.' For a moment Savage and the German confronted each other. Before either of them could move, Jean de Bernard had come straight to her and taken her in his arms.

'Sit down,' he murmured to her. 'Come over here.'

Instantly the guard was standing over them, menacing with his carbine. 'No talking!' he shouted. 'Go back to where you were!'

Jean de Bernard looked up at him. 'I am staying with my wife,' he said. For a second or so the German stared at him; then he turned and went back to his position by the door.

Louise found her husband's hand holding hers and his arm protectively round her shoulders. It was a sensation she suddenly remembered.

In the salon Adolph Vierken paused to pour himself a drink of wine from a decanter on one of the side tables. He had discovered nothing. Minden's alibi for the night was genuine; much as he would have liked to find a discrepancy in Roger Savage's credentials, they were faultless. There was nothing to keep him at the Château St. Blaize; he drank the wine, his attention caught by the exquisite engraving on the glass. It was a coat of arms with many quarterings. These were the people to whome Régine had not dared introduce him; the spineless French aristocrat with his armorial drinking glasses and his subservience to the conqueror, the moneyed American wife who had collapsed in frightened tears.

Vierken allowed himself a moment of congratulation. He had put them into their right perspective, these superior people. He felt a sharp regret that nothing suspect had come out in the investigation. Régine was different; she was not one of them. She belonged to his world, to him. On an impulse of spite he aimed the empty glass at the fireplace and smashed it to smithereens. He went into the hall, shouted for Kramm, who reported that there was nothing gained from the old servants or the invalid Comte. Vierken drew out a piece of paper and gave it to the Captain.

'Give that to the Swiss. Tell him to be out of St. Blaize by tomorrow or the pass will be revoked. I don't want any neutral hanging around here. The less witnesses we have the better. Give it to him now, and make sure he understands it's only valid for twenty-four hours!' Kramm saluted and went out; when he came back Vierken was already pulling on his gloves.

'He understands,' Kramm said. 'I made it clear to him.'

'Good. There's nothing more to be done here.'

'Pity about the American woman,' Kramm said.

'There'll be others,' Vierken said. 'Come on.' Minutes later their cars were sweeping down the drive, their headlights scarring the darkness.

'What happened?' Savage was beside her. 'You've been crying—what did they do to you?' He seemed unaware of

Jean de Bernard. She felt her husband's arm tighten around her. She got up, freeing herself.

'Nothing happened,' she said. 'Thank God. You were right,' she said to Savage. 'If it had got bad, I wouldn't have held out. I know that now.'

'That isn't true,' Jean de Bernard said. 'You were born with courage.' Looking from Savage to him, she felt an impulse to escape them both, to take the shock trembling inside her to some private place.

'I want to go to the children. I don't want them to be frightened. I'm quite all right. The main thing is, they've gone.' She went out and upstairs to the children's bedroom. Savage turned to Jean de Bernard.

'They've gone, but I'm damned certain they'll be back. I want to talk to you alone.'

'Yes,' Jean de Bernard said. 'I think the time has come for that. He gave you a pass. Why?'

'I have a nasty feeling he wants me out of St. Blaize,' Savage said. 'Me and anyone else who might be able to carry tales.' He took a cigarette. 'That's what I want to talk to you about. He picked out Louise tonight; I don't like it. And there's something else you should know. He's pretty friendly with your sister!'

'Régine! I don't believe it . . .'

'He told me,' Savage said. 'He knows her well; and she told him about all of us; me, Louise—the whole family. You'll have to watch out for her.'

'My God,' Jean de Bernard said. 'With a man like that . . .' "I've met someone—he's a German . . ." He remembered Régine saying that and the expression of defiance on her face. An S.S. commander. It was unthinkable. As unthinkable as Savage's allegation that she informed upon them. He saw the American looking at him and the contempt in his eyes, for him and for his sister. He turned away. 'Things have worked out very well for you,' he said. 'You can leave tomorrow; with the Gestapo's blessing.'

'I want to take Louise with me. She can't get out on this pass; that means I ask London to send a pick-up plane. I don't want to leave her here. Whatever your sister said about her, that bastard's got it in for her. She ought to go to England.'

'I see,' Jean de Bernard said. 'And have you asked her?'

'Yes, and she won't go. She won't leave you and the children. I hope you'll persuade her.'

'Then you're not going to use your pass?'

'Not if I can take Louise with me. And I tell you, she should go. They won't pin anything on you. If they are going to take hostages, my guess is you won't be considered. You're part of the pro-German establishment here, and your sister has made herself a very influential friend. But Louise is different. She's an American and she's known to be hostile to them. They just might take her. You can manage without her here.'

'Persuade her to leave with you . . .' Jean said slowly. 'You'd like that, wouldn't you? You've wanted her from the beginning. It would suit you very well to have her in England where you could take her away from me permanently. You must think I'm an imbecile!'

Savage felt a rush of anger so intense that it was hatred. 'You stupid bastard! You'd rather she played games with Vierken? I'll take her with me and you won't stop me!'

'You make any attempt to touch my wife,' Jean de Bernard said, 'and I'll kill you. I warned you before.'

'You wouldn't kill me,' Savage jeered. 'You wouldn't bloody dare,' he went on. 'But you'd sneak round to your pals the Gestapo and tell them who I really was—you wouldn't mind doing that, would you? That'd be more in character.'

'I have already thought of that,' Jean de Bernard said. 'Do you think I'd protect you, if I could save French lives and stop them punishing this village? But you've involved Louise; if they got you, that would come out. You think you're so brave and so tough, Monsieur Savage? A big, brutish American who knows all the tricks—you'd be crying like a child after they'd had you for an hour or two. You'd betray Louise and be glad to do it.'

Savage stepped close to him. 'Shut your mouth,' he said. 'Or I'll shut it for you.'

'Violence is your only answer.' Jean didn't move. 'To break and kill. You have more in common with the Germans than you know. I shan't denounce you because of my wife.

And I shall do whatever I think best to protect her. Turn out the lights when you leave.' He left Savage standing there.

Louise heard the door of her bedroom open and sat up. 'I want to talk to you,' Jean said. 'Can I come in?'

He sat on the edge of the bed, looking at her.

'I've been talking to Savage,' he said. 'He wants you to go to England with him. I think you should go.' Her hand was close to him, lying on the bedcover, the gold wedding ring circling one finger. He wanted to reach out and touch it.

'I'm not going,' she said quietly. 'I'm not leaving the children. Or you. He knows that.'

'Would you mind leaving me?'

This was the man I loved, she remembered, this was the man I left my country and my family for, the man who conceived our children in this bed. He's older and tired, and I know he's pleading. If I cry now, I'm a damned fool.

'Yes, Jean. I'd mind very much.'

'I'm glad,' he said. 'I'm glad you don't hate me. We had so much happiness till this filthy war. I love you; I shall never stop. But you're in danger and I'd rather lose you to him, than let you take a risk. Go with him.'

She shook her head. 'No, I'm very frightened; I have a feeling that something terrible is going to happen to us all. And we must all be together. You and I and Papa and the children; here at St. Blaize.' He caught hold of her hand; his was unsteady.

'Don't say that,' he begged her. 'It isn't true. These feelings mean nothing—it's just a reaction from what happened tonight. I heard something, something so shameful . . . I don't know how to tell you about it.'

'Go on.' Her hand had gripped his; she knew its pressure well, as well as she recognised the embrace of his arm when he rushed to her that evening. They had been very close for many years.

'Régine informed on us to the Gestapo.' He spoke slowly, not looking at her now. 'She knows that man Vierken; he told Savage. She must know him very well. He knew all about Savage being here.'

'I can't believe it,' Louise said. 'An S.S. commander—how could she . . .'

'I don't know,' Jean de Bernard said. 'But I can't deny my own example. I set the pattern; she followed it. You would say it was a punishment, wouldn't you?'

'Not now,' Louise said gently. 'I might have said it before but not any longer. It was easy for me to take the attitude I did. I wanted you to be heroic, the brave Comte de Bernard, shouting defiance from the battlements. I didn't visualise the reality. Now I've seen it. I felt it in our little study. I saw it on their caps; the symbol of death. You tried to keep it away from St. Blaize and from us. You failed. I wouldn't judge you any more. I only hope you won't judge me.'

He kissed her fingers. 'I admire you,' he said. 'You're brave and you have a proud heart. You were ashamed of me, and I can understand it. One day I shall ask you to forgive me.'

'If you can forgive me,' Louise said quietly. 'We've been enemies, haven't we? Now we're facing God knows what. Jean, there's something I've got to tell you. I want to get things straight between us. I got the key from Minden. I gave it to Savage.'

Her hand dropped out of his.

'Why should he give it to you?'

'He didn't. I got it when he was asleep. I put it back before he left me.'

She watched him turn away; he fumbled in his pocket for cigarettes and lit one, cupping the flame in his hands.

'You slept with him?'

'Yes. It was the only way. I want you to know it was the worst thing I've ever done in my life. It was nauseating, horrible. That's why they kept me so long tonight. He'd given me as an alibi. That man didn't believe I'd been with him. He kept on and on trying to catch me out. He knew I was anti-Nazi; he kept saying—you hate Germans.'

'I see.' Jean de Bernard examined his cigarette. 'I understand. Régine must have told him everything about you.' He sounded calm, but he wouldn't look at her.

'I didn't want to lie to you,' Louise said. 'You came to me in good faith, you wanted to make things up. You won't want to now, but at least I haven't cheated you. I did it, because Savage had to get that key. I thought of the children, children like ours, dying of that gas, and it didn't seem important whether I let one man make love to me or not. I'm sorry, Jean. I know you don't look on it the same way.'

'Savage . . . ?' he asked her, looking at her for the first time. 'Savage and you . . .'

'No,' she said. 'Not Savage. I promise you that.'

He blew smoke upwards, and suddenly he gave the cigarette to her. 'It's my last,' he said. 'We'll share it.' With the half-smoked end between her lips, Louise began to cry.

. . . . .

The following day was overcast; early in the morning there was a shower, brief but heavy. Paul and Sophie de Bernard left for school in Minden's car as usual, wrapped in their oilskins. He stood in the vaulted hall, ill at ease and irritable, while Louise kissed them goodbye and pretended not to notice him.

He wanted to talk to her, to make another effort to convince her that he was not responsible for the S.S. or for what had happened the night before. He had slept badly, struggling with the ache of his desire to make love to her again. He felt helpless and misjudged; he stood about in the hallway, until the children had gone.

'Good morning.' He had placed himself in her way. 'I hope you're feeling better.'

'Yes, I'm quite all right now, thank you.' Louise moved to step past him, but he blocked the door.

'Don't be angry with me. I couldn't sleep last night, I was so upset about you.'

'That's very kind of you.' Jean de Bernard had come up beside him. He took his wife by the arm. 'My wife is quite recovered now.' As Minden watched him, he kissed Louise on the cheek. In six months, Minden had never seen them touch each other. He saluted, his face turning red, and left the hall. Ten minutes later he was in his car, now empty of the children and on his way to the Château Diane. He couldn't get that proprietary kiss out of his mind.

At St. Blaize itself the day passed quietly; Louise spent the morning with her father-in-law. He was in bed, complaining that he felt too tired to get up and dress; bad weather depressed him. He didn't want to read or play his gramophone, so she offered to read to him. He watched her from his pillows, his eyes changing focus as they slid to objects round the room. She had a soothing voice and her company was a comfort. He felt an atmosphere in the house which he didn't understand, but which disturbed him. The children had babbled excitedly of Germans being in the Château, an S.S. officer had paid him a visit—already the Comte was confused about its purpose. Old Marie-Anne, who had never been a favourite member of his staff in the old days, insisted on sitting in his room in spite of his request to go away. That morning his son had come to him, and he too seemed different, anxious and more solicitous than usual. The old Comte decided that the reason for it all must be himself, and sank into a fit of petulant despair. He decided he was ill and therefore dying and could not get up.

After Louise had been with him a little while, his mood had changed. He felt comforted and safe, petted by everybody. He reached a thin hand across the bed and squeezed hers, his mouth curved into a smile. When she put down the book she saw he was still smiling and asleep. The room was very still; the smell was a mixture of the slight fustiness of age, and the fresh scent of soap and cologne from his morning blanket bath. Marie-Anne looked after him like a child; she didn't seem to notice that he disliked her and was querulous and petty. He looked very old, his hair so white and thin that it was hardly visible against the linen, the blue veins on his forehead pulsing under the tight skin.

Soon death would come to him; Louise put the book away and sat still for a moment. Death would be dignified and peaceful, he would leave the world in gentleness with love supporting him to the end. A different kind of death would come to St. Blaize. A harsh staccato, bullets tearing through flesh, the crack of pistol shots along the line of fallen figures . . . The nightmare came at her in the silent room, and she fought unavailingly against it. When would they make the first arrest? Had anyone been taken from St. Blaize already? In God's name, she asked out loud, why couldn't Savage have gone that day instead of having another day and night to wait . . . ?

She got up and the movement woke her father-in-law. He

stirred and his eyes opened, filmed with age and sleep.

'Louise? Louise . . .'

'I'm here, Papa. You slept for a while.'

She pulled the sheet straight; his eyes watched her.

'Where are the children?'

'They're at school. It's not lunch time yet. Go back to sleep; there's something nice for your lunch.'

'Not an omelette,' he said. 'I had one yesterday.'

'Veal,' Louise said gently. 'Jean Pierre got a small cut specially for you. You'll like that.'

'Yes.' He brightened at the idea of food. He pulled himself upright. 'I'm so sick of eggs. Thank you for reading to me, my dear. The sleep was good for me; I'm feeling better.'

'I'm glad, Papa.' She leaned over and kissed his forehead. 'Perhaps you'll get up this afternoon.'

'I think I will,' he said. 'Then Paul and Sophie can come and play up here. When will they be home?'

'About four o'clock. The usual time. I'll bring them up to you.'

The hours passed and the Comte de Bernard got up and dressed to wait for his grandchildren. Four o'clock came; he matched his pocket watch with the chimes of the bracket clock and they were in unison. He had a poor sense of time, but it seemed a short interval till he looked at his watch again and saw that it was long past five. And still the children didn't come.

. . . . .

There was no work for Minden to do. He and the rest of Brühl's staff were confronted with the wreckage that remained in the flooded cellar; the most cursory examination showed that nothing usable had survived. The worst tragedy from their point of view was the loss of the documentation. A massive filing cabinet, indexed and cross-referenced, containing nearly three years of experimental data and the latest developments on Formula XV had been penetrated by the water, and the contents were a congealed, sodden mess. At a conference called by Vierken at eleven o'clock that morning, it was decided to close down Brühl's section and return his staff to Germany. The Führer himself had ordered that the work should be resumed under the leadership of another scientist with a headquarters in the Fatherland. It was a useless decision, and Minden recognised its futility. He and his colleagues were given twenty-four hours to pack up, and issued with special passes, signed by Vierken without which not even an officer of the Wehrmacht could leave the area. The atmosphere in the mess at the Château Diane was gloomy; there was little conversation, except among the S.S. officers, who seemed in excellent spirits. Watching them, Minden supposed that, unlike himself, their activities were just beginning. He was sitting next to the red-headed Major who had questioned him the previous day. The Major was enjoying the food and the splendid wines and he was expansive, trying to talk to the disconsolate army officers and getting little response.

'You're going home, I hear,' he said to Minden.

'Yes. We're all leaving tomorrow morning.'

'Better than sticking around here,' the Major said. 'Nothing for you to do now.'

'No,' Minden answered.

'We won't be here long either.'

'Oh? Have you caught the murderer?'

'Not yet; we've searched all the villages, we've questioned hundreds of people. No doubt he came from St. Blaize—that's where the plane was circling and where the car came from. They haven't turned anyone in. But by tonight they'll change their tune!'

'Why? What are you going to do?' Minden didn't really want to know; he didn't want to talk at all. The question was a reflex and immediately he wished he hadn't asked.

'Operation Herod,' the S.S. Major said. He laughed; several of the other S.S. officers joined in. 'I'll give the Standartenführer credit for a sense of humour. He thought of the name for it.'

'What does it mean? Operation Herod . . .'

'Think about it; didn't you ever read the Bible?' There was a general laugh at this; the S.S. Major tipped his chair back and raised his wine glass.

'We'll teach the swine a lesson! They won't be so eager to help the English after this . . .'

'I don't understand,' Minden said. 'Operation Herod. There were several Herods.'

'It's a riddle.' The Major leaned towards him. 'I'll give you a clue. It's not the one that pissed himself over Salome!'

Minden didn't finish his lunch. He took a piece of cheese and cut it into squares, waiting until the senior officer present gave the signal to leave the table. He went outside and smoked a cigarette; the sun was shining and he walked slowly down a short avenue of trees to a stone seat. It faced a small fountain which no longer operated. The water in the basin was a stagnant pool a few inches deep, and the lead dolphin with two rollicking putti on his back was crusty with dried slime.

Herod. Minden threw his cigarette away. He knew the Bible well. Herod the Tetrarch had cut off the head of John the Baptist. Herod, King of Judea, had ordered the massacre of the children. Operation Herod. He looked at the putti, plump and joyous, riding the dolphin's back, and felt a surge of nausea, so strong that he choked into his handkerchief. The children. The children of St. Blaize. That was what they were going to do. Not hostages, not a few hundred adult males to be shot, but the children. 'By tonight they'll have changed their tune.' Tonight. His hands and neck were clammy, the hair stuck to his forehead. Hostages were logical; an enemy population had to be disciplined or no German soldier could walk the streets. Minden accepted that. He approved of it. If he had seen the mayor of the village and the priest and the doctor and anyone else in authority die he wouldn't have thought twice about them. But children. Sophie and Paul de Bernard.

'Major Minden—come and play ball . . . Major Minden, this is my drawing I did at school today . . .' The feel of a hand clutching on to his; Sophie sitting on his knee with her arms round his neck.

And the boy, the brave, open-natured child that reminded him of his own sons, the boy who didn't look at him with fear or hostility. Who accepted him and admired him. Tonight, that butcher had said, with his pansy laugh. Minden stood up. He wiped his hands and face and fastened the top of his collar. It was two-thirty-eight; by three o'clock he was in the back seat of his army car, the pass signed by Vierken in his briefcase, travelling at top speed towards St. Blaize en Yvelines.

. . . . .

The teacher was a widow; she had been born in St. Blaize, the daughter of the village notary, and married in 1940. Her husband had been killed during the German advance, and she had returned to her job at the school, a woman already old at twenty-six. There were twenty children in class that afternoon headed by the daughter of Camier, the Mayor, she was a clever child of eleven, responsible and studious, the idol of her family. Michele Giffier, the teacher, was in the middle of a geography lesson; she was unwilling to let Paul and Sophie de Bernard leave with the German officer. Her first reaction had been refusal; the officer appeared so agitated that she became afraid. But she accepted his explanation that their mother had sent for them, her reluctance overcome by the children's delighted welcome when they saw him, and at three-forty-one exactly they left the school building and climbed into the Major's car. Both children threw their arms round him; Sophie smudged a kiss on the side of his face. Even Heinz the driver looked over his shoulder and muttered something friendly.

'Why are we going home?' That was Paul, always the practical one. 'What does Mama want us for?' Minden was very pale; he looked grim and the children stared at him, suddenly anxious. 'What's the matter?' Paul said. On an impulse Minden put an arm round each of them.

'Nothing,' he said. 'Nothing's the matter, little ones.' The driver started the car and as it moved down the street there was a harsh engine roar from behind them. Minden looked back. An armoured car, the iron crosses painted black and white on its sides, was pulling up outside the school. S.S. troops armed with submachine guns spilled out of the back and ringed the building. Minden gripped the children tightly. Minutes; there had only been minutes to spare.

'Home, Heinz,' Sophie called out. 'Home please, Heinz.'

'We're not going home,' Minden said. 'We're going to have a surprise. We're going to Paris to see your Aunt Régine.'

. . . . .

'Cries and lamentations filled the land,' remarked the biblically minded Major. 'It was Rachel mourning her children.' He grinned and lit a cigarette. A ring of S.S. troops encircled the school; the entrance was blocked by the armoured car. The machine gun mounted in its turret swung slowly round, sweeping across the crowd which was gathered outside the school, kept back by the automatic weapons of the troops. There was a noise, a cry without words, coming from the mass of people, men and women of all ages. Fear, pleading, agony, frustration. The major saw Vierken arrive in a staff car; he spat the cigarette out and sprang to attention. The crying sound stopped suddenly; in silence Vierken stepped out of his car, flanked on each side by S.S. guards with guns at the ready. It was nearly sunset. He walked to the armoured car and stopped in front of it. There was a rush from the crowd.

The Standartenführer didn't move; he knew his men. They wouldn't be allowed to get near. He saw a small, fat man with a grey head, struggling with one of the soldiers, arguing and begging. The man turned to him and shouted.

'I am the Mayor! Let me speak to you, sir! For the love of God, let me talk to you!' Vierken made a signal. Albert Camier came stumbling forward; his pace suggested that he might fall on his knees. His face was streaked with tears.

'Standartenführer—why have you done this? Why are the children under guard? What have they done?'

'The children, Monsieur Le Maire, are quite innocent,' Vierken said. 'Unfortunately, it is often the lot of the innocent to suffer for the guilty. You are all guilty here.'

'But we've done nothing,' Camier cried out. 'Nothing!'

'You harboured a murderer, a saboteur,' Vierken said. 'He was dropped here and sheltered; by someone. Now you are going to be punished. I'm going to make an example of the people of St. Blaize.' He turned, as if there was nothing more to say. Camier seized his sleeve; his eyes were wild, his mouth slack and quivering.

'My daughter is in there. Let her go. Shoot me; shoot any of us, as many as you like! But for the love of Christ, let the children out!'

Vierken pointed to him. 'Put him back in the crowd. And bring me the hailer.'

When he began to speak there was a shiver and then silence from the crowd. Some of the women had been sobbing hysterically; even this was stilled.

'People of St. Blaize.' Vierken's voice came loud through the speaker. 'Two German officers have been murdered. A serious act of sabotage has been committed. We know that the criminal responsible for this was harboured in your area. He has not been found and no one has come forward. Therefore, it has been decided to punish you. You have shown yourselves enemies of the Reich, and while it would suit you to see a few of your fellow citizens shot for this outrage, this is not enough. You are going to learn that German blood is precious. German property is precious. As precious as your children. As a reprisal for your treachery, the children of this village are going to be deported to Germany. You will never see them again.' He put the hailer down and turned back to his car. There was a scream, one high-pitched shriek from the middle of the crowd; a woman fought to the front and ran at him, both hands outspread, the fingers curved into claws; she was screaming incoherently. Vierken paused for a moment. There was a single shot, and she fell, sprawling face downward. The revolver in his hand had a thin wisp of smoke curling round its barrel.

'Anyone attempting to go to the school building is to be shot.' Vierken gave his order to the Major. 'Nothing and no one is to be allowed inside or out.'

'What about the teacher? She's in there with them.'

'Leave her there. When the transport has come from Paris, she can go with them. Keep the men alert; they may try to attack when it's dark.'

'And if they do, Standartenführer?'

Vierken looked at him as if he had said something stupid.

'Set fire to the school. But let them know what'll happen if they start any resistance. I don't want a pitched battle here. I want an orderly operation, properly carried out. Heil Hitler!'

'Heil Hitler!'

Jean and Louise de Bernard had been waiting at the back of

the crowd. Jean had refused to be drawn into the hysteria. reminding himself that Paul and Sophie were inside the building and that shooting or violence must be avoided. He had his arm round Louise; she was silent, glazed with shock. 'They're all right,' he said to her. 'Nothing's happened to them. Nothing will happen.'

Louise turned to look at him. Tears were running down her face. 'You heard him; they're going to be taken away. He said we'd never see them again . . .' She was close to hysteria and Jean had seen one woman die already.

'It's a threat,' he whispered. 'They won't carry it out. It's just bluff. My darling, calm yourself now. This is blackmail. I am going to see him and find out the position. Then we'll make up our minds.'

'I want the children,' Louise said. 'I want the children back. I'll give myself up!'

'Hush,' Jean said gently. 'We'll get them. We'll get all the children back. I'll take you home and then I'm going to the Château Diane.' He had decided to wait, to judge the reaction of Vierken to the crowd. What he saw hadn't reassured him, but he still believed it possible to talk reasonably with the man when they were in private. The S.S. were putting on a show of strength for the people of St. Blaize. Alone, Vierken would take a different attitude. He stood watching the staff car reverse and drive away. The crowd waited, numbed; no one had moved to pick up the woman who lay dead in the road. 'Come home,' he urged Louise. 'There's nothing to do here now.'

'No. No . . .' She shook her head and pulled away from him. 'I'm not leaving here . . .' He was still arguing with her when a woman came through the crowd and ran up to him, grabbing his coat. She stood in front of him, her face contorted with hate.

'You bastard! You dirty collaborationist bastard! You got your brats out, didn't you?'

'No, Madame Barzain,' Jean said quietly. She was the wife of St. Blaize's carpenter. 'No, I didn't. Paul and Sophie are inside with the others.' Louise was staring at the woman, who didn't seem to see her. She was glaring at the Comte, her eyes wild.

'You filthy liar,' she screeched at him. 'I saw them leave the school—just before the S.S came! I saw that German from the Château come and take them away in his car! You knew what was going to happen, didn't you—you saved your own but you never warned us!'

'What do you mean—what German—who took them?' Without realising it, Jean de Bernard seized her by the arm. 'What are you talking about—for God's sake, woman, what did you see?'

'I saw them!' she shrieked. 'That German came to the school and took your children out! Just before the S.S. surrounded the others! I saw it—I'd come to collect my Pierre and Francine and I saw them go with him! God's curse on you, you filthy collaborationist pig!'

She drew her head back and suddenly spat at him. Louise gasped. Jean wiped his face with a handkerchief; Madame Barzain had begun to cry. He put his arm around Louise.

'If that's true,' he said, 'then my children are safe. But we knew nothing about it. We came down here like everyone else.'

'Minden,' Louise said; she felt dazed, too afraid to hope. 'It must have been Minden . . .' Marie Barzain looked at them and her hate died in her. The Comte didn't know beforehand. He hadn't cheated to save his own and left the rest of the village's children to fall victim to the Germans. She spoke to Louise.

'It was that Major,' she said. 'I know him by sight. He took your children away in his car.' She didn't look at the Comte.

'Before God,' Louise said to her, 'I swear we didn't know. I thought they were in there with the others. You shouldn't have done that to my husband. All he wants is to help you!'

'Forgive me,' Marie Barzain mumbled. 'Forgive me—I didn't mean it—they've got my little ones . . .'

'It doesn't matter,' Jean de Bernard said. He laid his hand on her shoulder. 'We must all do our best to get them out. Where is your husband?'

'In the crowd.' She began to sob. 'He's like a madman . . . Oh my God, Monsieur le Comte—what are we going to do?'

'I don't know,' he said gently. 'But they're not going to take our children away. Somehow we're going to stop them.

Go and find your husband and tell him to be calm. I shall go and see the S.S commander myself.'

'Oh, go now!' she begged him. 'Go right away—it'll be dark soon, they'll be so frightened!'

He turned to Louise. 'I'm going to talk to Camier and Father Duval. We must keep this crowd calm, or there'll be more shootings. Wait here; I'll come back and take you home.'

He found the Mayor comforting his wife; the priest came up to them. He was a big man, with a coarse peasant face and a heavy paunch. He had been curé of St. Blaize for thirty years, a typical provincial priest, looked after by a spinster niece; what he lacked in refinement was more than compensated by personal courage and a kind heart. He pushed his way through to Jean and the Mayor.

'What are we going to do? They can't do this—we can't stand by and let them take our children!'

'My Caroline,' Camier moaned. 'My little girl—my wife has fainted . . . Why have they done this—why, why? We never sheltered anyone!'

'Be calm,' Jean said. 'This is a punishment, a reprisal. But I don't believe they mean to do it. Father, I am going to see Standartenführer Vierken. I want you and the Mayor to come with me. We will be able to talk to him in private. I suggest that we offer our own lives and as many adults as he chooses as hostages instead of the children. I am prepared to pay a large fine, as well. We can give them men and money in exchange for the children. I think we will be able to strike a bargain.'

'They can have everything,' Carmier cried, 'everything I've got!'

'They can have *my* hide,' Father Duval said. 'And the church plate. That's all I've got. But you believe this, Monsieur le Comte? You think this is a bluff, to frighten us?'

'I am sure of it,' Jean said. 'What they're threatening is unthinkable. Nobody harms children. If we offer them a high enough price, we'll get the children back. I'm going to take my wife home, and then we should go to see this man. Are you agreed?'

'Yes,' the priest said.

Camier nodded. 'God knows I'm not a brave man. But to save my little girl—he can shoot me if he wants . . . I wouldn't want to live without her!'

'Good,' Jean said. 'Now Camier, tell the people we're going to plead with the S.S. commander. Tell them to be calm and wait here.'

The priest turned to him. 'Where is Madame? She must be terribly distressed—I'd like to speak to her.'

'She's waiting for us,' Jean answered. 'But she's all right. Our children are not in the school.'

'They're safe?' Father Duval stared at him. 'And you're going to stand as a hostage?'

'My first duty is to my family, Father. The second is to the people of St. Blaize. The fact that my children are not in danger alters nothing. We should go now.'

. . . . .

Jean de Bernard's aunt had lived in Paris since her husband's death. For twenty-three years she had been mistress of a large seventeenth-century château and an estate in the Loire Valley. Her husband was not concerned with the smart world to which his wife aspired. He was older by ten years and devoted to his home and his life in the country. The Baronne de Cizalle saw very little beyond the Loire valley until his death released her. She had relinquished her château to her son and a stalwart daughter-in-law who was obviously longing to manage it, and bought herself an apartment on the Rue St. Honoré. She didn't approve of Germans, but she was polite when she met them, since only the better connected officers came into her circle, and she ignored the unfortunate weakness some of her younger friends betrayed for handsome members of the Herrenvolk. To her credit, Pauline de Cizalle had never received the S.S. or actively courted the conquerors herself. So far as a member of her family was concerned, like Régine, she would have rigidly opposed any close relationship. She was dressing to go out to dinner when Minden arrived at her flat with the children. She heard the voices, and sent her maid to see who it was; the maid was followed by Paul and Sophie who rushed forward to embrace their aunt. Both children were too excited to explain why they were there. The Baroness hurried through the rest of her toilette and came into the salon. She paused at the sight of her neice Régine and a German officer, both looked strained and Régine positively stricken. There was a moment of awkward silence; her niece seemed disinclined to introduce the caller or even to speak at all. The Baroness collected herself and advanced upon the German, her hand outstretched, a polite if chilly smile upon her face.

Minden clicked his heels together and kissed her hand.

'Major Heinz Minden, Madame. Forgive this intrusion.'

'Not at all. I believe you've brought my nephew's children with you. I wasn't expecting them.

'You couldn't have been told.' Régine spoke suddenly. 'The telephones at St. Blaize have been cut off. The whole area is under siege.'

The Baroness forgot her social manners. 'My God! What's happened?'

Régine looked at Minden. 'You tell her,' she said. 'Tell her what you told me.'

'There's been two murders and sabotage,' he said. 'The S.S. have moved in and taken control. I brought Paul and Sophie to you for safety.'

'Safety?' Régine watched her aunt's well-pencilled eyebrows raise. She seemed bewildered. 'What do you mean, safety? What have the children got to do with the S.S.? There aren't any Jews there, are there?'

'No, Madame,' Minden answered her. He felt a pang of dislike, and he didn't know why. 'This doesn't concern Jewish children. It's been decided to punish the people of St. Blaize by taking their children. I don't know whether they're going to kill them or send them to an extermination camp. I just got Paul and Sophie out in time.' He made a gesture with one hand. 'I didn't know where else to take them.'

'Sit down, Major Minden.' It was Régine who suddenly took control. She looked plainer than he had ever seen her; the determination on her face made her look ugly. 'Sit down and tell us everything. Has anything happened to my brother? And my father?'

'Nothing,' Minden said. 'The S.S. came last night and questioned everybody, but they went away. They haven't found the saboteur, and they don't expect to now. The commanding officer is going to make an example of St. Blaize. I only heard it this afternoon. Operation Herod, that's what it's called. I couldn't warn your family; there wasn't time and anyway they'd have come to the Château to take the children. I just got to the school before the S.S. surrounded it.'

'Thank you,' Régine said slowly. 'Thank you, Major Minden.'

'This is so terrible,' her aunt stammered. 'I just can't believe it. I can't.'

'Nor could I,' Minden said. 'We've had to do many things, Madame, many harsh, regrettable things. But never this. Never using children as hostages. All I can say is that it's not us, not the German army. It's the S.S. and this man they've sent to St. Blaize. Adolph Vierken. It's him, not us.'

'Did you say Vierken?' He glanced at Régine; he wondered whether he might ask for a drink.

'Yes. Standartenführer Adolph Vierken.'

'Régine—are we going to stay the night with you?' Paul de Bernard stood in the doorway, behind him Sophie's little figure flitted past as she ran down the passage. Régine de Bernard looked at him. 'Yes,' she said. 'You're going to stay here for tonight and maybe tomorrow. Go and see if there's some cake in the kitchen. Ask Juliette to give you some.' She shifted on one foot and brought herself back to face Minden.

'You're sure it's Vierken?'

'Certainly. I've spoken to him. He's in our headquarters. He came to the Château and questioned your family himself.'

'Yes,' Régine said slowly. 'I see. I suppose he was curious.'

'Régine you talk as if you know this man?' Her aunt was staring at her. So too was Minden. A painful smile appeared on her lips. 'Yes, Aunt Pauline. I know Adolph Vierken. Major, you say they've shut up all the children in the village?'

'That was the plan,' he said. 'I didn't try to find out details. They were surrounding the school with armed guards when I left. Mademoiselle de Bernard, I must leave very soon. I'm on my way back to Germany. That's how I was able to get the children out; I had a special pass allowing me to leave. I made them lie down in the back of the car. They thought it was a game.'

'Your driver knows,' Régine said. 'What about him?'

'He's fond of the little ones,' Minden said. 'I know that. He saw the S.S. coming to the school. He wouldn't do anything to hurt them.'

'I'd better see what they're doing. Excuse me . . .' The Baroness got up. He had saved the children's lives. She couldn't feel gratitude; she felt only loathing and horror. It was a relief to go out of the room.

When they were alone, Régine said, 'You say the area's closed. No one can get out. Or in?'

'No,' he answered her. 'It's sealed off. How did you know Adolph Vierken?'

'Through music,' Régine said. 'He's very musical. We met at a concert. I'm going to St. Blaize. Tonight.'

'You can't,' Minden insisted. 'You won't be let through. You might even be arrested. For God's sake don't attempt it.'

'I'm going to see him,' she said. 'I'm going to stop him doing this.'

'You? You think because you've met him a few times you can hope to influence . . .'

'I've been sleeping with him for months,' Régine broke in. 'He loves me. We love each other. He won't do this when I've talked to him. Say nothing to my aunt. I'll need your car. Will you lend it to me—just to get me there? Your driver can leave me at the first checkpoint and come back here. I'll make my own way after that. Vierken will send transport for me. Please. I know what I'm doing.'

'I don't think you do,' Minden said. 'I don't think anything you say will make any difference. I don't think he'll even see you.'

'You don't know him,' Régine said. 'And you certainly don't know me. He'll listen. It's the only chance to save the children. If he shoots every man in the village I don't care. It's their own damned fault for meddling. But not the children. That mustn't happen. Lend me the car.'

'Of course,' Minden said. 'If there's any chance at all—Fritz will take you as far as he can. I'll wait at the George V till he gets back.'

The Baroness had returned.

To Régine he said, 'I'll walk to the hotel, it's round the

corner. I'll instruct Fritz to drive you. Good luck. And goodbye.'

She held out her hand and he bent over it.

'If you get through, let your sister-in-law know where the children are. And give her my respects. I hope in spite of everything she may think kindly of me sometimes.' For a moment his eyes stung. Truth pierced him through. Louise had never loved him; the impulse which had brought her to his room was nothing but a sexual whim. Now she could only hate him and blame him for the horror which had overtaken St. Blaize. Even his rescue of her children wouldn't atone for what was being done by fellow Germans. He bowed to the Baroness. 'If I might see the children for a moment, Madame? Just to say goodbye.'

'Please,' she said. 'I'll call them.' The sight of him bending down embracing Sophie while Paul hung on his arm made her want to cry and at the same time she felt like dragging them away. He left the apartment, and she went into her bedroom. Régine had a small overnight case already packed.

'I'm going home,' Régine said. 'I think I can do something to help. Now, Aunt Pauline, don't argue with me, please. I'm going. If I can get through to you I will. But don't expect anything. I'll come back when I can. Take care of the children.' Then the door closed after her too. The Baroness telephoned her friends and explained that a violent headache prevented her from joining them for dinner.

. . . . .

'Are you going to give him up?' Louise asked him. For a moment Jean de Bernard hesitated. He didn't want to see the look of anguish on her face, or to admit how deeply she was committed to the other man. He didn't want to see it because of what that knowledge might do to his judgement.

'I don't know,' he said. 'I don't know what I'm going to do; it will depend upon Vierken.'

'I was ready to do it,' she said, 'but that was when I thought Paul and Sophie were shut up in that school. Now—now they're not . . . Oh God, where could Minden have taken them? Why didn't he bring them home?'

'Because the S.S. would have come and got them,' Jean said.

'He knew that and he's taken them somewhere they'll be safe. He wasn't a bad man, I told you that.'

'I know,' she said. 'I want you to promise me something.'

'Not to betray Savage—is that what you want?'

'Yes,' Louise said slowly. 'I wouldn't have said it like that but that's what I meant. Don't give him up to them.'

'I don't think I'll need to,' her husband said quietly. 'As soon as he knows I believe he'll surrender himself. If he doesn't—and the children are at stake, I can't give you any promise. I'm sorry.'

'We sheltered him,' Louise said. 'We're the guilty ones.'

'I know that,' he answered. 'And I shan't let the innocent suffer. I'm going now; try not to worry.' They were in her bedroom and he came close to her.

'Will you trust me to do the right thing? And before I go will you believe me when I tell you something?'

'What is it?' Louise said. He stood in front of her and his hands moved as if he wanted to reach out and hold her, but they stayed at his sides.

'I didn't betray the Palliers,' he said. 'Will you believe that?'

Suddenly her eyes filled with tears. 'Yes; if you say so I believe you now. Oh Jean, Jean!' She was in his arms, holding tightly to him, weeping with remorse and fear, fear for him and a greater fear for Roger Savage. He held her, soothing and gentle, tortured by the knowledge that the pain he was comforting was on behalf of someone else.

'I'm sorry,' she said. 'I'm sorry for what I've done to you. I didn't understand you and I didn't trust you. But I trust you now. You'll do what's right.'

'I'll do my best,' he said, and kissed her quietly on the lips.

Louise came downstairs to find Savage waiting for her. He had a drink in his hand, which was unusual; he never helped himself or presumed on Jean's hospitality. He looked pinched and dangerous. He came straight towards her. 'I know what's happened,' he said. 'Marie-Anne told me. They have four grandchildren in the school. Don't worry, darling. I'll sort this out.'

'Paul and Sophie got away,' she whispered. She shouldn't have leaned against him but her body was trembling and weak. His was warm and his hold was strong. 'Minden came and got them out before the school was surrounded. I can hardly believe it.'

'Bully for him,' he said. 'He'd have gassed them to death but he didn't fancy the S.S. having fun with them—the bastard! The lousy stinking bastards! Children—that's about their level. What did they say they're going to do with them?'

'Send them to Germany. They'll never be seen again, that's what Vierken said. He was at the school house. One of the mothers ran out and tried to attack him. He shot her dead.'

'Germany,' Savage repeated. 'That means an extermination camp. Come over here. Listen to me, will you?'

'Jean's gone over to see him,' she said. 'To plead with him.'

'He's wasting his time,' Savage said. 'You don't plead with men like Vierken. He'll take those children out of here and they'll be gassed or machine gunned. Jean knows this.' He lifted her face and looked at her. 'Has he gone to turn me in?'

'I begged him not to,' she whispered. 'I don't think he will. He promised to do what was best. Oh God, you mustn't let them take you!'

Savage stroked her hair, twisting one dark strand round his finger. 'There isn't any other way, sweetheart,' he said gently. 'If they don't get me, those kids at the school are as good as dead. I'm going to give myself up!'

'You can't,' she protested violently. 'You can't do that! You know what they'll do to you . . .'

'I have my exit here,' he said, touching the cuff link. 'Don't worry, they won't have their fun with me. But they'll let the children go; that's all that matters.'

'You have a pass,' Louise said slowly. 'You could walk out of here and go back to Switzerland. You carried out your mission and that's all you were asked to do. What happens after you've left is none of your business. That's what some men would say.'

'And some men could live with themselves afterwards, knowing they'd left a lot of children to die for them? Maybe, but not this man. I love you, you know that, don't you?'

'Yes,' she said, 'and I love you. I don't know what to say . . . Isn't there any other way?'

'No,' Savage said. 'There isn't. And we both know it. I never expected to get out of this anyway. Finding you made me want to survive it—that can't be helped. I wish we'd made love.'

'I wish we had too,' she said.

'Don't cry for me,' Savage told her. 'I hate to see you cry. It's going to be tough for you and Jean, talking your way out of it, but I'll square things as much as I can for you both. I can say I *am* your cousin, but the OSS recruited me in Switzerland and sent me here deliberately. You knew nothing about it. They may believe me. There's no reason why they shouldn't. It could have been the truth.'

She couldn't answer him; she held on to him blindly, overwhelmed by an agony only equalled by what she had felt when she believed her children were in danger.

'I don't care,' she said wildly. 'I don't care if they arrest me too!'

'Don't you say that!' He sounded angry. 'Don't you dare talk that way—I came into your life without any right. I'm going out of it. But there's a future here for all of you; the children growing up—the war will be over and these bastards will be beaten now, I promise you that. You'll have a good life, my darling.' He bent over her and smiled. 'You can name the schoolhouse after me,' he said.

'Aren't you afraid?' she whispered.

'No. In a way I've expected it to end like this. And I've got the pill. They won't hurt me, so you don't need to worry about that. It'll be just like dropping asleep. Snap!' His fingers clicked. 'Like that. I think I'll walk down to the school,' he said. 'They can send me to Vierken from there.'

'No, wait, wait!' Louise begged. 'Wait till Jean gets back—he may have persuaded him to let them go! Oh, please don't leave me! Don't go down there yet!'

It was a useless stay of the inevitable and she knew it; instinct made her plead, the dread of that awful goodbye as he left her and gave himself into the hands of the enemy. He talked smoothly of escaping their revenge, of taking a pill and finding a quick death. But there was no guarantee. If he made an attempt and he failed . . . Her imagination fled from the situation; overcome with horror she caught his arm and held it.

'Wait till Jean gets back,' she said. 'Then you can go.'

And Savage realised suddenly that if the Comte were there it would be easier to leave her. She wouldn't be alone. 'All right,' he said. 'We'll wait together. And you take a grip of yourself. I'm going to get us both a drink.'

It seemed a long time before they heard the sound of the car in the drive. Men's voices murmured outside in the hall. A few moments later Jean de Bernard walked into the room. Louise sprang up and ran to him.

'Jean—what happened? What did he say?'

'Nothing happened.' He spoke quietly. 'I went to see him with Camier and Father Duval; I begged him to let the children go. He refused.' He took out a cigarette and lit it; his hands shook badly.

'He'll let them go,' Savage said. 'I'm going to give myself up. Thanks for not doing it first.'

'You needn't thank me.' Jean looked at him. 'It won't be any use if you surrender to them. The children are going to Germany. Whatever happens.'

'But why?' Savage demanded. 'They want the killer—they said so!'

'They don't expect to get him. What they want is to make an example of St. Blaize. To punish the French civilian population for sheltering the enemy. I asked Vierken if he'd let the children go if they found the saboteur.' Jean looked at Savage. 'I was going to betray you. I'm sorry, but when I saw he meant to take them, I made up my mind. He pointed his pencil at me and said, "Comte de Bernard, if the man stood in my office now, I'd send those children out of St. Blaize. A cattle truck is on the way from Paris. By tomorrow night they leave. And no French village will shelter the enemy again without remembering the children of St. Blaize." Those were his words. We offered everything, including ourselves. Money, our lives, anything. He just laughed. He actually laughed. "Go home and make some more." I am going to kill him. I don't know how, but I am going to kill that man.' He lit another cigarette from the stub of the last.

'There's no use you sacrificing yourself,' he said to Savage. 'They'd kill you and then murder our children anyway. You'd only throw your life away for nothing.'

'Paul and Sophie,' Louise said slowly. 'Just think if they were being held in there!'

'We wouldn't be able to think straight,' Savage said suddenly. 'And by God, that's what we've got to do. A cattle truck, eh? That means they'll go by train. And that's better than by lorry. Much better. Where's the Mayor and the priest?'

'In the library. I asked them to wait. Camier is completely broken down. That girl is his only child.'

'Get them in here,' Savage said. 'Breaking down isn't going to save her. And that's what we're going to do. We're going to bloody well save them all.'

'How?' Louise asked him. 'How can we fight the S.S. They'll kill anyone who tries to go near the school. They've proved that already.'

'We've no arms, no ammunition, nothing,' Jean de Bernard said. 'But the people will fight, they'll fight with their hands.'

'They'll have guns,' Savage said. 'I promise you. Call the others in here.'

. . . .

It was dark and inside the school most of the small children had stopped crying and were asleep, stretched out over their desks. The older ones sat mute, staring at the S.S. guard who lounged against the door, his carbine slung from his shoulder. Madame Giffier, the teacher, moved through the classroom, checking each child. Some were sobbing and she paused to comfort them, others whispered questions and she did her best to answer cheerfully. There was no heating and towards seven o'clock she had made the children put on their coats. There had been a hideous outbreak of hysteria when the crowd outside began to gather and the children heard their parents' voices. Three S.S. guards had driven them back, knocking Michelle Giffier to the ground when she intervened. There was an ugly blotch on one side of her face and her mouth had bled. The sight of her bleeding, sprawled on the floor, so shocked the children that they quietened. Fear overcame them all. They cringed in their seats, whimpering and shivering. Several of the smallest wet the floor; one adolescent girl was sick. They had no food and only water from the toilet to drink. Michelle Giffier looked at her watch; it was past eight o'clock. They had been shut up for four hours. She got up and went to the guard at the door. She moved stiffly; the fall on the floor had bruised her back. Shaken but determined she spoke to the guard.

'The children haven't eaten since lunch time. They're freezing cold. Let me go out and get some food for them.'

'Go back and sit down.' The German glanced at her. 'Nobody leaves.'

'But please—please, they'll starve—you can't mean to keep them here without anything!'

He shifted his carbine up on its strap and leaning a little forward he pushed Michelle Giffier in the breast with the flat of his hand. She stumbled and fell. He watched her legs displayed as the skirt rucked up. She saw the look on his face and covered herself, biting back tears. She went back to her desk; it was the daughter of Albert Camier who came and put her arms around her.

'Pigs,' she whispered. 'Don't cry, Madame. We're not hungry. We're all right.'

'I can't do anything,' the teacher wept. 'It's so cold and so long for the little ones. They won't let me out!'

'Never mind,' Caroline Camier said. 'It won't be long. They'll let us go. Don't worry.' She glanced across at the S.S. man and on an impulse stuck out her tongue. Her proper-minded mother would have been horrified. By ten o'clock a crowd of men and women had settled down outside the school to wait. This was in defiance of the curfew, but the major in charge decided that it was useless to enforce it. It would provoke a riot, and the Standartenführer had made it plain he wouldn't be pleased if there were trouble. He wanted a tidy operation. The parents were allowed to sit down in the road and keep their vigil. Nobody moved; women wept and prayed, a group knelt saying the rosary, the men sat dumb and helpless, waiting in front of the barred doors and shuttered windows behind which their children were imprisoned. The Major had spoken once over the loud-hailer, warning against any attempt to rush the guards or approach the building. A rescue attempt or any disturbance would result in the school being set on fire. As he told them, his men were pouring kerosene round the outside walls. There was a single shuddering wail from the watchers and then silence. The dead woman, mother of five children held inside, had been taken away and a dirty stain marked the place where her body had lain. It grew colder; a very few of the old were taken away to their beds. The sound of the rosary continued through the night. In the school building itself the children slept, and so did Michelle Giffier. The guards on duty yawned and changed watches. The one who had pushed the teacher over and seen her thighs, occupied himself with lewd thoughts. By the morning the children were crying and hungry. Nothing, not even a loaf, was permitted to come in from St. Blaize.

. . . . . .

The guards at the checkpoint had kept Régine de Bernard for three hours. When she refused to be turned back they threatened to arrest her. A particularly aggressive NCO poked her in the side with his carbine. White faced, thin lipped, absolutely determined, she withstood them and demanded to be taken to see Vierken. Her confidence shook theirs; finally it was the NCO, anxious not to make a mistake with someone who claimed to know the Standartenführer, who put a call through on the field telephone to the Château Diane. Vierken was out. Régine settled down to wait. The NCO tried to telephone again. An hour later he was handing her into a Mercedes flying the swastika from its bonnet and saluting her as she left. She sat in the back, smoking, hunched and small inside her coat. It all made sense. Vierken's insistence that she stayed away from home. He didn't want her at St. Blaize. He didn't want her to see what was happening or be caught up in his reprisals. He had tried to protect her because he loved her. And she loved him; in spite of what Minden said he was going to do, she still loved him. But she was going to persuade him to relent. The fools, she said it under her breath. The damned fools, meddling with saboteurs and the West. They deserved to be punished; they deserved to lose hostages and be taught a lesson. She had no sympathy with her fellow countrymen if they fought against the Germans, involving themselves in a useless struggle on behalf of an ally who was their traditional enemy. No sympathy and active hostility. But children. No, that couldn't be contemplated. Vierken must be bluffing. It might do the parents good to suffer, to sweat for their folly. But it must be terrifying to be inside the school; as Minden had described the armoured car and the running S.S. guards, she had an image of the Barzain boys, of Michelle Giffier, of Caroline Camier, and countless others whom she knew by name, cowering and whimpering in terror. She found she had picked a hole in her cigarette and savagely stubbed it out, only to light another moments later. She leaned forward and tapped the driver on the shoulder.

'I want to make a stop. Go to the Château St. Blaize; it's about eight kilometres from here.'

'I'm sorry, I'm not allowed to detour or stop, Mademoiselle. You are going direct to Château Diane. Those are Standartenführer Vierken's orders.'

Having said this, she felt him deliberately accelerate. She swore at him, not caring if he heard, and threw herself back against the cushion. All right then. He was probably angry; there would be a scene, explanations, a reconciliation. Immediately she felt weak at the anticipation of their making up. He would be fierce and strong, demanding subjection. Christ, she whispered to herself, her fingers clenching, Christ, I mustn't think of that . . . But she was still thinking of it, pale and moist-skinned with excitement, when they passed the school and she saw the kneeling women, the groups of dejected men.

'Stop!' She shouted at the driver. He braked sharply. Régine jumped out. Faces turned towards her, bodies shifted to make room. An old woman mumbled at her.

'Mademoiselle Régine—help us for God's sake. They've got our children and they're sending them away! They say we'll never see them again!' She recognised one of the estate workers from the Château. He caught at her hand; she gripped hard.

'I'll help you. Don't worry, Jumont, I'll help you.' For a moment she paused, looking towards the school. A temporary spotlight had been set up, to thwart a rush in the darkness. It showed up the familiar one-story building with its jutting porch under which she had sheltered as a child against the autumn rains, the window, shuttered and sinister, and the black uniforms of the guards who ringed it, carbines at the ready. The armoured car was drawn up down the side of a street leading towards the main road. She turned back to the car; the driver was out, holding the door for her. He gave her a look of dislike.

'Please . . .' he said sharply. 'Get in.' She drove away and saw the people watching her. They hadn't connected her with the Mercedes and the swastika pennant. Suddenly somebody realised its significance. A de Bernard was travelling in an S.S. car. A German had rescued the de Bernard children just in time. There was a howl from the crowd; the women thrust themselves forward and spat after her. She didn't see them. She had her eyes closed, as if it were possible to erase the sight of her village and its people, the school and the children held inside. Half an hour later she was in the Château Diane and face to face with Adolph Vierken.

7

THE Mayor, Albert Camier, Father Duval and Jean de Bernard were all seated; Savage stood by the fireplace. Jean Pierre had brought a bottle of wine; his eyes were red from weeping. When he left them Jean de Bernard spoke.

'My friends,' he said. 'This gentleman is my wife's cousin. He has a plan for rescuing the children. I ask you to listen to him.'

'We'll listen,' Camier said. He blew his nose and rubbed the handkerchief across his eyes. 'We'll listen to anyone, God help us!'

'Right,' Savage said. 'Let's look at the position. M. le Comte learned one very important fact tonight. Vierken wouldn't release the children but he told him how they were going to be taken away. Transport is coming from Paris to take them to Germany. By rail. My fear was that they'd use lorries. But rail means cattle trucks. One truck should be enough. You know what they're like; strongly built, completely closed. No windows. The destination is obvious. One of the extermination camps. I'd say Auschwitz; that's where they send your Jews.'

'God curse them!' Father Duval said. 'God damn them to hell!'

'There's nothing we can do while they're in the school. Any attempt to get them out will fail; we'll be shot down and they'll be massacred. But a train, gentlemen, is a different matter. Before I go any further I want to ask you something. You're not afraid to die?'

'We offered ourselves,' Camier mumbled. 'They could shoot every man in St. Blaize if they'd let the children go.'

'You can speak for the rest—say twenty men?'

'For all,' Jean de Bernard answered him. 'Every man, as Camier says.'

'And the women too,' Father Duval said.

'Good.' Savage drank some wine. 'In that case we've got a good chance. You know how to shoot?'

'With sporting guns, yes. We can use knives, clubs, anything. But we have no weapons. They were handed in after the capitulation.'

'I can get guns,' Savage said. 'I promised the Comte and I can get whatever we need.'

'How?' Camier stared at him. 'How can you do this?'

'That's none of your business,' Savage said. 'I'll get them and I'll tell you how to use them and when. But you've got to realise one thing. I'm running this affair and I know what I'm doing. No arguments and no questions. Agreed?'

They hesitated; both looked towards Jean de Bernard.

'You can trust Monsieur Savage,' he said slowly. 'Personally, I put myself in his hands. I have complete confidence in him.'

'That's enough for me.' Father Duval got up. He held out his hand to Savage. 'These are my children too.' He spoke quietly. 'I'll give my life to save them. Tell us what to do and we'll do it.'

'Anything,' Camier said. 'My daughter . . .' He blew his nose again.

'That's settled then,' Savage nodded to them. 'First I'll need men. Young men, fit. I want them at the Lavalliere airfield at dawn. How they get there and how they duck the curfew is up to you. But there's one condition. No woman is to be told. I don't give a damn how hard it is, but if you tell your wife, Mayor, or you start hinting to anyone, Father—we'll fail. The Germans will see or hear something. All it needs is one word in a village like this and the plan will be out. Let the mothers cry. For tonight. Is that clear?'

'It's clear. We won't say anything. The men will swear silence. But how will you get the guns?'

'By parachute,' Savage said. 'They'll be dropped at Lavallière.'

'Lavallière?' They stared at him, Camier's jaw slackened. 'But that's only ten kilometres away from St. Blaize—how could anything be dropped so close?'

'Since 1941,' Savage said, 'there have been two drops made and one actual landing. A man was rescued and flown back to England. From Chartres. You look surprised? It's perfectly true. That field is isolated, hidden from the road by a thick belt of trees. The road itself is seldom used by anything but farm traffic. And this area has been so thinly policed that it was relatively easy to land a plane on a full moon in a field that size. As for the drop—you had a British agent come here in '42, didn't you?' They nodded. 'He landed at Lavallière. So have others. You needn't worry about that field, it's never been discovered as a reception area. Our supplies will be dropped there.'

'With S.S. crawling all over the place?' Father Duval protested. 'It may have been thinly policed before but that's because we'd had no trouble. We're under curfew now!'

'Their troops are concentrating on the town and the main roads,' Savage said. 'And most important of all, they're not expecting help from outside. The stuff will get through. It's up to you to see there are men there to pick it up.'

'Do we attack the train?' Jean de Bernard asked him.

'Yes. But not till it's left St. Blaize. Again, they'll be expecting trouble at the station; a riot, an attempt at rescue. They'll be ready for anything. But not on the track. My guess is the station will be guarded at full capacity. But the engine and one truck can't accommodate more than six men at the most. Probably with a machine gun mounted on the roof of the truck. That's the only place they can place guards—the roof. Which means we can pick them off and there won't be any danger of hitting the children. What I need now is a railway map.'

'I have one in the desk here,' Jean said. 'I'll get it.' Camier turned to watch him; he pulled a handkerchief out of his pocket and ran it round his face and neck; he looked sick and his plump face seemed to have fallen in, leaving deep hollows round the mouth. He looked ten years older since the day began. Father Duval was looking at Savage. Many years in the parish and listening to the outpouring of human frailty in the confessional had given him a sound judgement of men. The Comtesse's cousin filled him with unease. He was a Swiss and the priest was inclined to equate them with Germans.

But there was something different about this man, something beyond the authority and obvious military connections which he wasn't troubling to conceal. He was a dangerous man, a type not normally found in a small provincial village or a nobleman's château. He moved with the taughtness of a powerful animal; there was a look in his face which worried the priest. And then he realised immediately that standing in the room with them was the man who had got into the Château Diane and murdered General Brühl. He cleared his throat and looked away.

'Now.' Savage opened the Baedeker. 'From here they'll go to Paris.' He ran his finger down the line. 'It's the direct route. I take it there's no transport in St. Blaize except bicycles and the station taxi?'

'My car has no petrol left,' Jean said. 'But Camier has a van.'

'I supply the Château Diane with groceries,' the Mayor said. He looked embarrassed. 'They allow me a little petrol.'

'How much petrol?' Savage asked him.

'A few litres.'

'Good; then that's what we use to pick up the guns at Lavallière. Get eight men together and you drive the van. If you're stopped by patrols, you're on your way to the château with provisions.'

'But Lavallière is nowhere near there,' Camier protested. 'How can I explain why I'm so far off the route . . .'

'You'll just have to talk your way out of it,' Savage said coldly. 'Unless you're too frightened to risk your neck for your daughter. If that's so, you'd better stay out of it altogether!' He turned away from him.

'No! No, no!' Camier grabbed at his arm. 'I'm not backing down—I'll do it, I'll think of something!'

Savage looked into the pallid face, greasy with sweat, at the trembling hand still clutching his sleeve. With a jerk he pulled free. 'I want you to know this,' he said. 'You talk about your child. She's not the only one. All the children are locked up in that school, and by tomorrow night they'll be on their way to the extermination camp. To be gassed or shot. Now listen to me, Monsieur Camier. You're frightened, yes? All right. But if you get so frightened that you ball this up, and those children can't be rescued, I'm going to kill you. I just want you to know that.' He turned away from the Mayor. 'Now what we do is this. We pick up the guns and go to this point on the railway line. Here; about eight kilometres out of St. Blaize. There's no signal box for another three kilometres and the place is isolated. Then we attack.'

'If we succeed and get them back,' Jean de Bernard said, 'where do we hide them? The S.S. will come looking for them.'

'The S.S.,' Savage said, 'won't know the train hasn't gone through for at least a day. If we clear up any evidence of the attack, run the engine and the truck off on a side line and leave them there, they might have pulled out of St. Blaize before word comes through that the children haven't arrived. These transports don't stop at stations, they go on for days; they only stop to refuel and change drivers. We'll have time to hide the children somewhere.'

'There isn't anywhere,' the priest said. 'There are no mountains, no caves. The woods are the only place, but it won't be possible to hide that many; there are children of five and six years old. What can we do?'

'I don't know,' Savage admitted. 'But we'll think of something. First, let's get them back. Now, Father, you'll be the liaison. Go back to the school, move round and select eight men—we haven't transport for more. Tell them to go to the Mayor's house and wait there. And don't give any details. Monsieur Camier, you go home. Check your van to see there's enough petrol. It wouldn't help if *you* ran out. What you must do is keep the men quiet when they get to you and wait till the Comte or I give you the word to move. Have you any questions?'

'No.' Father Duval spoke quickly. He didn't want Albert Camier's curiosity aroused. Fear and misery for his child had dulled his sharp wits and kept the obvious conclusion about the Comtesse's Swiss cousin from occurring to him. Father Duval knew Camier too well to trust him. If he connected Savage with the man the S.S. wanted, he might well make a deal to save his own daughter, if he couldn't help the rest. 'No, everything is clear,' he said. He took Camier by the arm. 'We will do exactly as you say. God bless you, Monsieur. I will pray for you.'

'Thank you,' Savage said. He shook the priest's hand. Jean de Bernard took them outside. When he returned Savage was sitting on the sofa, the empty wine glass held between his knees. He stood in front of him.

'Father Duval guessed who you were,' he said. 'I just hope Camier doesn't.'

'Giving me up won't help the children,' Savage said. 'They know that; anyway I've got to take that chance.'

'And will this rescue really work? Can you get arms and ammunition for us?'

'I don't know,' Savage answered. 'But by God I'm going to try. Starting right now.'

It was just dark when Savage came out through the door onto the rooftop. He shone the narrow pencil torch to find his way to the transmitter; a bank of cloud hid the moon and a light wind scurried through it, driving the wisps of smoky vapour away, until the moon hung revealed, the outline of the frozen peaks giving the semblance of a face to the luminous surface. For a moment he remembered his childhood excitement at discovering human features on something so distant and majestic, at being able to equate a planet millions of miles away in space with a mythical old man. Perhaps it was the human need to minimise, to scale down the universe to mankind's pigmy size. Yet men had looked as he was doing, on the ineffable beauty of the cold, dead star, and seen divinity in it. Again the wind came sweeping, rushing the clouds to veil the icy face. Savage uncovered the transmitter.

Once more before he began to use the keys, he glanced upward, watching the progress of the wind, trailing vapour draperies. For a second he paused, caught by a memory of long ago, by the line of a verse learned in his youth which had aroused his curiosity and touched him with a sense of beauty. 'My courses are set on the storm winds, I sail on the Lightning Stream'.

He adjusted his headphones. Like the man in the poem he was struggling against an intangible force of destruction, caught up in events which couldn't be left free to rage and wreck the lives of other people. He had come to St. Blaize and fulfilled his purpose; by right he should be free, free to take the chance of escape the pass with Vierken's signature could give him. Free to leave the village and its people, its children, to perish in the storm of events for which he was responsible. But the lightning stream was carrying him with it to an unknown end. He felt a sense of fatality, which he angily dismissed. There had to be a future for the children of St. Blaize; he had lost his own child, and the wife who hadn't found her happiness with him. But the innocent were not going to be sacrificed this time.

If he didn't much care what happened to him, he cared for them. He began to transmit. Deliberately he used the code which meant the message went to OSS rather than British headquarters. He remembered that snide, cold-blooded English Colonel; the request he was going to make wouldn't have an icicle's chance on a hot shovel if it went to him. He used General Heidsecker's code name. 'Geronimo. Geronimo from Apache. Mission completed, total success. Imperative assistance sent prevent reprisal against area. All children in village due extermination. Request drop of small arms, ammunition at Lavallière field by dawn, repeat dawn tomorrow. Reply confirming soon as possible. Apache.'

Huddled against a corner of the roof he settled down to wait. It didn't occur to him to pray; there was no God, no benevolent power somewhere in the arch of night sky above him. Nothing would come on angels' wings to save the children cringing in the school. Nothing had come to save his wife and child.

Only the courage and ingenuity of a few human beings might help them. And the policy decided in London. To send help or to refuse; to risk a plane and supplies for what he knew they would regard as a hopeless enterprise, or to ignore the message. Heidsecker was a good man. Savage used the word without analysing what it meant. It was a negative quality, meaning that the General wasn't a bastard, whereas Colonel Fairbairn was. Heidsecker was a family man, noted for leniency and humanity in his dealings with his troops. Savage smoked a cigarette; his mouth felt dry and stale. If they didn't send help—if they just didn't answer because there was a breakdown and they couldn't get through . . . He rubbed the cigarette out, exploding tiny red sparks on the slate. He looked at his watch again. Ten-thirty. He had been on the roof for an hour. The transmitter was silent. There was a noise behind him, and Louise said, 'It's me. I've brought you some soup.'

She came and sat beside him; her face was clear in the bright moonlight. 'Jean told me what you're going to do,' she said. 'Did you get through?'

'I did; now I'm waiting to get the answer. Sit close to me, keep me warm.'

'It sounds impossible,' Louise said.

'Nothing's impossible if you have the will,' he answered. 'And the luck. And something to fight with.' He looked at his watch again.

'You're a trained soldier,' she said. 'The people here don't know how to fight. They'll be massacred.'

'Desperation makes people do extraordinary things,' Savage said. He put his arm round her. 'You'll be surprised what these peaceful villagers will do when their children are at stake. I'm not worried about them.'

'If they don't answer you,' she whispered, 'or they won't help—what do we do then?'

'God knows,' he said. 'But we'll do something. You know I've been thinking about Vierken. Why did he tell your husband how they were going to move the children? And the time—I don't like that part. And why a cattle truck and a special engine, just for a few children . . . They're desperately short of rolling stock. It doesn't make sense. There's something wrong with it, but I'm damned if I know what it is!'

'There's nothing wrong with it,' she said. 'That's how they transport people to the camps; that's where the children are going.'

'Hundreds of people, yes,' he said. 'But not fifty children. It's not very efficient, and that smells bad to me.'

'I think you're imagining something's wrong,' she said. 'I believe it will be just as he said. Do you know, I feel so guilty because our children got away? I went to Minden's room tonight; nothing's been taken. He must have just picked up the children and run. I wish I knew where they were!'

'He's taken a risk,' Savage said. 'I have to give him that. If anyone finds out, he could be in real trouble.'

'He was always fond of them,' she said slowly. 'He didn't do it just because of me. I told Jean I'd slept with him.'

'Oh,' Savage said. 'Why? Why did you do that?'

'I felt I had to,' she said. 'I think he understood. You're the one he minds about.'

'And you,' Savage said. He turned her towards him. 'Where do you stand—with him or with me? I want you to come back to England with me.'

'I won't do that,' Louise said. 'I won't leave him alone here. After the war's over, it will be different. But I'm not walking out on him now.'

'I have a feeling,' Savage said, 'that you still love him. And you won't admit it.'

'If that were true, it would be easy. It might have been true if I hadn't met you. But you've changed my life. Nothing will be the same again for me, whatever happens.'

'How would you like to live in Mexico?' Savage asked her. 'I've had a bellyful of Europe and I don't feel like settling down in the States. How would Mexico suit you?'

'I don't know,' Louise said. She leaned against him. 'I'll think about it. What is your real name?'

'McFall,' he said. 'Brian Patrick John. I love you very much and I'm not going to lose you. I want you to know that. If you won't come back with me I'll come and get you.' He kissed her quietly. He looked at the luminous face of his watch. 'Christ! It's after midnight—why the hell haven't they answered!'

'It must take time,' she said. 'You've hardly given them time . . .'

'I've given them as much as we've got,' he said. 'If they can't cut through the red tape, then those children are as good as dead!'

'I want to come with you,' she said. 'I want to help.'

Savage shook his head. 'Not a chance, my darling. You're not going to be within a mile of this. It might surprise you, but I don't fancy you getting killed. You stay here and wait. This is for men only.'

'I don't want anything to happen to you,' Louise whispered. Her eyes filled with tears and she brushed them away. 'Or to Jean. Don't let him do anything foolish . . .'

'I wouldn't have thought it was in his character,' Savage said. 'He's not the reckless type.'

'You shouldn't despise him,' she said slowly. 'I made that mistake. I blamed him because I didn't know what we were up against. I know now, I've seen it for myself. He's not got your kind of courage but he's not a coward. And he loves St. Blaize and the people. Don't let him throw his life away.'

'All right,' Savage said. 'I'll look out for him, if that's what you want.' At that moment there was a buzz from the headphones and the answer from London began to come through.

• • • • •

Frank Heidsecker was having dinner at the Savoy when he was called to the telephone. It had been a tiring day, but stimulating. The weather reports were improving and the low cloud and winds which had bedevilled the first days of June seemed to have disappeared. Heidsecker left his office at seven and went back to his hotel to bath and change. He had a date with an attractive Englishwoman whom he had met at a cocktail party the week before. Her husband was serving with the Canadian division, which was at that moment waiting on the South coast for the order to sail. Heidsecker was happily married, but throughout that relationship he had enjoyed affairs with attractive women, and he was looking forward to sleeping with the charming wife of the Canadian Major, if he could persuade her to come back with him after dinner. Instead of going to bed and enjoying himself, the General spent the rest of the evening at his headquarters in St. James's Street while his disappointed guest went home intact.

There were four men round the table in the General's office, and a stenographer in WAC uniform. It was eleven o'clock and the room was thick with cigarette smoke. Of the four men one was in civilian clothes. He had a round, pale face and heavy spectacles. He looked grave and self-conscious.

'In my opinion,' Colonel Fairbairn spoke up, his voice on a higher register than usual as his indignation mastered him, 'in my opinion, this is a ridiculous request and highly improper! This man has no authority to interfere!'

'I don't think we can call it interference,' an American

Lieutenant Colonel interposed. 'This message says that our help is needed; otherwise if I get it right, they're going to kill the *children*. I'm not saying there's anything we can do, but I can't go along with your criticism of our operator.' He sat back in his chair and folded his hands on the table. He didn't like the English liaison officer from SOE.

A Group Captain in the RAF glanced up at him and then towards the General. 'If you want our help, sir,' he said, 'I can arrange it, provided we don't take too long to reach a decision.'

'And before we do,' the man in civilian clothes spoke up, 'we have to recognise that this has grave political implications.'

'As I see it,' Heidsecker spoke and everyone turned towards him, 'the issue here is very simple. We sent an agent into France with a mission so important that I can honestly say it has decided the outcome of the war. He accomplished that mission. Intelligence from Paris informs us that he went beyond his instructions and that there are rumours of serious sabotage at the Château Diane as well as Brühl's murder. Our man couldn't have done this without the co-operation of the French. And it's the people who helped him who are going to suffer.' The General looked round the table; Fairbairn pinched his lip between thumb and finger and avoided his eyes. 'Children, gentlemen,' Heidsecker said. 'Children are going to be murdered; that's what that message said. I for one will not refuse to help them.'

The official from the Foreign Office, who was only an observer and not as senior as he liked to pretend, coughed and said, 'I'm sure it would damage Anglo-French relations if the story got out after the war that we'd done nothing to assist them. I'm sure my department would agree with your decision, General.'

'And I'm sure mine wouldn't.' Fairbairn couldn't restrain himself. 'I think the whole idea is insane. We *knew* there'd be reprisals and we knew they'd be extreme. It's happened dozens of times before. People are taken as hostages and shot—we don't rush in with planes and guns to rescue them! It isn't possible. I want it on record that I think we should order this man to do absolutely nothing to draw attention to himself, but to get back by the recognised escape route as soon as he can. Of course it's admirable that he succeeded. Nobody, General, is more delighted than I am. After all, I helped to brief him. But I don't believe we should involve ourselves in French affairs. If I may put forward a practical view, that part of France is notoriously lukewarm towards the Allies, and an atrocity like this might be just what is needed to tip them over to our side!'

Heidsecker regarded him for a moment. 'I've noted your opinion, Colonel, and it's on the record. I reject it completely. Group Captain—you can arrange for a plane? I suggest we do the thing properly and send a transport in with the supplies. Lavallière field is big enough for it to land. If the operation against the Germans is successful we can airlift the children out.'

'You're going to take them *out*, sir?' That was the Lieutenant Colonel who had corrected Fairbairn.

'I am,' the General said. 'I'm going to give this rescue everything we've got! Those kids are going to be saved, and I'm going to be personally responsible!'

'In that case,' the Group Captain said, 'we've a lot to arrange and very little time.'

'Colonel Fairbairn,' Heidsecker said, 'we'll need your full co-operation.'

'Once a decision has been reached,' the Colonel said irritably, 'I shall abide by it. We will do everything necessary.'

'Good,' the General said. He flexed his shoulder muscles. 'Now, gentlemen, it's getting on for midnight. Let's get down to details.'

• • •

She knelt down beside him as he listened, taking the message down. Savage pulled the headphones off and swung round to her.

'They're sending everything,' he said. 'And a plane to take the children back! It's due at Lavallière at first light, around five o'clock. Come on, we've got to get going!'

They found Jean de Bernard in the library. He got up and looked at them, anger and suspicion on his face. 'You've been together? You know it's after one o'clock.'

'They're sending help,' Louise broke in on him. She went up and caught his arm. 'Jean, don't you understand, we've been on the roof, waiting—the message just came. They're sending guns and ammunition and a plane which can take the children back to England!'

'Thank God,' he said. He spoke to Savage. 'Camier and the others will be waiting. I'll go down on the bicycle; I know a way across our fields which will bring me to the edge of the village. I can get to his house from there without being stopped.'

'We both go,' Savage said. 'And then on to the field to wait for the plane.'

For a moment Jean hesitated. Then he came to Savage and held out his hand. 'I congratulate you,' he said. 'I didn't believe it could be done.'

'No more did I,' Savage answered. 'And until we see that plane take off with every child inside it, I wouldn't congratulate anyone, if I were you.'

• • •

'Why have you come here? I told you to stay in Paris!' Régine had never seen him look like that before. His face was grey with anger, the deep-set eyes were burning. He stepped close to her and she saw his right hand twitching. She thought suddenly that he was going to hit her, but she didn't move.

'Adolph, I had to come,' she said. 'Why are you so angry? Why did you send the car and let me through?'

'Because I thought something was wrong,' he shouted. 'I thought you were in trouble! Now I find there's nothing, nothing but an idea that you can interfere! You can go straight back—I'll send you back immediately!'

'Why don't you want me here?' she asked him. 'It's because of what you're going to do to the children, isn't it?'

'Children?' He seized her upper arm, his fingers crushing the flesh until she gave a cry. 'How do you know about the children? Answer me!' He slapped her so hard across the face that only his grip on her arm kept her from falling. Tears rushed into her eyes and streamed down her face. He raised his hand again. This was a stranger, a man she didn't know, a violent enemy prepared to beat her unconscious. But they were lovers. She loved him and he loved her. The ferocity of love was not like this. She shrank away, one arm flung up to protect herself. 'How did you find out?' He snarled the words at her. 'You'll tell me, or by God I'll call Kramm in here and let him get it out of you!'

'Minden,' she gasped. 'Minden told me. He came to my aunt's flat with my nephew and niece . . . He'd rescued them from the school just in time. He told me about Operation Herod . . .'

'Minden . . .' Vierken released her. She stood before him, weeping.

'He snatched the de Bernard children away, did he? By God he'll be sorry he did . . .' Without warning his mood changed. The fury he felt towards Régine suddenly veered away from her. He had another scapegoat. Minden: the brilliant bio-chemist who was one of Brühl's staff, the lover of Louise de Bernard. They were all the same—Vierken raged at the thought of him. He had completely forgotten Régine. Like all intellectuals, thinking themselves superior to the military élite of the Reich, naturally he could indulge his sentimental whim and flout the S.S., thwart them of their vengeance. *He* hadn't fought in Russia . . .

Suddenly he saw Régine, wiping her wet face, the ugly weal where he had struck her darkening on one cheek.

'Don't cry,' he said. 'I lost my temper. I'm sorry. Poor little one, come here.'

'It doesn't matter!' Régine said. Suddenly she threw her arms round his neck. 'Don't hate me, darling! Don't be angry with me! I can't bear it—I love you so much . . .'

He embraced her; she held on to him and sobbed.

It was not her fault; women were more sensitive about these things. He regretted having been unkind to her. He stroked her hair and soothed her. Minden, his mind said, Minden. So he went behind our backs, did he, and robbed us of two of them . . .

'Hush,' he said to Régine. 'No more tears. I'm not angry with you, sweetheart. It's all over. We won't quarrel.' He could feel the warmth of her body and the heat rose in him. He was tired and in need of relaxation. He pressed her against him. 'We'll have something nice to drink,' he said. 'And we'll stay together. I'm not angry you came—I'm glad.'

'The children,' Régine whispered. 'You're not really going to do anything to them, are you? It's only a bluff, isn't it?'

He was unbuttoning her coat, his fingers brushing against her breasts. 'Of course,' he mumbled, seizing the soft flesh, bending to kiss her. 'Don't worry about it.'

He ordered champagne; they drank it sitting on the bed. It was the same canopied bed in which Brühl had been murdered. Vierken was not superstitious about such details. It was the best bedroom in the Château and he took it.

She cried while they were making love; he was too absorbed and excited to see any significance in it. Lying in his arms, Régine stayed awake while he slept. She loved him; he was part of her. But so was St. Blaize; the Château where she had grown up, her father, fading out of life, her brother Jean, the children, who were now, thank God, asleep in their aunt's flat and not shut up in that school, like the others . . .

Nineteen years she had lived in the one place; she knew every villager by name. Jumont, clasping her hand and begging for help outside the schoolhouse. He had two grandsons and a grand-daughter, a great-niece . . . She turned over on the pillow and looked at Vierken sleeping beside her. He had said it was a bluff; he had told her not to worry. Doubt tortured her, an instinct stronger than her longing to trust him urged her not to believe it. She slid out of his embrace and lay on the edge of the mattress, huddled and cold. He couldn't mean to hurt them. He had children of his own; he had shown her a picture of them, two boys in Hitler Jugend uniform. He couldn't do anything to Jumont's grandchildren, to Caroline Camier, to dozens of others she kept seeing in imagination. He couldn't.

She was asleep when the telephone rang. She woke, startled and confused, to find Vierken gone. The ringing continued; she picked the receiver up and as she did so, Vierken answered from the extension; there was a sound of water running. He was in the bathroom, She held the receiver and listened. She had taken German as a major subject for her 'Bacchot'. She and Vierken spoke it when they were alone together. The caller was a subordinate; Vierken addressed him as Major.

'What's the position down there?'

'Quiet, Standartenführer. There was an alert about an hour ago, but nothing happened. We let them stay round the school, and at six this morning we moved them off the streets. A few protested but the rest went home. There were four arrests, three women and a man, and that convinced the rest of them. Everything is under control. The transport has arrived. It came at six o'clock this morning. It's ready for them.'

'Good,' Vierken answered. 'They're not expecting anything to happen till tonight. I told de Bernard we were sending the children out this evening. They won't have had time to prepare anything. You sent the special detail to Chemire?'

'Yes sir. The grave has been dug.'

'Good,' he said again. Régine lay back on the pillow, one hand pressed to her mouth, the receiver gripped in the other.

'I think I'll come down and see them go,' he said. 'Take the schoolmistress with them.'

'Right, Standartenführer.'

'And no trace is to be left, you understand? Nothing!'

'I told Grunewald to find a spot inside the woods,' the Major said. 'He reported an hour ago. Nobody will find them; it's completely hidden. There are no farmhouses anywhere near. Nothing will be heard.'

'Move them out in an hour,' Vierken said. 'I shall be there to watch it. Heil Hitler!'

Very carefully she put back the receiver; her hand was steady and she replaced it without making any noise. She lay back, her arms straight at her sides.

'The grave has been dug.' They weren't going to Germany; the children of St. Blaize were going to be taken off the train and marched into the woods at Chemire and murdered. She gave one cry of choking anguish and then stopped. He came into the bedroom, naked, with a towel over his arm, and stood looking down at her.

'You look pale,' he said. 'Go back to sleep. I'm going out and I'll be back in two hours. Then I'll wake you.' He bent over her and kissed her mouth, biting her lower lip. 'You're so bad for me,' he murmured. 'You take my mind off my work . . .'

'I'm not tired,' she said. She smiled and rolled away from him. 'If you're going out, couldn't I go to St. Blaize? I need clothes.'

'Not for me,' he said. 'I like you as you are.'

'Take me to St. Blaize,' she pleaded. 'I want to look nice for you. Please, Adolph.'

'All right; but not to stay. Just to pack what you want and then the car will bring you straight back here. I don't want you hanging about the village.'

'Why not? Are you expecting trouble?'

He shrugged. 'No, certainly not. But I want you here, waiting for me. I'll come to the Château with you. Get dressed then; we haven't time to waste.'

She sat in the back of the car with him; he reached out and held her hand. She smiled at him. 'I questioned your sister-in-law,' he said. 'I made it very disagreeable for her.'

Régine went on smiling. 'How disagreeable—did you hurt her? My brother?'

'No, no, my darling,' he protested. 'There wasn't any need. I'm a mild man, you know that. I just bullied her a little; to please you!' He squeezed her hand. 'It will amuse me to go there with you.'

'Yes,' Régine said. 'It will be most amusing.'

• • • • •

The sound of the plane woke Louise. She had refused to go to bed, but stayed in the salon in a chair. Jean de Bernard had come to her quietly and kissed her goodbye. She had given him her hand and pressed her lips to his cheek. Savage was standing in the doorway. She could sense him watching them, fighting against Jean. She looked into her husband's face.

'Take care; and God bless you. I wish I was going with you.'

'You have a long time to wait,' he whispered. 'Hours and hours before anything happens. Stay calm, and try not to be anxious. I believe we'll succeed.'

'Not if we hang around here,' Savage said. He came to Louise and she gave him her hand too. You love me, his eyes said. He kissed you like a brother.

'We'll be back,' he said. 'Just stay quietly here.'

Then they had gone. She got up, shivering because the fire

was almost out, and listened to the sound of the engine. And if it was seen to land . . . She turned and suddenly dropped on her knees. Her prayers were incoherent, helpless. She got up again and went upstairs to see if her father-in-law had awoken. His light was on and he was sitting up when she went in.

'An air raid? Are they dropping bombs?'

'No, Papa. It's just a passing plane. It means nothing. Go back to sleep.'

'I can't sleep,' the old man quavered. 'Jean hasn't been to see me—the children never came—nobody cares about me!'

'That isn't true!' Suddenly she lost her temper with him. 'Don't be so selfish—if you knew where Jean was tonight and what nearly happened to the children . . .' She checked herself. 'I'm sorry, Papa. I didn't mean to shout at you. But you're not being neglected. Go to sleep.'

'I know there's something wrong,' the Comte said. 'What do you mean? Where is Jean? What about the children?'

'You wouldn't understand,' Louise said slowly. 'And you're lucky. I'll go and make you a hot drink. Then you'll sleep.'

'It's the Germans, isn't it?' he said. He pulled himself upright. 'Go to my chest of drawers and get me my revolver. I won't let them hurt Jean. I'm not afraid. Go to the chest of drawers!'

'No.' Louise shook her head. 'Please, Papa, don't get excited. It's my fault for saying anything about it. There's nothing you can do. There's nothing I can do either.'

'I fought them in the First War,' the Comte said fiercely. 'I'll fight them now!' He threw back the bedclothes and before she could reach him he was stumbling to the chest. He pulled open a drawer and turned to her, triumphant. His face was very flushed and his eyes shone. 'There! You didn't believe me—but I've always kept it. Just in case we were in danger! And it's loaded, ready . . .' The long-barrelled revolver hung down in his hand, its weight too much for him. Louise ran forward and took it.

'Papa, for God's sake! Give me that. Lean on me now and come back to bed. You'll make yourself ill.'

He fell onto the bed and it was a struggle to lift him into it. At last he lay exhausted on the pillows; his high colour was receding, his eyes were still too bright. He breathed through his mouth.

'Hot milk,' Louise said to him. 'You'd like a nice glass of hot milk. I'll get it for you.' She took the revolver with her and went downstairs to the kitchen. Even the old had their secrets. Nobody knew of the gun's existence. The old man had kept it hidden in the drawer against some imaginary need. She picked it up and saw that it was fully loaded. She went upstairs and hid it in the bureau in the salon. Jean's revolver was gone; he had taken it with him. When she went back to the kitchen the milk had boiled over.

. . . . .

The Hudson stood on Lavallière field, the dawn light showing it up like a huge primeval bird. Savage ran to it first, followed by Jean de Bernard. The villagers hesitated; they seemed almost afraid to approach. Camier's van was hidden under some trees on the edge of the field. It had been pushed off the road. The trees round Lavallière provided an impenetrable screen of the field from the road. The moon still shone brightly, giving the scene a still, lunar quality. The sun had not risen yet. The pilot dropped down from the cockpit and Savage held out his hand. He was followed by his navigator and his airgunner. All three shook hands with him.

'Right on time. Where's the stuff?'

'Inside. Get your chaps together and we'll get it unloaded. I'm not too crazy about standing out in the open like this.' The pilot unbuttoned his helmet and took it off; he looked around him at the figures of men swarming round the plane. The big American was obviously in charge. And he knew how to organise. Within ten minutes the supplies were on the ground and being neatly stacked into piles. A Frenchman came up to him and spoke in excellent English.

'I'd like to express our gratitude to you for coming here. It's a tremendous personal risk for you, but the lives of every child in our village is at stake. The Germans have taken them and they're going to send them to Germany. Thanks to you, we may be able to stop them.' Jean de Bernard held out his hand. The pilot took it.

'Kids?' he said. 'They've taken your kids?'

'Yes,' Jean said. 'They're being held in the school.'

'The bloody bastards!' the pilot exclaimed. 'You can count me in on this. The Yank's in charge, isn't he?'

'Yes,' Jean said. 'He's coming now.'

'Let's get this stuff into the trees,' Savage said. 'Then we can sort it out; and this plane's got to be hidden. How the hell,' he swung round to the pilot, 'are we going to do it? It's like a bloody battleship!'

'The ops boys thought of that,' the pilot said, 'seeing I've got to hang around. You'll find some tackle inside for pulling her. And camouflage nets.'

It was obvious that there weren't enough of them to move the aircraft, but they tried. Heaving on the ropes attached to the undercarriage, Savage, the crew and the men of St. Blaize strained and struggled, but the load was too heavy. The pilot offered to start the engines and taxi, but Savage refused.

'Too big a risk,' he said. 'Something might pass on the road over there; we wouldn't hear it but sure as hell they'd hear us. Camier—get that van over here! The rest of you, move the guns into the trees. And be careful of that crate, it's full of grenades!'

Camier ran back to his van, his breath tearing through his heaving lungs. Sweat had soaked his shirt, his legs trembled. They had been stopped once on their way out of St. Blaize by an S.S. patrol. Luckily for him, the check point was at a junction which allowed him to insist that he was on an extra supply run to Headquarters at Anet. Sitting in the van, Camier allowed himself a moment of collapse. He sank against the steering wheel, his head supported on one arm, and closed his eyes.

He would never forget that moment, when the guards surrounded him and the face of an S.S. corporal peered through the window. He had felt physically sick with fear; at the memory his stomach heaved again. There were eight men hidden in the back of the van, crouched on top of each other. All the S.S. had to do was open the back doors . . . He had his papers ready and the pass which he had been given to enter the Château Diane; he had thrust them at the corporal, and the semi-darkness before dawn hid his livid face and the sweat running in trickles down his neck.

The van was well known at the Château. The pass was signed by the Wehrmacht commander of the Dreux district, General Fielder, and it was stamped and re-stamped for many journeys in the past weeks. The corporal had hesitated.

Camier had found a voice from somewhere.

'I shall be late,' he croaked. 'The Standartenführer wants duck eggs for breakfast. I'm bringing them specially . . .'

They had stepped back and let him go. He had no idea what made him think of the excuse. Duck eggs. He raised his head, drew a deep breath into his aching chest and wiped his oily forehead on his bare arm. Then he started the van, and bumping over the soft, uneven ground, he drove it slowly out towards the plane.

It was an old pre-war Renault; its chassis rattled and its engine protested at the strain being put upon it. But with the human power pulling on the ropes and the van dragging at the tow, the plane began to move across the open field until it came to rest under the shelter of some trees. Camier helped to spread the camouflage nets, instructed by the pilot. Savage ordered some branches to be cut, and these were laid along the wings; the tail was in deep shadow. They gathered to open the boxes of arms and the small wooden crate marked 'Grenades', with a skull and crossbones painted in red on one side. Every man present had experience of hunting. Hate and terror for their children sharpened their perception. Clumsy hands imitated the actions of Savage as he showed them how to use the sten guns.

To Jean de Bernard he tossed one fully loaded. 'Set a man to watch the road for patrols,' he said. 'And tell him for Christ's sake not to open fire on any Germans. Just report back here and run like hell if they look like stopping.'

'If they reckon I've landed,' the pilot said, sounding casual, 'how long would it take them to get here?'

'They'd have been here by now,' Jean de Bernard answered.

'Incidentally,' Savage looked up, 'being in uniform won't protect any of you from these boys. They don't go by the Geneva Convention. They'll kick your balls off and then shoot you. So get yours in first if they come.'

'Don't worry about us,' the pilot said. 'I've got my instructions. I know what to do.' Looking at the clean-cut, pleasant young face, Savage doubted it. Brave, cheerful, typically English. He had as much hope against the average S.S. soldier as a child threatening a man-eating tiger with a pop-gun.

'Right,' Savage said. The sun was rising; the sky was blushing on the horizon; obstinately, the silver moon still hung above them. 'Let's have a look at the grenades.' He glanced at the faces of Camier and the eight men. They looked gaunt and grim. Poor bastards. He was surprised to feel sorry for them. To him this was a well-practised exercise, something for which he had been trained. These people had lived in peace; their children's lives depended upon their learning skills in a few minutes which he took for granted. He reached in and took out a grenade.

He held it up for them. 'Pineapples,' he said. 'The pin has a ring in it; pull that, release the catch on the side, count to three and throw. I once heard of a man holding one of these in live training and saying, "But I never learned to count, Sarge . . ." There were so many pieces of him nobody else counted *them*. So remember. Pull, release catch, count, throw. I know they're pretty, but don't stop to admire them.' One of the men smiled; some of the tension relaxed. 'We'll use these for the engine,' Savage explained.

'Nobody tosses one near the cattle truck, whatever happens. We don't want any of the children getting hurt. A couple of these well aimed will bring the train to a halt. And get rid of our pals who may be inside the driver's cabin.'

'Would they use a driver from St. Blaize?' That was Jean de Bernard.

'Unlikely,' Savage countered. 'It'll be one of the regulars from Paris. He may be Boche or he may be French. Anyhow we can't worry about him. It's just his bad luck.'

'I'd like a cigarette,' the pilot ventured to Jean de Bernard. 'It's getting very light now. Have one?'

'Thank you.' Jean bent over the lighter flame.

'Have you got children in this too?'

'No,' the Comte answered. 'Mine were lucky. They escaped.' He looked at his watch. 'We've a long time to wait. They're not taking them out of St. Blaize until tonight.'

'Tonight!' The cigarette dropped. 'Christ, I'm willing to wait for an hour or even a bit over, but tonight! There isn't a chance—we're sure to be seen here! Look, it's daylight now . . .'

'Planes have landed here for the last two years.' Savage had come up to them. 'Not a Hudson, maybe, but aircraft carrying agents. Nobody guarded this place or gave it a thought. I landed here myself by parachute. You were told to wait. If we get the children out you'll fly them back to England. If we don't, you can get the hell out yourself. But not till tonight.' He turned away and called out to one of the villagers. The pilot looked after him. He replaced the cigarette and sucked on it.

'Nasty piece of work,' he remarked to Jean de Bernard. His tone was low. 'Typical Yank.'

He dug into the pocket of his flying jacket. 'I've got a drop of something here,' he said. 'Keep out the cold.' He offered a small flask to Jean, who shook his head.

'No thank you. You'll need it for the flight back. Why don't you relax now? Perhaps you could sleep.'

'I might.' The young Englishman stretched his back. 'I think I'll go and take a zizz inside.' He smiled at Jean and stamped on his cigarette end.

He climbed up into the belly of the aircraft and disappeared. Jean de Bernard stood apart, listening to Savage demonstrating and explaining the small-arms. There were pistols as well as the sten guns. He was a good instructor, precise, and patient. It was a side of his character which the Comte had not suspected. He couldn't understand Savage; the type was completely alien to him. But then he was too European. He hadn't really understood Louise either.

He only loved her. With the prospect of fighting the S.S. in front of him, he faced not only the fact of loving his wife, but of being killed before he could do anything about it. She had forgiven him; he knew that. The moment when he found her kissing Savage had roused him to contemplate murder. He looked at the American and wondered how deep his hatred of him went. Morality, sensitivity, nothing so effete as ethics would trouble Savage. He wanted Louise and he would do his best to take her. Unless, in the heat of the battle . . . Jean de Bernard dropped his cigarette close to the mashed stub left by the pilot, and stepped on it. Savage could have stood aside from what was happening. The children of St. Blaize were not his concern; his job was done. He could have used his permit and left them. Jean knew that there were men who would have done exactly that. He went over to the group and touched Savage on the shoulder.

'Let me help,' he said. The sun was up and it was growing warm. The time was six-twenty-three.

• • • • •

Inside the school Michelle Giffier formed the children into groups. There was a lot of crying, even among the older ones. Waking in their classrooms had unnerved them. The teacher organised the wailing little ones herself, helped by a few of the senior pupils. She took them to the lavatories, where she washed their faces and hoped that establishing a routine would calm them. Her own face was haggard and dirty; tears had dissolved her mascara and the split on her lip was now an ugly swelling. She found a hand-comb in her bag and began to tidy the children's hair, lining them up in front of her. Straggling bows were re-tied, frocks smoothed down, and hands inspected. An atmosphere of false security pervaded them, emanating from the slight young woman they had known all their lives.

She never glanced near the guard; the one who had manhandled her the night before had gone. A sullen robot stood in his place, his eyes staring at and through her and the children. She had a horrible sensation of being watched by a machine. It was obvious that he didn't regard her or them as human beings. The sensation was more frightening than the frank brutality of his predecessor. She beckoned Caroline Camier and Pierre Farrière.

'Get the books out,' she said. She smiled at them both. The boy was twelve, sturdy and dependable, the eldest of five. His mother had been the woman shot outside the school the night before. He and Michelle Giffier knew nothing of this.

'Since we're here, we might as well work. Caroline, you look after the little ones; set them some drawing to do. Pierre, we'll start with history. See that everyone starts at page twenty-seven of book three. St. Jeanne d'Arc. It was always my favourite lesson. Go on now.' Steadily she began to read aloud. The door opened after half an hour; she stopped and got up. The S.S. Major was approaching. She saw the children's eyes following him as he came to her desk. He saluted her.

'Madame. In twenty minutes you must be ready to leave. Gather any clothes together and have the children ready.'

'Leave?' Michelle Giffier went white. 'Leave for where? What do you mean?'

'You are being taken to a place of safety,' the Major said smoothly. 'You have nothing to fear.'

It was the formula with which he had calmed anxious Jews, awaiting removal to the gas chambers. It didn't work with the school teacher. She supported herself on the desk with both hands and said loudly, 'We are not going to any place of safety. Either you let my children go to their homes or we stay here.'

Her injured lip began to quiver; hate and terror brought the tears and they spilled down her face. The Major gave a little smile.

'The outside of this building has been soaked in kerosene,' he said. 'Within half an hour I shall order it to be set on fire. You may stay inside with the children if you wish. You have twenty minutes. Heil Hitler.' He gave a casual salute and turned away. Outside in the sunshine, he yawned. He had dozed in the back seat of the armoured car, but only for an hour or so and his temper was irritable. The cattle truck had arrived and waited at the station. Already a crowd of parents had returned to the school, reinforcing the group who had remained outside all night. The recitation of the rosary infuriated him. He had ordered his men to break up the kneeling group, but some distance away they had reformed, and the low murmur of voices rose and fell all night. He was waiting for the Standartenführer before he could actually load the children into the truck and take them to the station. He had sent the execution detail on ahead to Chemire, where they were waiting. It was all well organised and ingenious. He took his seat in the armoured car and settled down to wait for his superior.

• • • •

Louise had fallen asleep; she lay on her bed fully dressed, so exhausted that she didn't hear the car arrive. A hand seized her shoulder and shook her. She woke instantly and saw Régine bending over her.

'Wake up for God's sake!'

'What are you doing here?' Louise blazed at her. 'You filthy little bitch—get out!'

'Where's Jean? Where is he?'

'Why do you want to know? So you can tell your friend in the S.S.

'It doesn't matter what you say to me,' Régine said. 'Nothing matters but to help the children. That's why I've come. And keep your voice down. Vierken is downstairs!'

'You brought *him*!' Louise looked at her in horror. 'You brought him to St. Blaize! Well now you've done it, haven't you!' She turned away, overcome with despair. Jean and Savage were missing. If Vierken asked where they were . . .

'Listen to me.' Régine caught hold of her arm. 'Listen to me for the love of God! Minden came to the flat and brought Paul and Sophie—he told me what was happening! I came down to try and help. To plead with Vierken. He's my lover, I didn't believe he'd do anything to really hurt them.' She let go of Louise and hid her face in both hands. 'They're not going to Germany,' she said. 'They've dug a mass grave for them in the woods. They're going to be taken there this morning and murdered. I listened in on the telephone. He doesn't know I know.'

'They're not taking them to Germany?' Louise stared into the girl's face; her eyes were wild. 'They're going to kill them . . .'

'I told you,' Régine hissed at her. 'This morning. He's going down there now to send them off. For Christ's sake where is Jean? Someone's got to organise the village. They mustn't leave the school!'

'Jean has already organised a rescue,' Louise said slowly. 'He and Roger and Camier and others. But they're not expecting anything to happen till tonight. They're miles away from Chemire. Oh my God!' she cried out. 'What are we going to do?'

'I don't know,' Régine mumbled. 'I thought if I could tell Jean . . .'

'I'm going downstairs,' Louise said suddenly. 'I'm going to talk to him myself.' She stopped at the door. 'You'd better stay here,' she said. 'Keep out of this.' She went down the stairs; she felt calm, but icy cold. A mass grave in the woods. He had his back to her when she went into the salon; he was examining one of the family miniatures. He had taken it off the wall.

'Standartenführer Vierken!'

He turned round slowly, still holding the miniature. 'Madame? I was admiring the fine quality of this painting. Where is Régine? I told her to hurry.'

'Régine is upstairs,' Louise said. She walked away from him. 'You know what I'm going to ask you?'

'No.' He glanced up from his examination of the miniature. 'How should I know? Is this an ancestor—of your husband's, I assume. Americans can't trace themselves that far.'

'I'll go down on my knees and beg you,' Louise said. 'Let the children go home. Whatever the village has done, punish the adults. Shoot as many of us as you like—but don't murder the innocent!'

'I don't think your kneeling would make any difference,' he said pleasantly. 'It might be amusing to watch, however. I'm usually amenable to pretty women. Like your sister-in-law, for instance.' His eyes considered her, dark with hatred and contempt. 'You don't believe it's going to happen, do you, Madame de Bernard? You think I'm bluffing, don't you? Régine does. Surprising, because she knows me very well. You think you people can kill Germans and sabotage our war effort and we won't punish you as you deserve? You'll know better next time. I'm going to make an example of this place.'

Louise stood with her back to the bureau. 'You must have children of your own,' she said. 'How could you do this thing?'

Vierken laughed. 'My children have nothing to do with it, it's your children who are going to be re-settled.'

'That's a lie,' Louise said slowly. 'I know what re-settled means. You're going to kill them. Put down that miniature—

don't put your filthy hands on anything belonging to us!'

He half turned; the delicate seventeenth-century enamel smashed into the fireplace.

'Now,' Louise said slowly, 'either you let the children go home or I am going to kill you!' She held the old Comte's revolver in both hands. Vierken stood very still.

'You're being very foolish,' he said. 'You wouldn't hit anything with that.'

'You send a message,' Louise said, 'releasing them from that school. You've got a car outside. Write the order and your driver can take it. Now.'

'And afterwards?' Vierken asked her. His right hand was creeping inwards towards the holster at his side.

'Don't do that, Adolph,' Régine said from the doorway. 'She means it. She'll shoot.'

She walked into the room; her hair was brushed smooth and she had smeared a crimson lipstick on her mouth. She looked ghastly: 'Don't move,' she repeated.

'Do as she says. Send that note.' She didn't look at Louise, she was staring at Vierken. Her hands opened and closed at her sides. 'She'll shoot you—let them go!'

Vierken looked from her to Louise and then back to Régine. A smile of contempt twisted his mouth. 'Come over here,' he said in German. 'She can't shoot both of us. Be calm, sweetheart. Just take my gun.'

Régine walked up to him, she turned and faced her sister-in-law. 'I'm not going to let you kill him,' she said.

'Get back,' Louise cried out. 'Get away from him—he'll use you as a shield!' Régine didn't answer. She plunged her hand into the holster and brought out his revolver.

'Good girl,' Vierken said softly. 'Now step between us and give the gun to me . . .'

Régine looked at him and shook her head. 'No,' she said. 'No. You lied to me, Adolph.' She had stepped back and the black eye of the muzzle was pointing at his chest. 'I listened in on the telephone this morning. I know what you're going to do to the children. I know about Chemire.'

'You wouldn't hurt me, sweetheart,' Vierken said. 'You love me. You wouldn't shoot.'

'Send the message,' Régine said. Her voice trembled.

'Release them. For the last time, I beg of you . . .'

'Go to hell!' Suddenly his nerves snapped. 'They're going to be shot and buried! Every last one of them—give me that gun, you little whore, or I'll break every bone in your body!' As he leaped for her, the first shot cracked out. Louise screamed. There was a second shot and then a third. Vierken jerked backwards, his body jack-knifing as the bullets slammed into him at point-blank range. He crumpled and fell. Régine stood over him, firing repeatedly until the gun clicked empty. He didn't die at once. He twitched and choked, blood bubbling out of his mouth. His eyes opened, glaring and then suddenly they filmed over.

She stood and pulled the trigger. There was another useless click. Louise ran to her and wrenched the revolver away.

'Stop! Stop it, for God's sake!'

Régine fell on her knees beside him; she was moaning. 'Adolph . . . Adolph—oh God, oh God.' She held herself, rocking with grief.

Louise found the old servant Jean-Pierre standing in the doorway. He carried a little axe they used for chopping firewood. 'Madame—we heard shots . . . What's happened?'

'There's been an accident,' Louise whispered. 'Shut the door . . .'

'I had to do it,' Régine wept. 'I loved him but I had to do it. I couldn't let him murder the little ones . . .' She looked up and saw Jean-Pierre staring down at her in horror. ' "They're going to be shot," ' she said. ' "Shot and buried." When he said that I killed him.'

Louise caught hold of her. 'There's the driver outside,' she said. 'Get up, come away from here. Jean-Pierre, go and see if he heard anything!' She had half lifted Régine to her feet and was supporting her to the door. For a moment the girl pulled against her and looked back. There was no hysteria left in her; her eyes were dead.

'He called me a whore,' she muttered. 'I thought he loved me . . .'

'Come upstairs,' Louise begged her. 'Don't look at him any more. If you hadn't done it, I would have shot him . . . I wish to God I had!' The old man appeared beside them in the hall.

'The driver's still waiting by the car, Madame,' he said. 'He didn't hear anything.' The walls at St. Blaize were a foot thick. 'Is it true?' he asked her. 'Is she telling the truth—are they going to kill my grandchildren?' His mouth quivered.

'Yes,' Louise answered. 'I'm afraid it is. They're all going to be murdered. Unless I can get to the Comte in time.' She went to the window and looked out. Vierken's Mercedes gleamed in the sunshine; the driver leaned against the bonnet.

'I'm going to get that car,' she said. 'It's the only chance we've got. But you'll have to deal with the driver. There's a revolver in there.' She pointed to the salon. 'It's loaded. I must have dropped it. I'll send him inside. Make sure you don't miss!'

'I won't,' the old man said. 'Leave him to me, Madame. Marie-Anne, come here and take Mademoiselle Régine upstairs!' Louise ran down the steps and out into the sunlight. She went up to the car and the driver straightened himself.

'You're wanted inside.' she said. He turned and ran to the front door. She didn't wait to see what happened. She wrenched open the car door and slid behind the wheel. The keys were in it. She pressed the starter; it fired instantly, and a moment later the car skidded through the gates and swung onto the road to Lavallière.

8

THE woods at Chemire were full of birds. At the approach of the execution detail that morning, they had risen from the centre of the wood in a mass, screeching in alarm, streaking off in all directions. About two hundred yards into the wood itself, the S.S. scout car came to a halt at a natural clearing. A lorry was parked nearby. Above their heads was a circle of open sky, on all sides the massive trees surrounded them; underfoot the ground was soft and black with leaf mould. There were five men. They carried the machine gun in two parts. In the centre of the clearing a rectangular pit had been dug about twenty feet long and eight feet deep. The earth was piled into a huge mound on the far side. A group of men were squatting near the pit, smoking and talking. They were in shirt sleeves, their arms bare; earth stained them.

It had taken them three hours to dig the pit. Past experience made them as quick as professional gravediggers. They had stacked their shovels in a neat pile, and someone was boiling a metal coffee pot over a fire.

The noise made by the anxious birds continued for some minutes, while the S.S. NCO shouted directions to his five men. The machine gun was set up in front of a beech tree, its snout pointing at the yawning pit. To the execution squad it was a familiar routine. They had dug mass graves in Poland, in Russia, and in the makeshift camps set up for Eastern prisoners and Jews. They had shot and buried thousands of people of all ages and sexes. The cries of women and children had no meaning for them any more than the shrieks of the birds whose refuge they had disturbed. Some were married men with families; while they waited they joked among themselves and passed the time sharing cigarettes and talking.

Two men were occupied with a crossword puzzle. The NCO inspected the pit, decided on the placement of the gun, and then stretched out under a tree. He enjoyed the pattern made by the sunlight as it filtered down through the thick branches. The railway was about half a mile away. They would hear the train. It would take time to march the children across the fields and into the wood. Depending upon how small some of them were. He closed his eyes and let himself drift. It was a very warm morning.

One of the digging detail brought him coffee. He sat up and yawned, looking at his watch. It was nine o'clock. They were already late. He buttoned his uniform jacket, put his cap on straight and went to the edge of the woods, where he could see down to the railway line. There was no sign of the train.

• • • • •

The Major was also looking at his watch. He stood inside the doorway of the school, looking out onto the silent, sullen crowd. Behind him the schoolteacher and the children were ready. They waited with their satchels and books; a few were crying. He could hear them through the closed door and it irritated him. The Standartenführer was late. He had promised to be there in an hour, and it was already an hour and twenty minutes. The Major hesitated. The train was ready; the truck taking the children to the station was drawn up outside the school, surrounded by armed S.S. guards.

The longer he delayed in getting them out, the more the news of their removal was spreading through the village. There would be a crowd at the station. The Major smelled trouble. He was used to judging the temper of a crowd. He knew fear and indecision because he had seen it so often in the condemned. He also recognised revolt. He had been in charge of a group of Jewish and Polish prisoners once, when a riot broke out. Just before, he had seen a certain uniformity about the hungry, desperate faces. The same look was spreading through the crowd of men and women outside the school. The moment would come when they'd rush the lorry, regardless of the troops opening fire. And the Standartenführer had stressed his desire for an orderly operation. The Major made two decisions. He put the first into practice by going into the building. He came up to Madame Giffier. She was standing with an arm round two children who were in tears. He saluted her.

'Madame,' he said, 'it's time to leave. Before you go outside I have to warn you. There is a truck which will take you and the children to the railway station. There is also a crowd. If any rescue attempt is made, my men will fire. Not on the civilians but upon you and the children. I'm sure,' he said this with a slight smile, 'that you're not frightened for yourself, but equally you won't want those two you're holding now, for instance, to be shot dead. I want you to go outside and tell those people what I've told you. Warn them not to do anything to interfere with your departure. Tell them that their children will die if they move.' He opened the door and pointed with his cane. 'The responsibility is yours,' he said.

Madame Giffier looked at him. 'Where are you sending us? Tell me, before I go outside. Or I won't go.'

'To Germany,' the Major said. 'To a detention camp. Nobody is going to harm you or the children. But their parents must be punished. After a time you will all be released.'

'You give your word?'

'Of course. Go out and do as I've told you.'

She blinked in the strong sunlight; there was a loud anguished murmur from the crowd, and a movement towards her. It was checked by the S.S. using their gun butts.

'I've got something to tell you.' She raised her voice. 'For God's sake listen to me! We're going away in a few minutes. We're being taken to Germany but we're not going to be harmed. The children are safe and nothing's going to happen to them! But if you try and stop us going, they'll shoot the children! Don't make a move, don't try anything, for God's sake!'

There was a scream from the crowd. 'Janine—how's my Janine?' 'Pierre, Marie—are you all right!' 'Philippe . . .' 'Raoul . . .'

'That's enough.' The Major came beside her. 'Go back inside and bring the children out.'

'They're all right,' Michelle Giffier shouted. 'They're all all right, don't worry! I'll take care of them!' She turned back into the school. Inside, the ranks of children waited, faces upturned towards her. Tears made her blind and for a moment she faltered. It was Caroline Camier who saved her. She put her arm through the teacher's. 'Don't cry, Madame,' she whispered. 'We're not frightened. We'll be together.'

'You're a good girl,' Michelle Giffier said. She brushed her hand across her eyes and smiled; it was a painful grimace of her swollen mouth. The girl squeezed her arm. Her little face was set and stubborn; she was an ugly child who strongly resembled her father. She gave a look of hate at the Major.

'Children!' Michelle Giffier called out. 'We're leaving now. There's nothing to be frightened of, and we shan't be separated. We're going by train to a place where we'll stay for a few days and then we'll be brought home. File up in twos and do exactly as the soldiers tell you.' She turned to the Major.

'We're ready,' she said. This was the Major's second decision. Vierken had told him to move the children; that was more valid as an order than his remark about coming down to see them off. The Major's men were waiting at Chemire, the crowd were still subdued by the teacher's warning. He couldn't wait any longer and hope to avoid some incident.

'Good,' he said. He opened the school door. 'Outside!'

. . . . .

There was a group of S.S. about a hundred yards up the road. Louise saw them and for a second she braked. There was a motorcyclist and three men armed with machine pistols. They were at the side of the road, stationed to stop anything travelling towards St. Blaize. Since there were no private cars in use in the area and people travelled on foot or by bicycle, no road blocks were considered necessary on the subsidiary roads out of the village. The motorcyclist was enough. She had little time to think; her first reaction of fear made her slow down, the second was to slam her foot on the accelerator. If they chased her, she would probably be caught; the way was narrow and she wasn't used to the heavy car. But they wouldn't chase the Standartenführer's private Mercedes flying its Nazi pennant, unless they had time to see that a woman was driving it.

She gripped the wheel tight and pushed the pedal to the floor. All she glimpsed as she roared past the group was a blur with someone saluting. She rounded a bend and almost ran into the verge; it needed all her strength to wrench the wheel back and straighten up. Then she slowed, listening. There was no sound of a motorcycle. They'd seen the car, and the driver was as much a blur to them as they had been to her. Louise let the speed drop for a moment; her body was shaking, and her hands were so wet that they slipped on the wheel. Lavallière was only four kilometres away. She picked up speed again, guiding the car round the bends and twists in the road; it hit a rough pothole that jerked her out of the seat. Her mind kept trying to switch back to the Château, to Vierken lying dead on the floor with blood seeping out of his wounds onto the carpet; Régine, ashen with shock, weeping for her lover. It was like a nightmare. It couldn't have happened; she had a sensation of panic, imagining that it was all an illusion, that at some point while she slept for those few hours, her mind had given way and she had woken to a hideous hallucination. Panic came and she fought it off; she opened the window and the rush of air was calming. Lavallière; one kilometre. Less. There was the encircling belt of trees that hid the open field. After they were married, Jean and she drove out there and picnicked once. She suddenly remembered the smell of the grass and the dappled light above their heads. She braked, and stopped. When she got out there was complete silence. She began to walk into the trees. If they had left the field already . . . Nothing. No aircraft, no sign of life. A hand touched her shoulder; she wheeled round with a cry. Albert Dumois, who worked in the butcher's shop in St. Blaize, was standing in front of her, pointing a sten gun.

'Madame!' He was staring at her. 'When I saw the car stop I nearly shot you!'

'Where's the Comte?'

'Across the other side! There, under the trees, can't you see the plane?' Now it was visible, shrouded under the camouflage net. Louise didn't answer; she began to run.

It was Savage she saw first; he caught hold of her and held her for a moment. She pulled away from him.

'You've got to get to Chemire,' she gasped, breathless from

that wild run across the field. 'You've got to go now! They're going to shoot the children!'

By now she was surrounded; Jean de Bernard pushed towards her. He spoke quietly to Savage. 'Let go of my wife. Louise—what's happened! How did you get here!'

'In Vierken's car,' she said. 'He came to St. Blaize, with Régine. Don't ask any questions, just listen! She'd found out they were going to murder the children in the woods; taking them on the train was just a blind. Oh God.' She stopped, and Jean reached out for her. For a few moments she clung to his hands. Then she stood back and faced them.

'There isn't time to tell what happened. They were moving the children onto the train this morning. If we don't get there in time they'll be shot and buried in Chemire.'

'You're certain of this? It's not a trick?' She shook her head at Jean.

'No,' she said. 'It's the truth.'

'How did you get Vierken's car?' Savage asked quietly. 'Where is he?'

'At the Château. He's dead; Régine killed him.'

'That's good enough.' Savage looked round at the group of men. The RAF pilot and his navigator had come to join them; they couldn't speak French beyond a few words and they didn't know what was happening. 'Camier, you and the Comte take four men with you and ammunition. We'll use the Mercedes. How long will it take to get to Chemire?'

'By the direct route, twenty minutes,' Jean de Bernard said. 'But there's a longer way round. It skirts St. Blaize, and crosses the railway line about three kilometres down. There's a little hand-operated crossing gate.'

'There'll be Germans manning it,' Camier burst out.

'Why should there be?' Savage spoke to him quietly. The man's face was contorted; he looked as if he might fall down with a stroke. 'They're not expecting trouble. Who usually operates it?'

'Servard,' the Mayor mumbled. 'Servard. He's over seventy; half the time he sleeps . . . God knows why there hasn't been an accident . . . Caroline . . . Oh Christ Jesus help me!' He dropped to the ground and covered his face with his hands. There was a sound of sobbing, harsh and inhuman in its agony.

Louise went to him and shook him by the shoulder. 'Don't do that,' she said. 'It won't help. We may be in time still.'

Slowly he raised himself; he wiped his face with the back of his hand.

'Pardon, Madame,' he muttered. 'Pardon. I was overcome ...'

'How much longer by the railway route?' Savage turned to Jean de Bernard. The sight of Camier's collapse wasn't helping the morale of the rest of the men whose children were under sentence of death.

'Half an hour, forty minutes. Louise, how did you get through—weren't there any patrols, check points?'

'Only one; a motorcyclist and some S.S. I drove past at top speed and they didn't see me. They must have thought it was Vierken.'

'Then that's the route for the Mercedes. Jean, you go with Camier and take half the men with you in the van. I'll go with the Mercedes on the shorter route. If one of us gets stopped the other will get through.' He took a cigarette out and lit it; he handed it to the Comte.

'Camier drives, like last time. Go to the crossing and wait. If you're in time and the train stops to unload the kids, move in on them. If it's already done so, join us at Chemire.'

'And if we're too late?' Albert Dumois asked the question. He looked from Savage to the Comte. 'If they're dead, Monsieur—what do we do then?'

It was Jean de Bernard who answered. 'We attack and we kill every German we can find,' he said. 'None of us will survive, but if this thing happens, none of us will want to. Louise.' He reached out and took his wife's hand. He kissed it. 'God bless you. God bless you for your courage and resource in getting to us. Pray for us.'

'I'm coming with you,' she protested.

'No,' Jean said, 'you are not. You will stay here, with our friends from the RAF. Take good care of her, please.'

'Don't worry about that,' the young pilot said. 'But what's up? What's the panic?' In spite of his attempt at being nonchalant, he looked unhappy.

'We're going to get the children now,' Savage explained. 'The bastards are planning to murder them. Give us three hours, and if we're not back by then, get to hell out of here. And make sure you take Madame de Bernard with you.'

He didn't touch Louise. He raised the sten gun and saluted her. 'We'll get them,' he said. 'And we'll be back.'

Standing with the pilot beside her, Louise watched them running across the sunlit field and into the shadow of the trees. Minutes later, the sound of the Mercedes's engine was followed by the uneven rumbling of Camier's van. Then there was silence. The pilot looked uncomfortable; the woman was crying, and he didn't know what to do. He remembered the hip flask and quickly offered it.

'Drink this,' he said. 'It'll make you feel better—come on, don't upset yourself; there's nothing you can do about it.'

'Thanks.' Louise swallowed; the raw whisky made her cough. She wiped her hand across her eyes using the same gesture as Albert Camier. 'I'm sorry,' she said. 'It's just nerves. I'm all right now.' He had a young, worried face, its lack of comprehension suddenly infuriated her. She turned away from him.

'You're American, aren't you?' He had walked after her. He wanted company; he was personally brave in situations which he understood, but waiting around for three hours in German-occupied France while a group of inexperienced Frenchmen tried to attack the S.S. was not a contingency for which he had been trained. The navigator and gunner were back at the aircraft. The quiet, sunlit field and the surrounding trees was the most sinister place he had ever been. 'Where do you come from?' he persisted. 'How did you get here?'

'I live here,' Louise answered. 'I'm married to a Frenchman. They should have taken me with them. I can't stand this waiting.'

'It's pretty bloody,' he agreed. 'If the Jerries come I've got orders to set fire to the plane. You'll just have to run for it, I'm afraid.'

'It won't matter what I do.' Louise turned to him. 'One of their top men is lying dead in my house; my sister-in-law shot him. We're finished, whatever happens. And I don't care; I don't care about anything but saving the children. They've dug a mass grave for them in the woods.'

'Christ,' the airman muttered. 'You can't believe it, can you?'

'I can,' Louise answered. 'I can believe anything. Could I have a cigarette?'

'Don't worry,' he said. 'It'll be all right. Couple of hours and they'll be back here. Take the packet; I've got plenty more.' Louise saw him take a service revolver out of his jacket, load it and put it back. Together they sat on the grass under the shadow of the wings, to wait.

• • • • •

The engine sent from Paris was an old-fashioned steam locomotive, manned by a German army driver and two firemen from the depot. A single cattle truck was connected up behind. It was wooden-walled, creosoted black and the sliding door was drawn back. An S.S. guard stood at the entrance; he carried a whip of plaited leather. The first group of children climbed up unaided; a seven-year-old had to be lifted. The German swung him easily onto the top step. The boy hesitated and began to scream with fear of the darkness inside. The whip cracked as a warning to the rest to hurry up. The boy was pulled inside and only his persistent crying could be heard. Michelle Giffier was kept to the last; she stood near the Major, watching the pathetic file disappear into the black mouth of the cattle truck; she carried a five-year-old girl in her arms. Suddenly she turned to the Major. 'They won't be hurt—you promise?'

'My word of honour,' the Major said. 'Hurry up; we're running late and you have a long journey. There's food and water inside.' He saluted her. 'Heil Hitler.' She had a thin body, her clothes were creased and she looked dishevelled; she reminded him of many other women he had sent on a similar journey. The expendables, the inferiors, weeping Jewesses clutching their children and moaning, sections of humanity marked by nature for disposal by the strong.

The girl mounted the few steps and went inside. He gave an order and the door was dragged shut, its heavy batten secured. The cries coming from within were muffled. Three of his men climbed into the engine cab and stood with the driver. A third climbed to the roof of the cattle truck and crouched by the machine gun mounted on top. The Major gave a signal and the train lurched forward, hissing steam. Behind them, held back by a ring of S.S. guards, the people who had gathered at the station sent up a cry. The Major turned and addressed them.

'You've brought this punishment on yourselves,' he shouted. 'You know now the price of opposition to the Reich! Go back to your homes! Disperse or my men will open fire!'

There weren't more than twenty men and women; the stricken parents round the school had not had time to get there. Helpless, they began to drift away. Many of the women wept, the men looked back and cursed, a few waved their fists. One of the guards fired a burst over their heads and they scattered. The stationmaster had been locked into his office. Contemptuously they flung the door open; he staggered out. The S.S. piled into the lorries and drove off; their acceleration was an insult.

Down the line the rear of the cattle truck disappeared from view.

• • • • •

The group of men at the control point heard the car approaching. It was the Standartenführer's Mercedes being driven even faster than when it had passed them not long before. Automatically they saluted; it shot past them and the senior NCO peered after it. 'There must be something up,' he said 'He never drives like that. You, Fritche, go after him and see if everything's all right.' The motorcyclist kicked his machine and minutes later Savage heard the whine of its engine.

'They've seen us!' Dumois shouted. He was staring through the back window. 'He's coming after us! Go faster!'

'He'll catch up,' Savage said. 'Open your window—quick. Be ready, Albert, I'm going to slow down. Let him get close and then shoot him. Now!'

The Mercedes' red brake light showed so suddenly that the motorcyclist found himself shooting towards the car; he slowed sharply. He saw something glint at him from the nearside window and made an instinctive movement to swerve, but the reflex came too late. A burst from Dumois's sten gun ripped into him; his machine reared up and then went spinning off the road as he fell.

'I got him!' Dumois shouted with exultation. 'I got him!' Savage didn't answer. He snapped his foot down on the accelerator and took the road which branched to the left towards the famous hunting ground and beauty spot, Chemire.

. . . . .

'Lie down, Mademoiselle Régine—I'll make you something hot to drink.'

'No,' Régine said. She sat on the edge of her bed, her hands gripped together on her lap. 'I'm all right, Marie-Anne. Leave me alone.'

'Jean-Pierre said I was to sit with you,' the old woman protested. She had known Régine since she was born; the face looking up at her seemed to belong to a stranger. It was grey-coloured, as bloodless as if she were dead; the eyes were dilated, the lips trembled, but she no longer cried.

'I've told you I'm all right. Go away!'

Régine didn't move for some minutes; she sat on the bed and twisted her fingers together. The first hysterical storm had subsided, leaving her sick and drained. He was dead. She had gone on firing at him until the gun was empty. If she closed her eyes she could see his face, changing to the ghastly hue of death, the jaw falling slack, one hand grasping his side, blood trickling between the fingers. Blood coming from his mouth. She gave a low cry, and then stopped. His body must still be downstairs. An awareness of danger crept into her confused mind; she got up and went to the door. It was an instinctive movement, without real direction. She couldn't go downstairs and see him lying there. She couldn't call Jean-Pierre and tell him to take the body away...

She opened the door and hesitated. Her father. Her father was upstairs; she could go to him, sit with him. When she went into his room, he was sitting in his armchair, a book open on his lap. He smiled when he saw her. Memory often deserted him at the first sight of someone, but never with his daughter. He held out his hand, and said, 'Come in, my little one. Come in!'

She bent and kissed him and his hand clutched at hers, like the claw of weak bird. Tears filled Régine's eyes.

'How are you, Papa? How did you sleep?'

'Not well.' He shook his head. 'There was so much noise last night. The Germans are coming but you mustn't be afraid.'

'I'm not,' she said. 'Don't worry about me.'

'I won't let them hurt you,' the old Comte said. 'I fought them once before—I can do it again . . .'

He stroked her hair, his hand tremulous, his attention flitting from subject to subject. Emotion distressed him, anger made his heart race, and he sank quickly back into tranquillity.

'It's very warm Régie,' he said. 'Take this rug away, will you? I don't need it.' She took the rug off his knees and folded it. She turned and looked at him. 'You look pale, my darling,' he said. 'Is anything the matter?'

'No,' Régine said. For a moment she had thought to find a refuge with him. But it was a child seeking a child. She came and kissed him. Love. Love for this gentle old ghost whose body was still earthbound; love that consumed and burned for a man whose brutal sensuality had corrupted everything else. Adolph Vierken. If his body was discovered, they would all be shot.

'I've got a few things to do downstairs,' she said. 'Then I'll come back and read to you.'

'Don't be too long,' he said. 'Come back soon.'

She found Jean-Pierre in the hallway. He was pulling the driver's body along by the feet; the effort was exhausting him. Régine paused, and then looked away.

'Did you do that?'

'Yes,' the old man said. 'The swine—I nearly blew his head off! My grandchildren . . .'

'We've got to get rid of him,' Regine said. 'And of the one in the salon. I'll help you with this one first.'

The driver was a big man, and his weight was too much for them. Régine called Marie-Anne. Blood streaked the stone-flagged floor from the German's shattered skull. The old woman didn't blanch or even turn away. She looked down at the body and spat. Then she seized a leg and began to drag. They didn't speak; getting him out of the house required all their strength. There was a long garden trolley, which Marie-

Anne found, and heaving together they managed to get the German's body on it.

'This way!' Régine gasped. 'Down that path . . .' They dragged the trolley to the end of the garden path to the enormous heap of compost and leaf mould which had not been cleared for three years. Occasionally Minden's batman Fritz used to mow the lawns and tidy the kitchen garden, but there hadn't been a young gardener at St. Blaize since the war. The old man who kept the vegetables and weeded along the front of the Château was bent with rheumatism. Moving the compost heap was out of the question. Régine and Jean-Pierre heaved on the trolley and the body rolled off. They pulled it out of sight behind the mound.

Gasping for breath, with sweat running down their faces, the three of them paused. 'Now,' Régine said; her body was trembling with the exertion, and her clothes were sticking to her skin. 'Now let's get the other one. Marie-Anne, go in first and cover the face. I don't want to see it.'

Vierken seemed less heavy; the old woman had wrapped a kitchen towel round his head, Régine helped to half lift, half drag him without looking at him. She didn't realise that as she worked she was crying, the tears running down her face, her mouth screwed up with soundless sobs. Neither of the servants commented, even to themselves. Something terrible had happened to Mademoiselle Régine, but she was in command and they obeyed her.

At last the two bodies lay beside each other at the edge of the heap.

'What are we going to do?' Jean-Pierre mumbled. 'I can't dig a grave deep enough for them, I haven't the strength.'

'We don't have to dig,' Régine said. 'That's why we've brought them here. We'll move that earth on top of them. Three of us can do it. But first we'd better clean up the mess in the house. Marie-Anne, you go back and do that. Jean Pierre, get two shovels. We'll begin on this.'

'Won't they come looking for them?' the old woman asked. Her husband was still out of breath.

'Nobody knew where he was going this morning,' Régine said. 'He was expected at the school; they're probably still waiting for him. Madame has taken the car. There's nothing to connect him with St. Blaize except me; I can say he went on to the school. They'll think he was ambushed—or kidnapped! Anyway, we've got to do our best. We have the Comte to worry about.'

'They'll murder him,' Jean-Pierre said. 'They'll murder us all, if they find anything.'

'They're not going to find anything,' Régine said. 'What's done is done,' she muttered. 'I've got to protect Papa now. Get the shovels!'

• • • • •

Albert Camier's van rattled along the road; the men crouched in the back were bumped and jolted. It was a narrow country road, not much better than a track, and it wound its way across country until it joined up with the railway line and intersected it at the little crossing. Jean de Bernard was seated beside Camier; he carried his sten gun across his knees, covered by his jacket. His shirt sleeves were rolled up and his tie removed. As they rounded a bend the railway line came into view, not more than a hundred yards ahead of them. The engine stood at the crossing, steam idling from it; the cattle truck was open. A single figure in uniform straddled the roof, leaning against a machine gun.

'Stop!' Jean de Bernard yelled, and Camier stamped on the brake. For a moment they stayed immobile, staring at the scene; the old crossing keeper had seen the van and was moving slowly towards the gates to open them.

'Oh mother of Jesus,' Camier groaned. 'Mother of Jesus—we're too late!'

'The others won't be,' Jean said. 'They had the Mercedes and they took the short route. We've got to put these pigs out of action. There's three in the engine and one on the roof there. Drive forward and when you get to the crossing, stall the engine.'

The S.S. guard on the roof watched the van come close and trained the gun on it. Within his view, but hidden from Jean and Camier, a column of children was moving slowly across the field towards the dark lip of the wood at Chemire. It was a brilliant morning; the sun beat down upon the man on the wooden roof, making the metal parts of the gun hot to the touch. His collar was tight and a ring of sweat stained the edge; he ran one finger under it, his right hand crooked round the trigger of the machine gun. The van bumped over the level crossing and then stopped. The old keeper shuffled forward, waving his arm. 'Go on,' he shouted, 'You can't stop there—this train is leaving any minute!'

Inside the van Jean whispered to Camier. 'Get out—he knows you. Open the bonnet and fiddle inside. I'll follow. Don't do anything, just keep your head down.'

'Ah, good morning,' Serard saluted the Mayor. 'What's the matter—trouble?'

'Blasted thing's falling to pieces,' Camier muttered. 'I'll just have a look . . .' He threw up the bonnet and dived under it, pretending to grab at engine parts with shaking hands. He heard the van door open and a moment later Jean appeared beside him.

'I'm going to get the one on the roof,' he whispered. 'Stay where you are and for Christ's sake don't put your head up when it starts . . .' Then he was gone. He went to the rear of the van and opened one door. Inside the men huddled against each other stared at him from the dimness. 'Grenades,' he said softly. Two were passed to him; they went into his jacket pockets. 'A pistol; I can't hide the sten.' It was handed to him and disappeared under the jacket.

When Jean reappeared he saw the crossing keeper leaning beside Camier, looking at the engine. There was a shout from the train; the Army driver leaned out and yelled at them. 'Get that moving! Push it!'

Jean looked up at him and shrugged; the S.S. guard behind the machine gun was looking directly down at him. He slipped his hand in his pocket and found the sectioned surface of the grenade. He walked round the front of the engine, which placed him out of sight, and then, crouching, ran round the side of it. He pulled the pin on the first grenade, released the side catch and tossed it towards the cab. At the same moment he straightened and aimed his pistol at the man on the roof. The guard was not looking directly at him, his attention was focused on the van. Jean de Bernard sighted him; not daring to aim for the head in case he missed, he fired at the trunk. The sound of the shot cracked out, and he dropped on one knee. The blast of the grenade knocked him to the ground; there was a short stuttering burst of machine gun fire, the hiss and rattle of metal tearing and spinning lethally through the air. By now the van doors were open and the men inside were spilling out. Dazed, with his ears buzzing, Jean picked himself up. Above him the engine was hidden in smoke and blackened fumes; the cabin was shattered and as he watched, a dismembered arm, still wearing a rag of uniform sleeve, fell out and hit the ground. On the roof of the cattle truck, the S.S. guard lay forward, depressing his machine gun; he moved, and Jean de Bernard shot at him a second and a third time. He fell sideways and tumbled off the roof on the other side. Jean ran back to the van; he called to one of the men standing around it. 'Climb up and make sure they're finished inside that cab! Albert . . . Oh God!'

The Mayor of St. Blaize had fallen backwards; the burst of fire from the machine gun had sprayed the area in front of the train as the dying German pressed his trigger, and instinctively Camier had left the shelter of the van and tried to run. He had been cut down by a dozen bullets ripping into his chest. Serard lay riddled on the roadside a few feet away. Jean de Bernard knelt beside Camier. For a moment his eyes opened and he was conscious. Blood frothed in his mouth. 'Caroline,' he choked, and then his eyes rolled up and he died.

'There they are! Look, over there!' A hand seized Jean de Bernard by the arm and shook him. He looked, following the man's excited gestures.

Across the fields the dark caterpillar crawled, its pace the stumblings of the youngest who were still too big to carry. The man who had seen them burst into tears. 'We're in time, in time . . . Oh my God, my darling, we'll get you!'

Jean de Bernard didn't hesitate. He slapped him across the face.

'Get into the van!' he ordered. 'See if it's been damaged—if you can drive it, back it off the line and onto the road. Go on! Now.' He turned to the others. 'There are our children. Look, they've heard the shooting!' Larger figures could be seen running up and down the lines, and the procession began to hurry, faltering and uneven though it was, they were being made to run towards the woods.

'We've got to stop them!' There was a shout from the men.

'Wait,' Jean bellowed at them. 'Stay where you are, you fools—you can't shoot it out with them while they've got the children! Keep calm!'

There was silence then, except for the spasmodic bursts of steam from the engine. The van suddenly began to rattle as its engine turned and fired. It eased backwards away from the railway line and pulled up on the road.

'We can follow them,' Jean said. 'Spread out, and keep low. For God's sake, I know your children are out there, but you've got to keep your heads. If Savage has got through he'll be waiting for them in the woods. If not, then we'll try and pick them off one by one. Separate now and run; we've a hell of a way to go to catch them up!'

. . . . .

Chemire covered an area of about forty acres; as he approached the edge of the wood by the road, Savage slowed down. He spoke to Dumois, who was so excited by the death of the motorcyclist that he couldn't stop talking about it. 'You know the woods,' Savage said. 'Where could they bury the children? Looks as thick as hell to me.'

'On the other side,' Dumois said. 'There's a track about two hundred yards up, it goes through the middle to a clearing. It's a place for picnickers and courting couples. There's nowhere else which isn't stiff with trees. Poachers hide in there during the season and nobody can flush them out. Turn up here—here's the track.' Savage put the Mercedes into low gear and they began to bump through a rough pathway between the trees.

'How far?' Savage asked.

'Another five minutes or so.'

'We stop here.' He got out, closing the door quietly. The little group surrounded him; even Dumois, who was carrying his sten gun at a rakish angle over one shoulder, was subdued. It was very silent, with the feeling of oppressiveness and menace which is common to all woods whose tenure of the land goes back for centuries. The ground was soft and green with moss; tracks stretched ahead of them, rutting deep into the friable dark earth.

'They're up ahead of us,' Savage said. 'There are two sets of tyre marks there; one looks like a small lorry. From now on we don't make a sound. They won't be expecting anyone but they're no fools. They're professionals and if they hear anything, we'll never get within spitting distance of them.' He looked at his watch. 'It's ten o'clock,' he said. 'We made it in very good time. The children won't have got here yet. Check your weapons; Dumois, picking off a motorcyclist doesn't make you a crack shot, so don't get over-confident. I'll go in front and you follow in file. Walk carefully, and don't talk.'

'How do you know the children aren't already dead?' That was a heavy-set man whose name Savage had never learned. He looked tough and morose; his hands were huge and coarse and they gripped the sten gun like hams. Misery made him resentful of the stranger.

'I don't,' Savage snapped back. 'And there's only one way to find out. Come on!' He unslung his sten gun and began to walk, treading with catlike care, avoiding the branches which were lying on the path, dry and cracking underfoot. The rest began to follow. The man who had questioned him made the Sign of the Cross and began to mutter. He had three children, two nephews and several cousins among the victims. He hadn't prayed for thirty years.

• • • • •

The S.S. NCO had posted a lookout on the edge of the wood. He saw the train pull up at the crossing, and the children trickle out of the cattle truck. The men aroused themselves and the machine gunner began checking his weapon. The NCO decided he had time for a cigarette before the distant line of figures reached them. He went back into the wood, leaving his men to report on their progress. He ordered the fire under the coffee pot to be put out, and all uniforms to be properly fastened. He went over to inspect the machine gun. The sound of the grenade exploding and the short stutter of gunfire brought him running to the edge of the wood. Below him the train stood still, smoke pouring from the engine cab. He had a pair of field-glasses; seconds later they showed him the van and the men jumping out of it. Two were lying dead, and the machine gun on the roof of the truck leaned forlornly with its nose down.

He swung the glasses to the file of children. They were running, urged on by three guards, one of whom was using his whip. There was a woman with them, stumbling with a child in her arms; when she slipped there was a moment of total confusion. She was struck and kicked to her feet, the child torn out of her arms. For a brief moment the glasses held her and the scene and then swung back to the train's attackers. They had dispersed and were running after the file of children. The NCO shouted orders; his men came running, their weapons ready.

'They've bombed the train,' he said. 'There's five of them down there and they're on their way up here. Two of you take positions behind the trees. They won't catch the little bastards up, but as soon as you can get them in range pick them off!' He put the glasses up again; the children were within three hundred and fifty yards by now; he could hear shouts and cries. Some of the burial detail came out of the wood to watch. It was the machine gunner, wiping the barrel with an oily rag, who looked up and saw Dumois moving through the trees.

Savage knew they had failed when he heard the guttural yell. He froze behind a tree. They had crept up without making a sound, inching their way through the trees, guided by the voices. The burial pit gaped only a few yards in front of them, and the machine gunner caressed his gun, wiping the barrel with a rhythmic stroke. Then Dumois moved, shocked into forgetting that by now the trees were thinner and anything slipping between them could be seen.

The burst of fire caught him sideways on; Savage saw him spin completely round, both hands flung upwards, the sten dropping away from him. He gave a fearful scream and fell, blood spurting from terrible arterial wounds.

The S.S. training was superb; within seconds every man in the group had taken cover, the NCO was behind a big beech tree and the machine gunner crouched swinging the muzzle from side to side. Savage picked out a man lying flat on the ground, sheltering behind a trunk of beech with a fissure running down the side of it. He dropped to his knee and took aim.

'Come out!' It was shouted in French. 'You haven't a chance, we've got you all covered. Hands up and come out!' He looked over his shoulder and could see three of the men who had come with him, sheltering behind the trees, pointing their sten guns. They looked amateur and clumsy; Dumois was dying noisily only a few yards away from them. Savage slung his sten gun over his shoulder. He made a gesture to the three of them: stay where you are. Don't move. He felt quite cool, the chill of rage settled on him, as it had done when he killed Brühl. He took a grenade from his pocket, pulled the pin out, slipped off his jacket and held it in one hand. He held his sten by its sling in the other. He raised his voice. 'Kamerade! Don't shoot!'

Then with both hands raised to shoulder level, he stepped out from the shelter of the trees. They saw a big man, blond in the brief sunlight, and as he emerged into the clearing, he threw his sten gun away. The NCO stepped from behind the tree; he held his revolver pointed at Savage. His intention to shoot him was obvious.

'Don't shoot,' Savage cried out. 'I surrender!' Under cover of the jacket, his thumb pressed the three-second release catch on the side of the grenade. As the German pulled the trigger, Savage threw it at the machine gun.

The blast tore the gunner to pieces and dropped the NCO who caught it full on. Almost at the same moment, the three Frenchmen ran into the clearing, firing wildly and indiscriminately; the big labourer leaped over Savage's body and the mangled machine gun, he caught two of the S.S. in his fire and dropped them. A third killed him, and was exposed in doing so. The other two of Savage's men shot him together. Then they flung themselves behind trees, and the first grenade fell in the direction of the remaining S.S. composed of the gravediggers, two of whom had been wounded by cross-fire. Screams followed the explosion; the younger of the two Frenchmen, a chemist's assistant, who had done military service and been wounded in the back and invalided out, yelled to his companion and a barrage of grenades fell into the trees around the area. For three minutes they threw, and the forest was shattered by explosions. Wood splinters and human fragments flew; dust covered the clearing, blotting out vision.

Then there was no more sound. The chemist's assistant, who was named Pellissier, and had twin sons, slowly came from behind his tree. There was a groan from the left. He gestured to his companion to follow; moving very carefully he approached the sound. For a moment he disappeared from the other's view behind a clump. There was a short burst of fire and then he stepped out. The two men looked at each other. 'We got them,' Pellissier said slowly. 'They're all dead now.'

He dropped his sten, and went to Savage.

The NCO's bullet had caught him in the chest; its impact had thrown him to the ground just before the grenade exploded. The blast had concussed him, blood was staining the front of his shirt.

'He's dying,' the second man said. 'If he hadn't got that swine with the machine gun . . .'

'I don't know how bad the wound is,' Pellissier said. He had opened the shirt and was swabbing with a handkerchief. 'I've nothing to dress it with. Don't move, friend, for God's sake, you've been hit.' Savage had opened his eyes.

'Get the kids,' he said. 'Never mind frigging about with me.' He spoke in English and neither of them understood. His eyes closed again. Pellissier took off his own shirt and tore it in strips; he bandaged Savage's chest, but within minutes the dressing was soaked through. He shook his head. 'I can't help him,' he said. 'It's no use. We'd better go and look outside the wood.'

At the first sound of firing, the S.S. had halted the column of children. Michelle Giffier was sobbing, embracing the children nearest her. One of the guards yelled at her. 'Shut up! Shut up, you bitch, or I'll smash your jaw!'

The firing in the wood was suddenly interrupted by a series of explosions. The children began to scream. The senior S.S. guard, a man in his forties with service in the East and a corporal's rank, bellowed at them to lie down. Michelle ran among them, dragging them to the ground.

'You!' the corporal shouted. 'Come here!' He seized her by the arm, pulling her in front of him. The sound of fighting in the wood had stopped. The children were crying and moaning with fear. The corporal looked back down the field to the train. There was no sign of the men who had attacked it. The ground was uneven; they might well be within range of him and hidden by the terrain. He had twenty children, one trembling woman as a human shield, and only two men. He swore, and jerked savagely at the woman, in his rage. He cupped a hand to his mouth and yelled, 'Comrades! Show yourselves! Are you all right up there!' There was no answer. No one appeared.

Somehow the French had discovered their plan and mounted an attack. The silence showed him that it must have been successful. They were waiting for him in the wood. Behind him, the attackers of the train were moving after him. If he obeyed his common sense and abandoned the brats, he would be shot for cowardice and disobeying orders. Discipline was merciless. His only salvation was to carry out his orders as much as he could and then run for it. He made up his mind. He shouted an order in German to his two subordinates. 'Start shooting the little bastards—then we'll make a run for it!'

It was part of Michelle Giffier's youthful curriculum to know two foreign languages. She understood and spoke both English and German. He flung her aside and she fell. As she watched, he grabbed his machine gun. She gave a wild scream and with a speed and strength that was beyond her frail physique, she sprang up and threw herself on him.

He was a powerfully built man, trained to a high pitch of physical fitness. He would have thrown a man off in one movement. The ferocious woman who attacked him drove her nails into his face, raking for the eyes, the gun went off, and it was a moment or two before he swept her aside and smashed his elbow into her. As she fell, Jean de Bernard came over the rise in the ground and shot him. The children lay sprawled on the ground. The two S.S. men were on their feet; both were dead before they had a chance to fire, killed by Pellissier and his companion who had come out of the wood above them.

For a moment nobody moved; Jean de Bernard stood with his gun slowly pointing downwards. Michelle Giffier lay in a heap by the dead German. Then he walked forward, joined by the rest of his group; one of them gave a cry and began to run. Jean de Bernard stopped by a small child, who knelt on the ground hiding its face and sobbing with terror. Very gently he lifted him up. It was the child of Dumois, whom he did not know was dead. 'Oh, oh,' the boy wept, and flung his arms around his neck.

'It's all right, little one,' Jean said gently. 'It's all right. You're safe now. You're safe . . .'

. . . . .

The navigator and the gunner were conferring with the pilot. He walked over to Louise. 'Look,' he said, 'it's three hours. There's no sign of them.'

'Please,' Louise begged him. 'Just a few more minutes . . . they'll be here! You can't leave without them!'

'Your chap gave me the time limit; I ought to start the old girl up and get us out of here.' He frowned and looked at his watch again. Louise had taken turns in watching by the roadside from the shelter of the trees. No traffic at all had passed in the last hour.

'I'm not going,' Louise said. 'I'm staying here. What will you feel like if you take off and you see them coming back with the children?'

'Oh for Christ's sake,' the pilot said. 'I'll give them another fifteen minutes and then I'm off. We're going to get the nets off her.'

'Thank you,' Louise said. 'I know they'll come.' She started pulling the camouflage netting down. It had seemed like days while they waited. They had nothing to say to each other; it was a relief to wait, hidden, by the roadside, praying that every motor sound was either the Mercedes or the van. Once a military ambulance raced past her, and she had given way to momentary panic. Chemire was miles away, and nearer to St. Blaize than the Lavallière field. They wouldn't send an ambulance along that route. Twenty minutes later it returned, travelling more slowly. Inside, the dead body of the motorcyclist was strapped to a stretcher. There were so many injuries that the bullet wounds which had sent him spinning off his machine were not obvious on the first examination.

When the plane was free of camouflage, the pilot turned to Louise. He looked awkward but determined. 'Five minutes to go,' he said. 'I'm going to start her up. I'll help you inside.'

'No!' Louise backed away from him. 'I'm going to look again . . .' She ran into the trees before he could stop her. The road was deserted; she leaned against a tree and suddenly all hope left her. They had failed; Jean and Savage, Camier and the others. They had been butchered and the children were already tumbled in the grave at Chemire. . . . The Mercedes came into view first. Then a small German lorry, its canvas sides and body marked with the Iron Cross, followed by a small field car and then last of all, rattling as if it were going to fall to pieces on the road, came Camier's little delivery van. Louise ran into the road; behind her there was a roar as the aircraft propellers began to turn in the field. She waved wildly at the Mercedes, tears blurring her sight of who was driving, and then dashed back into the belt of trees, shrieking at the pilot to stop . . . stop . . .

Within the shelter of the trees the cavalcade jolted to a stop. Louise came running back, followed by the airmen. The first person she saw was Jean de Bernard; she threw herself into his arms. 'Oh Jean—Jean, thank God! I'd given up! The plane was leaving . . .'

The Comte kissed his wife. 'Don't cry,' he said. 'We got them all; they're all safe. Come and help get them out.' Children were being lifted down from the inside of the German lorry; they came tumbling out of Camier's van. The men who had rescued them were calling for their own sons and daughters; Pellissier found his twins and knelt on the ground, hugging them, openly crying with relief.

'Papa—papa . . .' The cries were repeated as fathers and children were reunited. Michelle Giffier, her face so bruised and sallow with shock that Louise hardly recognised her, watched the scene, with a wailing toddler by the hand.

'Madame Giffier—what did they do to you? Come here, little one.' Louise tried to take the child. Instantly it clung to the teacher with both hands, its face screwed up in terror.

'I'm all right,' she said. 'Thank God none of the children was hurt. Don't make that noise, Ninie, there's nothing to be frightened about now . . . Oh Madame, I can't tell you what might have happened . . . In the clearing they'd dug a huge pit for us . . .' She turned away and Louise saw her shudder.

She spoke calmly but hysteria was very close. Louise put an arm round her. She was a proud, self-contained woman who would have resented the intimacy in other circumstances. Now she burst into tears on Louise's shoulder. 'It was so terrible,' she said. 'The firing, I thought we'd all be killed. And then one of them was going to open fire on us—just at the last minute!'

'Don't think about it,' Louise said. 'You're going to England with the children. They'll be safe there till the war's over. Get them together and we'll lift them inside. Come on; the pilot's got some whisky. I'll get you some.'

The plane stood out in the field, clear of the trees 'Children,' Jean de Bernard called, 'line up and come over here. You're going in the aeroplane with Madame Giffier.'

Shepherded by fathers and the teacher, the children formed a queue; many were too dazed to understand what was happening to them. Others began to cry and protest. There were heart-breaking cries. 'I don't want to go—I want Maman—Maman!' One boy broke free and had to be caught, struggling and kicking against being lifted into the plane. Jean de Bernard came to Louise.

'It was Savage who saved them,' he said. 'Pellissier told me. He deliberately sacrificed himself.' Shock robbed the scene of reality; she didn't say anything for a moment. Jean didn't touch her.

'He's dead?'

'He's dying,' he answered. 'He wanted me to leave him behind.'

Louise moved back from him. 'And you did?'

'No, he's in the scout car. He's going back on the plane.' She turned and ran, back into the belt of shadow where the car was standing. A man who was the notary's clerk in St. Blaize was bending over someone on the ground. Louise pushed past him. Savage lay with his head on a folded jacket; his shirt had been cut away and Pellissier's blood-soaked bandage replaced. His face was grey and cold with sweat, his eyes closed. The notary's clerk got up and made way for her.

'He's been asking for you, Madame,' he said. 'I was just going to call you.'

'Go away,' Louise whispered. 'Please, go away.' She caught at the slack hand lying by Savage's side. 'Oh God,' she held it tight and her tears fell on him. He opened his eyes; there was a glaze over them which cleared as he recognised her.

'It worked,' he said. She had to bend close to hear him. 'We got every child back. And we killed all those bastards . . . I take it back about the French . . . they were bloody marvellous.'

'Don't talk,' Louise begged him. 'Please, don't say any more. Lie still . . .'

'That son of a bitch knew how to shoot.' Savage grimaced. 'I love you—can you hear me?'

'Yes, yes, I can hear you.' Louise felt a pressure from his hand.

'I'm not through yet. He's a good guy, that husband of yours; but he made a mistake. He should've left me behind . . .'

'You're going home,' Louise said. 'You're going on the plane and you'll get proper care—oh darling, don't die—I couldn't bear it . . .'

He didn't seem to hear; his eyes had closed. Suddenly she felt his hand tighten on hers. 'Louise . . . I'll be back. Remember that.'

She felt Jean de Bernard come behind her; she turned round to him, still holding Savage's hand, and as he watched she bent and kissed it.

'He must go now; the plane's ready.'

'Be careful,' she said. 'Try not to hurt him . . .' She saw them lift him; he was unconscious and her last sight of him was masked by the navigator who reached down from inside the plane to lift him up.

At the edge of the field she waited in the little group of men, as the propeller turned and then idled, turned and then swung into full power. The noise was a hideous assault, the airstream tore at their clothes and sent them staggering, holding to each other for support. Fathers with children waved and shouted; Jean de Bernard put his arm around her and held her steady. The plane was taxi-ing fast down the field, bumping and lurching over the uneven surface; suddenly its nose lifted, and the clumsy progress became a smooth, miraculous ascent into the sky. The machine rose steadily, easily topping the trees, climbing until it became smaller and smaller and the noise of its engine a distant throb.

Nobody spoke for some moments. Men who had seemed extraordinary, with guns on their shoulders, slipped back into their normal selves. They looked upward, disconsolate and lost without their children. Out of the ten who had started out from St. Blaize, six were left. The notary's clerk blew his nose and found a packet of cigarettes. He came and offered one to the Comte and more hesitantly to the Comtesse. Louise refused. Jean de Bernard inhaled into his lungs. He wiped his face with his forearm and looked round at them.

'Our children are safe,' he said. 'Whatever happens to us, they'll have their lives and they'll come back to St. Blaize when the war is over. That is what matters.'

'What do we do now?' Pellissier asked him. 'Where do we go?'

'Home,' Jean de Bernard said. 'Home to collect money, food, everything we'll need for the next few months. We have two alternatives. We can wait at St. Blaize for the murder squads to come and pick us up, or we can go into the countryside and fight. Thanks to the British we have guns and ammunition. We have the lorry and that car. We may not last long but we'll give some account of ourselves.'

'I'll go with you,' the clerk said. He was a gentle, precise man who usually wore wire-rimmed spectacles. 'And me,' Pellissier said. One by one, with one exception, they came and shook his hand. The lone dissenter also shook it.

'My wife is ill,' he said. 'I can't walk out and leave her. I have to make sure she's all right with her sister. If I can join you, Monsieur, be sure I will. But I have to look out for her first.' He came and shook hands with Louise; the others followed.

'I'll stay here,' Jean de Bernard said. 'The rest of you go back to St. Blaize in the van and take my wife with you. Pick up what you need and come back here as quickly as you can. There won't be much time before they realise what's happened at Chemire. When nobody reports back they'll start searching. We have an hour or two start.'

He threw the cigarette away.

He turned to Louise; they were alone, as the others dispersed and somebody started Camier's van. 'I thought you would have gone with him,' he said.

'No,' Louise answered. 'I'm staying here; with you and Papa and Régine. The children are in Paris, they'll be safe there. But I loved him, Jean. And I'll never know what happened to him.'

'I know you did,' the Comte said. 'Thank you for staying. God knows what the end will be for us all. Will you take care of St. Blaize and Papa and Régine for me?'

'You know I will,' she said. He took her hands and held them. Tears came into his eyes.

'At least now you can be proud of me,' he said.

'I will always be that. God bless you, Jean. Come back to us.' She came close, and for a moment they held each other.

'I don't want to say goodbye,' Jean de Bernard said. 'So just go with them now, my darling. Just go . . .'

Louise pulled away and ran to the little van; the passenger door was flung open for her and she jumped inside. She sat, tears running down her face, refusing to look back until they came to the edge of the road. Then suddenly she couldn't bear it. She leaned out of the window, staring back through the trees. It was too late to see him. There was nothing visible but shadow.

• • • • •

They were all silent. Paul was standing in front of the fireplace, looking down at the ground; there was a frown between his eyes; his wife was sitting with her hands clasped on her lap, staring at Louise. Suddenly Sophie got up, flung her cigarette into the fire and went over to her mother. Louise glanced up and felt her daughter's arm slip round her shoulders.

'All right,' Sophie said. 'Now you've told us. What a hell you must have gone through. All of you.' She bent down and kissed her.

Louise's eyes filled with tears. 'Thank you, darling. I hoped you'd understand.'

'Perhaps it's easier for her.' Françoise de Bernard spoke in a strained voice. 'Sophie wouldn't mind anything coming out —she hasn't got a family and a position to think about. But we have!' She faced Louise. 'What about Paul and the election? What in God's name would his enemies make of a story like that? His father was a collaborator who only resisted at the end—his aunt was the mistress of that dreadful butcher . . .' She stopped suddenly, both hands to her mouth. 'Oh my God —under that big rockery—is that where those bodies were buried?'

'Yes,' Louise answered quietly. 'I'm afraid so. They're still there.'

'Oh my God! It's horrible!' Her daughter-in-law was sheet white. She stared at Louise, 'And you lived here—knowing that!'

'Let's keep it in proportion,' Paul de Bernard said. 'Forget about the rockery. After all these years there's nothing left there anyway. What you've told us, Mother, is exactly what that woman Minden hinted at. Only worse. She didn't know that Régine murdered that man Vierken.

'They'll bring it out that you slept with that German, and that's why he risked his life to save your children,' Françoise said. 'They'll make it as sordid as they can. Two of you, you and Régine. Nobody will believe it was only once—you know what people will think . . . We'll be disgraced, Paul's career is as good as over now, if even a whisper of this gets out.'

'I don't believe that,' Paul said. 'They've nothing to gain by dragging mother through the dirt. All they want is a case for mitigating the sentence on Minden, something to prove he was personally humane. Saving Sophie and me is just what they need. They'll concentrate on that. Nothing else need come out in court at all. Don't worry about it, Mother.'

'I think we're trying to delude ourselves,' Louise said. 'That woman threatened to bring every detail out in court. And in telling the story of what Heinz Minden did, she'll see that my part in it, his relationship with your father, Régine and Vierken, everything will be exposed. I believe she'll do it. If she's told the defence council all this, and I refuse to testify, they'll have to make a big drama out of it to emphasise his heroism. But if I go to court, I need only say that he was fond of you both, and risked his own life to save you. My presence there to speak for him will have tremendous impact. That's why not even an affidavit will satisfy them. I shall have to go and give evidence at the trial.'

'No you won't!' Sophie said loudly. 'You're not going near any court! How do you know what they'll ask you when you get up on the witness box—what do you think the prosecution's going to try and make of this? They'll tear you to pieces! As for you, Paul, if you let her do this, I'll never speak to you again! To hell with your political career—Mother's not going to be sacrificed.'

'I shall be sacrificed anyway if the truth comes out,' Louise said to them all. 'I could bear that, but not to see you hurt, Paul's future destroyed. Your father's good name smeared. He was a hero, decorated for his work in the Resistance. To hear him called a collaborator would break my heart. To see your Aunt Régine's memory disgraced . . . I can't do it. I knew that even before I came down here, but I suppose I was hoping to escape. I'll have to go to Germany.'

'No!' Sophie interrupted. 'I won't let you!'

'I think you've made the right decision,' Françoise said. She stood up, and linked her arm through her husband's. 'Paul would never ask you, but I know how much his political career means to him. I know how hard he's worked for St. Blaize, and this would ruin everything for him. The whole family would be disgraced. As it is now, the Comte is a hero, his sister a Resistance heroine, killed fighting the Germans. Please, please let us keep this between us. Go to Germany and speak for this man. Otherwise we're destroyed.'

'No, Mother,' Paul said. 'Don't do it. Not for me. I'll withdraw my candidature. Then they can say what they like. It was a very long time ago. People won't be all that interested if there's no political capital to be made out of it. It'll soon be forgotten.'

'I've made up my mind,' Louise said to them. 'There's nothing else to be done. I'll telephone Ilse Minden in the morning.' She smiled at her son. He looked strained and guilty. His arm was still linked to his wife's, and as she watched, Louise saw them clasp hands. They were in agreement, and she couldn't blame either of them. Paul had built his own life at St. Blaize; whether Louise and she had little in common or not, didn't denigrate the efforts of Françoise to be a good wife and to advance his chosen career. Louise might not like her, but she appreciated her loyalty to her husband. And she even understood the shock and condemnation which the younger woman hadn't been able to conceal. She had been brought up in the post-war world, married into a family with a reputation for heroic resistance in the late war, and had never imagined that all was not exactly as it seemed. In Françoise's conventional world, people did not fornicate and kill, or invite a German into their bed, however patriotic the motive. She glanced up at her daughter, and saw with a pang that the face was pale, the mouth taut. Sophie had been shaken too, although she was too loyal and protective to her mother to reveal it. Not by the infidelity, but by the unconsummated love for Roger Savage. Instinctively Louise knew that to Sophie that love was a betrayal of the father she had loved so deeply, and knowing this had hurt her.

'Thank you,' Françoise said. Her tone was final, discounting any possibility of second thoughts. 'I know you've made the right decision. Now let us go and have some dinner.'

She led the way out of the salon, into the panelled dining room. It was a silent meal, and immediately afterwards Louise excused herself and went upstairs. At the door she turned and said gently to Sophie, 'Come and say goodnight to me.'

'Of course.' Love flowed between them; forgiveness was implicit in the way her daughter squeezed her and the kiss she gave was warm. 'I'll look in,' she said. 'If you're asleep I won't disturb you. Goodnight, darling. And don't worry.'

But when she came Louise was wide awake. It seemed to Sophie that her mother looked much younger suddenly, sitting up in the bed with her hair hanging down like a girl's, her face slightly in shadow.

She must have looked like that during the time when Roger Savage was at the château. She had always been aware of her mother's beauty and elegance; now, with a sense of shock, she recognised the sexual quality that distinguished her. Louise held out her hand.

'I'm glad you came; come and sit beside me. You're hurt and disappointed, aren't you?'

'Not about Minden.' Sophie brought out the Gauloise packet and lit a cigarette. She had chain-smoked throughout the evening.

'You did the right thing. But the American—I was surprised, that's all. I never thought for a moment you'd ever looked at anyone except Father. You seemed the most devoted, loving couple.'

'And we were,' Louise said quickly. 'After the war when he came back, so terribly hurt and helpless, I realised that I had always loved him. And we were happy, right to the day he died. You know that.'

'I know,' Sophie said. 'You did everything for him. I used to watch his face when you came into the room. It was quite something to see. I suppose I knew I'd never be able to affect anyone that way. Maybe that's why I've never wanted to get married. It would never be like that for me. That's what I thought.' She blew smoke into the air. 'I'd like to ask you something. If you don't mind?' She glanced at Louise, awkward and anxious not to hurt her.

'You can ask anything you like,' Louise said gently.

'Did you ever see Roger Savage again?'

'Yes,' Louise answered. 'For months I thought he was dead. Your father was fighting, the Allies were advancing. Régine and I were here with your grandfather. I couldn't forget the last time I saw Roger. I was sure he'd died, even on the journey. I went through a very bad time, Sophie. I wouldn't have left your father while there was any danger, and I'll answer one question I know you won't ask me; I never had an affair with him. But I loved him. I loved him with all my heart.'

'Poor Mother.' Sophie reached out to her. 'How awful for you. Don't talk about it any more. It doesn't matter.'

'Months later I got news that he was alive and recovering. He'd been sent back to America. And then he came to St. Blaize.' Louise paused. 'You wouldn't remember it, but you saw him arrive. I can see you now, running into the hall, calling for me. And he followed behind you. I sent you out into the garden. He'd kept his word. He'd come back for me.'

'And you didn't go,' Sophie said. 'But you wanted to, didn't you?'

'Yes,' Louise said. 'He wasn't an easy man to refuse. When

he wanted something he got it. But I didn't argue with him, Sophie. I just took him into the salon and showed him your father sitting in the garden in his wheelchair. He understood why I couldn't ever leave him. He left here and I've never heard from him since. That's many years ago.'

'It's sad,' Sophie said. 'Terribly sad for both of you.'

'I never regretted it,' Louise said. 'Your father was happy. That's all that mattered.'

'Darling,' Sophie said suddenly. 'Don't go to Germany. Never mind about Paul and his bloody silly election. Don't put yourself at these people's mercy. I really mean it. I'm afraid of what could happen to you.'

'Nothing will happen to me,' Louise said. 'I'll give my evidence and it'll all be over very quickly. Then I'll come straight home.'

'I'll come with you,' Sophie said. 'But I have a very nasty feeling about the whole thing.'

• • • • •

On the 3rd of October, exactly two weeks after Ilse Minden had come to the house in the Rue Varenne, Louise took the Lufthansa flight to Bonn. Normally she found flying peaceful; unlike many women whose nerves objected to the speed and altitude in jet flying, she was relaxed and calm in the air. On this journey she spent the hour and ten minutes in taut discomfort, wishing she had allowed Sophie to come with her. The more she tried to convince herself that the ordeal would be minimal, the more uneasy she became. Minden's wife had been brief and non-committal on the telephone. She didn't thank her for agreeing to help, or say anything but that Minden's lawyer would be in touch with her. The letter, signed Siegfried Kopner, had arrived within three days; it was friendly and courteous and said all the grateful things which Ilse Minden had omitted. Temporarily Louise was reassured. Paul and Françoise accepted the tone of the letter with relief; only Sophie was sceptical. The affair with Gerard was coming to a graceless close; there were rows and mutual walk-outs, and Sophie looked pale, and had lost weight. Louise refused to have her travel to Germany. She had installed her in the Rue Varenne, where she could escape the importunities and tantrums of her lover, and promised to send for her when the trial began. At Bonn airport she found a uniformed chauffeur waiting with her name written on a card. He bowed and spoke in clumsy French, 'Herr Kopner's compliments and I'm taking you to your hotel.'

The gesture was unexpected. So too were the flowers she found in her hotel room. Welcome to Bonn. Siegfried Kopner. It was a luxurious hotel, the Steigenberger Hof; smartly decorated in modern style without extremes of taste. She dined alone in the large dining room, watched by groups of business men who interrupted their conversations and negotiations long enough to admire the elegance and beauty of the new arrival. She felt lonely and conspicuous, more of an alien in the atmosphere than she had ever felt before, and since Jean's death she had travelled every spring. Her last trip had been to Mexico. She was neither shy nor self-conscious about going anywhere alone; but in the heavy chic of that German hotel dining room, Louise felt a sense of total isolation. The food was excellent, the service impeccable; she ate very little and didn't look round her. A large middle-aged man at a nearby table was staring at her openly. There was an appointment with Siegfried Kopner for the next morning at eleven. If it wouldn't inconvenience her, he preferred the meeting to be in his office.

This country and these people, clean, efficient, polite, were the background of Heinz Minden, who had worked on a project to kill millions, and yet risked himself to save two children of whom he had grown fond. It was the birthplace of Adolph Vierken.

It was impossible to fault them or to explain the feeling of disquiet which was increasing. Perhaps it was the reflex of the war, of years spent equating the sound of German with tyranny and fear. Perhaps the sight of that schoolhouse ringed with armed men, and the huge empty pit at Chemire, which she had gone to see after the Allies took St. Blaize in their advance, had prejudiced her for ever. She didn't know the reason, but she found it very difficult to sleep that night.

The next morning was crisp and sunny; she went for a walk, hoping to admire the city. The charm of the old University City was being eroded, its shape deformed by modern buildings, post-war constructions without beauty or tradition, but there was no attempt to hide its affluence. The cars were sleek and expensive, the shops full of luxuries, priced very high. She found nothing to admire except the weather, which was beautiful. At ten-forty she found a taxi and went to Kopner's office on Hofgarten Strasse.

It was a twenty-storey block, built in granite and glass, and it glittered in the sunshine like an iceberg. His office was on the nineteenth floor; she went up in a soundless lift, arriving in seconds without any sensation of having moved at all.

A smart, attractive secretary showed her into a private waiting room. It was sparsely but beautifully furnished in contemporary style, and there was a fine Klee drawing on one wall. She lit a cigarette and waited. She insisted, almost angrily, that there was no reason to be nervous.

Her watch showed that she was early, by three minutes. At eleven o'clock exactly the secretary came in, smiled and said, 'Come with me, please. Herr Kopner is expecting you.'

He was a tall man, with receding fair hair and bright blue eyes, soberly but expensively dressed, and when they shook hands, he smelt strongly of toilet-water. He made no attempt to hide his admiration. He kissed her hand and gave a little bow. 'This is a great pleasure, Comtesse. Please come and sit over here. Cigarette?'

Louise took one out of the handsome aluminium box and he was beside her immediately with a light. The smell of his toilet-water or after-shave, whatever it was, was overpowering.

'I am delighted to meet you,' Siegfried Kopner said. He had great confidence in his capacity to charm, and he exerted it to the limit. He thought the American woman exceptionally attractive; he had a weakness for good legs, and hers were beautiful, showing discreetly under the dark sealskin coat. Feet also appealed to him; hers were narrow and high arched, clad in hand-made calf shoes. He looked at her and smiled. No wonder poor Minden had made a fool of himself. If she was this striking now, how much more at that time . . .

'Thank you for the car,' Louise said. 'And the flowers. It was very kind of you.'

'I hope your hotel is comfortable?'

'Yes, it's very nice.'

'I have all the data for the defence here,' Kopner said; he laid his hand on a thick hessian folder. 'I saw Heinz Minden yesterday and I told him you would be coming. He was very grateful.'

'I want to help if I can,' Louise said. 'Could you explain exactly what the charge against him is?'

'Certainly. He's accused of crimes against humanity in that he was working on a nerve gas, which is a weapon outlawed by the Geneva Convention. Unfortunately experiments were carried out upon political prisoners in the early stages of testing the formula, but my client was not concerned with the development of the gas until after this had happened. Otherwise, I'm afraid we would not have any defence to offer.'

'No,' Louise said. The image of a woman, clasping a child in her arms as she died in terrible convulsions, passed through her mind as he spoke. 'No, you couldn't possibly defend that.'

'Believe me, Madame de Bernard, I wouldn't try.' He leaned towards her earnestly. 'I assure you, I abhor the crimes committed by the Nazis. It's because I know that Heinz Minden is an honest man who was misguided, that I've agreed to take his case. You must believe that.'

'I'm sorry for him,' Louise said. 'He was never a bad man, Herr Kopner. He had human feelings; that's more than you could say for some of the others.'

'Adolph Vierken?' He said the name with a slight smile, a suggestion of sympathy, on his mouth. 'A monster; a psychopath. Every country in the world has them, but it was just Germany's misfortune to be ruled by the biggest madman of them all. I must say, Frau Minden's story is a little hard to believe. Would you mind if I asked you some questions?'

'No. If you feel they'll be helpful.'

'In order to make the most of your testimony, Madame, I must have a clear picture of the facts, all the facts, in my mind. Then the prosecution can't spring any surprises. Not, I assure you, that your evidence will be contested. Now, may I ask you something very personal—was Heinz Minden in love with you?'

'Yes,' Louise answered quietly. 'He was.'

Kopner cleared his throat. 'His wife says that you had an *affaire* with him. Is that true?'

'He made love to me once; that was all.'

'I see.' Again he cleared his throat. He half rose from his desk, holding the cigarette box towards her. Louise shook her head.

'May I ask you how it happened?'

'I'd rather not discuss it. It hasn't any relevance to your case.'

'I understand,' he nodded. The look of friendly sympathy had never left his face. He watched her with caution, even with respect. One night. She didn't want to give the details. She could refuse to answer now, but when they were in court . . .

'And your sister-in-law Régine de Bernard—she was killed fighting for the Resistance, wasn't she?'

'Yes,' Louise said. 'She was acting as a liaison for my husband's group, when she was stopped by an army patrol outside Chartres and shot trying to escape.'

'Yet according to Frau Minden, she told Heinz Minden that she was not only Adolph Vierken's mistress but that she was in love with him. Is this the truth? I have to ask you these things, Madame, because I have only Frau Minden's word, second hand from her husband. He won't discuss any of it, even with me. I have to be sure she's not exaggerating.'

'She's not,' Louise answered. 'It is perfectly true. When Vierken disappeared and Régine discovered what he had planned to do to the children, she changed completely. She became a patriot.'

'His disappearance has always fascinated me,' Kopner said casually. 'But then the Resistance knew how to hide their victims.'

The word victim stabbed at her, sharp with warning. She looked into the blue eyes and saw nothing there but friendliness, good will.

'I'd hardly call Adolph Vierken a victim.'

Kopner mentally kicked at himself. Hard. This was not a woman to be treated carelessly. She was far too intelligent; and not afraid to speak her mind. He was unused to being corrected so sharply and a little colour came up under his well-barbered skin.

'An unhappy choice of words,' he said. 'My English is not as good as I would wish. What was the relationship between Heinz Minden and the rest of the family? Did he get on well with your husband, for example?'

'Very well,' Louise said. She took a cigarette out of her case and lit it, forestalling him by seconds. 'He was very generous at a time when we could get very little of anything; he was friendly and never intruded. My husband liked him. He used to play with the children and even go up and sit with my father-in-law. He was an invalid and rather senile. Everyone liked Heinz Minden in the house.'

Yes, Kopner thought, watching her, everyone except you. You didn't like him and it shows by the way you speak. You're trying to be sorry for him, to be impartial. But you hated him; you used his love for you, and because of that love he endangered his life to save your children . . .

'Would you ever have described him as a typical Nazi? You know the type, arrogant, bullying?'

'No, never. He was a quiet man, anxious to be friendly.'

'Good,' Kopner said. 'Excellent. And you will say all this in court? You will speak of him as you have done to me?'

'If you want me to, yes. Because it's the truth. He was like that.'

'When did your husband die, Madame?'

'Ten years ago. Why do you ask?'

'Just for my file,' Kopner said. 'He was a very brave man, highly decorated, wasn't he?'

'Yes. He was shot in the back during a battle with a German patrol, and he spent the rest of his life in a wheelchair.'

'Heinz Minden thought very highly of him,' he said. 'He often talked about him to his wife. He described him as a man of peace.'

'And so he was,' Louise said. 'He always hoped to find a reasonable solution to any problem. He hated war and he hated the waste of life.'

'So it was really the S.S. action against the children that changed him?'

'Yes it was. It changed the whole village, overnight.'

'Overnight,' he repeated. 'Naturally. What an unspeakable crime—it's almost incredible that my countrymen could contemplate such a thing. To murder children. Madame de Bernard, I would like to say something to you.' He stood up; it was a little theatrical as if he were facing an audience.

'I think it is wonderful of you to come and give evidence on behalf of a German, after what happened at St. Blaize en Yvelines. It shows a truly generous spirit.'

'I owe it to him,' Louise said quietly. 'I didn't want to come, to open up the past again. But he deserves to be judged on the good as well as the bad. There is one point I would like you to clarify, Herr Kopner. My evidence will consist only of an account of how he took my children from the school and brought them to Baroness de Cizalle in Paris? Nothing else will be mentioned?'

'Nothing,' Kopner said. 'You will be asked for those details and nothing more. Anything else we have discussed is quite irrelevant. You can be assured of that.'

He pressed his intercom button and spoke in German. A woman's voice answered him. 'I have ordered you a taxi,' he said. 'I'll take you down to the front hall.'

'That isn't necessary,' Louise protested. She didn't want to stand about with him, making small talk. 'I know you're terribly busy. Please don't bother.'

'It will be a pleasure.' He took her elbow and walked with her out of the offices into the passage. The same atomic type lift shot them to the ground floor, and there, drawn up by the pavement, a taxi cab was waiting. He took Louise's hand and made the obligatory pretence of kissing it. 'One thing,' he said. 'Would you be prepared to see Heinz Minden before the trial? I can get permission.' She hesitated. The idea of going to a prison to see someone who must now be an old man repelled her. Kopner looked as if he expected her to agree.

Despising herself, Louise said, 'If it would help, but I'd rather . . .'

'Thank you,' he said quickly. 'I think it would help him. I'll arrange a visiting time and telephone you later. This evening—about eight o'clock?'

'All right.' Louise got into the taxi. 'Would you tell him to take me back to my hotel, please.'

He closed the door, made her a little bow, and spoke rapidly, and in a brisk tone, to the driver. He waved his hand a little as she drove away, and then vanished back into the building. She knew, without being able to rationalise it, that agreeing to see Heinz Minden was the first mistake.

At twelve-thirty Siegfried Kopner left his office. He used a taxi rather than the chauffeur-driven Mercedes which was garaged in the basement of the office block.

He had decided to let the Comtesse de Bernard find her own way to the appointment; the same quirk of meanness which smoked the disgusting cigarettes, resented saving her money on taxi fares. Being met at the airport and greeted by flowers in the hotel should surely be enough to make the right impression. His reason for not using his own car was different; he didn't want anyone to know where he was going. Chauffeurs talked; so did secretaries. His appointment was extremely confidential. He arrived at one o'clock at a large house in the Venusberg district, a smart residential complex, with large expensive houses and gardens. He ran hastily up the steps of a big red sandstone house, built within the last ten years, and disappeared inside. Nobody saw him go in; it was the lunch hour and his compatriots were devoting themselves to eating lunch. Meals in Germany were a serious ritual. It was almost more important to enjoy food than to enjoy life.

The house was heavily furnished, mahogany and gilt, ugly pictures, a massive bronze equestrian group in the hall. He was shown in to a study by a manservant, who didn't ask his name. A man, slightly built, with white hair and a proud face, rose from an armchair and came to meet him. They shook hands. Kopner was stiff, deferential. For a moment or two his host kept him standing. They discussed the weather for two or three sentences, paying tribute to some convention that would not allow them to mention their real business immediately. Then the old man asked him to sit down.

'We will have some wine,' he said. 'And we lunch in fifteen minutes. My wife and family are unfortunately not at home.' Kopner, who had not expected anything else, expressed regret. The man he had come to see was one of the most influential politicians in Bonn.

'Well, Herr Kopner,' he said. 'What happened this morning?'

'I had a very useful interview with the lady,' Kopner said.

'And what sort of impression will she make in court?'

'Exactly what we want. She is extremely attractive, very poised. The contrast between her and Minden should strengthen our case. She admitted that they had been lovers. Also that her sister-in-law was the S.S. commander's mistress. She described her husband, the Resistance hero, as a man who hated war and always sought a compromise whenever possible.'

'That's very encouraging,' the old man said. He had poured a glass of iced Riesling for Kopner and a slightly larger one for himself. He sipped it, showing appreciation. 'I hope she didn't suspect what line your questions will take?'

'I'm sure she didn't. We parted on friendly terms and she has agreed to see Minden. I'll arrange a visit tomorrow morning. She didn't want to go, but I persuaded her.'

'And you think that's wise?'

'I think the newspapers will make a very interesting item of it,' Kopner said. 'After all, here is a man accused of war crimes, being visited in prison by the Frenchwoman with whom he was in love during the war. A wealthy lady with a title, prepared to come and testify for him. That alone will blur the public image of a Nazi murderer.'

'Not the tabloids, I hope. We mustn't have sensationalism at this stage.'

'The *Frankfurter Allgemeine Zeitung*. Very respectable. There will be foreign syndications, of course.'

'I look forward to reading it.' A smile flitted over his mouth and then disappeared. 'I have great confidence in your ability, Herr Kopner. If you can manœuvre this case in the way that our party wants, your political future is assured. You have my word on that.' Kopner bent forward from the waist; it was difficult to bow when sitting down, but he accomplished it.

'My one wish is to serve my country,' he said. 'I have lived with shame and reproach all my life, and I have refused to deny my pride in being German. It's time what happened in the war was seen in its true perspective. The vindictive hounding of men for doing their duty in defence of their country has gone on unchecked for all these years. If we can gain an acquittal for Heinz Minden, or a suspended sentence, there may be an end to these trials. And a political rebuff to the people who advocate them. It's time we stopped hiding from the past, and cringing before the world. What happened at St. Blaize en Yvelines was a military operation, a so-called atrocity, which in fact never took place, and Germans are vilified while the people who collaborated and battened off them are described as heroes. There will be no heroes left by the time this case is over. Just let me get Madame de Bernard into the witness-box.'

'That, my dear Herr Kopner,' the old man said quietly, 'is what we are waiting for. Now let us go in to lunch.'

• • • • •

Bonn prison was a dark stone block, situated in the old part of the city. It was approached by electrically operated gates, and guarded by armed men. Kopner had collected Louise at nine that morning, and passed the short travelling time in explaining to her that she would find Minden very much changed. She was annoyed and embarrassed by the sympathy in his tone, as if he were preparing her for a reunion which must by its nature be a painful one. Without saying so, he conveyed the impression that her relationship with Minden had been more prolonged than the single incident she had described. Her discomfort changed to dread when they passed through the gates, Kopner being quickly recognised and admitted, and were actually within the precincts of the prison itself. It was horribly oppressive, dingy and impersonal, a dungeon for the mind as much as the body. More electrically operated gates, more men with dour faces in grey-green uniforms, horribly reminiscent of men she had known years ago, with the same harsh look of authority. Then they were in a small room, with a plain table and two chairs, lit by fluorescent lighting. The walls were painted a dull slate blue; the effect was chilling and metallic. She turned to Kopner. 'What a dreadful place—how long has he been in here?'

'For two years.' The bland face smiled at her. She thought suddenly that to this pleasant, highly cultured man, there was nothing offensive about the stone cage in which his fellow men were shut away. A warder opened the door; there was a brief conversation between him and Kopner, and when he returned a moment later he brought a third chair. 'Sit down,' Siegfried Kopner said. 'They've gone to bring him up. I'm afraid smoking is forbidden.' There was a large notice on the wall, printed in Shcrift, of which the prohibition of smoking was only one of the rules.

Louise sat down; the chair was wooden and hard. She gripped her handbag tighter than she realised, and waited for the door to open. When it did, she didn't recognise the man who came in, a warder behind him. He was quite short, whereas her memory of Heinz Minden was of a tall man, well built. His hair was grey and his eyes sunken into his face. Kopner came towards him. He spoke to him in German, and then in French. 'Here is Madame de Bernard. She's come to help you.'

Louise stood up and slowly they approached each other. He looked at her without saying anything. She held out her hand, and after a second's pause he took it. His hand was dry, and it trembled.

'You shouldn't be here,' Heinz Minden said, and the voice was the same. 'This is no place for you.' He let her hand go and turned to Kopner. 'You shouldn't have done this. I told Ilse and I told you. I don't want Madame de Bernard mixed up in this.'

'Sit down,' the lawyer said. 'Madame de Bernard wanted to come. She wanted to see you. For old times' sake.' He turned away and walked over to the notice. His back was to them, leaving them alone as far as he could.

'How are you?' Louise said at last. 'How are you bearing up?'

'We'll sit down,' Heinz Minden said quietly. 'I only have twenty minutes; they don't count this as a legal visit. They're very strict about visitors.' He shook his head suddenly; the hair was very white. 'I won't see Ilse today; I'm only allowed one visit a week.'

Kopner spoke without turning round. 'You'll see her tomorrow. I got special permission for Madame de Bernard to come.'

'I'm going to give evidence for you,' Louise said. 'I'm going to tell them how you saved Paul and Sophie.'

'They told me,' he said. Now the eyes were fixed on her; they were bright in the prison-grey face, and the look in them was the same as it had always been. She had a sudden flash of understanding for his wife. 'You're as beautiful as ever,' he said. 'You haven't changed at all. How are the children—they're grown up now, of course, but I still think of them as they were . . .'

'Paul is married, he has two children. He lives at St. Blaize now. Sophie isn't married; she's very modern about these things.'

'That's a pity,' Minden said. 'The world is changing. I haven't seen my sons since I was arrested. But my wife has been very loyal to me. I wish you'd go home!'

'I can't,' Louise said quietly. 'You need my evidence. I want to give it.' Now, having seen him, it was true. On an impulse she put out a hand to him. 'Don't worry about me,' she said. 'Your wife told me you'd had a very bad time since the war. I was so sorry things turned out like this for you.'

'You shouldn't be,' he said. 'I deserve it. Me and people like me who supported them. I've had years to think about it. I deserve to be punished.' Behind him, Siegfried Kopner's back went stiff.

Minden looked at Louise and smiled slightly. Old and physically broken, he had a strange dignity. 'I am quite resigned to what will happen,' he said. 'It is very kind of you to try to help me. But any human being would have done what I did. I was very fond of your children. And of you. I never forgot you.'

'If you lie down, you'll be walked on.' Siegfried Kopner spoke suddenly. His voice was cold and he looked impatient. 'If you go into that court and hang your head and ask to be punished, you'll stay in here for the rest of your life. One letter a month, one visit every three months. Solitary confinement as a special case. Madame de Bernard! For God's sake, try and convince him that he's got to fight. He wasn't responsible for what he was making—it was a weapon of war!'

'Gas was forbidden under the Geneva Convention,' Minden

said. 'You know that, Herr Kopner. It won't do you any good to defend me. You'll be accused of sympathising with the Nazis. Enter a plea of guilty, let Madame de Bernard go home to her family, and leave me in peace!'

'Think of your wife and your sons,' Kopner urged him. He shrugged in Louise's direction. 'He mustn't take this defeatist attitude. He will be his own worst enemy.'

'Try not to give up,' she said. 'What's done is done now. And Herr Kopner said in the car coming here he thought you'd get a suspended sentence. That wouldn't be too bad.'

'Herr Kopner is an optimist,' Minden said. 'Tell me, how is the Comte?'

'He's dead,' Louise said. 'He died ten years ago.'

'I'm sorry to hear that. He was a good man.'

'Yes,' Louise said. 'He was.' They both heard the door open, and the warder come into the room. He spoke to Minden, who got up.

'You have to go now,' he said. He held out his hand, and she shook it. He didn't bow, or kiss it. He was very much changed.

'I am glad to have seen you,' he said. The moist brown eyes gazed at her and the years fled. 'But if you really want to help me, don't listen to Herr Kopner or my wife. Go home. Stay away from this. And God bless you.'

Then he was gone. Kopner came to her side. 'He's been here too long,' he said. He sounded a little brusque, as if he were trying to minimise what Minden had said. 'He's given up hope of justice.'

'Perhaps,' Louise answered him slowly, 'perhaps it's justice that he wants.' They walked out of the main building in silence. As they reached Kopner's car, Louise had an impression of a group of men converging on them from the gates. Seconds later the first photographer ran up and snapped his camera in her face.

• • • • •

Sophie looked at her mother's old friend Raoul Delabraye. She had dismissed him for years as a dull, conventional man, plodding on in pursuit of Louise. She had made fun of him and worried in spasms in case he persuaded her mother to marry him. She remembered that morning when Ilse Minden came to the Rue Varenne, he had just telephoned to take Louise to the Opera and she had made a slighting remark about him. Now, sitting opposite him in the Ritz lounge, she saw why Louise liked him, and why he was her most regular escort. Grey haired, very well dressed, impeccable manners and a gentle voice; none of these appealed to Sophie who saw them as varieties of stuffiness. But there was strength and reliability; and kindness. She had come to ask his help and she felt ashamed of her intolerance. She carried a copy of *Le Monde*.

'Have you seen this?'

'Yes,' Raoul said. 'There was another photograph in *Figaro* and the story was worse. "Comtesse to defend war criminal." It was almost libellous.'

'It's terrible,' Sophie said. 'The whole slant that's been put upon it is making Mother look like this bloody man's mistress. As if they'd been lovers! I'm very worried for her, Raoul. I felt I had to come and see you—you're such an old friend.'

'What can I do?' he asked her. 'If she'd told me, I'd have done my best to stop her going there. I don't trust these people; a war crimes trial is a very nasty business. I wish you'd come and told me before—why didn't your brother go with her? I can't understand it.'

'My brother is so terrified of being connected with it, Mother wouldn't hear of it. He did offer, I must admit that. But she was blackmailed into going; that's why she didn't tell you. Minden's wife threatened her if she didn't give evidence. And because of Paul and his career, Mother gave it. I'm going to fly to Bonn tomorrow; the trial opens the day afterwards, but I feel she needs a man there with her. I want you to come with me.'

'What was the blackmail? Can you tell me?'

'No,' Sophie answered. 'I'm sorry. But it doesn't reflect any blame on Mother. You must believe that.'

'Knowing her as I do,' Raoul said, 'I couldn't believe anything else. I've been thinking about this story. It must have been a planned leak to the press. Somebody wanted the spotlight to turn on Louise, and show her in a certain light. And you're right, my dear. She is going to need help. Would you pour me some tea—I'm afraid it may be cold. We quite forgot it.'

'I'm sorry, I wasn't thinking.' Sophie poured him a cup and some for herself. Tea at the Ritz was a pleasant ritual, enjoyed by little groups of people sitting in the handsome lounge. Silver, fine porcelain and delicious small cakes; an atmosphere of placid elegance. Sophie lit a cigarette. 'Will you come?'

'Of course,' he said. 'But I don't think I'm the one to help in this. Moral support won't be enough. When she goes into that court she's going to need more than a faithful old friend sitting in the background. Neither of us, my dear Sophie, are what she needs. We weren't at St. Blaize, we've nothing to contribute. She will be at the mercy of the prosecution; perhaps even of the defence. I know this man Kopner's reputation. He's an ambitious politician, a self-publicised lawyer who's putting himself up for election to the Bundestag. He's undertaken this man's defence because it's going to be a major trial and he will be centre stage. The very thought of Louise being in the hands of such people horrifies me. No; I won't be much help to her. But I know exactly who would. And I'm sure he'd come to her, wherever he is, if he knew what was happening.'

'I don't understand,' Sophie said. She had flushed, without knowing why. Even before she heard the name, she had tensed up against it.

'Roger Savage,' Raoul Delabraye said. 'The man who was there at the time. And he is a lawyer too.'

'How did you know about him?' Sophie said. She crushed out her cigarette. 'Why did Mother tell you?'

'Because he is the reason she won't marry me,' he said quietly. 'Or anyone else. She still loves him.'

'She loved my father,' Sophie said. 'That other man was years ago. She can't still care about him. It's not possible.'

'I wish I could agree with you. I've been in love with your mother ever since I met her, but I know I haven't got a hope. I've learned to be content with being her friend. And as her friend I know she needs this other man to help her now. It will be ironic, don't you think, for me to bring them both together?'

'He's probably married,' Sophie said angrily. 'He won't care what happens to someone he knew all that time ago. Men aren't that faithful.' She had a painful memory of Gerard as she said it. He had left her life as abruptly as he had come into it. Without the courtesy of goodbye. She was not hurt, she insisted, only angry. He had also left her apartment in a filthy mess. Then she thought of something. 'You'll never find him,' she said. 'Roger Savage wasn't his real name. It was the name of Mother's cousin, who'd died.'

'It was his wartime name,' Raoul said. 'I have a very good friend in the State Department. I'm sure he could find him for me. He received a decoration for his work against the Germans. I think we'll manage it, between us. And in that case, I should go now. I'll put in a call to Washington when I get home; the time difference is about right.'

'If he does come back,' Sophie said, 'and he isn't married . . .'

'I will lose what little of your mother I have now,' he said gently. 'But if it saves her being hurt in any way, then it is worth it.'

Sophie stood up. She despised the social habit of kissing on the cheek; she held out her hand.

'I take it back,' she said. 'Some men are faithful. I suppose I've been picking the wrong ones.'

'Go to Bonn and look after her,' Raoul Delabraye said. 'And try not to worry. Say nothing to her about this. Just leave it with me.'

• • • • •

The court was full; when Louise, Sophie holding her arm protectively, came in to take her seat, there was a loud hum of interest; people turned to stare at her. The trial had been in progress for four days. On Kopner's advice, Louise stayed away until he decided it was time to call her evidence, and she was only too relieved not to be present. The newspapers and German Television carried daily reports. Minden's chances looked poor; the prosecution had made out a damning case against him. His participation in Brühl's hideous project was established earlier than the six months he had spent on the staff at Château Diane. He had been engaged on research work the previous year, although not part of the team which had operated in Auschwitz. His membership of the Nazi party was lifelong, his record of allegiance to it unswerving. For years he had lived in hiding, fully aware of his criminal record. The prosecutor was a flamboyant personality, who was presenting the court with a picture which Louise herself knew to be grossly exaggerated. The Minden she had known at St. Blaize bore no relation to the callous Nazi fanatic portrayed at the trial. On the morning when her own evidence was to be given, there was an early telephone call from Siegfried Kopner.

'Just to assure you, Madame de Bernard,' his voice said briskly. 'You needn't be nervous. I will see you in the court. My car will come for you at nine o'clock.'

Before she had time to ask any questions he had said good-bye and hung up. The court was a large one, decorated in pale green; the panel of three judges and six jurors sat on a raised platform at the far end. The chair for witnesses was to their left. It was the first thing she saw, apart from the crowded rows of seats. At the entrance to the Criminal Court itself, they had run a gauntlet of photographers; Sophie had swung her shoulder bag at one who tried to block their way. Shaken, Louise hurried into the building, where they couldn't follow her, and was met by one of Kopner's clerks. She took her place in the front of the court on the defence side. It was pointed out, politely, that Mademoiselle de Bernard would have to sit in the body of the court. Louise sat down, and immediately Siegfried Kopner came beside her. The same flowery toilet water smell enveloped her; she leaned a little away from him.

'I open the defence this morning,' he said. 'And you are my star witness. You mustn't be nervous. And answer my questions as fully as you can.'

'It's going badly for him, isn't it?' Louise asked.

'The prosecution has made a strong case,' Kopner said. 'But they've said no more than I expected. You are his only chance, Madame.' For a moment the blue eyes were cold, the look of friendliness was gone. There was a suggestion in his tone that somehow she was to blame for something.

'I'll do my best,' Louise said. The sensation of being stared at was overpowering; she lowered her head for a moment, seeking to hide from it. The feeling increased. She glanced towards the left of the dais, and recognised the prosecuting lawyer from his photographs. He looked at her with hostility. On an impulse, Louise turned round and found Ilse Minden seated behind her. There was no smile, no nod of recognition. She looked thinner, more lined, and there was a tense expression on her face. As her eyes met Louise's glance, there was hate in them. And expectation. Louise turned to the clerk beside her. The heat seemed overpowering suddenly . . .

'Could I have a glass of water? Thank you.'

Two doors at the side of the raised platform opened; everyone stood up, with a regimented unanimity, and the three judges came in. They wore loose black robes and white neckties. The most senior took his centre seat as President of the Court. There was a command called out in German; the spectators sat down again, and through a second door, on the opposite side of the judges, Heinz Minden came into the court and took his place on the right.

He wore a dark suit and a white shirt, the collar of which stood away from his neck; it made him look old and pitiable. Kopner, who knew the value of visual impressions, had told his wife to bring a size larger than the normal. He didn't look at the judges; immediately he searched the front rank, and when he saw Louise, an expression of distress was clearly visible. She smiled at him, trying to show encouragement. In return he shook his head. Then he clasped his hands and stared down at them. Siegfried Kopner got up, pushing his chair back; the court was so quiet that it made a loud rasp on the floorboards.

He faced the judges, one hand tucked into his gown. 'If it pleases you, Herr President, I shall open the defence case for Heinz Minden by calling my first witness. My only witness.' There was a sharp hiss of breath from behind him, coming from the tightly packed hall. 'I shall call someone who has travelled from Paris at her own behest to speak on behalf of the man you have heard described by my learned colleague as an inhuman monster, a man who worked on an infamous weapon without a scruple of conscience for its effect upon helpless human beings. I call the Comtesse de Bernard to come before the court!'

There was a touch upon Louise's arm; one of the court officials had come up to her, and with an outstretched hand was showing her the way to the witness chair. As she walked the short distance, passing under the judges' eyes, there was a low murmur from the crowd. She took her place in the chair, and swore the oath. Kopner advanced towards her. He walked slowly, his gown swinging round his legs, his head thrust forward. He came to a stop in front of her.

'Madame de Bernard, you are the widow of Comte Jean de Bernard, a hero of the wartime French Resistance, are you not?'

'Yes, I am his widow.'

'Would you tell the learned judges how you came to know the accused, Heinz Minden.'

'He was billeted in our house, the Château de St. Blaize, at St. Blaize en Yvelines.'

'During what period of time?'

'About seven months; from November 1943 until June 1944.'

'What was his attitude to you and to your family while he was living in your house?'

'He was very friendly.'

'What does "friendly" mean, in this context, Madame? Describe what forms this friendliness took, if you please.'

'He used to bring us things—things we couldn't get. He got his batman to help in the house.'

'When you say "things" I assume you mean food and drink? Luxuries, perhaps.'

'Yes, that would be correct.' He wasn't looking directly at Louise, although she was impelled to watch him, trying to anticipate his questions. At present their purpose seemed confused. He moved about, shifting from one foot to the other, addressing his questions more to the judges than to her.

'And you accepted these presents from Heinz Minden?'

'My husband did.' It was said before she realised that she had made the distinction. Kopner paused, and looked at her.

'Your husband accepted presents from Major Minden? Can I assume he wasn't in the Resistance at this time?'

'No,' Louise said. 'He wasn't.'

'So up to June 1944, your husband, who was afterwards so heroic, was not engaged in any anti-German activity at all?'

'No.'

'Describe the relationship between you, and your family and Major Minden. Please address yourself to the judges, Madame, and not to me.'

She moved a little in the chair. Nervousness made the judges' faces seem a blur. She had said something which had put Jean in a false light, but how—what . . .

'I will repeat the question.' Kopner raised his voice. 'Did you and your family get on well with Major Minden? Did he take meals with you, for instance?'

'He dined with us every evening.'

'As a person, Madame de Bernard, how would you describe him?'

'He was very quiet; he never intruded.'

'He didn't force his company upon you then?'

'No. He was invited.'

'By your husband—they got on well, didn't they?'

'Yes.'

'The prosecution has described Heinz Minden as an ardent Nazi, a man without humanity. Was that your impression of him?'

'No. He seemed perfectly ordinary to me.'

'Perfectly ordinary,' Kopner repeated, raising his voice. 'A typical German from a middle-class background, serving his country in a war. Would you agree with that description?'

For the first time Louise hesitated. 'I can't say that exactly. I know nothing about typical Germans. I only knew Nazis occupying France.'

'Nazis like Adolph Vierken, the S.S. commander who was sent on a punitive expedition against your village?'

It didn't seem to need an answer and she didn't say anything. One of the judges leaned towards her.

'Please answer the defence counsel's question.'

'I suppose so.'

'A lot has been written about that incident at St. Blaize en Yvelines. It might be described as one of the most publicised Resistance operations in Europe. The battle with the S.S. The rescue of the children who were being deported.'

Deported. Suddenly she was stiff with alarm; her hands gripped the chair seat. He had said deported. It was a deliberate misrepresentation. The face looking down at her was harsh and full of enmity; the mask had been ripped away.

'They weren't going to be deported,' Louise protested. 'They were going to . . .'

'The witness will confine herself to answering questions. She is not allowed to comment.' The President's voice cut across her reply. 'Proceed, Doctor Kopner.'

'Your Honours, members of the jury.' Kopner addressed the judges above him. 'In order to establish the case for my client, I need to elaborate on the situation in which he found himself. I assure the court I have a definite point to put before you.'

'Proceed,' the senior judge said again. Kopner turned back to Louise.

'Heinz Minden was on General Brühl's staff at the Château de Diane when he was billeted with you. Were you aware of the nature of his work?'

'No. God forbid.'

'When did you become aware of it?'

'When I was told what he was doing. In May.'

'Until then he had impressed you as just another army officer? You had no suspicion that you were in fact entertaining in your family a fanatical Nazi scientist, bent on destroying the human race with a nerve gas?'

'No.'

'Up till that month of May, everyone at the Château and in the village itself had lived at peace with the occupying German forces, isn't that so?'

'Yes, it is.'

'Until just before the invasion, in fact. There was no sabotage, no outbreaks of violence against the army?'

'Nothing. But then two years before . . .'

'You have answered my question already,' Kopner interrupted her. 'Nothing, you said, no resistance, no hostility to the German troops. They can hardly have been such brutal Nazis, can they? Any more than Major Minden, who was made so welcome in your house. Would you tell the court what changed this state of affairs, apart perhaps from the imminence of the Allied invasion . . .'

In the body of the court Sophie de Bernard watched her

mother. At one stage in the questioning, Louise had flushed; now she was terribly pale. The atmosphere in the court was quivering with tension. It was obvious to those observing that Minden's counsel was treating Louise de Bernard as a hostile witness. And it was even more apparent to Sophie that his questions were taking a completely different direction to the one her mother had anticipated.

'Why did Adolph Vierken come to St. Blaize?'

'To punish the village.'

'And what crime had this peaceful, might I say, collaborationist community committed, to bring the S.S. upon them?'

'There had been two murders,' Louise said slowly. Her throat felt tight, and she swallowed. Now she was on guard, watching her answers, trying blindly to protect herself from a menace that she didn't understand. He wasn't defending Heinz Minden so much as attacking her. Attacking the people of St. Blaize. And Jean de Bernard.

'Explain, if you please. Who was murdered, and by whom?'

'General Brühl,' Louise said. 'He wasn't murdered, that was the wrong word. He was killed, by an Allied agent. To stop the gas being made.'

'I see,' Kopner said. 'And the village sheltered the killer: isn't that right? They hid a man who broke into the Château Diane and murdered two Germans with his bare hands. And they were not aware that General Brühl was anything but an ordinary serving officer in the Wehrmacht at the time?'

'Nobody knew what he really was,' Louise said.

'So, perhaps understandably, the German authorities were angry. They sent Adolph Vierken with his S.S. troops to investigate. Was Adolph Vierken known to you?'

'No,' Louise said. Visibly, Kopner sneered. He half turned his back on her, almost addressing the spectators. There was a movement among the prosecutor's seats. She didn't look at them; she saw only Heinz Minden staring at her.

'Not to any of you? To your husband?'

'No,' Louise said. Régine. She knew what was going to happen. She knew now that she had been tricked and lied to, that whatever this man wanted, it was not so much the vindication of Heinz Minden as the ruin of the de Bernard family.

'You did not know Adolph Vierken. Your husband, who was so friendly to the German officer staying in his house, he didn't know him either. But your sister-in-law Regine de Bernard did!'

'I object to this line of questioning!' The prosecutor was on his feet, advancing over the floor towards them. For a moment Louise's vision swam. 'It is completely out of order. It has no relevance to the case!'

'It has every relevance,' Kopner snarled at him. 'Heinz Minden is on trial for crimes against humanity. I am going to prove that he was more humane than the people who accuse him! That in the sordid and despicable story I am going to lay before the court, his was the only honourable, decent action!'

'Your objection is overruled.' The President spoke to the prosecutor. 'Continue, Doctor Kopner.'

'Your sister-in-law, Régine de Bernard, was another Resistance heroine, was she not?' Now his tone was soft, insinuating.

'Yes,' Louise answered boldly. 'She died fighting for her country. And whatever you say won't alter that.'

'But she was still the mistress of Adolph Vierken?' Kopner raised his voice to a shout. 'There we have this typical French household in this typical French village; the aristocrats at the château pretending friendship to Heinz Minden while they battened on his generosity to supply themselves with rationed goods, the sister of the heroic Comte de Bernard, Grand Cross of the Legion d'Honneur, herself a posthumous heroine, sleeping with a notorious S.S. commander! And it was to people like these that Heinz Minden showed much more than generosity! But we will come to that, Madame de Bernard. First let me ask you one more question. Was Major Minden in love with you?'

Down in the court, Sophie de Bernard clenched her hands. 'Oh you bastard,' she said out loud. 'You bastard!' A man sitting beside her hissed at her fiercely to keep quiet.

There was a gasp from the crowd; she half rose from her seat to see what had caused it. Heinz Minden was on his feet.

'I wish to change my plea.' His voice rang out, loud and strong. 'I plead guilty to the charges against me!'

Siegfried Kopner opened his arms wide.

'There is no need for you to answer, Madame de Bernard. The officer you duped has answered for you. Even now he tries to shield you! I ask that this interruption be stricken from the record of the trial. The plea cannot be changed except through me.'

The senior judge spoke for a moment to his colleagues. 'There will be a recess,' he announced, 'while you speak to the accused. We will reassemble in half an hour.'

A moment later Sophie de Bernard had fought her way through to the front and seized Louise's arm. Behind them the silence had changed to an excited babble; reporters were struggling to get to the exits and the telephones in the main hall. 'Darling!' Sophie threw both arms around her. 'Come on —we're getting out of here!'

But Louise didn't answer; she didn't seem to feel the pressure on her to move forward. A man was coming towards them. Sophie saw her mother's face and stepped away, letting her go. She knew, before either of them spoke, that Raoul Delabraye had succeeded.

. . . . .

'Now,' Siegfried Kopner said, 'you asked to see me. What can I do for you, Senator?' There were five of them in the little side room. Outside the door a policeman stood on guard. Heinz Minden and his wife were seated side by side; Louise, with Savage near her, sipped a glass of water. Kopner examined the American. He was a tall, strongly built man, middle aged but without a grey hair. Kopner had the card with his name on it in his pocket. Senator Brian McFall. He had come into the room with Louise de Bernard on his arm, and there was something about him which alerted Kopner. He sensed that this was a different type to the suave American politicians of his acquaintance, anxious to ingratiate themselves and prove their lack of bias towards Germans. 'What can I do for you?' he repeated. Savage put a hand on Louise's shoulder.

'You can change your client's plea to guilty,' Savage said, 'and save yourself and him a lot of trouble.' He lit a cigarette and passed it to Louise. Kopner smiled unpleasantly.

'Really? And are you qualified to give me such advice?'

'Better qualified than you know,' Savage answered him. He looked for a moment at Minden, who was staring at him.

'I have no idea why you make this suggestion,' Kopner said coldly, 'but I can assure you there is no question of changing the plea. I shall resume my examination of Madame de Bernard as soon as the court reassembles. Major Minden has been under a great strain. He's not responsible for that outburst in the court.'

'I am responsible.' Minden spoke suddenly. His voice sounded tired. 'I want to plead guilty. And don't keep calling me Major. It was only a sham rank.'

'You should be proud of it.' Kopner rounded on him angrily. 'Proud to have served your Fatherland! I will not change the plea!'

'Then I shall take the witness stand for the prosecution as a special witness.' Savage didn't raise his voice. 'They have the right to call me. And by God you'll regret it when I get up there. I've watched you bullying this lady for the last half an hour, Herr Doctor. I only hope you try to cross-examine me!'

'If that's a challenge,' Kopner said contemptuously, 'then I accept it. But I have yet to see how your testimony could make the slightest difference.' He turned away and lit one of his cheap cigarettes.

'As I understand it,' Savage said, 'your defence will be that your client was a patriotic German, acting under orders, that he was an unwilling subordinate who had no choice but to work on the project, that he showed no enthusiasm for it, and everything about his character confirms that he wouldn't willingly hurt the proverbial fly—right?'

'You should conduct the defence for me,' Kopner sneered.

'You're going to prove he was a humanitarian, aren't you? That's why you brought Madame de Bernard here—to testify to his saving her children's lives? First you show up the French as a lot of self-seeking, double-crossing bastards, turning on the Germans when they thought the Allies were going to win—you crucify Madame de Bernard and her family—then you present Heinz Minden as the true Teutonic Knight, bravely risking his own safety to rescue the children of the woman he loved?'

'Really,' Kopner shrugged, 'I need hardly go into court at all. You have won my case for me, Senator.'

'I'm the one who'll lose it for you,' Savage said. 'Because I saw Minden's notebook. I saw the work he was doing on Brühl's formula. They were having trouble with it; water neutralised it. It was all there, written out in Minden's own handwriting. And one phrase. I can testify to that one phrase, and how in his anxiety to perfect this filthy weapon, he had underlined it. "We must find a solution". That shoots the hell out of your unwilling subordinate plea!'

'How did you see it?' Kopner asked the question slowly; his look narrowed.

'Because I am the Allied agent who killed Brühl,' Savage said. 'And the people who sheltered me were the de Bernard family. He knows me.' He spoke to Minden. 'You knew who I was the minute I walked in here, didn't you?'

'Yes.' Minden's voice was listless. 'I recognised you. Her cousin. That was a lie then?'

'It was a lie,' Savage said quietly. 'I went to your room, opened your briefcase and read your notes.'

'I did write that,' Minden muttered. '"We must find a solution". I remember it well. God forgive me.' He hung his head again.

'You listen to me,' Savage said. He stepped close to Kopner, who did not recoil. 'Whatever the dirty game you're playing—and being a politician myself I guess it's a nice little job of whitewashing the Nazis for political ends—you might as well give up. I haven't gone to the prosecution yet and offered myself as a witness. But believe me, I'll make a hell of a good one. I'll give them a picture of Heinz Minden and the gas he was so anxious to make perfect that will send him to prison for the rest of his life. And leave a very dirty smell around anyone defending him. Especially when I describe how that gas was used to kill my wife and child at Auschwitz!'

For a moment Kopner fought back, silently, using an intangible force of will, he struggled against Savage and against his own conviction that he faced defeat.

'Change the plea to guilty,' Savage said. 'Otherwise I'll go in there and blow your case and your political future to smithereens!'

'Don't listen to him!' Ilse Minden had leapt to her feet; she confronted Savage and Louise, her face blanched and contorted with hate. 'You swine! You dare to threaten what you'll do to Heinz—you who killed in cold blood! My husband isn't pleading guilty to please you—or to save her! She was just a whore who made a fool of him, and it's all going to come out—she's going to stand in front of the world for what she is!'

'Be quiet!' Kopner shouted at her. 'Hold your tongue! Minden, we have no choice. The plea will be changed to guilty. I'll ask the court for mercy. There's nothing more I can do now.' He flung the cigarette on the floor and trod it to pulp. For a moment he looked at Louise. He seemed as if he were going to say something, but Savage stepped between them. He took Louise by the hand.

'Come on,' he said quietly. 'We've finished here.' With his arm around her shoulders, they left the room.

• • • • •

Sophie de Bernard was watching as they came out of the side room. She started forward to meet them, and then stopped. Neither her mother nor the tall man, unmistakably American, had seen her. They appeared oblivious of their surroundings; he was bending over Louise, with one arm around her, she was looking up at him. A pang of jealousy caught Sophie by surprise; this was the man who had meant so much to her mother that even now, after so many years, there was no place in her life for anyone else. They had paused in the corridor, talking quietly. He had taken his arm away from Louise and was holding her hand, they faced each other. Sophie stayed in her seat, watching them. He was not a conventionally handsome man, but there was power in the way he held himself, authority in the face. Her father had been slim and graceful, elegant even in the captivity of a wheelchair. This man was hard and big boned; there were no fine edges about him. Beside him, her mother looked small. Sophie got up and walked towards them.

'It's all right, darling!' Louise said. 'He's pleading guilty—

it's all over! This is my daughter, Sophie. Senator McFall—Roger Savage!'

He had a deep voice. 'The last time I saw you, you were a little girl,' he said. He held out his hand and Sophie shook it. She saw her mother's radiant smile.

'Thank you for coming,' she said to him. She had never felt awkward or inadequate with a man before. Her jealousy retreated in shame, and with it the regret that none of the men she had known would have crossed the world for her.

'I hope you'll have lunch with us,' Roger Savage said. 'Then we can tell you all about it.'

'That's very kind of you. Can I ask you one question?'

'Of course.' He was looking as happy as Louise. She felt he would have gone on smiling whatever she had said.

'Are you married?'

'Sophie!' She ignored her mother.

'No,' he said. 'I'm not.'

'Then in that case,' Sophie said, 'you and Mother had better lunch alone.' She took out a cigarette and lit it, throwing the empty Gauloise packet away. 'I'll join you for dinner tonight.' She kissed Louise quickly on the cheek and walked away.

Savage looked down at Louise.

'It's taken a very long time,' he said. 'But I think you'll be happy to come home?'

'Yes,' she said. 'I think I will.'